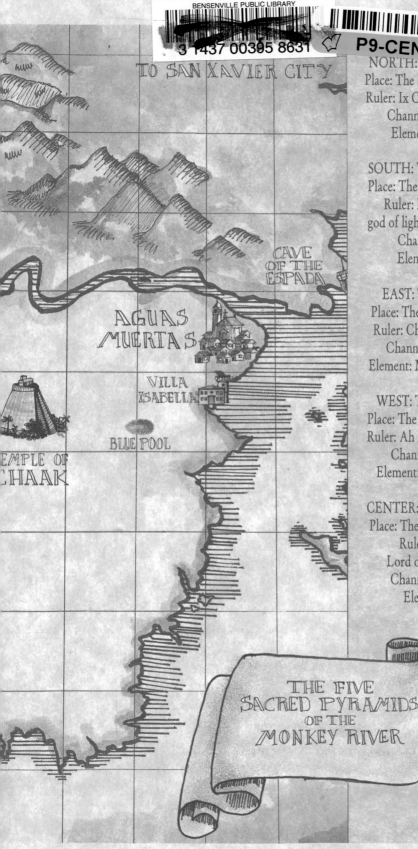

TO SAN XAVIER CITY

NORTH: The White Jaguar
Place: The Pyramid of Visions
Ruler: Ix Chel, moon goddess
Channels: Creativity
Element: Alabaster

SOUTH: The Yellow Jaguar
Place: The Pyramid of Blood
Ruler: Bolon Tz'akab,
god of lightening and lineage
Channels: Truth
Element: Amber

EAST: The Red Jaguar
Place: The Pyramid of Rain
Ruler: Chaak, the rain god
Channels: Prosperity
Element: Mexican Fire Opal

WEST: The Black Jaguar
Place: The Pyramid of Death
Ruler: Ah Pukuh, god of war
Channels: Courage
Element: Black Obsidian

CENTER: The Green Jaguar
Place: The Pyramid of Time
Ruler: Itzamna,
Lord of the Heavens
Channels: Wisdom
Element: Jade

CAVE OF THE ESPADA

AGUAS MUERTAS

VILLA ISABELLA

BLUE POOL

TEMPLE OF CHAAK

THE FIVE
SACRED PYRAMIDS
OF THE
MONKEY RIVER

THE JAGUAR STONES: BOOK ONE
MIDDLEWORLD

J & P Voelkel

SMITH
&SONS
A SMITH AND
KRAUS IMPRINT

To Harry, Charly, & Loulou,

k yahkume'ex.

THE JAGUAR STONES

DEAR READER,

Like many of the teenagers who reviewed this manuscript, you may object to one of the names in this story. You can't have a hero called Lord Six-Rabbit, you may say. It's not regal enough. Why, to modern ears, he sounds more like a cuddly toy than a fearsome warrior king.

You're right, of course. But if this book leads you to read more about Maya civilization, you'll meet other strangely named kings such as Stormy Sky, Smoke Monkey, Green Macaw, and Smoking Frog. Then you may be glad that our hero was inspired by a great eighth-century ruler called Eighteen-Rabbit, and not by Stormy Sky's father, the ingloriously named Curl Snout.

Here are some more things you should know before you read on . . .

The Ancient Maya called our world Middleworld, because it was sandwiched between the upper world of the heavens and the underworld, which they called Xibalba.

The Jaguar Stones are fictional, as are all the main characters except for Friar Diego DeLanda. He was the true-life Spanish priest who, in 1562, reduced the sum of Ancient Maya knowledge to ashes by making one huge bonfire of all their hundreds of folding bark books. (As far as we know, only three books and a fragment of a fourth survived.)

San Xavier is a fictional country based on present-day Belize.

Maya or Mayan? We have followed the scholarly precedent of using Maya as both noun and adjective to describe the people and their culture, reserving the word *Mayan* for the family of thirty languages still spoken by the six million Maya living in Central America today.

J&P Voelkel
Norwich, Vermont
5 Kib, 8 K'umk'u

CONTENTS

It's not easy being
fourteen. Especially
when your parents
have accidentally
unleashed the forces of
chaos and destruction into
the world — and left you
to sort out the mess.

This is the story of an ordinary
boy (you know — a bit lazy, rather
selfish, fond of pizza) who gets
caught up in an epic battle between
good and evil in the jungles
of Central America.

It's set in the present day,
but it all begins on a
moonlit night,
twelve hundred
years ago,
in the Ancient Maya
city of Itzamna . . .

I

PREFACE: THE DREAM

LORD SIX-RABBIT was awakened by the sound of his own screaming.

For a few moments he lay still on his sleeping mat, trying to shake off the memory of the dream. He told himself to calm down, but still his body trembled and the sweat ran down his forehead. (No small journey, as his mother had strapped his head between two boards when he was born to lengthen his skull like a cob of corn.)

A monkey . . . ?

Suddenly the door curtain was ripped aside and the royal guards burst in to investigate the noise. They filled the tiny room.

Lord Six-Rabbit quickly composed himself and signaled to them that all was well.

Then it occurred to him that perhaps all was *not* well.

As soon as the guards had gone, he examined himself all over, looking for monkey fur. Only when he was sure that his muscular body was still as smooth as a turtle shell, did he start to relax.

But a monkey . . . ?

It was unthinkable.

He was the famous Lord Six-Rabbit — most powerful king, most fearless warrior, most handsome hero of the mighty Maya. Yet in his dream, he'd been a stinking, flea-infested baboon. What did it mean? If dreams were messages from the gods, surely this one had gone astray in the cosmic sorting office.

Then again, perhaps it was not the gods who had sent this dream. Only yesterday, Lord Six-Rabbit's advisors had warned him about the growing power of his half-brother Tzelek. It was no secret that Tzelek coveted the throne. As a high priest, he was also an accomplished sorcerer. Could he have sent this dream?

Lord Six-Rabbit sighed. It seemed his advisors were always warning him about something. If it wasn't the machinations of Tzelek, it was a challenge from a neighboring kingdom or some impending natural disaster. One court astrologer had even foreseen the fall of the whole Maya civilization.

No wonder everyone was jumpy.

Vowing never to tell another soul about his dream, he rubbed his heavy-lidded eyes, blew his huge hooked nose, and went outside for some air.

The royal sleeping quarters were at the top of the palace and Lord Six-Rabbit could see for miles from the terrace outside his room. All around him, the silhouettes of other pyramids rose out of the jungle. Facing him, across the plaza, loomed the massive temple that his own father had designed and built. And below him, still and quiet, lay the beautiful city of Itzamna — jewel of the Monkey River. Its citizens slept peacefully tonight, trusting the young king they worshipped as a living god to protect them from all misfortune.

Lord Six-Rabbit shivered, even though the night was warm.

Stars were twinkling in the jungle sky and a big round moon was shining down. It reminded him of another night, long ago, when he'd stood here with his parents, the king and queen, Lord Punak Ha and Lady K'an Kakaw. They were pointing out the image of a leaping rabbit on the surface of the moon. But little Six-Rabbit couldn't see it. It looked like the face of a man to him. How they'd laughed and teased him.

It was strange to remember his mother as young and happy. Since Punak Ha's death, she'd turned into a bad-tempered old woman. It was as if she blamed her son for her husband's murder. She seemed to hate Six-Rabbit these days. It was war between them now.

"Where's that idiot son of mine?"

As if on cue, Lady K'an Kakaw came running onto the terrace, flaming torch in hand, four long gray braids flying behind her. She slapped her son hard on the head.

"That's for waking me with your screaming."

"I am sorry if I disturbed thee, Mother," said Lord Six-Rabbit.

"Sorry if I disturbed thee, Mother," she mimicked in a singsong voice. "Why must you talk in that old-fashioned way?"

"I believe it is fitting for a king to use the language of his ancestors."

"Well, you'll never get a wife. You sound ridiculous."

"I do not want a wife. I have dedicated my life to avenging my father's death."

"Very noble, I'm sure — except that you caused his death in the first place."

Six-Rabbit braced himself for the usual litany of accusations, but she seemed distracted. She was staring across the valley, as if mesmerized by the rustling of the treetops and the screeching of the monkeys in the jungle.

"Is something out there, Mother?" he asked.

"No, of course not!" she said, a little too quickly.

He tried to follow her gaze, but her crossed eyes made it impossible. (Crossed eyes were a sign of beauty and, as was the custom for females in the royal household, his mother's eyes had been trained to focus inwards by tying a bead to hang between them when she was a baby.)

But Lord Six-Rabbit didn't need to look his mother straight in her old red eyes to know that she was lying.

"What dost thou look at? I command thee to tell me!"

"There's nothing to tell."

"Speak — or I will bid Tzelek to rip out thine old heart in one of his rituals."

"You wouldn't dare," she said.

"Art thou sure? The day of 12 Knife approaches and the people expect a human sacrifice. They would be most impressed if the chosen one were of royal blood. Thine image would be painted on souvenir plates, the poets would write odes in thy memory . . . unless, of course, thou hast something to tell me, old woman?"

She gaped in disbelief.

"How dare you speak to your mother that way?"

"I am the mighty Lord Six-Rabbit. I will speak to thee any way I wish."

"Even you are not mightier than the gods, Six-Rabbit, and tonight I have found favor with them. Treat me with respect or you may feel their wrath."

Lord Six-Rabbit inspected his mother more closely. There was something different about her tonight. She seemed younger, happier, almost girlish.

"What is this nonsense? In thy deluded old head, how dost thou believe the gods hath favored thee?"

"Oh, I am not deluded. For tonight, the gods blessed me with the most wonderful dream. In fact, before you so rudely awakened me, I was happy for the first time since your father died."

To her son's amazement, the old woman began to whirl around like a temple dancer, her crossed little eyes as bright as two shiny cocoa beans.

"I was swinging through the trees and howling at the top of my lungs," she intoned, as if in a trance. "I was sucking on wild plums and spitting out the stones. I was picking the lice off my head and eating them." She paused theatrically. "Yes! I was a jungle baboon — and I loved every moment of it!"

Then she seemed to remember where she was and her performance ended abruptly. "It's not something a cold fish like you would understand," she said.

If she had not hung her head at that moment — whether in shame or to hide her happiness — she would have seen how intently her son was gazing at her.

Now Lord Six-Rabbit was the one who was mesmerized.

He could hear his mother talking in the background. But whatever she was rambling on about could not distract him from the small insect that had landed on her head and was now crawling over her hair.

Very slowly, almost tenderly, he leaned over and picked it off.

Then, before he knew what he was doing, the mighty Lord Six-Rabbit opened his mouth and popped it in.

THE SUN RISES,
THE EARTH TURNS,
THE MAYA EMPIRE FALLS.
TWELVE HUNDRED YEARS
(OR, IN MAYA TIME,
THREE BAK'TUNS)
PASS FROM THAT NIGHT
IN THE ROYAL PALACE
OF ITZAMNA.

OUR STORY BEGINS AGAIN IN
BOSTON, MASSACHUSETTS,
WHERE 14-YEAR-OLD
MAX MURPHY
IS HAVING A BAD DAY...

CHAPTER I

THE END OF THE WORLD

TUCKA-TUCKA-TUCKA!

Max Murphy ducked behind the tree trunk as the three men burst out of the rainforest in a blaze of machine-gun fire. One of them pushed a hostage, a young girl, in front of him. The other two shot at anything and everything as they ran across the clearing, toward the steps of the pyramid.

The noise was terrifying — guns shooting, men shouting, parrots shrieking — but Max tried to stay calm, waiting for the right moment. He knew he would only get one chance. And, armed with only a blowgun, he also knew the odds were against him.

In the end, it happened so quickly that he hardly had time to think.

Just as the men reached the bottom step, something caught their attention high above Max's head, and they stopped to blitz the treetops with gunfire. He crouched behind the log, not daring to breathe, as leaves and twigs exploded and rained down onto the forest floor. An animal shrieked and fell through the branches, landing with a thud somewhere behind him.

It was now or never.

Adrenaline pumped through his veins as he fired his three darts in quick succession.

Yes! Yes! No!

He'd hit the hostage — again.

GAME OVER.

Max threw down the controller in disgust. He'd been replaying this scene all afternoon and he couldn't get past this level.

What was he doing wrong?

What was that cross-eyed monkey trying to tell him?

He grabbed the case and studied the rules again. Nope, definitely nothing about cross-eyed monkeys. In fact, hardly any rules at all.

Stupid game.

Where had it come from anyway? It was just lying on his bed when he came home from school. The case looked new, but it had a slight musty smell like rotting fungus. Or like the gym lockers at school. Maybe one of his friends had left it behind.

As Max's hand reached for the controller again, a vacuum cleaner roared into life outside his door. No one could shoot a blow-gun with that racket going on. He decided to go downstairs for a snack.

On the landing, he stepped around Zia, the housekeeper and wielder of the vacuum. As usual, she didn't look at him. Or maybe she did. It was hard to tell.

Max had never seen her eyes because she wore heavy black sunglasses, even on the grayest of days. In her fist, she carried a crumpled handkerchief to wipe away the tears that often rolled down her cheeks. Max's mother said it was dust allergies and not to mention it. (A housekeeper with dust allergies, just what you need, thought Max.)

Zia had lived with Max's family for as long as he could remember. She rarely spoke, except to discuss household matters with his mother or to whisper in some strange language on the phone. She was just someone who cooked and cleaned and slept in the room over the garage. She never sat with the family or ate with them, and Max was so used to her flitting around the house like a little dust mite herself that he hardly registered her existence.

At the bottom of the stairs, he paused by the hallway mirror to check out his hair. (He was trying to grow it, and he'd got into the habit of reviewing its progress in every reflective surface he passed.) It was thick hair, not quite straight and not quite curly, the color of roasted chestnuts.

Kids at school called it red.

Max called it brown.

His father's hair was exactly the same color — apparently, it ran in the Irish Murphy side of the family, along with pale blue eyes. But since Max's mother was Italian, he'd inherited her brown eyes and long black eyelashes. One of these days, he intended to dye his hair rock-star black and disown the Irish gene altogether.

He combed his floppy bangs with his fingers and struck a moody pose in the mirror. Then he slunk into the kitchen and opened the fridge.

Just a dish of Zia's homemade tamales and a piece of dried-up salami.

No contest. He reached for the salami.

He'd tried one of those tamales once, just once, when he was little. They'd looked so tempting in the dish: a neat row of yellow corn-husk packages, each one tied up with twine like a little surprise present.

Yeah, the worst surprise of your life, thought Max.

On that fateful day, he'd excitedly unwrapped a tamale and

sunk his teeth into the greasy dough. MISTAKE!!! His tongue probed the sticky filling — which seemed to expand in his mouth like insulation foam — and sent desperate EVACUATE signals to his brain. He'd only just reached the sink in time. The worst thing was that Zia had witnessed the whole thing. Come to think of it, that was possibly why she didn't speak to him.

Max's mother said he was a picky eater. But she was from Venice, Italy, where the local specialty was boiled tripe. Tripe! The stomach lining of a cow! Why would anyone eat tripe in the country that invented pizza?

But tripe aside, Max's Italian grandmother — Nonna — was a fantastic cook. And as soon as school finished for the summer, they were flying to Italy to see her for a long vacation. As Max tried to slice through the rock-hard salami, he thought about Nonna's pizza, the dough thin and crisp and chewy all at the same time, homemade tomato sauce, bubbling mozzarella . . .

Max was still daydreaming about pizza when the back door flew open and his parents, Frank and Carla Murphy, burst in. They were chattering and laughing like excited schoolchildren.

"Mom . . . Dad . . . what are *you* doing home?"

It was only four thirty and they were never home before seven. Often much later. They were archaeology professors at the university — specialist subject, the Ancient Maya — and they'd practically been living there lately. Max zoned out when they talked about work, but he gathered they were on the verge of some sort of breakthrough.

But, really, who cared?

The Maya had died out hundreds of years ago and no amount of archaeology would bring them back. Max didn't understand his parents' passion for dry-as-dust ancient history. And the Maya seemed particularly boring. All they'd left behind were a few pots and some tumbledown pyramids. Yet, judging from the amount of time his parents had been spending at work lately, Frank and Carla Murphy obviously found a bunch of long-dead Maya to be better company than their own living, breathing son.

Max sometimes wondered if his father would be happier just camping out in the archaeology department, surrounded by old stuff. He seemed to have no interest in twenty-first-century Boston. Max was sure he couldn't name the mayor, the Red Sox manager, or even Max's homeroom teacher. He was always deep in thought, lost in the past, with a faraway look in those pale Murphy eyes.

Max's mother, on the other hand, took an active interest in the world around her. She was always dragging her reluctant husband to museum functions and galleries and opening nights at the theater.

She studied fashion magazines avidly and she loved to take Max shopping for clothes. Sadly, her taste ran more toward the preppie look than the punk-rock vibe Max was aiming for.

"*Ciao, bambino!*," she said now, as she rearranged his collar and attempted to plant a kiss on his cheek.

"Mom, I've told you, cut it out!"

"*Si, si,* you think you're too old for my kisses. But what about that little blond girl across the street, eh? You wouldn't mind if she tried to kiss you . . . ?"

"I'll be in my room," said Max, scowling at his mother.

"No, I'm sorry for teasing, please stay. We need to talk to you, *bambino.* Here, let me make that sandwich for you. Do you want mustard?"

Max nodded sulkily and sat down next to his father at the breakfast bar. Together they watched as Carla scrutinized the mustard label, then turned the nozzle this way and that, all the while holding the bottle at arm's length to avoid squirting her pale-green silk shirt. Nothing came out.

"Incredible, isn't it?" murmured his father. "She's the world's foremost expert on Maya glyphs, but she can't read the instructions on a mustard bottle."

"I heard that," laughed his mother, attempting to swat her husband with the salami. Max watched, appalled. If they ever acted like this when his friends were over, he would curl up and die of embarrassment.

Max found many things about his parents embarrassing. He hated that they were nerdy archaeologists instead of something cool and overpaid — like website designers or advertising executives. He hated watching TV with them because they never knew who anyone was. Most of all, he hated that they looked different from other people's parents.

For example, his mother never wore old jeans like the rest of the mothers. She said Italian women liked to look smart. Even when she was dressed for a dig, she'd add earrings or a silk scarf to her khaki shirt and trousers.

His father, on the other hand, went too far the other way. He didn't seem to care what he looked like. His thinning hair was tied back in a ponytail because he hated getting haircuts. Sometimes there were cookie crumbs or bits of popcorn in his beard. Worst of all was the hideous beige cotton safari jacket that he wore every day, even in the coldest Boston winter. It was covered in pockets, more pockets than any normal person could ever need, and every pocket bulged with scraps of paper, notebooks, and leaking pens.

Only a few days ago, Max had seen his mother try to seize the jacket for dry cleaning and his father had refused to let it go.

"It's time you sorted it out once and for all, Frank," she'd snapped, in a voice that sounded too angry to be talking about laundry. But that was Italian mothers for you. She was always getting hot under the collar about something.

Right now, Max could hear her cursing under her breath as the mustard shot out in one big splat. She saw him looking at her and composed her mouth into a smile.

"Did you like your new game?" she asked brightly.

"Pyramid of Peril? Did *you* buy it?"

"No," she said. "Zia brought it home it for you. She said it would be educational. I think she found it in a yard sale or something."

"A yard sale? Well, that explains the smell. I can't believe that Lenny-next-door gets the new Collectors Edition Hellhounds 3-D, and I get garbage from a yard sale."

"There's gratitude for you," said his father.

"He has a point, Frank," said his mother. "Perhaps we should buy him this . . . " she paused, wincing in distaste at the title . . . "Hellhounds." (She pronounced it in the Italian way, *'Ell 'Oundz*, which made it sound a bit more sophisticated.) "It would keep him busy while we're away."

Away? What did she mean? Max didn't know what she was talking about, but he nodded furiously in agreement.

"Shopping is not the answer, Carla," said his father. "You buy him far too much as it is. He needs to learn to make his own entertainment."

"I just thought, with the trip and everything . . . " said his mother, defensively.

"What trip?" said Max. "Do you mean Italy?"

"No, *bambino*, that's what we wanted to talk to you about. We've had such good news today." She looked so happy that Max couldn't help smiling with her.

"What news?" he asked.

"It's like a dream come true. We've talked about it for years, but we never thought it would happen. Then, suddenly, today, the permits for the dig came through."

"The dig?" said Max, dully. This didn't sound like good news at all. It sounded like very bad news.

"Yes, we leave in a few hours' time," beamed his father, rubbing his hands together with excitement.

"Tonight?" echoed Max in disbelief. "You're *both* going? For how many days?"

He saw his parents exchange glances.

"We're . . . um . . . we're not sure, Max," said his father.

"But what about the end-of-year concert? My drum solo?"

His mother put an arm around him. "I'm sorry, *bambino*. We'll ask Lenny's mom to tape it for us, and we'll have a party and all watch it together the night we get back . . . "

Max shook off her arm.

"You're the worst parents in the world!" he yelled. "You've missed every single performance of the school band! You *promised* you'd come to the end-of-year concert. I've been rehearsing for weeks . . . "

"Calm down, Max," said his father. "We didn't plan it this way. It's out of our control. We said we're sorry."

He didn't sound sorry.

Max kicked the fridge. "Why can't you just wait a couple of weeks till the end of school?" he said. "Then *you* could come to the concert and *I* could come on the dig?"

"Not possible, I'm afraid," said his father. "These permits are like gold dust. They're only valid for a few weeks, and they could be revoked at any time. It's now or never, Max. We won't get another chance at this."

"I'll cut school and come with you," suggested Max. "I've got all summer to catch up. I won't be any trouble, I promise. It'll be fun, like that conference in Palm Springs."

Aaah, Palm Springs.

His parents had been in meetings every day and fancy dinners every night. They'd paid Melissa, the sixteen-year-old daughter of one of their colleagues, to look after him. Melissa. He still kept a photo of her under his mattress. It had been one of the best weeks of his life.

"We're going to San Xavier, *bambino*. It's not like Palm Springs."

"San Xavier?" said Max. "Isn't that where you grew up, Dad? You always said you'd take me there some day."

"But not this time, " said his father firmly. "This trip is work. Hard work."

Max turned to his mother in resignation. "Well, just hurry back," he said, "so we can go to Italy."

She didn't reply. She seemed to be too busy fiddling with the gold hoops in her ears to even look at him. Why wouldn't she look at him? Alarm bells went off in his head. "We *are* still going to Italy, aren't we?" he asked anxiously.

There was a moment's silence and then his father said: "We may have to take a rain check, Max." He seemed oblivious to his son's disappointment. "Let's face it," he was saying, "you're probably getting a bit old for family vacations anyway. You teenagers want to be with friends your own age, not boring old folk like us."

Tears pricked Max's eyes. He could hardly say so now, but he'd really been looking forward to Italy and spending some time with his parents.

His mother read his thoughts. "I was looking forward to it too, *bambino*. We wouldn't be doing this if it wasn't very important," she said.

Some people think their kids are important, said a sulky little voice inside him. But on the outside, he shrugged as if he didn't care. He opened the fridge and looked inside. Then he took out the milk and gulped it down straight from the carton.

"Massimo Murphy!" roared his mother. "Use a glass!"

Massimo was the name on Max's birth certificate. It was Italian, after his grandfather. But Max was always called Max and no one ever called him Massimo, except his family in Italy and his mother when she was angry with him.

Max wiped his mouth with the back of his hand — "Massimo! Use a napkin!" — and replaced the milk. He slammed the fridge door hard enough to make all the cans and bottles rattle inside and gave it another little kick for good measure.

Then he had an idea.

"If you two are working," he said, "can I go to Florida with Lenny?"

Another exchange of parental glances.

"It seems," said Max's father, "that Lenny's family are going to Florida without him this year. They're sending Lenny to camp for a few weeks instead. They're hoping it will improve his behavior."

"What?" said Max in outrage. "What's wrong with Lenny's behavior?"

"They say he's been a bit difficult lately. Shouting at his parents, slamming doors, kicking fridges . . . that sort of thing."

Max narrowed his eyes. "What's that supposed to mean?"

"Just that it can do a fourteen-year-old boy a lot of good to test his inner resources once in a while —"

"But Dad, it takes a lot of inner resources to play Hellhounds 3-D . . . "

"What *you* need," said Frank, "is a *break* from the consumer society. When I was your age, I wasn't lazing around indoors playing video games. I was off climbing trees and exploring ruins and swimming in waterholes . . . "

Max groaned. "But we live in the middle of Boston. You grew up in the jungle."

"That's true. And your Uncle Ted and I had a fine old time running wild, while your grandpa was managing the banana business."

"I thought you didn't get along with Uncle Ted," said Max. "If you had such a fine time together, how come you don't speak to him anymore?"

Carla looked up, interested to hear her husband's reply.

He didn't take the bait. "All that fresh air and freedom was the making of me, Max, and I think it would be good for you, too."

"So bring me with you on the dig."

"I told you, Max, it's not possible. You need proper supervision — trained counselors who can teach you new skills and help you use your time productively."

Trained counselors? Max did not like the sound of this.

"Which is why, continued his father, "when school ends, you'll be going to camp with Lenny until we get back"

"Camp?" protested Max. "I'm too old for camp."

"It's for boys up to eighteen years old," said his father.

"And girls," added his mother.

He looked at her. "So where is this camp?"

His father coughed in an embarrassed sort of way. "Maine," he said, "the Great North Woods."

"Maine?" groaned Max. "I'll be eaten alive. Don't you remember the black flies, when we went hiking that time?"

"You'll be fine, said his mother firmly. "I'll pack some insect repellent."

"Don't bother," said Max, "because I'm not going to . . . to . . . what's the name of this camp, anyway?"

"Camp Wilderness," said his father.

"Camp Wilderness!" exploded Max. He felt like he was plummeting in freefall. "You can't be serious? I saw it on a reality TV show. It's the toughest camp in the country. They made them eat fried slugs for dinner. Slugs, Mom, *slugs!*"

Surely even a mother who ate tripe would draw the line at slugs?

Carla grimaced, but she did not back down. "I promise we'll hurry back," she said, "and you'll be eating Nonna's pizza before you know it."

"I'll be dead by then!" yelled Max.

"Oh grow up, Max!" said Frank angrily. "It's not the end of the world."

But it was the end of the world. That's exactly what it was.

Max was so angry, he hated his parents at that moment. They didn't seem to care about his feelings at all. They just wanted him out of their hair. They'd be drinking cocktails and living it up on business expenses, while their only son was being poisoned and tortured in the wilds of Maine.

"I'm sorry, *bambino*," said his mother, reaching out to stroke his arm.

"Don't baby him, Carla," said his father. "He's not a *bambino* anymore and it's time he stood on his own two feet. Most boys his age would be looking forward to a few weeks at Camp Wilderness."

"Didn't you do *any* research on this place?" said Max indignantly. "They call it Brat Camp! It's like a prison with cookouts."

"Nonsense. A bit of discipline never hurt anyone," said his father. "You'll build some of that strength of character I'm always talking about. Believe me, Max, you'll soon find out that old-fashioned fun is much more exciting than any video game!"

"I'm not going and you can't make me!"

Max stormed out of the kitchen and slammed the door behind him. Then he stomped up to his room and slammed that door too. He grabbed his iPod, turned his current favorites, The Plague Rats, up to full volume, and threw himself on the bed, fuming with rage.

After a while, his mother came in to talk to him, but her voice could not compete with the throbbing bass in his ears. Max just lay there, nodding along to his music and staring at her contemptuously. She looked at her watch and rushed out of the bedroom, gesticulating in that Italian way of hers.

When she returned, she was carrying a tightly stuffed backpack.

His kit for Brat Camp, no doubt.

One by one, she took out the contents to show him. Spare clothes. Towel. Flashlight. Bug spray. Mosquito net. Shades. Sun cream. Then she held up his Red Sox cap, and she pointed up at an invisible sun. Yeah, yeah. He knew what she was saying. She was obsessed with wearing hats in the sun. He doubted they even got any sun in northern Maine. Some disgusting health food granola bars completed her impromptu show-and-tell.

She put the pack down on the bed, then leaned over and attempted to ruffle his hair. He fended her off and nudged the pack with his foot until it fell to the floor with a thud. Then he straightened his hair and resumed his contemptuous stare.

There were tears in his mother's eyes as she left the room.

Serves her right, he thought. She wanted to go to Italy as much as I did. She should stand up to Dad and tell him that his own family's more important than the stupid Maya.

As Max lay there, a calculating expression replaced his blind anger and he glanced around the room, appraising his possessions. There was his new laptop, a present from his father to atone for missing Max's middle school graduation . . . his top-of-the-line games console, bought to keep him happy over one spring break . . . his electronic drum set on which he could pound away without disturbing anyone . . . shelves of CDs, DVDs, model kits, video games . . . all the trappings of an only child whose parents were guilty about not spending enough time with him.

Max cheered up a little. His mother was already feeling guilty. If he put his mind to it, he was sure he could persuade her to buy

Hellhounds 3-D. Then he'd talk her into cancelling Brat Camp and letting him stay behind in Boston with Zia.

One advantage of being an only child was that he usually got his own way in the end.

So the next time his mother came into the room, he took off his headphones and composed his features into a soulful expression.

"I'll miss you, Mom," he said. "I wish you weren't going."

She stroked his hair. "I'll miss you too, *bambino* . . ." The rest of her words were drowned out by a furious honking in the street below.

"Taxi's here, Carla," called his father. "Time to go."

Time to go? Quick, think of something.

"Please don't go right now, Mom," he whimpered. "I don't feel good."

She felt his forehead. "He does look pale, Frank."

"Of course he looks pale," snapped his father impatiently. "He always looks pale! He spends whole weekends in his room! There's nothing wrong with him that a few days in the great outdoors won't cure. Look, I'm sorry you're not happy about this, Max, but we'll have to talk about it when we get back."

"I won't *be* here when you get back. And I won't be at Brat Camp either."

"Remember to wear a hat in the sun," said his mother.

"Like you care."

"Don't *do* this, Max," said his father, exasperated.

"What am *I* doing? You're the ones who are walking out on their only child."

"You're fourteen," said his father, "hardly a child. There were Ancient Maya kings younger than you."

Outside, the taxi was revving its motor.

"Don't worry if you don't hear from us straight away," said his mother. "I'll call or e-mail as soon as I can, but it's like the Stone Age in San Xavier — nothing ever works."

"Come, Carla," said his father. "Zia will look after him. We need to go."

As her husband chivvied her out of the door, Max's mother turned back and called: "I love you, *bambino*."

She looked at him imploringly, willing him to say one nice thing.

He looked away in silence.

And when he looked back, they were gone.

Max lay on his bed for a while, mulling over the injustice of it all. Then he remembered that he hadn't had any dinner, and he felt even more sorry for himself. He went down to the kitchen. No sign of Zia. Nobody cared if he starved to death.

He put a frozen pizza in the oven. As he waited for it to cook, he replayed the evening's drama in his head. He couldn't believe they'd gone. If only he hadn't wasted so much valuable negotiating time in arguing. His father said it was his Italian blood that made him so temperamental. His mother said he got his temper from the hotheaded Irish Murphys.

Either way, everything was totally his parents' fault.

Satisfied with this conclusion, he took the sizzling pizza and a huge bowl of ice cream into the sitting room. The house had never felt so empty. Yet as he rooted under the sofa cushions to find the TV remote, he felt he was being watched.

He looked around the room. His mother's prized collection of Ancient Maya sculptures looked back at him. Usually these little pottery figures blended into the wallpaper, but, tonight, they seemed to be perched on the edge of their shelves, following his every move with their hollow clay eyes.

He made a face at the nearest one and noticed, with surprise, that it had the head of a crocodile and huge lobster claws for hands.

What did his mother see in this stuff? Why was it any better than all the misshapen pottery he'd brought home from school over the years? If she liked ugly, deformed figurines so much, why were none of *his* creations on display?

He felt a stab of jealousy. Maybe he'd auction them all online while his parents were away and spend the money on a huge plasma TV. That would teach them.

Meanwhile, he switched on their pitifully small, ordinary TV and started slurping down his food. He was still slumped on the sofa watching rock videos when Zia marched in at midnight.

"Bed!" she said, switching off the TV.

When he didn't move straight away, she reached behind him, pulled out the cushion he'd been leaning on and started beating it furiously. Max got the impression she'd like to beat him as well, so he meekly went upstairs.

He could still hear her beating up cushions when he got into bed and switched out the light. After a week alone with her, I'll be looking forward to Brat Camp, he thought, before he fell asleep.

Next morning, Friday, Max awoke to the smell of bacon frying. Instead of his usual toast and cold cereal, he found a cooked breakfast and fresh orange juice waiting in the kitchen. When he came home from school, a juicy homemade cheeseburger, corn-on-the-cob, a big piece of blueberry pie, and a glass of milk were set out on a tray. Both times, the food was hot but there was no sign of Zia.

He was about to take the tray upstairs, when he heard a familiar snuffle from the sitting room.

"Zia!" he called. "Zia! I'm home!"

She didn't hear him. She was kneeling down with her back to him. She'd arranged some of his mother's Maya figurines like an audience in front of her. On the floor between Zia and the figurines, there was something on the carpet. Pebbles, maybe, and bits of yellow corn. She looked like a little girl playing with dolls. Was she trying to feed the statues? Had she lost her mind?

"Zia!" he shouted. "What are you doing?"

She jumped at the sound of his voice. Putting on her sunglasses, she turned quickly around. She looked frightened.

"You are early," she said.

"I ran all the way, in case Mom phones. What are you doing?"

With trembling hands, she picked up all the bits on the carpet and put them into her apron pocket. Then she pulled a duster out of her other pocket and started wiping the figurines.

"I clean," she said.

"But . . . " began Max.

"Eat!" she commanded. "I clean."

She was the weirdest housekeeper in Boston, all right. Shaking his head, Max put two large scoops of chocolate ice cream on the pie and carried the tray up to his room, where he played video games till the early hours.

Next morning, his cell phone rang.

He grabbed it eagerly, expecting it to be his mother.

It was Lenny.

"Yo, Max."

"Yo, Dude."

"Ready for camp?"

"Not going."

"Your mom said you are."

"*Your* mom said they're going to Florida without you."

"Whaaaat? She said no Florida this year."

"No Florida for *you* is what she meant."

"Gotta go!"

Lenny slammed down the phone. Max didn't hear from him again, but there was a lot of shouting coming from his house.

For the rest of the weekend, Max lay around playing video games, bashing on his electronic drums, checking out girls on MySpace, gelling his hair into spikes, and waiting for a phone call or an e-mail. At mealtimes, Zia would bring up his tray and take away the dirty dishes in silence. He felt a bit like an animal in a zoo.

His mother finally called on Monday night.

"Mom?"

"Max! I've been trying to call since we got here!"

She sounded like she was speaking down a wind tunnel. He could hardly hear anything she said. To make matters worse, they kept getting crossed lines and other voices would cut in on top of her.

"Where are you, Mom?"

"We're at Uncle Ted's tonight. Tomorrow we're going to . . . " the rest of the sentence was lost in the wind tunnel. The only other thing Max caught was about wearing a hat in the sun. At one point, the line improved and she shouted, "I love you, Max!" Then there was a beep and the line cut out altogether.

"I love you, Mom," said Max, but he knew she hadn't heard him.

That night, he lay on his bed trying to remember everything he knew about Uncle Ted. It wasn't much. Only three things:

1. He was Frank Murphy's older brother.

2. He'd inherited Grandpa Murphy's banana business in San Xavier.

3. Frank Murphy hated him.

Max knew that the two brothers had fallen out many years ago, but he didn't know why. (For someone who was supposed to love history, his father was annoyingly tight-lipped about his own past.) So why would his mother be calling from Uncle Ted's house? Had the brothers buried the hatchet after all these years? And where were his parents going tomorrow? Hopefully to somewhere with a decent phone system.

But the days went by and he heard nothing more.

On the Friday morning, a week and a day since his parents had left, he came down to a breakfast of cereal, dry toast, and an e-ticket to San Xavier with his name on it. The flight was departing in a few hours' time.

"Zia!" he yelled.

She walked calmly into the kitchen with an armful of laundry.

He waved the piece of paper at her.

"What's this, Zia? Where did it come from?"

"They tell me to buy it," she said. "They say you must go there."

They? Who's they? My parents? What else did they say?

"They say you are special," said Zia with a shrug, as if this was the most baffling statement she had ever heard. Then she reached into her apron pocket and pulled out Max's passport.

"Take it," she said. "Go! You must not keep them waiting."

CHAPTER II

THE CURSE OF THE MAYA

TORRENTIAL RAIN BEAT against the windows of the small plane as it rolled to a stop. Max wiped away the condensation and peered out. Water was streaming in waves over the runway. It wasn't exactly dry land but he was glad to be on it. It had been a bumpy ride.

"Welcome to San Xavier City," said the pilot, glumly. "The local temperature is 95 degrees and the forecast is rain."

At least English was the official language here, thanks to some British pirates who'd settled this coast 300 years ago and eventually laid claim to the whole country. Before them, the Spanish had ruled San Xavier. And before them, it had been home to the Ancient Maya, whose kingdoms had stretched across Central America from the Caribbean to the Pacific.

Max hadn't known any of this when he'd boarded the plane. In fact, having always hated the Ancient Maya for monopolizing his parents' attention, he'd made a point of avoiding all knowledge of them. But a few minutes of flicking through the in-flight magazine had taught him the history of San Xavier — plus more than he wanted to know about the Ancient Maya enthusiasm for human sacrifice.

What an eye-opening read that magazine had been.

Max had opened it eagerly, looking for alluring photos of luxury hotels on palm-fringed beaches. But all he found were blurry old snapshots of ruined temples and gloomy caves, plus the occasional artist's (gory) impression of a sacrifice or a bloodletting in progress.

Even the article on flora and fauna was unnerving.

It seemed that all the biggest, nastiest, ugliest insects in the world had chosen to live in San Xavier. The black flies in Maine seemed harmless compared to these monsters. Max was particularly daunted by the picture of a hairy brown spider as big as a dinner plate. And how could such a small country be home to so many species of poisonous snakes?

It was as if the San Xavier tourist board wanted to keep people away.

But here he was.

And boy, did his parents have some explaining to do.

Max's only luggage was the backpack his mother had packed for camp. He pulled it down from the overhead locker and shuffled down the narrow aisle toward the door. Most of the other passengers stayed in their seats, glumly watching as the ground crew pushed a set of rusty steps toward the plane through the blowing rain.

Finally, the steps clanged into place.

No one else seemed anxious to disembark, and Max was first in line when the steward swung open the door. It was like standing behind a waterfall. The roar of the rain was deafening, and the wet wind blew in a thick, musty smell of earth and decaying plants. Max hesitated, savoring his final moment of being dry before ducking into the torrent. He was planning to dash down the stairs and across the tarmac as quickly as possible, but as soon as he stepped out of the plane, he lost the power of forward motion. While the rain lashed his face, the wind pounded at his body with invisible fists. It was almost pushing him back onto the plane.

Eventually, the steward gave him an impatient shove and the momentum propelled him down the stairs. He kept going, fighting the elements every step of the way, until he reached the small concrete terminal building.

He was literally soaked to the skin. He couldn't have been wetter if he'd sat in a bath of water with all his clothes on. Shuffling uncomfortably across the floor, he joined the line at the immigration desk, where a puddle quickly formed around his feet.

One by one, the passengers were called forward, interviewed, and waved through until only Max remained. The uniformed official snatched his passport from him and began studying it with great interest.

Without taking his eyes off the passport, he made several muffled phone calls. Then he made a big show of looking back and forth between Max and his passport photograph. Was something wrong? Max began to get annoyed. He knew the photo wasn't great — his hair had come out a lurid orange — but it was definitely him.

Eventually, the official put down the passport, leaned back in his chair, and began staring at Max in person.

As Max stared back at him, he realized that the man looked familiar. Where had he seen that high forehead, those heavy-lidded eyes, that huge nose before?

Then it hit him.

This guy was the embodiment of one of his mother's Maya figurines. Max looked around the airport. And there they all were. Behind desks, in lines, slumped in chairs, leaning against walls. Wherever he looked, faces from ancient history stared back.

And they didn't look entirely friendly.

The official's voice, when it finally came, made Max jump.

"Massimo Francis Murphy?"

Max cringed. He hated his full name. Massimo was bad enough, but he would never forgive his parents for slipping in a Francis (after his father). He looked cagily around, hoping no one else had heard.

"Yes?"

"What brings you to San Xavier?"

"I'm here to meet my parents."

"Ah, the famous Frank and Carla Murphy."

"You know them?"

"I know *of* them."

"What does that mean?"

"It means that your parents make life difficult for government officials like myself. They ignore our warnings. They think they are above such things."

This was news to Max. He'd always thought his parents were the most boringly upright and law-abiding citizens on the planet.

"Have they done something wrong?"

"Tell them from me," said the official, as he cracked his knuckles menacingly, "that they are not welcome here. They may have procured the necessary permits" — he rubbed his thumb and forefinger together to suggest a bribe — "but some things are better left alone."

A chill ran down Max's spine. The official's eyes were as cold and hard as flint. It wouldn't be difficult to imagine him conducting a human sacrifice.

At last, Max's passport was stamped.

"Take care," said the official as he handed it back. It sounded more like a threat than a friendly farewell.

Max walked into the arrivals hall. It was a sea of people, noise, and color. He scanned the faces of the waiting throng expectantly. Somewhere in there, his mother would be waving and calling to him — "Over here, *bambino*, over here!"

Why couldn't he see her? Both of his parents were taller than most of the locals who crushed around the barriers. He looked again more slowly.

His confident smile faded.

It was unbelievable. Here he was, ready to forgive his parents and make a fresh start by a hotel swimming pool — but where were they?

Not here, that was for sure.

They were late.

Late for the big reunion scene.

It was the last straw.

All Max's feelings of forgiveness evaporated. First his parents abandoned him, then they made him fly 2,000 miles on a rickety plane to some snake-infested dump in the rainy season, and then they couldn't even be bothered to pick him up on time.

He watched miserably as the other arriving passengers were swept away in happy, laughing groups. But no one came for him.

How could his mother leave him waiting in a strange airport? For all she knew, he was being mugged or kidnapped at this very moment. Max inspected the people around him again. They all looked like crooks to him.

Then, through a gap in the crowd, he noticed a wiry, nervous-looking little man holding up a cardboard sign. It had something written on it in small, neat handwriting. Max had just deciphered his own name when the man saw him and darted over.

"Mister Max Murphy?"

"Yes?"

"I am pleased to meet you. I was beginning to think you had missed the plane." Here, the man wiped his forehead with a handkerchief to dramatize the worry Max had caused him.

"You might want to get a bigger sign," said Max. He looked around. "So where are my parents?"

"They could not come."

"Why not? Too busy with work, I suppose? Typical!"

The little man was obviously taken aback by this outburst, but he patted Max reassuringly on the arm. "You are tired from your journey. Please not to worry, I will take care of you."

Max looked him up and down. "Who *are* you?"

The stranger fumbled in his pocket for an identity card. "My name is Oscar Poot," he said. "I am the Head of the Maya Foundation here in San Xavier City. I have the privilege to work with the great Frank and Carla Murphy."

Max returned his handshake distractedly. He was still half expecting his parents to materialize.

"Come," said Oscar, trying to lead Max away.

Max shook him off.

"I'm not going anywhere until you tell me where my parents are."

Max sat down in the nearest chair, folded his arms and tried to look immovable.

Oscar glanced nervously around as if to check they weren't being watched. Then he sighed in resignation and sat down heavily beside Max.

"It is going to be OK," he said.

"What's going to be OK?"

Oscar looked at the floor. Then he studied a cockroach that was burrowing into a corner. Then he folded his handkerchief into geometric shapes. Max was ready to explode with impatience by the time Oscar finally spoke.

"I last spoke to your parents four days ago. They were calling on the satellite phone from the Temple of Ix Chel." (He said the name slowly, and the way he pronounced it, Eesh Chell, reminded

Max of the wind that whistled every time the terminal doors were opened and the angry rain that lashed the windows.)

He shivered. "Where's Ix Chel?

"Way up in the north. It's a very remote site, Late Preclassic . . . "

"But what did they say?" Max interrupted impatiently.

"It was a bad connection, but I understood they had made good progress and they were planning to carry out an experiment that night to test their theory . . . "

"What experiment? What theory?"

"I do not know. To tell the truth, I was a little hurt. It's not like them to keep such things secret from me. But Frank said he would explain everything when they got back."

"So when will that be?" said Max. He felt like he'd been kicked in the stomach. No happy reunions today. His parents were off somewhere with their beloved Ancient Maya and, once again, he was on his own.

"They should be back already," said Oscar. "But the weather has been so bad and Ix Chel is far away. We have been trying to contact them, but no luck. Of course, communications often fail in the jungle — especially in bad weather."

"Knowing Mom and Dad, they probably decided to stay a bit longer at their precious temple. I bet they lost their phone or forgot to switch it on or something."

"That's the spirit," smiled Oscar. "Nothing to worry about."

Something in his voice told Max he was very worried indeed.

"Is there something you haven't told me?" asked Max.

"Of course not," said Oscar. "It's just that . . . " His voice trailed off as if he'd thought better of whatever he was going to say.

"What?" said Max, impatiently.

"You must forgive me, I have always had a big imagination. But I can't help feeling that your parents are mixed up in something . . . dangerous."

First the immigration official, now this guy. What was wrong with people in San Xavier? This was the second time today that someone had referred to Frank and Carla Murphy as if they were criminal masterminds.

"Get real," laughed Max. "My parents are just boring archaeologists, not secret agents. There's nothing dangerous about old pots."

Oscar raised an eyebrow. "Let's go," he said.

"Wait a minute," said Max. "If you haven't spoken to my parents lately, how did you know to meet me? Zia only bought my ticket the day before yesterday."

"Zia? Ah yes, it was this Zia who called me."

Max's head was spinning. "It was *Zia*? Then Mom and Dad must have made contact with her somehow. She said they wanted me to come."

"*They*?" Oscar narrowed his eyes suspiciously. "Who is *they*?"

"My parents, of course. Who else?"

Oscar opened his mouth to answer and then thought better of it. He picked up Max's backpack and gestured for him to follow.

"Where are we going?"

"To the bus station."

Max groaned. He'd been looking forward to checking into a hotel, having a hot shower, ordering room service, and watching some TV.

"A bus? Give me a break! I've just been sitting on a plane for five hours . . . "

"You are to stay at the house of your uncle, Mr. Theodore Murphy."

"Uncle Ted? Where does he live? Can't you drive me there?"

"I am sorry, but it is far from here, over the mountains. My car would not make it. The bus is the only way. Your uncle will meet you at Aguas Muertas."

"*Aguas Muertas*?" Spanish was one of Max's least favorite subjects at school, but a few words had seeped into his brain. "*Dead Waters*? What kind of name is that?"

"It is a long story," said Oscar. "I will tell you sometime, but right now we must go to the bus station. Are you ready to run?"

His car was parked just a short sprint from the terminal doors, but the rain was so fierce that once again Max got soaked.

"How do you like this rain?" Oscar gestured at the dark gray sky as he tried to start up the engine of his battered little car. "It is most unusual for the time of year. Even the old people say they have never seen anything like it."

"It's not much drier inside," muttered Max. His window refused to roll all the way up and his face was stung by the rain that pelted through the gap. His feet were sitting in a pool of water at least three inches deep. He groped for his seat belt and realized there wasn't one. But Oscar didn't seem to notice anything amiss and they roared off into the rain, narrowly missing a collision with an airport fuel tanker. The stubby wipers struggled to cope with the volume of water and Max wondered how Oscar could see anything as he wove crazily through the traffic. Suddenly the car in front stopped at a red light and Oscar jumped on the brakes. Max slammed his hands on the dash to stop himself flying through the windshield. As the car skidded to a halt, he was thrown back against the seat, wrenching his neck.

Oscar turned to Max and smiled.

"Hungry?" he asked.

Max considered the question. His primary emotion right now was terror at Oscar's driving. Next to that, he was wet, tired, and confused. But underneath it all, he was amazed to detect the ever-present flicker of hunger.

A surprisingly short time later, they had parked at the bus station and installed themselves at a table in the nearest café.

Max looked around in distaste. It was the least appetizing eating place he'd ever seen. There was no counter or bar, just a small, low-ceilinged room containing a few ill-matched tables and chairs. The walls were yellowed with cigarette smoke and sticky with grease. A naked lightbulb hung from the ceiling, illuminating the cockroaches that scuttled across the dirty floor. Max tried not to think about the class on food hygiene he'd taken last term.

A volley of curses issued from a doorway at the back, which presumably led to the kitchen. Then an ancient waitress in bright red lipstick, a miniskirt, and carpet slippers made her way over. Max looked at the silvery gray roots of her stringy blond hair as she flicked the crumbs off the table and onto the floor. She looks like Madonna's great-great-grandmother, he thought.

While Oscar ordered the Daily Special for both of them, Max tried to dry himself out with some paper napkins. He was surprised to notice that he'd already acquired several nasty insect bites on his arms.

When the waitress had shuffled back with their drinks (a bottle of Coke for Max, a bottle of rum for Oscar), Oscar proposed a toast.

"To your parents," he said. "May they return safely."

Max didn't even bother to raise his glass. "Honestly, I'm sure they're fine," he said. "When my father's thinking about the Maya, he forgets everything else. And he's *always* thinking about the Maya. He forgot to come home for my birthday party once. He's so selfish and Mom lets him get away with it."

"How can you speak like this about your parents?" protested Oscar, sounding shocked. "It is not respectful. And they are such wonderful people."

"So wonderful," said Max sarcastically, "they just flew off and abandoned me."

"You feel abandoned? But your parents talk about you all the time. How we laugh at the Foundation to hear the story about when you were little and you took off all your clothes in the supermarket and . . ."

"Stop!" said Max, who didn't like to be laughed at. "I don't want to hear it."

Oscar looked surprised at his rudeness. He gazed around the room in silence, radiating hurt feelings and wounded pride.

Max cast around for a less sensitive topic of conversation. "Why don't you tell me how Aguas Muertas got its name?" he suggested.

Oscar cheered up slightly, took a large gulp of rum, and began.

"It used to be called Santa Aguada. It was just a little trading post at the mouth of the Monkey River. Then the Spanish found logwood upriver. You know of this, yes?"

"No," said Max.

"Logwood trees contain a red dye that Europe was crazy for. A single load of logwood was worth more than a whole year's cargo of anything else. Almost overnight, my people were enslaved in logging camps and Santa Aguada became a prosperous port." Oscar's eyes shone with emotion. "As the Monkey River ran red with the blood of Maya slaves, the hands of the Spanish were stained bloodred with logwood dye."

Max became aware that diners on nearby tables were listening in.

"Could you talk more quietly?" he whispered. "Everyone's looking at us."

If anything, Oscar got louder.

"So the logwood was floated downriver to the port, where it was loaded onto galleons and shipped back to Spain — along with anything else the Spanish could steal from us." He paused dramatically and dropped his voice. "One day, the cargo on the dock included a sea chest belonging to Friar Diego DeLanda."

At this name, the restaurant fell silent.

Now all the tables were hanging on to Oscar's words.

He took another swig and poked Max in the chest.

"Your parents have told you about DeLanda?"

"I don't remember," said Max.

"You would not forget if you were Maya," said Oscar. "Diego DeLanda was a putrid devil, oozed up from the most slimy depths of hell to destroy my people."

This story was getting more interesting.

"What did he do?" asked Max.

Oscar thumped on the table. "He tortured us, he burned our books, he looted our inheritance."

A murmur of assent went around the room.

"But worst of all," continued Oscar, "he tried to steal our Jaguar Stones."

"Jaguar Stones?" said Max. "What are they?"

The old waitress wheeled around and fixed him with a glittering eye. She looked different now. She was standing up straight and proud, like a ballet dancer. Her shoulders were back, her chin was up, and Max could see that once she had been beautiful. She seemed surprised to find herself holding a tray of dirty plates. She set it down quickly, as if it was burning hot, and pulled up a chair at the nearest table.

Meanwhile, Oscar stared at Max in surprise. "You have never heard of the Jaguar Stones?"

Max shook his head.

Oscar addressed the room. "He has never heard of the Jaguar Stones."

The diners gasped with incredulity. A whisper went around the room. It sounded like *"baa-laam-toon oh ob."* The waitress pulled a handkerchief from her pocket and wiped away a tear.

"What are they saying?" asked Max, but Oscar had begun his story.

"Once the five sacred stones gave us dominion over all the land," he declaimed. "At the five sacred pyramids, they made our kings as powerful as gods. DeLanda knew that, with the Jaguar

Stones, we were invincible. If all five stones had been brought to-gether, no force on Earth could have beaten us. There would have been no conquest. My people would not have endured these five long centuries of slavery and oppression. But thanks to the evil of one man, our past and our future have been destroyed."

Oscar sat down and buried his head in his hands. A gloom set-tled over the restaurant. Some diners pushed away their plates, too miserable to eat. Others called to the waitress for more drinks. She got slowly to her feet, old again and haggard, and shuffled off to serve them. Max hadn't thought this place could get anymore de-pressing. But now it was like Suicide Central. He had to get Oscar talking again.

"Mr. Poot?" he said. "Oscar? You were telling me how Aguas Muertas got its name . . . ?"

Oscar slowly looked up. "Then listen well," he said, "for I am about to tell the story of our doom."

Despite this somber opening, the mood in the restaurant bright-ened instantly. The other customers nudged each other and mur-mured their encouragement, for Oscar was a masterly storyteller and they were eager to hear the next installment. The old waitress sat down again to listen, her eyes shining with emotion.

"Imagine the scene," said Oscar. "We are on the wharf at Santa Aguada. A brisk wind tugs at the *Espada*'s sails as the Maya slaves load her up with logwood and other plunder. A sea chest sits ex-pectantly on the dock, but none of the slaves will touch it. It bears the crest of Friar Diego DeLanda and among its ill-gotten contents are said to be two of our sacred Jaguar Stones."

Heads shook in despair all around the room.

"The slaves are whipped and beaten, but still they refuse to load the chest. Eventually, the captain and his first mate lug it aboard themselves, determined to sail with the tide. But just as the ropes are cast off, a Maya warrior appears on the dock. He is tall and hand-some. His skin is painted black and he wears the battle gear of kings: a quetzal-plumed headdress and a jaguar-skin cloak."

Oscar was enjoying himself now. His audience was riveted, as he continued: "Who is this mighty warrior, you ask? He never speaks his name. But some say it is the greatest and most fearless of them all, the immortal Lord Six-Rabbit."

Max quickly moved out of the way as Oscar pushed back his chair and jumped up to act out the scene.

"The Maya king points at the captain of the *Espada*. '*Unload the ship*,' he commands, '*or these will be the waters of thy death* — las aguas de su muerte. *This ship will never leave these shores. And this accursed town, built by the suffering of my people, will forever be the home of misery and despair.*'"

"Ay," moaned the waitress, stifling a sob.

Encouraged by this reaction, Oscar put his hands on his hips to imitate the swagger of a Spanish sea captain.

"Of course, the captain laughed at the crazy native and the *Espada* set sail for Cadiz. It was a perfect day. Her sails soon caught the wind and she headed for the open sea. She rounded the point of the bay and disappeared from view. She was never seen again. A week later, the body of the captain was found floating in the harbor."

Oscar dropped his voice to a dramatic whisper.

"On his forehead was the mark of the Jaguar."

There was a moment's dramatic silence before the whole place burst into wild applause. Oscar signaled for quiet. "This was no happy ending," he said. "If DeLanda couldn't steal our stones, he robbed us of their power. Lost, buried, hidden, separated, the Jaguar Stones were soon forgotten. And when we lost our sacred stones, we lost our fighting spirit. Our Golden Age was over, never to return."

The waitress sobbed more loudly.

Oscar raised his glass in the gesture of a toast. "To the Jaguar Stones," he said.

"And to Lord Six-Rabbit," added another customer.

For one brief shining moment, the entire restaurant stood and raised their glasses. Then the spell was broken and they downed their drinks and slumped back into their seats.

Oscar smiled at Max. "And that, my friend, is how Aguas Muertas got its name."

"What happened to the galleon?" asked Max.

"No trace of the *Espada* — nor DeLanda's sea chest — has ever been found. Some say it was dragged down to the underworld by the weight of the sacred stones. Others say the crew mutinied and scuppered the ship after stealing its precious cargo. Who knows?" Oscar shrugged. "The official explanation is that the ship hit a reef and sank. Certainly, these waters are treacherous. Ah, here comes the food."

The waitress set down two steaming plates.

The iniquities of history were forgotten as Oscar sniffed the food appreciatively and rubbed his hands together in anticipation. "Mmm," he murmured, "who doesn't like tamales?"

The revenge of Zia, thought Max.

Tamales, it turned out, were quite a favorite in San Xavier. There were at least three tamale stands in the bus station, adding their distinctive moldy aroma to the already toxic mixture of exhaust fumes, cigarette smoke, and sweat.

But it was the noise that made Max's eyes water.

Horns blared, doors slammed, adults shouted, children wailed, babies screamed, and underneath it all, tinny piped music screeched out from loudspeakers on poles.

A never-ending convoy of buses streamed into the flooded parking lot, each one gaudily painted in bright colors and inscribed with a woman's name.

"They look like old school buses," said Max.

"That's what they are," said Oscar. "We buy them from North America. The tourists call them 'chicken buses.'"

"Why?"

"I suppose, because the locals use them to carry chickens to market."

Max watched as Lidia, the bus in front of him, disgorged twice as many people — and chickens — as could possibly have fit inside. Were they all running around the back and getting on again to trick him? It was crazy.

Oscar saw his astonishment.

"We have a joke," he said. "How many people can you fit on a chicken bus?"

"I don't know," said Max.

"The answer," smiled Oscar, "is 'Always one more.'"

Lidia had railings around her roof for the luggage. A young boy climbed up and began throwing down all the wet bags and threadbare cases with a muddy splat. At the same time, a barrage of identical pieces was thrown up at him from all sides, as if he were a goalie in some manic soccer practice. Meanwhile, at ground level, another heaving mass of humanity fought to get onboard.

Oscar pointed to a ramshackle pink- and green-striped vehicle that was just pulling in. The name *Estelly* was painted on its side.

"That is your bus. Push your way on as soon as the doors open. You have to be quick, they sell more tickets than seats." Oscar handed him a greasy paper bag of something and shoved him into the crowd.

"Aren't you coming with me?" called Max, but he was already being carried along in the throng toward the steps of the bus.

He fought his way onboard, elbowing everyone who got in his way, and he was instantly enveloped in the reek of too many unwashed bodies packed into too small a space. The odor was unpleasant, but oddly reminiscent of roasting peanuts. He found an empty seat at the back and slid in. It was a tight squeeze. He put his backpack on the seat next to him to discourage anyone from sitting there.

Moments later, a fat man in a cowboy hat eased in and would have sat on the backpack if Max hadn't grabbed it and pushed it onto the floor. He was now pinned against the window and, with his feet on his backpack, his knees were under his chin. A woman, carrying a sleeping child, made her way to the back of the bus and eyed the same seat. Soon — impossibly — the four of them were crammed onto a hard plastic bench originally designed for two schoolchildren.

The rest of the bus filled up just as quickly. And when no one else could squeeze even part of a buttock onto a seat, they sat between the seats in the aisle.

Max's eyes were the only parts of him that could freely move, so he swiveled his gaze to look out of the window, expecting to see Oscar out there. But all he saw was darkness and chaos. He remembered that Oscar had given him something. Moving slowly, extricating first one arm and then the other, he managed to open the paper bag.

Tamales.

The fat man in the cowboy hat made a little grunt of pleasure.

Max passed him the bag. The fat man deftly unwrapped the little cornhusk packages and devoured the contents greedily. Then he nodded at Max and went instantly to sleep, the crumbs on his lips fluttering in time to his snores, like flowers dancing in the breeze.

There was nothing to do but wait for the bus driver.

One hour later, when he finally appeared, the first thing the driver did was switch on a radio. Jangling, distorted Caribbean music was pumped into every corner of the bus. Max groped in his backpack until he found his iPod. But even with The Plague Rats at full volume, he could still hear the tinny hiss of bus music.

A conductor, who didn't look more than twelve years old, jumped on and banged on the side of the bus with his fist. With a blast on the air horn, the driver revved the engine, crashed the gears, and splashed out of the parking lot.

Max Murphy was on his way to Aguas Muertas.

CHAPTER III

AGUAS MUERTAS

THE BUS TRAVELED on through the night, stopping and starting, stopping and starting. For every two people who got off, three more always seemed to get on. Maybe, thought Max, it was called the chicken bus because they were all crammed into tiny spaces like chickens in cages.

The body heat generated by the fat man was becoming unbearable. Max was stuck to the plastic bench with sweat. His iPod ran out of juice, but he kept the earphones on to try and block out the radio. He tried to sleep; but every time he drifted off, he was jolted painfully awake by his head smacking against the window as the bus bumped through the rutted course of mud and stones that was the road.

Max passed the long hours until dawn by watching the gyrations of the little conductor as he squirmed and burrowed through the huddled bodies to collect his fares. When a hazy pink sunrise broke through the rain clouds, Max was grateful for the prospect of daylight so that he could watch the world go by.

After five minutes, he realized darkness was preferable.

In the dark, you couldn't see all the hairpin bends. You weren't so aware of other traffic and how your driver liked passing it at top speed on blind corners.

As they hurtled along a narrow precipice, Max tried not to think about the little picket fence of crosses along the roadside, each one marking the scene of a previous accident. He tried not to look at the mangled wreckage of overturned cars and buses that dotted the mountainside below him, giving it the air of a modern sculpture park. He tried instead to concentrate on the valley floor where brightly painted wooden houses punctuated the lush green fields. He could see men working in the orange groves, children chasing dogs, and women bending over cooking fires.

Then his worst fear came true.

Around the next corner came another chicken bus. The two vehicles faced each other in the rain on the narrow mountain road, both blasting their air horns, neither one slowing down.

Max couldn't look.

Now he knew why they were called chicken buses. Because their crazy drivers liked to play chicken with their passengers' lives.

Somehow they made it.

Maybe the other driver had given way. Maybe the two buses had scraped past each other. Max would never know, as he'd had his hands over his face the whole time.

By the time the little conductor yelled, "Aguas Muertas!" late that afternoon, he'd stopped thinking altogether. His only emotion was an intense desire to get off the bus. But as they rumbled through the outskirts of town, his heart sank even further. Aguas Muertas was far worse than he could ever have imagined.

How did the Maya king put it in Oscar's story? *"This accursed place will forever be the home of misery and despair . . . "*

Well, the king's curse had certainly come true.

What a dump.

The streets were lined with dilapidated wooden shacks. Their tin roofs were rusty and patched. Their walls, once gaily painted, were cracked and stained.

On nearly every corner was a dimly lit bar where men hunched over their empty glasses. Old women in black sat in porches and doorways, but none bothered to look up as the bus went past. Even the scrawny little dogs lay still, their heads on their paws, while flies buzzed half-heartedly around them.

A fat finger poked him in the ribs.

His neighbor in the cowboy hat was telling him to open the window. Although the sky was still heavy and gray, the rain had finally stopped. Max pulled down the window, took a deep breath, and

almost choked on it. The salty sea air and the leafy smell of jungle were overpowered by the stench of rotting fish and diesel oil.

"Aguas Muertas!" yelled the conductor again.

With a final squeal of brakes, the bus skidded to a stop in a rubbish-strewn square. The only indication that this was the center of the town — and the only reminder of its wealthy colonial past — was a crumbling cathedral at one end of the square, fronted by a statue of some long-forgotten Spanish general on his horse.

How the mighty had fallen.

Once the general and his compatriots, flush with looted treasure, had built their lavish palaces in this square. Once their wives had paraded round it in the latest European fashions.

But now the looters themselves had been looted.

Their palaces were scrawled with graffiti and festooned with washing lines. Their cathedral was an empty shell. As for the general, he and his horse were just the droppings-encrusted roost for the pigeons that scratched a living in the square.

Max took off his earphones and discovered they were no longer plugged into anything. Someone had stolen his iPod. It must have happened in the night, while he was dozing. Tears of rage pricked his eyes. He suspected the little conductor, but he knew it was no use accusing anyone.

He deliberately trampled on the fat man's toes as he squeezed out of his seat and then punished the whole bus by "accidentally" hitting as many people as he could with his backpack as he edged toward the door.

Leaving a chorus of protests and curses behind him, Max jumped off the bus and surveyed the wretched huddle of people waiting on the sidewalk. Was one of these hapless peasants Uncle Ted?

All along the line, Max's hopeful smile was met by hostile scowls.

"Hey, Americano!" called a voice. It was the little conductor. He was on the roof of the bus, throwing down bags. "Catch!" he yelled, pretending to take aim at Max with a sack of corn cobs.

Max ducked in spite of himself and instantly felt foolish. Everyone was laughing and pointing at him. His face burned with rage, and he was filled with an intense loathing for Aguas Muertas: the place, the people, and even the pigeons in the square.

As soon as the last bag hit the ground, the bus gave a blast on its air horn and lurched away in a grinding of gears. When the cloud of black exhaust smoke cleared, the other passengers had gone and Max was left standing alone.

Once again, there was no one to meet him.

He felt like a sailor who'd just stepped onto dry land after months at sea. His body was buzzing from the last fifteen hours of ceaseless vibration.

He looked unsteadily around and noticed two men loitering on a corner, smoking. They were watching him like cats watching a mouse.

Uncle Ted, where are you?

Aware of the men's scrutiny, Max tried to look less like a stranger. He put his hands in his pockets and sauntered shakily down the street. This attempt at nonchalance was severely hampered by a swarm of yellow butterflies, which, it seemed, had never seen a tourist before. They dive-bombed him and flapped madly around, trying to land on his head, his face, his hands, any piece of exposed skin they could find.

After several minutes of swatting butterflies, Max glanced back. The men were walking toward him. A knife glinted in the sunlight.

Max pulled out his cell phone. He knew it wouldn't work outside the States, but he jabbed at it anyway.

"Hello," he said loudly, "Police?

Just then, a shiny new Mercedes with blackened windows rolled into the square and pulled up across the street. The butterflies took off in a yellow cloud. The men melted into the shadows.

Max stared at the car. It looked so out of place in that little squalid town, it could have been an alien spaceship.

The door of the Mercedes opened and the driver slowly got out.

He was the biggest person Max had ever seen: a massive block of solid muscle in a black suit and dark sunglasses.

He wasn't that old, but his twenty or so years had obviously been hard-lived. A long scar ran down his haughty Maya face from his high, sloped forehead to the bottom of one ear. His bulbous nose looked as if it had been on the losing end of a fight with an iron bar. From his big bull neck to his barrel chest and his legs like tree trunks, every inch of this giant exuded menace.

Was this guy the Maya Mafia or what?

Max was telling himself to keep calm, but his heart was beating like a jungle drum and his brain was in panic overdrive. He stood there, rooted to the spot in terror, as the driver strode over — staring at him all the while — and snatched his backpack.

"Is that the police?" Max babbled again into his dead cell phone.

The driver slung the backpack into the trunk, then came back and stood in front of Max, staring at him quizzically.

"Take it, take it," stammered Max, handing over his cell phone, "but, p-p-p-please don't hurt me. My uncle will be here any minute."

Trying not to cry, he sniffed so hard that a wet snort was sucked up into the deepest cavities of his head, only to crash back down his nostrils in a bubbling tsunami. He wiped his nose on the back of his hand. This was not his coolest moment.

The rear door of the Mercedes opened and a hand emerged holding out a crisply ironed white handkerchief. The hand was followed by its owner, a handsome but slightly haggard man in a cream linen suit and Panama hat. A wisp of dark reddish hair was just visible beneath the brim. Two pale blue eyes regarded him sadly.

"Max Murphy, I presume?" said the man.

"Uncle Ted?" whispered Max.

The man nodded. "Could you blow your nose?" he asked, with distaste.

Max took the handkerchief and gave a long, honking blow, scrutinizing Uncle Ted all the while. He looked much older than Max's father. There was only a year or two between the brothers, but Ted had deep furrows etched into his brow and down the sides of his mouth. Besides his wrinkles and his melancholic air, Max was relieved to see that Ted Murphy had something else distinctive about him. From his immaculately casual suit to his neatly manicured fingernails, it was the unmistakable glow of wealth.

Max tried to hand back the wet, grimy handkerchief. Uncle Ted grimaced and the driver stepped in to take it, with evident disgust.

"This is Lucky Jim," said Uncle Ted.

Lucky didn't seem he right name for this ugly, battle-scarred man-mountain.

"Hello," said Max.

Lucky Jim gave a big smile full of gold teeth. "Nice cell phone," he said.

"Yeah," said Max, "except it doesn't work here."

"You mean you weren't really talking to the police?" Lucky feigned surprise.

Max scowled at him, which made both men laugh rather unpleasantly.

"I wouldn't get on the wrong side of Lucky if I were you," warned Uncle Ted. "He comes from a long line of fierce Maya warriors."

Max swallowed hard. They weren't exactly making him feel welcome. "Have you heard from Mom and Dad?" he asked.

"No," said Uncle Ted. "I was going to ask you the same question. I'd like to know how long you'll be staying with us. It's most inconvenient. We're very busy at the moment." He looked at his watch. "Speaking of which, we need to get going."

Max slid into the Mercedes. He was stiff and bruised from the chicken bus and his bones sank gratefully into the soft leather cushions. Enveloped in luxury, with the electric windows tightly closed and the air conditioning gently fanning him, he felt safe at last from the horrors of Aguas Muertas. He sat back and put his feet up against the seat in front of him.

This was the way to travel, all right.

"Feet down," barked his uncle, getting in next to him. He leaned over and carefully wiped the imprint of Max's dusty shoes off the leather seat back.

Lucky drove them out of town on another rutted, muddy road.

The Mercedes rolled smoothly over the rocks and potholes until they came to a driveway marked Gran Hotel de Las Americas.

"Do you live in a hotel?" asked Max.

"Of course not," snapped Uncle Ted. "I have a business meeting here."

Max groaned. He just wanted to collapse into bed.

"It won't take long. And the view from the terrace is spectacular."

"I'm too tired for sightseeing. Can I wait in the car?"

"No."

"But . . . "

"You'll do as I say. There are some dangerous people around."

As they rounded a curve in the drive, an imposing colonial style building came into view. It hadn't seen a coat of paint for a hundred years, but somehow it managed to be charming rather than depressing — quite a feat in Aguas Muertas.

They drew up at the colonnaded entrance and a liveried doorman came running over to open the car door. "Welcome, Mister Ted," he said.

Uncle Ted gave a slight nod and strode past him into the hotel.

Max sat stubbornly in the back seat.

"Out," said Lucky Jim. "Now."

Reluctantly, Max climbed out of the car and went into the hotel.

"This way," ordered Lucky Jim, leading him briskly through the rundown lobby and out onto a stone terrace overlooking the sea.

Although they had the terrace to themselves, Uncle Ted had chosen a table tucked away in the far corner. He sat down with his back to the wall and pulled out a chair for Max. Lucky Jim took up a lookout position in the garden. They certainly took security seriously in the banana business.

A waiter in a starched white jacket glided out of a side door and set down little dishes of olives and roasted cashew nuts.

"Good afternoon, Mister Ted. May I bring your usual?"

"Thank you, Victor. And for you, Max?"

Max perked up a little.

"Do you have Coke?"

"Yes, sir."

"And vanilla ice cream?"

"Of course, sir."

The waiter bowed and was gone.

Maybe Aguas Muertas wasn't so bad after all, thought Max.

He got up to look around. From the terrace, steps led down through formal gardens to a small pebble beach.

"Come back and sit down," said Uncle Ted. His eyes were darting all over the gardens as if he were looking for someone.

Max came back. He leaned over the side terrace wall. The clouds were clearing now and the estuary below sparkled like emeralds in the sun.

"Sit."

Max sat on the terrace wall. "What's that river down there?" he asked.

"This is a business meeting," said Uncle Ted. "Please sit at the table like a civilized human being. When my client comes, I want you to stay in your chair and don't move. Lucky Jim will watch you. I will take a walk with my client."

With a heavy sigh, Max did as he asked. "So what's the river?' he repeated sulkily.

"That's the Monkey River," said Uncle Ted, "the main artery of San Xavier. It flows right across the country to the Caribbean sea."

"Oscar Poot said it used to flow red with the blood of the logwood slaves."

"Oscar Poot must have a vivid imagination."

"He said he thinks Mom and Dad might be mixed up in something dangerous."

"Well, I just wish they'd made proper arrangements before they embarked on their little adventure."

"What do you mean?"

"I don't wish to sound inhospitable, Max, but I'm not running a guesthouse. Your parents stayed here last week and that was bad enough. Then I get a phone call out of the blue, and I'm supposed to drop everything and play babysitter to their son."

"Who phoned you?" asked Max.

"That madwoman who lives with you," said Uncle Ted. "You call her Zia, don't you? I told her not to send you here, but she wouldn't listen to reason."

Max shifted uncomfortably.

"And here I am," he said, eventually.

"And here you are," echoed Uncle Ted coldly.

Max could feel his temper rising. He squeezed his hands into fists and pressed his fingernails into his skin to stop himself from saying anything he might regret. He wasn't going to let Uncle Ted know how lost and alone he was feeling right now.

He took a deep breath and focused on the boats bobbing on the green water. "Is the Temple of Ix Chel near here?" he asked.

"No," said Uncle Ted.

"Did my parents tell you what they were doing at Ix Chel?"

"No," said Uncle Ted.

"Look," said Max, "I get it. You don't like my parents and you don't like me. But the sooner I track them down, the sooner we'll all be out of here. So you might want to be a bit more helpful."

Uncle Ted surveyed him coolly. "It's a deal," he said.

"So what do you know about Ix Chel?" asked Max.

"The Temple of Ix Chel was one of the five sacred pyramids of the Monkey River. Ix Chel herself was the moon goddess. Her name means Lady Rainbow, which sounds nice enough, but don't let that deceive you. The Maya thought rainbows were bad omens from the underworld. You certainly didn't want to make Lady Rainbow angry."

"Why not?"

"She had a nasty habit of emptying her water jar on the earth and causing floods and rainstorms."

Above them, the sky was clouding over again.

"You seem to get a lot of rain here," said Max.

"Tropical climate," shrugged Uncle Ted. "Although I must admit it isn't usually this wet. The farmers will be worried if this carries on much longer."

"Do the farmers still believe in Lady Rainbow?"

"If they do," smiled Uncle Ted, "they might want to make some offerings to her. She's obviously not happy about something."

"What kind of offerings?"

"I'm joking, Max. The farmers get their weather reports from the TV these days."

"But what kind of offerings did they *used* to make to Ix Chel?"

"Oh, you know, the usual. Jade, incense, sacrifices, that sort of thing."

"*Human* sacrifices?" asked Max. "That's so gross." He shook his head in disgust. Then a horrible thought occurred to him. "I hope Mom and Dad are all right."

"Frank knows how to survive in the wild," said Uncle Ted. "Ix Chel is pretty inaccessible at the best of times, and with all the damage caused by the storms, the trails will probably be impassable. But I'm sure they'll be back in a day or two."

They sat in silence until Victor came back with their order.

Max poured half the coke into his glass and carefully dropped a large spoonful of ice cream into it. Then he closed his eyes and sucked it all down until his straw made loud gurgling noises on the bottom of his empty glass.

When he opened his eyes, he realized that Uncle Ted and the waiter were staring at him appalled.

Get a life, thought Max, it's hardly the Ritz-Carlton.

"I'm sorry, Victor," said Uncle Ted to the waiter. "I can only apologize for my nephew's table manners."

Victor smiled indulgently at Max. Then he leaned over to Uncle Ted and whispered, "Have you heard anything from the police yet, sir?"

Uncle Ted froze. His eyes darted nervously toward Max to see if he'd heard.

"The police?" sputtered Max. "Is this about Mom and Dad?"

Victor shot an apologetic glance at Uncle Ted and scurried away.

"Calm down," said Uncle Ted. "The chief of police is a friend of mine. I asked him to send a few men up to Ix Chel, just to check there was nothing untoward."

"What do you mean, *untoward*?"

"Oh, I don't know. Things are never what they seem around here."

"Like what?"

"Forget it. It's superstitious nonsense. I wish I'd never mentioned it."

"Tell me . . . please . . . you *have* to tell me."

Uncle Ted sighed. "It's just that many people claim to have seen a strange light over Ix Chel last week."

"What? Like a UFO or something?"

"I told you it was nonsense, Max."

"But what did it look like?"

Uncle Ted's voice took on a husky quality. "It was like a glowing white cloud against the night sky, it was long and thick, and it reared over Ix Chel like a ghostly serpent."

"A serpent? Why would they say something like that?"

"Who knows? The locals have a problem distinguishing past and present. It's all the same to them."

"But I don't understand . . . "

"Hundreds of years ago, the king would go to the Temple of Ix Chel to seek guidance from his ancestors. They spoke to him through a ghostly snake called the Vision Serpent. That's what people believe they saw in the sky that night. So the local witch doctors are saying that your parents did something to anger the goddess Ix Chel and that's why we've been having so much rain." Uncle Ted noticed that several gardeners and waiters were plainly eavesdropping. He spoke louder this time for their benefit. "Of course, it's bull. You always get this sort of thing at a dig."

"So why did you call the police?"

"I want to put a stop to the gossip before it holds up work at the banana plantations. But I'm sure Frank and Carla will come strolling home before the police even get to Ix Chel." He looked at his watch and shook his head. "Where's my client got to? He should be here by now. I can't abide lateness."

Suddenly, a shout rang out from the gardens. Uncle Ted spun round and Lucky Jim pulled out a gun. There was another shout, a flash of steel, and then one of the gardeners held up the headless, writhing body of a snake.

"Good thing Dad's not here, he hates snakes," said Max, in horror. Suddenly, he felt ill. He wished he hadn't drunk his float so quickly. "Where's the restroom?"

After a few wrong turns, he found it upstairs.

Max looked at himself in the tarnished mirror. His face was white as death. He told himself it was exhaustion from the journey but, deep inside, he knew he was creeped out by this whole Ancient Maya thing.

Human sacrifices, ghostly snakes in the sky . . . he didn't want to stay in San Xavier a day longer than he had to. Maybe when his parents came back, they could all fly up to Florida for a proper vacation. It was the least they could do to make up for everything they'd put him through.

He turned on the tap. After a lot of banging in the pipes, some weak brown water trickled out. He splashed his face and rinsed his mouth. The water smelled of drains and it tasted awful. He stumbled into the corridor, intending to stick his head out of the nearest window for some fresh air. But what he saw made him jump back.

There were men with guns all over the garden. They were dressed in black, and they seemed to be focused on something that was happening directly under the window.

Max flattened himself against the wall and peered down.

There were two men on the path. One was his uncle. The other was a swarthy, dark-haired man with a neatly trimmed beard and a moustache that curled up at the ends. Like his bodyguards, he was dressed in black, with a short cape around his shoulders and black leather gloves.

This must be Uncle Ted's client.

But why all the guns and the bodyguards?

Voices drifted up to the window.

"I understand you have certain, shall we say, *objects* for sale," the dark-haired man was saying in a strong Spanish accent.

"Objects?" repeated Uncle Ted cagily.

"Let us not play games, Señor Murphy. I have heard that you recently sold a sword, a fine blade of Toledo. I must know where you found this piece."

"I'm afraid I cannot divulge that information."

The Spaniard clicked his tongue impatiently. He seemed to be having a problem controlling his temper. "*Bueno*. But you will confirm that it was the sword of Friar Diego DeLanda?"

"It was sold as such," conceded Uncle Ted.

"If that sword is authentic, Señor Murphy, it was last seen in the hold of the ship *Espada* that sailed from this very port in 1563 and was lost en route to Cadiz." (He pronounced it cad-eeth.)

"I am aware of the history of the sword."

"Then you will know that the same cargo was said to include some Maya stone carvings?"

"Ah, so you're a collector of stone carvings?"

"Señor Murphy, let us get to the point . . . "

The Spaniard clicked his fingers and one of his bodyguards came forward, carrying a metal briefcase. He tripped slightly on the terrace steps and before he could regain his balance, the Spaniard had grabbed the briefcase from him, pulled out a gun, and pistol-whipped him across the face. As the guard fell to the ground in pain, the Spaniard kicked him savagely in the stomach. "Clumsy pig," he screamed.

This guy's a complete psycho! thought Max.

Uncle Ted was staring at the scene in horror, but the Spaniard turned back to him as if nothing had happened. "The stone that I seek . . . " he began and then he noticed a drop of the guard's blood on one of his black leather riding boots. *"Momentito,"* he said, clicking his fingers again. Another guard materialized to wipe away the offending stain.

"Bueno," said the Spaniard, "and now to business. As I was saying, the stone that I seek must match this one, *exactamente.*"

With that, he placed the briefcase on the garden wall and unlocked it. The breeze died down and the birds stopped singing as he threw back the lid.

A faint glow emanated from the case, and Max could see that it was lined with foam. Nestled inside was a glassy black stone about the size of a grapefruit. It was carved to look like a jaguar's head with the mouth open, ready to bite. An unpleasant smell, like rotting meat, wafted up to the window.

Uncle Ted gasped. His face looked even more deeply wrinkled in the glow of the stone. "The Black Jaguar . . . lost for centuries . . . ," his voice was an admiring whisper, " . . . but where did you get it?"

The Spaniard snapped the briefcase closed.

"I, too, have my secrets, Señor Murphy. But I see that you recognize the stone. Tell me, do you have any of its brothers?"

"If I did," said Uncle Ted, "I'd be a fool to sell."

A songbird trilled noisily in a nearby tree. The Spaniard wheeled around and shot it dead. "Everything has its price, Señor Murphy, every thing and every body."

His tone had changed from unpleasant to threatening.

"Ah, qué bella," he said, strolling over to admire a rosebush in a beautiful painted pot. He picked one perfect red rose and sniffed it delicately. "A rare hybrid grandiflora, if I am not mistaken." He let the flower drop to the ground and crushed it with the toe of his boot. It lay on the path like a smear of blood.

"It touched me in the heart to hear that your brother and his wife are missing, Señor Murphy. How unfortunate. And your nephew is with you now, is he not? What a comfort, since you have no children of your own. It is to be hoped that your nephew does not also . . . disappear."

At this, Uncle Ted stiffened and looked like he might punch the Spaniard. Max was mentally egging him on, his own fists clenched in sympathy.

"I warn you not to make another mistake you will regret," hissed the Spaniard.

What did he mean, wondered Max, *another* mistake?

But there was no time to think, because next minute the Spaniard was cocking his gun and pumping one bullet after another into the painted flowerpot, until it lay in tiny, broken pieces. He kicked the rosebush out of the way, impatiently. A lizard darted out to hunt for beetles in the spilled dirt. The Spaniard tried to shoot that as well, but he'd run out of bullets. He threw the gun at it and missed.

"Sell me the Jaguar Stone or you will be sorry," he hissed in a fury.

Uncle Ted put up his hands to signal defeat. "May I at least inquire with whom I am to do business?"

"*Si, como no,* why not?"

In a moment of pure pantomime villainy, the Spaniard threw back his cape, stuck out his chest, and looked down his aquiline nose. It was a wonder he didn't twirl his moustache. "Count Antonio DeLanda," he announced, making an elaborate bow, "at your service."

"DeLanda?" repeated Uncle Ted in surprise.

"Yes, Señor Murphy, your ears do not play tricks. I am the direct descendant of the famous Friar Diego DeLanda. So you see, I am merely seeking the return of my family's rightful property."

Uncle Ted's eyebrow shot up as if to dispute that claim, but he quickly masked his skepticism. "Of course, this changes everything," he said, in a cold, flat voice. "It will take me a little time to retrieve the object, but I will contact you tomorrow to arrange the details of the sale."

"A wise decision," said DeLanda. "*Hasta luego.*"

Then he turned on his heel and was gone.

All this time, Max had been crouching out of sight at the window. He knew he should get back to the terrace, but his head was spinning from what he'd just overheard. He stood up and ran his fingers through his hair.

There was an ominous click right behind him.

He turned around to see one of DeLanda's black-suited body-guards standing in the corridor, pointing a gun right at him. The thug's lips went "bang" like a child pretending to shoot. Then he blew away the imaginary smoke and smirked. "*Hasta luego*, Max Murphy," he said. "Say nothing about what you have seen — or next time, I will not play games."

Max waited until he'd gone back downstairs. Then he went down himself and hurried back to the table on the terrace.

"Are you all right?" asked Uncle Ted. "You look like you've seen a ghost."

Max was considering telling him about the encounter, but decided to say nothing as instructed. "I'm just tired," he said.

"Let's go then," said Uncle Ted. "My business here is done."

"Uncle Ted, what exactly *is* your business?"

"Bananas, of course," answered Uncle Ted. He clapped an arm round Max and guided him back toward the hotel doors. Behind them, Max could see the gardeners sweeping up the damage wrought by DeLanda. There was clearly more to his uncle than bananas.

Uncle Ted lived about five miles up the coast. It was a beautiful drive, with fields of banana trees on one side and rolling surf on the other. But Max saw none of it. As soon as his head touched the cool leather of the backseat, he fell fast asleep in the Mercedes. As they drove along the rutted highway, a rainbow arched in the sky above them.

CHAPTER IV

THE VILLA ISABELLA

ALL THAT NIGHT and late into the morning, Max dreamt about snarling jaguars prowling the streets of Boston. He was finally awakened by the tropical sun streaming in through the French windows. He lay there basking in its rays for a moment and taking in the details of Uncle Ted's guest room.

He'd been too tired the night before to register anything, except that the room had a bed in it. Now he looked approvingly at the white walls, wooden furniture, and striped woven rug. An old wooden fan whirred on a ceiling joist. It was all very tasteful and a lot more welcoming than the Murphys' tiny guest room in Boston.

Max stretched out luxuriously. Then he remembered that his parents were missing. And that his uncle was doing deals with trigger-happy Spaniards. And that a black-suited thug had pointed a gun at him the previous afternoon and threatened to kill him. It wasn't the most promising start to a summer vacation.

He threw back the sheets and got out of bed.

The tiled floor was pleasantly cold on his feet. He wandered into the bathroom. Nice. Piles of thick white towels sat beside huge jars of bath salts and bottles of French cologne. There was evidently plenty of money to be made in the "banana business," he noted approvingly.

After a hot shower, Max wrapped himself in a fluffy white bathrobe. Then he opened the French windows and stepped onto

the balcony. The air hit him like a blast from a blowtorch. It was hotter than the shower he'd just left.

A toucan with a beak like an upturned canoe was sitting on the railing. When it saw Max, it gave a croak of protest and flapped off into the jungle. A bright green insect the size of a toy helicopter hovered menacingly above Max's head, before landing on a purple flower as big as a frisbee. And everywhere Max looked, yellow butterflies were dancing in the sunshine. Everything was so big and bright and colorful, he couldn't quite believe any of it was real.

Uncle Ted's house looked like a film set, too. The Villa Isabella sat on a ridge at one end of a sheltered bay. It was an old colonial mansion, built of honey-colored stones that glowed in the sun. But despite its blue-painted shutters and flower-decked balconies, the villa also had the aspect of a fortress.

Max estimated from the depth of the window recess that the walls were two feet thick. He could see a tall, battlemented tower on one corner of the house and, by leaning out as far as he dared, he noted that the lowest floor had slits for windows like a medieval castle.

It was hard to imagine why this beautiful place needed such extreme fortifications. Max guessed that whoever built it was protecting his family from those marauding British pirates he'd read about on the plane — or maybe from hostile Maya warriors, like the ancestors of Lucky Jim. You'd need thick walls to hide behind if he was on the warpath.

From his second-floor balcony at the end of the house, Max could see the bay and all the way across the gardens, to the rainforest and the mountains. The villa's grounds were encircled by an old fortified stone wall. Was that built to keep predators out? Or to keep Maya slaves in?

Faint animal sounds — whoops and cackles — floated over from the rainforest. From his high vantage point, Max could see the tops of the trees packed tightly together like giant broccoli. Max hated broccoli. It made the rainforest seem evil by association. It was like a brooding presence, biding its time for the moment when it would reclaim the grounds and house.

Max wondered if somewhere in its dark and tangled depths, his parents were making their way back to him. More likely, he told himself with a stab of self-pity, they hadn't given him a thought and they were still happily ensconced at Ix Chel with their precious Ancient Maya.

A blast from a ship's horn made him look toward the sea. The bay was wide and horseshoe-shaped, a perfect natural harbor. A small, rusty freighter was anchored close to shore, while a big white yacht sailed farther out in the turquoise water.

Only the beach spoiled the picture. Instead of fine white sand, this was black and gritty. It was littered with palm fronds, old tires, strips of plastic, and all sorts of other garbage that had washed up in the storm. Nobody would want to sunbathe on this beach. But then this was a work zone, not a tourist resort.

Along the curve of the bay, about half a mile from the house, there was a large warehouse connected to a pier. Another freighter was docked at the pier and a crane was loading crates into the hold. This must be the banana business in action. But given the opulence of Uncle Ted's house and the conversation he'd overheard yesterday at the hotel, Max couldn't help wondering if those crates all contained bananas — or something a little more valuable.

His musings were interrupted by a low rumbling growl from his stomach. Time to go and find some breakfast.

He got dressed and peered out of the bedroom door. His room opened onto a long corridor lined with shining suits of armor and oil paintings of stern-looking men with little pointed beards, all richly dressed in ruffs and capes. They reminded him of that De-Landa guy from yesterday.

Max followed the corridor down to the main staircase. His footsteps echoed loudly as he ran down the huge slabs of carved stone into the Great Hall.

Wow. He must have passed through this room the night before, but he'd been so tired he hadn't taken it in. Now its size and scale amazed him.

The Great Hall was arranged as a reception room with clusters of antique sofas, dark wood tables, and uncomfortable-looking chairs. Against the far wall was an enormous stone fireplace that could have burned a small forest in one go. A heraldic crest with crossed swords and rampant lions was carved into its stone overmantel.

Max would have thought he was in a castle in medieval Europe, were it not for the Maya sculptures that looked out from every ledge, every side table, every niche. In pride of place, on the floor in the center of the room, were two gigantic stone heads.

It was only when he stood in front of these heads that Max realized how big the Great Hall really was. The heads were each taller than a school bus and yet not out of proportion for the room. As he looked from one hook-nosed face to the other, they seemed to stare right back at him — one with sadness, one with anger.

Max began to feel uncomfortable. There was a sense of tension between the statues that gave him goosebumps. He reached out to feel the stone.

"Please do not touch," came a voice behind him.

Max turned to see an immaculately groomed old man in a black tailcoat.

"Welcome to the Villa Isabella, sir. I am Raul, head butler and household administrator. You slept well, I trust?"

"Yes, thank you," said Max. He turned back to the heads. "Who are these guys?"

"The one on the left is Lord Six-Rabbit."

"Isn't that the dude who cursed the Spanish at Aguas Muertas?"

"The very same, sir," said Raul, sounding impressed by Max's knowledge.

"He was a king, wasn't he?" continued Max, showing off what little else he remembered from Oscar's story.

"He was indeed, sir. He ruled the Monkey River region at the peak of the Maya Classic period, in the ninth century AD."

"The ninth century?" queried Max. Something didn't sound quite right. He tried to dredge up some Central American history from the muddy depths of his brain. "But didn't the Spanish come later than that?"

"Yes, sir. They first arrived on our shores in 1517 AD."

"So it couldn't have been this guy who cursed them? He'd have been at least six hundred years old."

"The Maya believe that Lord Six-Rabbit returns to Middleworld to help his people at times of crisis," said Raul.

"Middleworld?"

"Middleworld is what the Maya call this mortal realm, sir."

"I see." Max turned his attention to the other head. "And who's Mr. Angry?"

"That's Lord Six-Rabbit's half brother, Tzelek the Black Priest."

"What's his problem?"

"In a nutshell, sir, he's a bad loser."

"Does he return to Middleworld too?"

"One hopes not."

"So what happened between them?" asked Max, looking quickly from one head to the other, as if to catch them blinking.

"It's a classic case of sibling rivalry, sir. In a bid to seize the throne, Tzelek conjures up a demon army and attacks Lord Six-Rabbit, who counterattacks with his veteran Jaguar Warriors. It is the greatest battle between good and evil in Maya history."

"A classic case of sibling rivalry."

Max liked the way Raul told the story in the present tense as if he was a sports commentator and it was all happening right there and then.

"In the final stage, both armies spent, the half brothers are locked in mortal combat. Finally, Lord Six-Rabbit gains the upper hand and hurls Tzelek into the underworld. But the great king has been gravely wounded and, soon after, dies. In all the annals of the Maya, there will never be another king as feared by his enemies nor as well-loved by his people."

Raul rubbed his hands together briskly to indicate that his story was finished. "And now, sir, would you care for some brunch?"

Max nodded enthusiastically.

"Please make yourself comfortable on the terrace," said Raul, pointing toward some glass doors. He vanished as quickly as he had appeared.

Max was about to go outside when, through a half-open door, he glimpsed a circular room off the hallway. Aha! That must be the base of the battlemented tower he'd seen from his balcony. He thought he'd have a quick look for the stairs to the top.

He peered round the door and stopped dead in his tracks. If the rest of the house was channeling medieval Spain, this room was like something out of a James Bond movie.

With varnished wood paneling from floor to ceiling, it had the sleek, tight feel of a luxury yacht. Large windows had been cut into the stone outer walls to give a panoramic view of the coast and the sea. Plasma screens hung from the ceiling beamed in radar pictures and security shots of the house, the grounds, and the warehouse. On the desk were a laptop computer, some night-vision goggles, and an array of high-tech communications equipment. It was obviously his uncle's office. Max was surprised that the banana business required such an impressive control center.

An American passport was lying on some papers.

Must be Uncle Ted's.

Eager to laugh at someone else's bad photograph, Max flicked through it and caught a glimpse of lurid orange hair. Ha-ha! Uncle Ted had the same problem with camera flash as he did!

Wait — that *was* him.

It was Max's own passport!

That was odd. He didn't remember giving it to Uncle Ted. But then again, he'd been so tired, he'd didn't remember much about the night before.

He picked up the passport and looked round for a way up to the tower. Nothing. There were no stairs and the only door in the room was the one he'd entered by. Oh well. He'd ask his uncle about it later.

His eye was drawn to a poster-size aerial photograph, showing the locations of various Maya ruins. Max tried to find the Temple of Ix Chel, but there were too many sites and the captions were too small.

On another wall was a framed diploma from the Royal College of Art in London and some old photographs. There were Ted and Frank as teenagers, striking cool poses in the jungle, and there was Ted holding a red-haired baby. Uncle Ted had no children, had never been married as far as Max knew, so that baby had to be him — little Max. The thought that Uncle Ted kept his picture on the wall made him feel more at home and he looked around for any other family mementoes.

In front of one of the windows was a brass telescope on a tripod. It was pointing out to the bay. Max squinted through and saw that the high-powered lens was focused on the luxury yacht he'd seen from the balcony. He could just make out the lettering on the back: *La Espada, Cadiz.* That's a coincidence, he thought, same name as that old Spanish galleon. But this yacht couldn't have been more twenty-first century. It was bristling with electronic masts and radar dishes.

He was trying to find the zoom for a closer look, when a hand tapped him on the shoulder. Max nearly went through the roof.

He turned to see Raul standing behind him. What was this guy's problem? That was the second time today he'd sneaked up behind Max and scared him half to death.

"This is Mr Murphy's *private* office, sir," said Raul frostily.

"I was just looking at that big yacht in the bay," said Max. "Whose is it?"

"It belongs to Count Antonio DeLanda, sir — a most unsavory character, by all accounts, with an interest in the Black Arts. They say he killed his own brother to inherit the family estate in Spain. And now, sir, if you don't mind —"

As Raul ushered Max out of the room, he registered the passport in the boy's hand. He said nothing, but he pulled the office door tightly shut behind them and stalked imperiously back to the kitchen.

Max went out onto the terrace.

It was surrounded on three sides by frescoed stone walls and shaded by a yellow canvas awning that stretched halfway to the ground and gave the light an unreal quality, as if everything was inside a tent. Wooden ceiling fans whirred in the rafters. In front, the stone balustrades were lined with neatly tended flower boxes.

In the center of the terrace, there was a large round table covered with a starched white linen cloth. It had been set for two, with china plates, sparkling glass, and heavy silver flatware. A newspaper was placed to one side. Even the newspaper looked ironed. It was the most immaculate table setting Max had ever seen.

He took a seat and Raul appeared instantly behind him.

"Tea, coffee, or chocolate, sir?"

"Chocolate," said Max.

Raul looked at him expectantly.

"*Please*," said Max.

Raul nodded and went inside.

Max was making faces at the butler's back when, through the glass doors, he saw Uncle Ted come out of the circular office. How odd. There was definitely only one door to that room. How had Uncle Ted snuck in without Max noticing?

Now Raul was saying something to Uncle Ted and gesturing toward the terrace. (Uh-oh. Max could guess what that was about.)

"Good morning, " said Uncle Ted frostily, when he came out.

Max braced himself for the rebuke he knew was coming.

It came.

"I hear you've been doing some exploring."

Before Uncle Ted could continue, Raul reappeared with a platter of scrambled eggs and smoked salmon, a bowl of freshly sliced pineapple, and a big basket of toast, rolls, and pastries.

"Thank you, Raul," said Uncle Ted, unfolding the newspaper and scanning the headlines. While his uncle was reading, Max shot Raul his fiercest glare. This seemed to amuse the butler greatly. He smiled to himself as he poured hot chocolate for Max and coffee for Uncle Ted. Then he gave a small bow and withdrew.

Uncle Ted put down the paper and folded it neatly.

"I must ask you not to poke around. Raul runs a tight ship and I don't want you making more work for him. Do you understand?"

"Yes," said Max, sulkily.

"And please give me your passport for safekeeping."

"I can look after it myself."

"There's a booming black market for American passports in San Xavier. I insist we keep it in the safe. Neither of us wants you to get stranded here."

Max reluctantly handed over the passport.

"Thank you," said Uncle Ted. "Please eat."

Max guessed this would be a bad time to ask about the stairs to the tower, so he concentrated on breakfast. He took a large spoonful of eggs and picked out the salmon. Next, he cut the crusts off a piece of toast and removed all the raisins from a danish. Then he settled down to enjoy what was left, surrounded by little piles of rejected food.

Uncle Ted ate nothing. He had picked up his newspaper again, but Max noticed that he wasn't turning the pages. He seemed to have something on his mind. Max hoped it wasn't bad news.

"Uncle Ted," he ventured, "has the chief of police called yet?"

"It's too soon to know anything," Uncle Ted said gruffly, from behind the paper. "You need to be patient."

"But did he call?"

"Only briefly."

"What did he say?"

"Not much."

"But what, exactly?"

Uncle Ted put down the paper. Then he took a bread roll, tore it into pieces, and threw it to the little birds that hopped around under the table. He seemed to be sifting through the facts in his mind, looking for something positive to say. "He did mention that a local archaeologist had been at the camp with Frank and Carla — Herman something or other. A splendid fellow, by all accounts, knows the jungle like the back of his hand — so he's probably leading your parents back to safety, as we speak. Would you like some more eggs?"

"So was the camp deserted?"

"Yes. More toast?"

"But what did it look like? Did Mom and Dad leave in a hurry?"

"Let's leave the detective work to the police, shall we? Orange juice?"

Max waved all offers of seconds away. "But was everything packed up or not?"

Uncle Ted gave an irritated sigh. "It's hard to say. Things were strewn around, probably from the storm."

"Aha!" said Max, pouncing on this clue. "So we can assume that Mom and Dad left the camp *during* the storm. Otherwise, Mom would definitely have tidied up. She even makes her bed in hotel rooms. She hates mess."

"So do I," said Uncle Ted, pointedly eyeing the piles of discarded food around Max's plate and the drips of hot chocolate on the white cloth.

"I think *I* should talk to the police," declared Max. "I might be able to fill in a few details about Mom and Dad for them. It might speed things up a bit."

"No, Max. That's not a good idea."

"But why not?"

Uncle Ted was getting flustered. "I said no. The police know what they're doing. If you want to help, the best thing you can do is let them get on with it."

At that moment, Raul came out with a phone. "I'm sorry to interrupt your breakfast, sir, but they said it was urgent."

"Hello, Ted Murphy speaking."

As soon as he heard the caller's name, Uncle Ted scraped back his chair and scurried to the far corner of the terrace, stretching the phone cord to its limit. He lowered his voice and cupped his hand around the receiver. "It's not a good time . . . "

Max could hear everything, but pretended he couldn't. He assumed it was another of Uncle Ted's shady business contacts on the line.

"Yes, he *is* here, but . . . ask him what? . . . no, absolutely not . . . "

Max looked up. "It's the police, isn't it?"

Before Uncle Ted could stop him, Max had run over and grabbed the phone.

"*Max* Murphy here? Can I help you?"

It *was* the police.

They had some questions for him.

When he'd answered everything as best he could, Max handed

the phone back to Uncle Ted. Then he went back to the table on shaky legs and sat down. He waited for Uncle Ted to hang up before he spoke.

"You knew all along," he said, bitterly. "You knew and you didn't tell me."

"At this point, it's pure conjecture. I didn't see the point of worrying you."

"But the police said the camp was littered with used gun shells."

"A few shell casings don't mean anything."

"There were more than a few — there were hundreds."

"It was probably Frank shooting at the snakes. You know how he hates them."

"Oh yeah, the snakes. Something else you didn't tell me. The policeman said there were snakeskins all over the place." Max shuddered.

"It's a natural phenomenon. They don't usually shed en masse like that, but it's probably a reaction to the drop in atmospheric pressure caused by the storm."

"So how do you explain Mom's earring?

"It probably *wasn't* Carla's earring. Most women in San Xavier wear gold hoops."

"Where was it they found it again? I couldn't understand what he was saying."

"In the cenote," said Uncle Ted quietly. (He pronounced it sen-oaty.)

"That's the word. What does it mean?"

"It's the local name for a sinkhole. The jungle's full of underground lakes and rivers. When the cave roof over one of them collapses, you get a cenote. It's like a deep well."

A bell rang in Max's brain. "Didn't the Maya use them for human sacrifice?"

"How did you know that?" said Uncle Ted in surprise.

"I read it in the magazine on the plane."

"Well, they like to lay the human sacrifice story on thick for the tourists, but I'd advise you to take it with a pinch of salt. Cenotes were an important source of drinking water. Those skeletons were probably thirsty villagers who fell in and couldn't get out."

"What skeletons?"

Uncle Ted obviously regretted saying that bit. "This is an old country," he shrugged, "they're bound to find skeletons from time to time."

"Did they find skeletons at Ix Chel?"

"No! They found an earring. Period. And even if it is Carla's, I'm sure it fell in when she was exploring the site. And I said *if* it's Carla's, which I very much doubt. This is why I didn't want you talking to the police. I knew you'd start imagining the worst. It's going to be impossible having you stay here, if you're going to whine about everything."

"It looks bad," said Max.

"Nonsense," said Uncle Ted briskly, "it looks good. Whatever happened, your parents obviously got clean away. I'm sure they're on their way back right now."

"Don't patronize me," said Max.

Uncle Ted had the grace to look embarrassed.

"Is that it?" asked Max, wearily. "You've told me everything?"

"Yes," said Uncle Ted, but he didn't meet Max's eyes.

"Do you swear on my father's life?"

"That's a little melodramatic, isn't it?"

"Do you swear?"

"I swear."

Uncle Ted sat back and looked around the garden. He looked at the flowers. He looked at the trees. He watched a lime-green lizard scaling a terracotta plant pot. "Oh, there was one more thing," he said, as if it had just occurred to him. "Did the police happen to mention the jacket to you?"

Max's blood ran cold.

"Dad's jacket?"

"Yes."

"They found Dad's jacket?"

"Yes, that disgusting old thing with all the pockets."

"But he never takes it off."

"Maybe not in Boston, but it's hotter here — in case you hadn't noticed."

Max shook his head. "I've seen him wearing that jacket at noon in a heat wave in Palm Springs," he said. "Was there anything in the pockets when they found it?"

"Not as far as I know. Why do you ask?"

"That's where Dad keeps his research notes."

Max knew his father would never willingly be parted from that jacket. This was very bad. He tried to calm himself by taking a sip of hot chocolate, but his hands were shaking too much to hold the cup.

"Did you know," said Uncle Ted, "that the Ancient Maya were the first to make a drink out of chocolate? They served it on special occasions like we serve champagne."

Max pushed the cup away.

"If the police didn't know how important that jacket was to Dad, why did they mention it particularly?"

Uncle Ted tried to sound casual. "It had a mark on it. They thought it might be a clue. But I told them, that old jacket was so dirty, it was always covered in stains."

"What mark? What was it?"

"Now Max, don't go —"

"Tell me."

"It was blood, but —"

"BLOOD?"

"Don't panic, it's not Frank's blood. In fact, they don't think it's human."

"Not human? I don't understand."

"No one understands. We must wait for forensics to finish their tests."

"When will that be?"

Uncle Ted shrugged. "Who knows? Things don't move as quickly in San Xavier as they do in Boston."

"But surely there's something you can do?" said Max. "You're a rich man, you must have connections. Shouldn't you be out there looking for my parents yourself?"

"The jungle is a dangerous place. We must leave it to the police," said Uncle Ted. "Unfortunately, you may be staying here for quite a while."

"Well, I'm not happy about that either," snapped Max. "You don't even have cable TV." He felt jet-lagged and tired and confused. He was angry at his parents, he was angry at Uncle Ted, he was angry at the yellow butterfly that was fluttering in front of his face.

"More hot chocolate?" said Uncle Ted.

"No."

Max tried to wave away the butterfly and accidentally knocked the chocolate pot out of his uncle's hand. It smashed on the tiled floor. Chocolate dregs spattered Uncle Ted's suit and shards of bone china flew everywhere.

Raul ran out with a dustpan and brush.

Uncle Ted poured some water onto a napkin and dabbed at his suit. "I must ask you to be careful while you're staying here, Max," he said. "I like an orderly house."

But Max didn't care about a few hot chocolate stains.

It was the blood on his father's jacket that preoccupied him.

As they sat there, the sky darkened to a purple bruise and raindrops began drumming on the canvas awning. When Uncle Ted finally spoke, he had to shout to make himself heard above the rainstorm. "I'm running a banana business, not a hotel. You can't sit around all day under Raul's feet. So, as from tomorrow, you'll start work in the warehouse."

Max looked at him warily. "How much will you pay me?" he shouted back.

"Hard work is its own reward," replied Uncle Ted, rather shocked at the question. "You're living here at my expense. You should be glad to earn your keep."

"That's child labor!" protested Max.

But Uncle Ted didn't seem to hear him. "That's settled then," he said, as if he were winding up a business meeting. "Breakfast at five tomorrow and report straight to Lucky Jim in the warehouse."

"Breakfast at *five*? But it's summer vacation. I sleep late when school's out."

"At your age, Frank and I were always up at the crack of dawn. You have to rise early in the tropics to beat the heat. So Lucky Jim will be expecting you at 6 AM sharp and you can look forward to a productive day's work."

Hard work is its own reward? Breakfast at five? Look forward to a productive day's work?

Max stared at his uncle open-mouthed.

"Something wrong?" asked Uncle Ted.

"You sound just like my father," said Max, accusingly.

Uncle Ted said nothing. But the expression on his face reminded Max of the day his mother had stepped in dog poop on Boston Common.

CHAPTER V

MAX GOES BANANAS

"There's only one way to learn the banana business," said Lucky Jim. "And that's from the bottom up."

"Does that mean I get to drive one of those? asked Max, pointing to the little forklift trucks that zoomed around the warehouse moving pallets of green bananas.

"No," said Lucky, "it doesn't."

The bottom, as it turned out, was one dirty job after another.

It was only eight o'clock in the morning — Raul had finally dragged him out of bed at seven — and Max had already refused to break up the old wooden pallets ("I'll get splinters."), mop the warehouse floor ("No way!"), or clean the workers' bathrooms ("Forget it!").

Lucky scratched his head, perplexed. "The boss isn't going to like this," he said.

"Well, the boss should pay proper wages," said Max. "I'm not his slave. Besides, this is my summer vacation."

"Is that so?" said Lucky. "Well, how about working on your suntan? You tourists like that, don't you?"

Max nodded. This was sounding more like it.

"Good, you can clean up the beach. See all the old tires and palm fronds and dead fish, washed up by the storm?"

"But that's a huge job," spluttered Max. "It'll take weeks. I shouldn't be out in the sun for so long. I have sensitive skin. I burn easily."

"Wear your hat," said Lucky, passing him the rake.

Max knew when he was beaten.

As he glumly set to work, he consoled himself that at least he'd escaped the confines of the warehouse. It was better to be outside in the open air.

Unfortunately, the teeming insect population of San Xavier agreed with him.

No matter how much bug spray he used, they attacked him relentlessly. They even bit through his clothes. He soon had so many bites, he looked like a human dot-to-dot puzzle. He hadn't felt like such a geek since second grade. He was only grateful there were no girls around to witness this deeply uncool turn of events.

As he worked — or more accurately, as he didn't work — Max wondered what had really happened at Ix Chel. The more he went over things in his mind . . . the gun shells, the snakeskins, the bloodstained jacket, the earring . . . the weirder it all seemed. He tried to work out a rational explanation, but his head was filled with visions of bloodthirsty rituals and ghostly serpents.

Oh come on, he told himself, get real. This is a dumb little Third-World country where people believe in all kinds of stupid superstitions. Forget all that talk about human sacrifice. In real life, the only thing archaeologists die from is boredom.

Still, it was hard to get his head round the present situation. It was only a week since his parents had come home early from work and turned his world upside down. Now they were missing and he was an unwelcome guest at the Villa Isabella. He felt so helpless, but all he could do was pretend to clean the beach and wait for news.

But *was* that all he could do?

Perhaps he could call Zia and ask her — what? Communication with the crazy housekeeper was hard at the best of times. And the thought of trying to make himself understood on the phone was too daunting.

But she'd said his parents needed him.

Why did she say that? What could he do? He was a stranger in San Xavier.

A stranger . . . that was it!

He'd phone the American Embassy! They probably had all sorts of high-tech equipment for finding American citizens who got lost in the jungle. And it would be good to talk to someone who didn't believe in all this Ancient Maya garbage.

As soon as he could escape Lucky's eagle eye, Max threw down his rake and sprinted back to the house. He ran straight into Raul in the Great Hall, almost knocking him over.

"Where's the phone? I need to call someone . . . "

"Did your uncle give you permission?" asked Raul.

"I didn't ask him," said Max, pushing past. "Where's the phone?"

"You must ask your uncle for permission," insisted Raul.

Max lost his temper. "I'm a guest here, not a prisoner," he shouted.

"What's all the noise?" asked Uncle Ted angrily, emerging from his office.

"I need to use the phone," said Max.

"Ah," said Uncle Ted, exchanging glances with Raul. "And whom do you wish to call?"

A sixth sense told Max not to tell the truth. He had a feeling that anyone who conducted underhanded business with psychopathic Spaniards in seedy hotels would not want to attract the attention of the United States government.

"I need to talk to my friend Lenny in Boston," he said, trying to sound casual.

Uncle Ted studied his nephew's face. "The thing is, Max, I wouldn't want you alarming anyone at this stage. The San Xavier police are doing everything they can to find your parents. The last thing we need is an international incident."

"I understand," said Max, nodding earnestly. "It's not about Mom and Dad. It's just that Lenny borrowed some money from me, and I don't want him to think I've forgotten about it."

"A businessman after my own heart," smiled Uncle Ted. "Please show Max to the phone, Raul, and see that he has everything he needs."

So far, so good. The phone was sitting on a console table near the kitchen. It was like a miniswitchboard with an LED screen and flashing lights. Raul pulled a directory out of the drawer and checked the international calling section.

"Dial 1 for USA, then 617 for Boston," Raul said frostily. "I assume you know your friend's number?"

Max nodded and held out his hand for the phone.

Still clucking with disapproval, Raul punched in an access code, carefully shielding the numbers from Max's view. Then he did a lot of tapping and jabbing to get a dial tone. Eventually, he handed Max the receiver.

"Thanks," said Max. "I'll be fine now."

If the butler would just stop hovering over him, he could look up the Embassy number and make his call. But Raul showed no intention of moving.

"Is there something in the oven?" asked Max. "I think I smell burning."

Raul hurried off toward the kitchen.

OK . . .

Max grabbed the directory, found the page, and ran his finger down it . . .

United Bank . . .

United Oil & Gas . . .

United States Embassy . . . Got it!

He took a deep breath and dialed the number.

It rang. And rang. And rang.

Suddenly — "This is the United States Embassy in San Xavier."

Max plunged in. "I need to report my parents missing. They're U.S. citizens —"

"For English, press 1; for Spanish, press 2; for a choice of Mayan languages, press 3."

Max pressed 1.

"Welcome to the United States Embassy in San Xavier."

"Hello, it's about my parents, Frank and Carla Murphy, they're archaeologists, last seen at Ix Chel a week ago. I was hoping you could —"

"For Consular Services, press 1; for the Emergency Desk, press 2."

Max pressed 2.

"This is the Emergency Desk of the United States Embassy in San Xavier. Office hours are 9 to 10 AM, Tuesday and Thursday. Outside these times, please leave a message. Your call will be returned as soon as possible. Speak clearly after the tone."

"Beeeeep."

"My name is Max Murphy and I need to report . . . "

"Beeeeep. Beeeeep. Beeeeeeeeeeeeeeeeeeeeeeeeeeeeeeeeeeeeeeeeep."

The answering machine was either full or malfunctioning. Either way, Max's time was up. He could hear Raul's footsteps coming back through the Great Hall. He sprawled back in his chair and laughed loudly into the beeping phone. "Ha ha, good one, Lenny! See ya!" Then he hung up on his chance to get help from the outside world.

"Everything all right?" asked Raul. Max looked at him closely. Had he been listening in on the call?

"I also need to send an e-mail," said Max. "You do have e-mail, don't you?"

"Of course."

"So can I use Uncle Ted's laptop?"

"It might be possible under normal circumstances."

"Is that a yes?"

"Unfortunately, due to the storm, our Internet connection is down. It may be out for some time."

No phone calls. No e-mail. No passport.

So what *was* he — a guest or a prisoner?

Next morning, for want of a better idea, Max reported for work again on the beach. As he pushed the rake half-heartedly around, he had the distinct sensation of being watched. He couldn't actually catch anyone spying on him, but he guessed that Lucky Jim had the binoculars trained on him at all times. He was glad, midmorning, when it rained and he could run off in search of shelter.

He was headed toward the warehouse, when he noticed the space under the loading pier. The tide was out and the rocks were dry. It was the perfect place. He could sneak under the pier and laze around on the rocks without being seen by anyone. Plus this hideout had the advantage that he could hear everything that was happening on the dock above him, which would help him keep tabs on Lucky Jim.

Surrounded by a curtain of rain, Max sat and thought things through for the billionth time. It was obvious that Uncle Ted wasn't going to lift a finger to help find his parents. He was on his own, as usual. All he needed was a new plan.

Max's thoughts were interrupted by noises above him. He realized that the downpour had stopped and work had resumed on the dock.

He heard his uncle's voice.

"It's all hands on deck tonight, Lucky. We load at 2 AM."

"No worries, boss, the shipment is ready."

"Splendid! And how's that nephew of mine shaping up?"

"I'm sorry to say this about your own flesh and blood, boss, but he's as lazy as a three-toed sloth."

Both men laughed heartily.

"Bit of a spoiled brat, eh?"

"He's not used to hard work, boss, that's for sure."

"He's an only child — I think he's used to getting his own way."

"Should I go easier on him, boss?"

"Absolutely not. It could ruin everything, him showing up like this. We have to keep him out of the house, at all costs. Raul caught him snooping round the office the other day — and you know what that could lead to. Work him till he drops, Lucky — make sure he's too tired to cause any trouble."

"Whatever you say, boss."

Max couldn't believe what he'd heard. He was shaking with rage.

So his uncle thought he was a spoiled brat, did he? And cleaning this stinking beach was just a ruse to keep him out of the house? Well, Uncle Ted's game was up. As of this minute, Max was officially on strike. He'd sit here till the tide came in and then . . .

. . . and then . . .

. . . and then . . .

. . . What?

Suddenly, he knew what he had to do.

He'd expose Uncle Ted for the crook he was.

There was obviously something hidden in the office that Max wasn't supposed to see. Something incriminating. Max thought back to the day he'd looked around in there. Had he noticed anything strange? Then, suddenly, he remembered seeing Uncle Ted emerge from the office without ever going in.

And, just like that, he knew what he was looking for.

A secret door.

Maybe it led to the tower. Maybe there was a money-laundering operation up there. Or a factory churning out counterfeit Maya artifacts. Or — an idea struck him like a knock on the head — maybe, just maybe, his parents were being held prisoner up there.

Now Max was tingling with excitement.

If they were loading a shipment at 2 AM, he'd make his first search tonight. Everyone would be out of the house long enough for him to have a good look round. A spoiled brat indeed! For once Max was proud of the anger that burned in his veins and spurred him on to vengeance. Uncle Ted was going to regret the day he'd ignited the wrath of Max Murphy!

That afternoon, Max worked with a new energy and enthusiasm. Even Lucky Jim noticed his efforts and signaled his approval from the pier. Max waved to him cheerily. And as he raked, he laid his plans.

Dinner that night was eaten in silence, with both Max and Uncle Ted lost in their own thoughts.

Straight afterward, Uncle Ted excused himself. "I need an early night," he said.

Big, fat liar, thought Max. "Sounds good," he said. "Me too."

As soon as he reached his room, he started putting his plan into action. He found a flashlight in the side pocket of his backpack (thanks, Mom!) and changed into a dark T-shirt and jeans. Then he set his alarm clock for quarter to two and lay down on the bed to get as much rest as possible before zero hour.

When the clock went off, he felt as if he'd just gone to sleep. He forced himself out of bed and staggered to the window.

No movement at the pier.

He looked up and down the coast.

Still nothing.

Wait, what was that?

A flashlight was bobbing in the grounds. Max's heart was in his mouth until he recognized the night watchman doing his rounds. What an anticlimax.

Maybe the rendezvous had been cancelled.

Maybe Uncle Ted really did get an early night.

The minutes ticked by.

Max was just about to call the whole thing off and get back into bed, when he realized that what looked like a shadow on the water was actually a boat slowly and silently making its way to the pier. When it finally docked, dark figures emerged from the warehouse and started loading crates onto it.

This was it. His big chance. He guessed he had at least twenty minutes before they finished loading and came back to the house.

He stuck his head out of the bedroom door. All was still. The only sound was the beating of his own heart and the tick of an antique clock. He crept into the corridor, past the suits of armor, past the disapproving frowns of the long dead Spaniards and down the big stone staircase to the Great Hall.

Uncle Ted's huge collection of Maya sculptures shimmered in the moonlight. With the furniture receding into the darkness, they seemed to hover in the air like ghosts. A faint chatter of insects from outside the window fell quiet as Max entered. He felt as if he'd walked in on a secret meeting, presided over by the two great stone heads.

Max hesitated. The heads looked even more alive tonight. Luminous in the moonlight, they seemed to glow from within. He told himself that their animated expressions were just the flickering shadows of the palm fronds at the window.

But they were looking straight at him.

And they did not look pleased to see him.

"Excuse me, guys," he said under his breath and steeled himself to walk past them. (Were their eyes following him? *Don't think about it.*)

On shaking legs, he reached the door to his uncle's office.

It was closed.

Worse than that, it was locked.

No, wait, it was just stuck.

He gently eased the old door open with a creak that seemed to reverberate through the house. He froze, listening for any sound or movement. Nothing. He breathed again. But time was passing. He had to hurry.

Quickly. Get inside and close the door.

Now, where to look?

He didn't dare switch on his flashlight in case they saw him from the dock. So with only the moon for light, he started searching the room. He tapped walls, looked behind shelves, scoured the floor for a trapdoor, but he found nothing.

What had he missed? How can you hide a whole door?

He sat down on a wide, low bookcase that ran under the window, and looked around one last time. It was no good. He'd have to try again another night — but who knew when he'd get the chance? He yawned and shivered at the same time. The prospect of aborting his mission and going back upstairs was suddenly quite appealing. He was exhausted from his afternoon's exertions on the beach and there was a cold draft in this room that had brought him out in goosebumps. Time for bed.

He put a hand on the edge of the bookcase to push himself up and, as he did so, the icy rush of the draft took his breath away. It was coming from directly behind him.

Wide awake now, he got down on his hands and knees to inspect the woodwork. There was a crack where the bookcase joined the wall. He pulled at the bookcase and felt a slight movement, just enough to tell him that he'd found his secret door. Now he had to find the lock.

Heart thumping, he started taking the books off the shelves and feeling around inside the bookcase. His fingers closed on a small lever. He pushed it down and, with a click, the shelf unit swung away from the wall. He'd done it!

Still on his hands and knees, Max was now looking into a narrow steel staircase that spiraled steeply down into the bowels of the Earth.

Down?

This was not what he'd been expecting at all. He'd been looking for an entrance to the tower, not the dungeons.

He shone his flashlight into the blackness. Perhaps this wasn't such a good idea, after all. But then he imagined Uncle Ted in handcuffs and the spirit of revenge drove him on.

He took a few steps down and pulled the bookcase back into position behind him. When it clicked shut, dim green lights came on to illuminate the stairwell. He listened carefully, but he could hear nothing but a faint dripping.

Down and down he went, trying not to slip on the wet steel treads. With every step, the temperature dropped another few degrees.

At the bottom of the staircase it was as cold and clammy as a tomb.

Max stepped under a small archway into a tunnel hewn out of the rock. All he could hear was the soft hum of machinery and the dripping of water, louder now. The tunnel seemed deserted, but he could see arched openings at regular intervals all the way along. Anyone — or anything — could be inside them.

He crept down the tunnel and looked through the first archway. It opened into a large room, dimly lit by rows of computer screens.

The walls were papered with charts and maps. Long metal tables supported stacks of computer hardware and electronic boxes covered with dials and switches. Cables and wires snaked across the ground and lay heaped in coils.

Was he dreaming? This was crazy. There must have been a million dollars worth of equipment in there. What on earth was going on?

The next archway revealed a locker room, packed with camouflage gear and wet suits.

After that, came a smaller tunnel that sloped steeply downward.

Max followed it for about twenty paces. He tripped on something. The beam of his flashlight revealed several rusty iron rings embedded in the cobbles. As he circled them, trying to work out what they were, he realized that he'd backed into water. *Ah, so they were boat moorings.* The rest of the tunnel was flooded, and Max guessed it led to the open sea.

He quickly retraced his steps back up to the main tunnel.

What was next, he wondered. A weapons cache? An underground firing range? A submarine dock?

But it was none of those. In fact, the next room was more extraordinary than anything Max could ever have imagined.

He was standing in the entrance to an Aladdin's cave.

The long vaulted space was lined with shelves. On them, nestled in foam rubber and laid out as carefully as a museum display, was a magnificent array of Maya artifacts and pieces of Spanish armor and weaponry.

Max stepped in to have a closer look. Nearer the doorway, the pottery was chipped and the swords were broken and rusty. But the farther back he went, the more perfect — and, presumably, more valuable — the artifacts became. At the far end, displayed on double thicknesses of foam, were pieces of jade jewelry, inlaid masks, ornately painted bowls, and beautifully carved stone figurines.

Max had seen it all before.

How many times had his parents dragged him round museums, oohing and aahing over this kind of stuff?

He hated it.

He was just turning to leave and go back to the techno-room, when he saw a small metal suitcase on a high shelf. It seemed to be calling to him. Without thinking, he reached up for it.

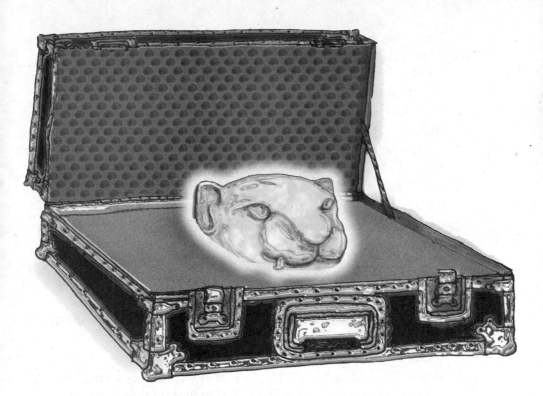

It was heavier than he expected and he nearly fell backward as he pulled it down. Then he flipped open the latches and lifted the lid.

A warm breeze blew out of the case and filled the air with the earthy smell of jungle. Inside the case, nestled in foam, was a life-size jaguar's head carved in blood red stone. It was so realistic, it almost seemed to snarl.

At that moment, Max felt cold metal on the back of his neck.

A voice whispered, "Don't move or I'll blow your head off."

Max knew that voice.

It was Lucky Jim. And he didn't sound like he was joking.

"Put your hands on your head and turn around slowly."

Max did as he was told.

When he turned round, he was looking into the barrel of a gun. He started to stammer an explanation, but Lucky snapped: "Silence!" He looked furious. A vein as thick as a jungle vine was throbbing in his forehead.

"You're in big trouble, boy," he said. "If you weren't the boss's nephew, I'd have shot you on the spot. Now move!"

There was no escape. Lucky Jim nudged him with the gun to direct him back to the flooded tunnel.

"Where we going?" asked Max, but Lucky said nothing until they reached the iron rings in the ground.

"Get down," commanded Lucky, "Lie on your side."

"It's all wet," complained Max, "the tide's coming in."

Lucky cocked his gun. "Do as I say." Then he handcuffed Max's hands behind his back, looping the chain through one of the rings, so he couldn't get away.

He smiled his gold tooth smile. "Look at you, all trussed up like a chicken. I reckon the boss might just take you for a swim and feed you to the sharks."

His laughter echoed down the tunnels and bounced off the vaulted ceilings.

Max was thinking fast.

"Lucky Jim, you're descended from the Maya, aren't you?" he asked.

Lucky Jim stopped smiling. "What of it?"

Max looked straight into Lucky's heavy-lidded brown eyes.

"So why are you allowing Uncle Ted to loot your own treasures? This stuff should be in a museum. Don't you want your children and grandchildren to see the amazing things the Maya were doing when Europe was still in the Dark Ages?"

Max thought it was a brilliant speech for the spur of the moment. He waited expectantly for Lucky to realize the error of his ways and turn on his employer. But Lucky showed no trace of shame. Instead, he drew himself up to his full man-mountain height, folded his arms, and sneered down at Max.

"You don't know what you're talking about, little boy," he said. "If I ever have any kids, I'd want to keep them as far away from this stuff as possible. I want them to break free of the past."

"B-b-but what about their heritage?" Max said weakly.

Lucky Jim was beyond anger. He was so angry he was almost calm.

"Heritage? If you want heritage, go to one of those Maya theme parks in Mexico. You can watch a Maya show, eat Maya food, have your picture taken with a Maya warrior, the complete Maya experience. It won't be the real thing, of course, because you tourists don't want the real thing."

"What's the real thing?" whimpered Max.

"Time for a history lesson," said Lucky Jim, bending down until that huge pulsing vein on his forehead was just inches from Max's face. "Those old Maya may have been good at pottery and math, but they were ruled by violence and superstition. Problem is, they're still alive. And they're still trying to run things around here. You can call that heritage, if you like, but I call it a dangerous reality."

"You're crazy!" blurted Max.

Lucky Jim laughed like a crazy person.

"You tourists don't get it, do you? Maya time is different from your time. Our world is different from your world."

He sat down and leaned back against the tunnel wall.

"Take those pyramids in the jungle, like the one your parents were working on. You think they're just old, abandoned ruins, don't you?"

He prodded Max with the gun.

"Don't you?" he prompted.

"I guess so," said Max.

"So when you see a parked car, do you automatically assume it's abandoned?"

More prodding. Max shook his head.

"Our temples are like parked cars. They're waiting for their owners to return. You tourists wouldn't be so quick to climb all over them if you understood how many doors to the underworld they conceal. And those doors are still open. Your parents knew that . . ."

"What else did my parents know?" whispered Max.

Lucky Jim grabbed Max by the neck of his T-shirt and pulled him so close that his shackled arms were stretched out painfully behind him.

"*Bahlamtuuno'ob*," he hissed.

Max had heard that word before somewhere. But before he could make any sense of it, there was a sound of approaching footsteps.

Lucky Jim loosened his grip on Max and stood up, brushing himself off. "I've seen some bad things in the jungle," he said, backing out of the tunnel, "but I wouldn't like to be in your shoes now."

As Lucky Jim's footsteps faded away, the other footsteps got louder until Uncle Ted stood over his terrified nephew.

"Got a little lost on our way for milk and cookies, did we?" he said coldly.

Max started spouting excuses, but Uncle Ted held up a hand to silence him.

"The only question now is what to do with you. Lucky thinks we should dump you in the ocean . . . tell the police you went looking for your parents in the jungle and never came back. It's an interesting idea, don't you think?"

This was really not the time to make a stand. But for Max Murphy and his hotheaded Italian-Irish temper, thinking before speaking had never been a strong point.

"Now I understand why my father hates you," he said.

"To hell with your father," said Uncle Ted. "It's your own skin you need to worry about."

CHAPTER VI

FAMILY SECRETS

"To hell with your father."

That's what he'd said.

The words were still ringing in Max's ears as Uncle Ted unlocked the handcuffs and pulled him to his feet. He suddenly knew, with a horrible certainty, that Uncle Ted had killed his parents.

"Walk," said Uncle Ted. "And don't try anything. The villa is crawling with security guards tonight. And their orders are shoot to kill."

"You'll go to jail for this," said Max.

"Silence!" said Uncle Ted.

Pushing Max in front of him, Uncle Ted guided them back through the tunnels and up the steps. When they emerged into the office, the sun was rising over the sea. Max shivered in the dawn light. He was wet and cold and weary to his bones.

"Sit!" said Uncle Ted, pushing him into a chair. Then he opened the desk drawer and took out a vicious-looking hunting knife.

Max gasped in terror. Was this the knife that Uncle Ted had used on his parents? He couldn't take his eyes off its glinting blade. He thought about running, but he was too weak to move. In any case, where would he go? This was it. His parents were dead. And now it was his turn to die.

There was just one thing he had to know.

"Why did you kill them?" he asked dully.

"What?"

"Why did you kill my parents?"

Uncle Ted looked at him blankly. "What on earth makes you say that?"

Max looked at the knife.

Uncle Ted followed his eyes. Then he started to laugh.

"Don't be ridiculous," he said. "Did you really think I was going to chop you up and feed you to the fish? This rusty old thing couldn't cut butter."

Still chuckling to himself, Uncle Ted pulled a large storage chest out from the wall. He knelt down and starting working the blade under the lid. "I keep the knife handy for this," he explained. "Darn thing always sticks. The sea air warps everything."

Eventually the lid came free, and Uncle Ted pulled a blanket out of the chest. He wrapped it around Max's shoulders.

"I'll admit I'm not happy about your staying here," said Uncle Ted, "and I'll admit that I don't like your father. But I wouldn't wish either of you actual bodily harm. In fact, the reason I'm so angry is that you could have got hurt tonight. I just want to keep you safe until I can wash my hands of you and give you back to your parents."

"So having Lucky Jim stick a gun in my neck was keeping me safe?"

"He was just trying to scare some sense into you. It's one thing when you ignore orders at the banana warehouse, but tonight's little escapade was unforgivable . . . you could have been killed."

"I just want to go home, I hate this place."

"Believe me, the feeling's mutual," said Uncle Ted. "But no matter how uncomfortable this situation may be for both of us, the fact remains that I am your legal guardian in the absence of your parents. I must therefore offer you my protection."

"What, by tying me up and threatening to shoot me?"

"It was for your own good, you stupid little boy."

"I'm not stupid and I'm not a little boy!"

"That's a matter of opinion."

"Oh yeah? Well, in my opinion, the police will be very interested to hear about what happened tonight."

"Sorry to disappoint you, Max, but the chief of police is a friend of mine, remember?"

"So what are you going to do with me?" asked Max. "Throw me in the dungeons?"

"It's tempting," said Uncle Ted.

They glared at each other for a while, then Uncle Ted wheeled around and stared out of the window at the ocean.

"Here's what I suggest," he said eventually. "Since we are stuck with each other for the foreseeable future, we will have to find a way to live together. From now on, you must obey my rules to the letter. You will stay in your room at night, and you are forbidden to set foot in my office. Agreed?"

"What's in for me?" asked Max, sensing an opportunity to manipulate an adult.

"What do you want?"

Max considered the question. He was about to demand cable TV, a new iPod, and the Collectors Edition Hellhounds 3D, when he realized there was something he wanted even more.

"Just tell me the truth," he said.

"About what?"

"About the treasure trove in your cellar. About what's going on around here."

"Why should I trust you?"

Max had seen enough gangster movies to know the answer. "Because I know too much," he said in his toughest voice. "And because I'm family. They say blood is thicker than water, don't they?"

They faced each other for a moment, like Al Capone and his biggest rival.

Then, to Max's surprise, Uncle Ted started to laugh. "You know," he said, "if you weren't my brother's son, I think I could get to like you. You're a Murphy, all right."

"What does that mean?"

"Hasn't Frank told you our family history?"

"No," said Max. "He doesn't like to talk about it."

"Then," said Uncle Ted with a wicked smile, "it will be my pleasure to tell you everything he doesn't want you to know."

Which is how, ten minutes later, Max found himself tucked up on a sofa in the Great Hall, as Raul brought in a tray of hot chocolate and buttery, freshly baked croissants. Max avoided the butler's eyes, but he could feel their disapproval beaming down on him.

Uncle Ted pulled up a chair and leaned forward to pass Max a mug of chocolate. As their mops of red hair touched, you could almost imagine they were father and son.

"It all started," began Uncle Ted, "after Patrick Murphy — my father and your grandfather — returned to the family farm in Ireland after World War I. He was just nineteen years old and haunted by what he'd seen in the trenches. He tried to settle back on the farm, but the war had changed him. He needed to cut loose. So he headed to America to seek his fortune, working his passage on a tramp steamer. From New York City, he hustled and brawled his way south until he finally ended up in San Xavier."

"I'd always imagined Grandpa as a businessman in a suit and tie," said Max, delighted to have a renegade in the family.

"He looked more like a cowboy in those days," said Uncle Ted. "And this place was like the Wild West — full of adventurers and opportunists, the kind of place where a man can be anything he wants to be. Your grandpa tried big game fishing and logging before eventually settling on bananas."

"Why bananas?" asked Max.

"Who knows?" said Uncle Ted. "But it was a lucky move. Bananas became big business and he did very well indeed."

"Was he a millionaire?" Max was now very interested.

"Probably. But he spent it all on renovating this house and filling it with beautiful things. He turned it into the finest mansion on the coast."

"What a waste of money," said Max, disappointed.

"Not for Grandpa," smiled Uncle Ted. "He was trying to impress someone."

"A girl?" guessed Max.

"Otherwise known as Grandma," nodded Uncle Ted. "Her name in those days was Isabella Pizarro, and she was the beautiful daughter of a wealthy local landowner. Her family could trace their lineage back to the original conquistadors who arrived from Spain with Hernan Cortez. Patrick Murphy was descended from dirt-poor Irish farmers. Needless to say, Isabella's father did not approve of the match. But Patrick bought this house and lavished money on getting it ready for her and eventually her father agreed to the marriage."

"The Villa Isabella," mused Max. "So Grandma Isabella was a Spanish aristocrat? Why did Dad never tell me this?"

"Think about it. Leading Maya scholar is direct descendant of the very people who tried to wipe out Maya culture. It doesn't look good on his résumé."

"But he could have told *me*," said Max indignantly.

"I think there's quite a lot your parents haven't told you," said Uncle Ted.

"Please go on," urged Max. "You were saying that Patrick and Isabella got married?"

"That's right. I was born a year later and your father came along a year after that. We were so close, people often thought we were twins. We went everywhere together."

"I can't believe Dad's never mentioned any of this," said Max.

"As I said, there's a lot you don't know about your father. But there's one thing that's never changed — he's always been obsessed by the Ancient Maya. We used to go camping together in the jungle, when this area was pretty much off the map. Sometimes we'd stumble on some Maya ruins and Frank would teach me about them. He could bring history to life with his stories . . . "

"So you weren't always enemies then?"

"Far from it," said Uncle Ted. For a moment, he looked almost happy. Then his face clouded over, his wrinkled frown reappeared, and he continued.

"In the summer that changed our lives, Frank and I were camping with a friend when we discovered a different kind of ruin. Not a Maya temple this time, but a Franciscan monastery from the days of the conquistadors. There wasn't much left of it and we wouldn't have stayed, but it started to rain. So we took shelter in the ruins and built a fire against one of the old walls. I don't know if it was the heat of the fire or a gust of wind, but the wall suddenly collapsed. We were lucky not to get crushed. When the dust settled, there, in the rubble, was a small cedar box. It must have been hidden in a hole in the wall. We forced the box open, expecting to find gold coins and jewels. What a letdown! It was just some rosary beads and an old book wrapped in deerskin! I was disappointed, but Frank was dancing a jig like he'd just scored the winning touchdown in the Superbowl."

Max groaned. "I've seen him do that dance at weddings."

"Forget the dance, Max. Your father had realized that the old book he held in his hands was none other than the private journal of Friar Diego DeLanda!"

"I keep hearing that name," said Max.

"Where? " asked Uncle Ted sharply.

Max panicked. Although he couldn't admit it, he'd last heard the name DeLanda on the lips of the crazy Spaniard in the garden of the Hotel de Las Americas. But now he thought about it, he'd heard the name somewhere else too.

"Oscar mentioned him," he said. "Called him a putrid devil from the slimiest depths of hell — or something like that."

Uncle Ted relaxed.

"That's him. He was a priest sent from Spain to convert the Maya — which he attempted to do by torturing them and burning all their books. In one huge bonfire, he reduced the sum of Maya knowledge to ashes. Can you imagine? Even the authorities in Spain were shocked and had him imprisoned in the monastery."

"Did you find his skeleton in the ruins too?" asked Max.

"No, he was sent back to Spain to face charges."

"So what happened to the diary?"

"Well, that's the awkward bit. It was one of the greatest archaeological finds of the century, but I'm afraid your father couldn't bear to part with it."

"What? Where is it now?"

"Let's just say that its existence is known only to a select few."

Max could not believe his ears. His father had been hiding stolen goods all these years. He was an archaeological outlaw, a desperado in a safari jacket.

"The jacket!" spluttered Max.

"What jacket?" asked Uncle Ted.

"Dad's old safari jacket! I bet that's where he kept the diary!"

"Surely not?" said Uncle Ted. "How could he be so stupid as to bring the diary back to San Xavier? I'd always assumed it was locked in a safe." He sighed. "If you're right, Max, this is very bad news."

"Why? Because it's worth so much money?"

"No, because it has between its covers the power to destroy this world and everything in it."

"Sure it does," said Max cynically.

"If you're not taking this seriously, I have work to do," said Uncle Ted, brushing the crumbs from his shirt and looking at his watch.

"No, please go on," said Max, genuinely sorry.

Uncle Ted cleared his throat.

"That old weasel DeLanda may have been sent by the church, but he had no interest in saving souls. The Maya had something very precious and unique, and DeLanda was determined to steal it. He tortured thousands of men, women, and children just to get what he wanted."

"It was the Jaguar Stones!" guessed Max.

"You've heard of them?" said Uncle Ted, surprised.

"Oscar Poot told me a story about them. But you don't really think that a piece of old stone can have special powers, do you?"

"One thing you learn around here, Max, is to keep an open mind. But the point is that *DeLanda* believed in the Jaguar Stones. He wrote in his diary that they could turn men into gods — and he gave full instructions."

"So why did Dad keep the diary? Isn't that against some kind of archaeological code of honor."

"Honor doesn't come into it, Max. Ever since your father read DeLanda's diary, he's been obsessed by the Jaguar Stones. But I don't think any of us actually believed in their powers until your parents went to Ix Chel. I saw the beam of light over the jungle that night, and I'm telling you, it was not of this universe. And neither was that rainstorm. It was terrifying, like the end of the world. I thought we were going to get washed away. In all the time I've lived here, I've never seen or heard anything like it."

"What do you mean, *until my parents went to Ix Chel*? Are you saying that my father had a Jaguar Stone?"

Uncle Ted slowly wiped his mouth with a napkin, which he carefully refolded before putting it down next to his cup. When he could no longer avoid answering the question, he spoke in a whisper. One word. One word that changed everything.

"Yes."

"What?" Max sat bolt upright.

"He had the White Jaguar."

"Where did he get it?"

"From me."

"But where did *you* get it from? Do you forge the stones?"

"No, Max, my Jaguar Stones are the real thing. Surely you saw that last night?"

Max shuddered to remember how the Red Jaguar had seemed to throb with blood and muscle and sinew.

"So where did you get them?" he persisted.

"It's another long story, I'm afraid."

"You said you'd tell me everything," Max reminded him, settling back into the sofa and pulling the blanket over him, like a child waiting for a bedtime story.

Uncle Ted sighed and began again.

"About twenty years ago, your grandpa had a stroke. At the time, I was at art school in London, and Frank was in Boston working on his doctorate. Your grandma had died some years before and Grandpa was living alone. As the elder son, it was my duty to come home and look after things. Sadly, Grandpa never recovered. When he died, he left the business to me."

"Why did he leave it all to you? Why didn't Dad get half?" asked Max, indignant that Patrick Murphy's fortune had passed his family by.

"Because I'd been working here every summer while Frank was off on his digs. Like it or not, I knew the banana business inside out. Besides your father had only ever wanted to be an archaeologist."

"It doesn't seem fair though, that you got all the money," said Max.

"That's what your father has always thought," said Uncle Ted. "But the truth is, there was no money. When I inherited the business, it was on its last legs. There was a blight in the banana trees and production was at an all-time low. I was tempted to just pack up and leave, but a lot of people were depending on me."

"Like who?" said Max, still peeved that his father had missed out on the inheritance.

"Like Lucky Jim's family. Lucky's father was my father's foreman for forty years. Lucky is the youngest of ten children, and they've all worked here at one time or another. I couldn't walk away from those kinds of ties. And I was sure the business would take off again once the blight was over. I just had to find the money to keep it going in the meantime. Then I could go back to London, make my name as an artist, and never eat another banana as long as I lived. Suddenly the solution came to me . . . "

Uncle Ted rubbed his hands together in pleasure.

"In a flash of inspiration, I realized that my regular banana shipments to the States were the ideal cover for a little sideline. So I decided to put my artistic training to good use and start dealing in Maya artifacts."

"Smuggling them, you mean?" said Max.

"There's your father talking again!" said Uncle Ted with a smile.

"Dad's always saying how much he despises smugglers and looters."

"Yes, we had a big argument about it. He called me greedy and ignorant. He said I was no better than a thieving conquistador. I thought that was a little over the top, given that he's secretly hoarding the greatest treasure of them all. So I called *him* a few names too. You could say that we both went too far. But, to cut a long story short, things have been frosty between us ever since."

"But Dad's right. What you're doing is illegal."

"Look, Max, I don't expect Frank to condone what I do, but he doesn't have to be such a hypocrite about it. He's just worried that, if I get caught, he'll never get permission to excavate another site. This isn't about ethics. It's about Frank's fixation with the Jaguar Stones."

"So that's why you and Dad don't get along. I understand now. He does get very focused on his work."

Ted shrugged. "Work . . . women . . . the villa . . . whatever . . . Frank has always been jealous of me for one reason or another. It's younger brother syndrome."

"Like Tzelek and Lord Six-Rabbit," said Max.

Uncle Ted looked surprised. "You learn fast," he said.

"Yeah, I was never interested in the Maya in Boston. But now I'm here . . . "

"Your father would be proud to hear you say that, Max." Uncle Ted gave a bitter laugh. "You know, the joke is that I've always been jealous that he got to live out his dream and I had to stay in San Xavier."

"So why didn't you go back to London when the banana blight was over?"

"The usual story . . . *cherchez la femme*."

"What?"

"I fell in love."

"Who —?" began Max.

"It's not important, it didn't work out," cut in Uncle Ted. "But the experience changed me. It nearly destroyed me. I resolved never again to get close to another human being. You can't be an artist without passion, so I threw myself into running the business. Maya artifacts are just another commodity to me — like bananas. I don't understand why people get so worked up about objects and possessions. It's the things money *can't* buy that are important in this life."

"Hmmm," said Max. He wasn't convinced. "Do you have an heir?" he asked.

"What? Yes . . . I'm planning to leave my estate to Lucky. Why?"

"Just wondering," said Max. He looked around the richly decorated Great Hall. "For someone who doesn't rate possessions, you have an awful lot of them."

Uncle Ted shrugged. "One of these days, I'll probably donate it all to a museum. I know Lucky wouldn't want to be surrounded by antiques. He prefers modern art."

"Dad says all modern art is rubbish," said Max.

"Oh, so now he's an art expert too, is he?" sneered Uncle Ted.

"You know Dad," said Max. "He has a lot of opinions."

"Ignorant opinions," said Uncle Ted. "To be honest with you, Max, after seeing him last week, I wouldn't care if our paths never crossed again."

"But he's your brother."

"Frank and I are like oil and water. We don't agree about anything, these days. He may be my brother, but I don't have to like him."

"So why did you give him a Jaguar Stone?"

"I didn't have much choice. He was blackmailing me."

Max's mouth fell open. "You're kidding!"

Uncle Ted shook his head. "Your father had me over a barrel. He threatened to blow the whistle on my smuggling operation unless I gave him what he wanted. The penalties are pretty stiff for that sort of thing in San Xavier. Even with friends in high places, I'd be looking at spending the rest of my life in jail."

"And what did he want?"

"He wanted a Jaguar Stone. He made me promise that if I ever came across one in my dealings, I would pass it straight to him, no questions asked. Of course, that conversation happened years ago. I never dreamed, for one moment, that one of the stones would actually fall into my hands."

"Why did he want it so badly?"

"It's what he needed to make use of DeLanda's diary."

Max shook his head in disbelief. He still could not imagine his father being caught up in all this drama and intrigue.

"Where did *you* get the stone?"

"Pure chance." Uncle Ted leaned forward conspiratorially. "One day last year, we'd just set sail with a load of bananas and our 'special cargo,' when the local coast guard pulled alongside to board us for inspection. Luckily, we were using the old Chinese smugglers' trick of towing the loot in a crate underwater. We cut the rope, the crate sank to the bottom of the sea, and there was nothing for the coast guard to find."

"But didn't you lose everything?" asked Max, fascinated by this master class in smuggling techniques.

"No, that's the clever bit. We fit our crates with small transmitters. If we have to cut one loose, we can track it with a GPS — a global positioning system. The waters around here aren't deep, so we just send down a diver to retrieve it."

"Why don't the coast guard see the signal?"

"They do. But there are so many environmentalists tracking whales and dolphins with the same system, no one pays any attention. Even so, we thought it would be wise to lay low for a while. So we left the crate down there for several months and monitored the signal. That's when we noticed something strange."

Max sat up again. "What was it?"

"The crate was moving toward land. You expect things to drift with the current, but this was like a magnetic attraction. Eventually the signal indicated that the crate was no longer underwater. Yet the depth gauge showed it was still way below sea level. It didn't make sense."

"Did you send the divers in?"

"Yes, and I went down with them to see for myself. We entered the ocean where the seabed drops sharply just offshore. There was a strong current, but we fought our way through and soon found ourselves in an underwater tunnel. We followed it for a hundred yards or so, until it opened into a huge cavern. And I mean *huge*. I'm talking about a space the size of Madison Square Garden. When we surfaced and shone our lights around, we couldn't believe our eyes. Washed up on the rocks on the far side of the cavern was the wreck of a Spanish galleon. It was the long lost *Espada*."

"That's the ship that was cursed by Lord Six-Rabbit!" yelled Max excitedly. "She disappeared after sailing out of Aguas Muertas!"

"Exactly! And can you imagine the riches that were in her hold?"

When Uncle Ted shielded his eyes from the morning sun, it looked as if he were blinded by the glare from the *Espada*'s gold.

"It took us months to bring up the haul. But the best was yet to come . . . "

Uncle Ted paused for dramatic effect.

"On our final dive before the tides changed, we found an old sea chest at the back of the hold. It was perfectly preserved, something to do with conditions in the cave I suppose, and there, burned into the wood, was the crest of Friar Diego DeLanda! Can you believe it? It was so heavy, we had to call for more divers to help us shift it. But remembering that old box in the wall, I was braced for disappointment."

Uncle Ted's face was glowing with excitement, and Max knew that, this time, DeLanda's box had contained something more than rosary beads and books.

"As soon as we cut off the padlock and began opening the lid, a ghostly glow lit up the entire cavern. Inside the chest, along with

a jeweled sword and some solid gold candlesticks, were not one, mark you, but two! — of the legendary Jaguar Stones. One in pure white alabaster and one in a ruby-red Mexican fire opal. I couldn't believe it. There in front of me were the White Jaguar of Ix Chel and the Red Jaguar of Chaak."

Uncle Ted laughed at the memory. "So there you have it. Not only did I make good on my promise to your father, I even used my connections to get him permits for the dig. And was he grateful? No, he was not. He came to collect the White Jaguar last week, and he took it from me as if it was his birthright. Not one word of thanks. It wasn't the most comfortable of meetings, but I'd fulfilled my side of the bargain and that was all that mattered to me. I assumed that Frank and I would have no further contact. I wasn't expecting his son to turn up on my doorstep a few days later."

"I'm sorry," said Max.

Uncle Ted smiled ruefully. "I'm the one who should be sorry, Max. I've enjoyed our little chat. Maybe blood *is* thicker than water. But I haven't been a very good host so far, have I? It's just that, when it comes to houseguests, I tend to agree with Jean-Paul."

"Jean-Paul? Is he another one of your servants?"

"Jean-Paul Sartre," smiled Uncle Ted, "the French philosopher. He said, 'Hell is other people.' Well, of course, he said it in French. But my point is, I don't like visitors at the best of times and seeing your father always puts me in a bad mood."

"To be honest," said Max, "he sometimes has that effect on me, too."

He sipped his chocolate and looked around the room again. What a waste to give all this stuff to a museum. It must be worth millions. "You know, just because you don't like my father, it doesn't mean you have to cut *me* out of your will."

This time, Uncle Ted laughed out loud. "I like a man who speaks his mind, Max. I think I might enjoy having you here, after all. I hope we can make a fresh start."

"I'd like that," said Max.

"But you must promise to obey my rules. I'm selling the Red Jaguar tomorrow night, and I need to know that you're safe in your room. My buyer is a nasty piece of work and anything could happen."

Max guessed he was talking about DeLanda the younger, the gun-crazed Spaniard from the hotel.

"Why deal with those kind of people?" he asked.

"I'm a businessman. I don't choose my customers, I just sell to the highest bidder. Besides, if I refused to sell the Red Jaguar to this particular collector, his goons would steal it from me anyway. At least this way, I get paid for my trouble."

"I'll help you!" said Max, still trying to ingratiate himself with his rich uncle.

"Help me? Absolutely not. I'm warning you, Max, stay in your room."

"But why do *I* have to miss all the excitement?"

"To stay alive," said Uncle Ted, grimly.

"Well, let me do something safe then, like keeping a lookout. There's a great view from my balcony and I could use those night-vision goggles I saw in your office."

Uncle Ted thought for a moment. He seemed to be warming to the idea. "At least I'd know where you were. But you'd have to promise to stay in your room, whatever happens. These thugs mean business."

"I promise."

"That's settled then." He shook Max's hand.

Raul, who'd come in to clear away the breakfast things, looked curiously from one to the other. It was a long time since he'd seen his boss looking so happy. The sight of it made him happy too, and he smiled to himself as he loaded the plates onto a tray.

"Thank you, Raul," said Uncle Ted. "Have you packed the boy's lunch?"

"What?" said Max, eyes wide with indignation. "I thought we were making a fresh start? You mean, after all this, I still have to go and rake the beach?"

"Absolutely," smiled Uncle Ted. "Now get to work."

CHAPTER VII

THIEVES IN THE NIGHT

THAT EVENING MAX sat on his balcony, waiting for it to get dark enough to try out the night-vision goggles and thinking over everything Uncle Ted had told him. His head was throbbing from information overload. If he were a computer, he would have crashed for sure.

Back in Boston, life had been black and white. Parents led dull lives and went to bed early. Smugglers were lowlife jerks. The Maya were dead as dodos.

Here in the jungle, none of that was true. All bets were off. How had Uncle Ted put it at the hotel? "Things are never what they seem around here."

It made Max feel nervous, but it also made him feel excited. He liked the sense of possibility, the idea that he could be anyone he wanted to be. He could have hair that never looked red . . . he could be irresistible to girls . . . he could . . . he could . . . (dare he even think it?) . . . perhaps he could be an interesting enough person to make his parents want to spend more time with him.

If they ever came back.

He sighed. He'd read somewhere that the trick to getting what you wanted in life was the power of positive thinking.

Trying to think positively, he took stock of his current situation.

He'd traveled all this way on his own. He'd survived tamales and chicken buses and that goon at the hotel and Lucky Jim's gun on his neck. He'd even bonded with Uncle Ted.

It wasn't a bad start.

In fact, tonight, standing on the balcony of his rich uncle's beautiful house, he felt like a new person.

Older, wiser, more mature.

That's the spirit, he encouraged himself.

He smiled, a sardonic James Bond kind of smile.

Out here, with the waves lapping the shore and the echoing sounds of the rainforest beyond the garden wall, it was easy to feel like an international playboy.

Max Murphy, Man of Mystery.

It had a ring to it.

A loud buzzing in his ears abruptly interrupted his daydream and sent him scurrying inside for the bug spray.

Where had he put it this time? As he rooted through his backpack, he found a bit of paper tucked into an inner pocket. It was a note from his mother.

> *Ciao, Max!*
> *I hope you're having fun and wearing your*
> *hat in the sun. Look up at the Moon Rabbit*
> *(remember?) and I'll be looking at it too.*
> *I love you, Mom*

She must have written it when she was packing his bag for camp. He kept telling her he was too old for that stuff, but she was always tucking embarrassing little notes into his lunch box or under his pillow.

Mothers.

But what was that about the Moon Rabbit?

It sounded familiar, but he couldn't place it . . .

And then it came to him.

It was an evening long ago. He was sitting on the window seat in his bedroom in Boston. His mother was pointing up at the night sky. "We see the man in the moon," she was telling him, "but Ancient Maya children saw a leaping rabbit, the pet of the moon goddess."

After that, little Max had waved to the Moon Rabbit every night.

Big Max cringed at the memory and stuffed the note back into his bag.

Night had fallen while he'd been inside and he went back onto the balcony. The moon was shining weakly behind the clouds.

There would be no Moon Rabbit tonight.

He inspected the night-vision goggles. They looked like heavy binoculars attached to a web of straps. It took him a while to get them on, but once he did . . .

Boy, did they work!

It was fantastic! Everything was cast in a green glow, but he could see almost as well as in daylight. In fact, thanks to thermal imaging and infrared detectors, he could see some things even better than usual.

Ha-hah! Those guards patrolling the beachfront thought they were keeping a low profile, but their body heat made them stand out like luminous green ghosts!

Excited, Max turned his gaze onto the rainforest. Surely tonight he'd be able to spot an animal in its normally inscrutable mass.

Nothing.

Nothing.

Nothing.

Wait.

He saw a movement out of the corner of his eye.

He focused in on it.

Gotcha!

Something was coming out of the jungle and heading this way. As he watched, the faint green glow formed itself into two distinct heat spots. Max increased the magnification on the goggles until he could make out two large monkeys.

With their long tails curved in the air behind them, the monkeys loped quickly toward the perimeter wall. For a few minutes they disappeared from view, but soon they appeared again on the edge of the wall. Max smiled to himself. They must sneak in all the time to steal bananas.

The monkeys certainly seemed to know where they were going, but it was not toward the banana warehouse. They were headed straight toward the house. Max was tingling with excitement. Seeing animals in the wild felt very different to seeing them in the zoo. He kept absolutely still so as not to frighten them.

What were they up to? They seemed to be interested in a particular stone pillar in the garden. Was there some sort of tasty vine growing on it? What was the special attraction? Max's smile faded as he watched the monkeys remove a metal grate off the side of the pillar and climb inside.

What were they doing? Where had they gone?

Suddenly, Max understood that the pillar must conceal a ventilation shaft for the underground rooms. He kept his eyes fixed on it, but the monkeys had vanished. Just when he was wondering if he'd dreamed the whole thing (had he fallen asleep for a moment?), the monkeys reappeared.

But what was that? They were carrying something. Max's jaw dropped when he realized it was the metal case containing the Red Jaguar.

This was not remotely funny anymore. It was deadly serious

and Max seemed to be the only one who was aware of it. Where were the guards? Where was Lucky Jim? Where was Uncle Ted?

If only someone would come before it was too late . . .

The monkeys moved awkwardly across the lawn toward the perimeter wall. The case was very heavy and they were having difficulty lifting it. But even so, they would soon be over the wall and into the jungle.

Max was in turmoil. Should he shout for the guards and try to convince them that two monkeys had staged a commando raid? Or should he go after the monkeys himself and break his promise to Uncle Ted about staying in his room?

Max made his decision.

A promise was a promise.

Last night, he felt like he and Uncle Ted had bonded. His uncle hadn't liked him at first, but Max had won him over. He felt proud of himself for that and he didn't want to blow it now. Besides, it would be a lot easier to find his parents with Uncle Ted on his side.

He basked in a glow of self-righteousness.

For once, he would act in a mature and responsible manner. He would do as he was told — even if the monkeys got clean away.

He ran to the door to raise the alarm.

It was locked.

Uncle Ted had locked him in! What a jerk!

So much for mutual trust and respect! As of now, all promises were null and void.

In a hotheaded rage, Max grabbed his backpack and reviewed the jumbled contents: flashlight, penknife, towel, mosquito net, shades, and — what was that, at the bottom? — ugh, those health-food granola bars. (He would never, *ever* be that hungry.) Anything else? He threw in his Red Sox cap for good luck.

Ready to go.

But how was he going to get down?

His balcony was too high to jump off.

Think. Think.

OK. Time for a trick from the movies. He'd seen it done a million times.

He pulled the sheets from his bed and knotted them together. Tying one end to the balustrade, he threw the other end into the darkness. Then he swung the backpack over his shoulder and eased himself over the balcony railing.

It was higher than he'd realized.

Telling himself not to look down, he started climbing clumsily down the sheets, hand over hand. It wasn't as easy as it looked in the movies. His head was weighed down by the night-vision goggles. His arms ached. The sheets made a terrible groaning noise. Or was that sound coming from his own mouth?

Worst of all, when he finally got to the bottom, he was still ten feet from the ground.

Max closed his eyes and let go.

He landed on his back in a flowering bush.

He was alive. He was down.

He got to his feet unsteadily and looked back up at the balcony. The sheets were fluttering in the moonlight like a luminous white flag. So much for Max Murphy, Man of Mystery. If the guards hadn't actually seen him climbing down, they'd certainly know about it now.

Uncle Ted was going to be mad.

Very mad.

But there was no going back now. Besides, if Uncle Ted had trusted him and not locked him in his room like a naughty child, he wouldn't have attempted this crazy escapade. Now he was master of his own destiny. And if he could just get those monkeys to drop the Jaguar Stone, Uncle Ted would have to kiss his feet and beg his forgiveness.

Through the night-vision goggles, Max spotted the monkeys disappearing over the perimeter wall. He raced across the garden toward them. Steps led up to a battlemented walkway that ran along the top of the wall. Max took the steps two at time and peered over. There was about forty more feet of lawn between the wall and the start of the jungle. He could see the monkeys slowly dragging the case toward the tree line. They seemed to heading for a gap in the undergrowth, maybe some sort of trail.

Max swung over the wall and found footholds to climb down in the crumbling stone. Then he sprinted across the lawn toward the trees, just as lights came on all over the house. The alarm had been raised. There was no going back.

He plunged down the trail and into the forest. His pace slowed. It was like entering a tunnel. The noise was incredible. *Whook-whook. Whook-whook.* At first, he thought a search-and-rescue helicopter was circling above him, but then he realized that this deafening sound was coming from the tiny pop-eyed frogs that looked down at him from every tree.

Though no competition for the frogs in the decibel stakes, nocturnal birds were shrieking, insects were buzzing — and every so often something a whole lot bigger would let out a hungry growl that shook the air like a subway train passing through.

Max told himself that the creatures were more scared of him than he was of them, but he doubted it were true. He wanted to turn back. But which would he rather face — a wild beast or an angry Uncle Ted?

He decided to keep going.

With every step, the din of the jungle grew louder. The trees rustled and shook. Bats darted in front of his face. Lightning bugs and click beetles lit up his goggles with their fluorescent green trails. He seemed to be surrounded by creeping, crawling, jumping things.

OK. Concentrate.

Max could clearly see the path and he picked his way carefully over the tangled mass of roots and rotting leaves. It was lucky for him that the Red Jaguar was so heavy. If it had been lighter, the monkeys could have swung through the trees and he wouldn't have had a chance of following them.

As it was, they continued their slow, shuffling progress until they came to an open space under a tall stand of bamboo. Then they inspected the ground fastidiously before choosing a place to set down the suitcase, like two old ladies getting ready for a picnic.

Max hid behind a tree, hardly daring to breathe. He noticed that one of the monkeys was bigger than the other. Any minute now, he thought, I'll run into the clearing, frighten them away, and grab the suitcase. But as he stood there, gathering his nerve, the bigger monkey opened its mouth and began to roar.

Max couldn't believe the sheer volume of it. It was like something out of *Jurassic Park*. If he couldn't see that it was coming from a monkey, he would

have thought a T-Rex was loose in the jungle. Make that a T-Rex with a megaphone.

But who or what was this monkey calling?

A human figure, dressed all in black, emerged from the forest. The monkeys jumped up and down excitedly. The figure patted them and gave them each something to eat. The monkeys grabbed the food and leapt into the trees, whooping and screeching at each other.

Then the figure opened the case and took out the Red Jaguar.

Its glow illuminated the whole clearing.

Suddenly, the air was silent. The insects, the birds, even the tree frogs, ceased their calling. The whole jungle seemed to be waiting and watching.

Quickly, the figure wrapped the stone in a cloth and put it into a small backpack. Then he started digging in the ground, scooping out the dirt with both hands until he'd made a hole big enough for the metal case. Only when the both the stone and the case were hidden from view, did the jungle cacophony resume.

Who was this mysterious thief who trained monkeys to do his dirty work? Was it one of DeLanda's henchmen? Or a business rival of Uncle Ted's?

An unearthly growl made Max jump out of his skin.

Whatever it was, it was close.

He peered around the tree trunk in terror.

It was the thief talking to the monkeys. With his hands cupped around his mouth, the thief was making a series of inhuman noises. Loud growls and grunts rained down from the trees in reply. While Max was trying to locate their source in all the foliage, the thief suddenly took off again.

Max followed, trying to be as quiet and light-footed as he could.

It was harder than before, because the pace was faster now and the trail much less distinct. Even with the night-vision goggles, he had to use all his wits and concentration to keep the figure in view. Roots tripped him, clinging vines clung to him, branches pulled at him. But none of these obstacles seemed to bother his quarry who made the trek look as effortless as a stroll in the park.

They came to a stagnant river with a layer of green scum floating on top. A large tree had fallen across it, creating a natural bridge. The thief ran nimbly over the tree trunk and continued up the path.

Max paused before crossing. Two columns of big, fat ants were marching across the tree trunk. In the line approaching him, each ant carried a piece of leaf several times its own size. In the other line, the ants were marching back unencumbered, presumably to get more leaves. There was no end in sight to their ranks in either direction.

They're only ants, he told himself and stepped gingerly onto the log. It was perilously slippery. Max inched his way along, concentrating every fiber of his being on keeping his balance. He had made it about half way across, when he felt a searing pain in his legs, like being jabbed by invisible knives. He looked down to see ants all over his sneakers. They were crawling up inside his jeans and biting his legs! Before he thought about what he was doing, he leaned over to swat at his jeans and fell headfirst into the murky river.

It tasted disgusting. Max spluttered to the surface and stood up on the oozy bottom. The water came up to his waist. He couldn't see much because his goggles were smeared with mud, but the pain in his legs seemed to be subsiding so he guessed that the ants had been washed off. On the downside, who knew what else was lurking down there? There could be piranhas or crocodiles or leeches or . . .

He told himself to stop thinking and get out of there fast.

The muddy riverbed made every step a struggle. At one point the suction pulled off a sneaker, and he had to crouch down and feel around in the mud until he found it. The thick, green water stank like rotten eggs, and his whole body shook with revulsion.

Something slimy touched his face.

A piece of weed? A water snake?

Splashing hysterically, he made it to the bank. There was a large rock and he sat down on it. His heart was pounding. Where was he? What had he done? What would become of him? Dripping wet and trembling with fear, he rammed his sneaker back on. Then he ran his hands all over his body to wipe down every inch of himself. He didn't want any creepy jungle thing to touch any bit of him. This was it, the end of the line. He could make himself go no farther. He would sit here until he was found.

Or until he starved to death.

Or until something ate him.

It was at this low point that Max realized what an idiot he'd been. He was lost in the treacherous forest, alone, wet, bitten, scared, and hungry. Now the police would have to break off their search for his parents to look for him instead (if Uncle Ted had even bothered to report him missing). He just hoped that someone would find him before DeLanda's thugs did.

Then he drew his feet up, put his head on his knees, and hugged himself. His clothes smelled sulphurous and moldy. He was overwhelmed by self-pity.

He unzipped his wet backpack and looked inside. It seemed to be pretty dry in there. He pulled out a damp towel and dried his head. Then he stuck his hand in again and groped around. Among the tangle of mosquito netting and odd socks, his fingers closed on something unnaturally hard and dense.

The granola bars.

It had come to this.

Miserably, he unwrapped a bar. He brought the dense, brown mass slowly to his lips. With a heavy heart, he opened his mouth and prepared his tongue to receive the foul-tasting grunge. And then, in the nick of time, he recovered his fighting spirit.

Things were bad, but not that bad.

He still wasn't desperate enough to consider eating one of those bars.

So he sat on the rock and pulled himself together and thought about what he should do.

The most sensible thing would be to retrace his steps. But going back over that ant-covered log was not an option. Nor was wading back through that slimy river. And they both paled in comparison to the terror he felt about facing Uncle Ted without bringing back the Jaguar Stone

He wiped the last of the mud off his goggles and looked around.

Trees, trees, nothing but trees. Big, thick trees with root clumps that were taller than he was. Tall, thin trees with sinister, twisted trunks and long, sinewy roots.

He looked harder. Now he was seeing things.

In the unreal green light of the goggles, he could see a shape hacked into one of the tree trunks.

It looked a bit like an arrow. And it was freshly carved.

He wished he hadn't watched that zombies-in-the-woods movie at Lenny's house a few weeks ago. He shuddered.

"We've been expecting you, Max Murphy . . . " cackled the zombies in his head.

Stop it. There must be a natural explanation, some burrowing insect or the scratchings of some demented rodent, but it spooked him all the same. He had a sense of being watched, the same feeling he'd had on the beach. He was just about to start panicking when he noticed a faint trail at the base of the arrow-scarred tree.

Was that the continuation of the trail he'd been following before? Come to think of it, where *was* the trail he'd been following before?

He put his head in his hands. He was lost in the middle of a jungle.

He felt about as safe as the last jelly doughnut in a school cafeteria.

Any moment now, he supposed, something big would come along and tear him limb from limb. Or maybe nothing would eat him, and *he'd* be forced to eat the granola bars. In any event, the future was looking grim.

He got up and looked more closely at the arrow-scarred tree.

Maybe it's a good sign, he told himself.

Oh sure, he answered himself.

He thought he saw something move in the bushes ahead. Whatever it was, he decided to follow it.

His feet squelched as he walked, but he no longer cared if he made any noise. He was miserable and tired and his quarry was long gone. The important thing now was to stick to the trail and try to find somewhere to sleep. He just tramped along on autopilot. He told himself it was no worse than a forced march at Brat Camp. At least here, there were no bossy counselors to order him about.

At last, he came to a part of the forest that was quieter and airier and didn't seem quite so creepy. By now, he was bone tired. His legs ached, his feet ached, his arms ached, his head ached.

He looked around and saw a massive tree trunk, easily twenty feet in diameter. The bottom of the trunk was bare, but its higher reaches had some kind of vine growing down them. The vine had big leathery leaves and exposed roots that dangled from the tree like bits of frayed rope. Where the trunk split into two, about ten feet off the ground, the crook was cushioned by a thick green mattress of leaves that seemed to have been flattened down, just for him. In Max's exhausted state, it looked as cozy and inviting as a feather bed.

Summoning his last reserves of energy, he climbed the tree, using the dangling roots to pull himself up. When he reached the crook, he wedged himself between the branches. Then he hung his mosquito net over him as best he could and lay back, using his backpack as a pillow.

He knew he'd never be able to sleep in this position, but at least he was relatively safe and his clothes were beginning to dry out.

In fact, it was surprisingly comfortable.

Max began to relax. He'd been awake for two days and it felt good to finally rest.

The busy hum of the jungle arranged itself into a soothing lullaby.

His eyelids felt heavy. He'd close them just for a moment.

Soon he curled up like a baby bird in a cozy nest and nodded off to sleep.

"Ow! Ow! Ow!"

The next thing he knew, he was screaming in pain and terror.

He'd been attacked as he slept.

He woke up to find great black hairy hands all over him, pinching him, squeezing him, pulling out his hair by the roots.

CHAPTER VIII

THE MONKEY GIRL

THEY WEREN'T HANDS, they were paws. Great hairy paws with long fingers.

Max tried to bat them away, but he was tangled up in his mosquito net and he fell out of the tree. He landed in a heap on his backpack.

Seconds later, the night-vision goggles landed next to him with a crash of broken glass.

He peered up to see what had attacked him.

Two monkeys were sitting high in the branches. One was big and black. The other was smaller and lighter in color. The bigger one was wearing Max's baseball cap. They both had thick hair and wispy beards that would have made them look quite intellectual had they not been baring their teeth and screeching with monkey laughter.

"Scram," shouted Max angrily, picking up a stick and throwing it at them. He missed by a mile, but they took the hint. In an instant they were off, leaping from branch to branch, still screeching raucously.

Max looked around. The leaf canopy above him was so dense that no sun could penetrate. Though not as dark as night, the light was murky. It was the energy in the air that told him it was morning. Thousands of busy little life forms scuttled around, intent on getting breakfast before it got too hot to move. Bugs buzzed and

"They weren't hands, they were paws."

whirred and clicked. Birds shrieked and squawked and whooped. Flowers pumped out their heady scents, competing with each other to lure the passing insects like those salespeople who lurked in Macy's doorway with sprays of perfume.

Everything was shrouded in a humid mist. In the dim light, Max felt like he was underwater, but with butterflies instead of fish.

It was the most amazing morning of his life.

On the negative side, he was lost, sore, itchy, hungry, and caked in mud. He'd also run out of steam. Sheer, hotheaded anger had carried him this far. But now, in the calm light of day, he realized that he had no choice but to go back and face the wrath of Uncle Ted.

He felt sick at the thought. If only he could return in triumph, having rescued the Red Jaguar. But it was too late for that now.

Thud!

A wild avocado, hard as a rock, landed at his feet.

Deep in the foliage he heard monkey laughter.

What was it with these guys? Why were they tormenting him? Weren't animals supposed to be afraid of humans? Wait! What if these were the same monkeys who stole the Red Jaguar last night? They were comfortable around people. They were light-fingered enough to extract his cap from his backpack. It *was* them, he was sure of it.

Max felt a ray of hope. If the monkeys were hanging around, maybe the human thief wasn't far away either. Maybe the triumphal return scenario was still a possibility.

He started up the trail.

Although it was just after dawn, the air felt wet and heavy. There was an insistent drumming sound that Max could not identify. As the noise grew louder and louder, water began to drip from the leaves above. Soon the drops became a downpour. Of course! The drumming sound — it was rain on the forest canopy!

Max ducked under a huge leaf for cover. He watched the rain running down the center of the leaf in front of him, and he caught as much as he could in his cupped hands. It was the sweetest water he'd ever tasted.

When the deluge was over, Max set off again into the dripping jungle. With his wet clothes chafing him, bugs biting him, and thorns tearing at his skin, his high spirits soon plummeted. He trudged along, trying to ignore the voices in his head that were telling him how lost he was, how stupid he was, how doomed he was. The voices were right, of course, but there wasn't much he could do about it now.

A shaft of sunlight burst through a gap in the tree canopy.

At the same moment, Max rounded a turn in the path.

In front of him was an ancient stone slab, about eight feet tall, standing in a spotlight of brilliant sunshine. Brushing aside the purple flowers that clung to it, he saw that the slab was covered in worn hieroglyphics. A swarm of yellow butterflies danced around his head, and the sun bathed the whole incredible scene in a golden glow.

Max paused for a moment to take it all in . . . the stone, the butterflies, the smoky scent of the flowers . . . Smoky? Wait —

He caught the unmistakable whiff of campfire.

His quarry was at hand!

But what now?

He'd been so intent on the chase that he hadn't considered what he'd do if he ever caught up. How exactly would a fourteen-year-old boy — with no knowledge of any combat technique that wasn't computer-generated — overpower this thug and steal back the Jaguar Stone?

It might be safer to just keep following and hope the police would soon show up. But first, he'd take a closer look at the enemy.

Grabbing a fallen branch as a makeshift weapon, his every sense on high alert, Max tiptoed down the path. The trees were starting to thin out, and he was coming to some sort of open space. For the last ten yards, he crept forward on his hands and knees. Then, using a large tree as cover, he peered into the clearing.

What he saw took his breath away.

Above the tree line, facing him, a Maya pyramid rose out of the jungle. It was covered in vegetation, but it was still possible to see the stepped terraces soaring up to the blue sky. It was incredibly tall and steep. Max felt dizzy looking up at it. After all these hours of traipsing through dense, tangled jungle, it was extraordinary to come upon something so angular, so precise, so . . . man-made.

In the plaza leading up to the temple were more stone slabs like the one Max had seen by the trail. Some were leaning at crazy angles; others had fallen to the ground. In the middle of the plaza, the remains of a campfire smoldered.

Still hiding behind the tree, Max scanned the area.

No one.

Perhaps he'd arrived too late.

Secretly, he hoped so.

But hey, he'd been hot on the trail and he took pride in that. For his first time in the jungle — with no map and no compass — he'd done really well to get this far. Brat Camp would be a piece of cake compared to this.

He was so busy congratulating himself that he didn't hear the swish of a machete behind him, didn't hear the thief creeping up on him, until a voice whispered in his ear: "Looking for me?"

Max spun around.

There in front of him was the mysterious figure in black.

It was a girl.

A pretty girl.

She was taller than him and probably a little older. She had the amber-colored eyes and straight black hair of the Maya. She was wearing black cargo pants, a Ramones T-shirt, and hiking boots. A black sweatshirt was knotted around her waist. She held the machete loosely in one hand with the ease of one who knew how to use it.

Max had the strangest feeling he'd seen her somewhere before.

She spoke again. "What took you so long, Hup?"

Max was speechless. So many questions were going through his mind. He stood there with his mouth open, until one question formed itself into words.

"Who are you?" he stammered.

"My name is Ix Sak Lool." (To Max, it sounded like Eesh Sock Lowell.) "It's Maya for Lady White Flower. But most people call me Lola."

"But who are you? Why did you steal the Red Jaguar?"

She ignored his questions. "Come and sit down, Hup."

He couldn't move. He just stood there, staring at her.

"Oh, I'm sorry, do excuse my manners," she said, affecting a formal bow. "Please be seated, Massimo Francis Murphy. Perhaps you would care for some jungle soda, otherwise known as water?"

"How do you know my name?" he asked.

She led him into the clearing and passed him a canteen of water.

"Massimo is Italian, after your grandfather," she said confidently. "And Francis is after your father."

Max stopped drinking and gawked at her in amazement.

"I met your parents at Ix Chel last week," she laughed. "My friend Hermanjilio" — she pronounced it Herman-*hee*-lio — "was working with them. I helped him set up camp before your parents arrived."

"They're missing," said Max. "They haven't come back."

"Yes, I heard about it. I think Hermanjilio might be with them."

"Do you know what happened?"

"No, I had to leave for Aguas Muertas, so I wasn't there when . . . you know . . . I'm sorry, Hup . . . " her voice trailed off.

There was an awkward silence and Max looked away.

Another question formed in his addled brain. "Why do you keep saying Hup?" He tried to copy her pronunciation, which sounded a bit like *hope* but shorter.

Lola smiled. "That's what I called you in my head, when I was following you. It's short for *hiri'ich hoop* (hee-ree eech hup), which means 'matchstick' in my language. With your red hair and your thin little legs, that's what you look like!"

"My hair is brown," said Max coldly. "But what do you mean, when *you* were following me? I was following *you*."

"Hah! You'd have been eaten by jaguars if I hadn't kept an eye on you. And what about that crocodile's nest you nearly disturbed when you fell in the river? Or the vampire bat that was hovering around while you slept — in the strangler fig bed that I made for you? Not to mention keeping the crazy count at bay."

"Liar," said Max, but he swallowed uncomfortably.

"Well, how about the arrow I cut into the tree for you? You can't tell me you didn't see that? You'd still be sitting on that rock, feeling sorry for yourself, if I hadn't shown you the way. Which reminds me," she said, handing him a mud-caked towel, "this, I believe, is yours."

He recognized it instantly. He must have left it by the stagnant river. He shook off the dried mud and pushed it into his backpack.

"I think the phrase you're looking for is *thank you*," said Lola.

"What should I thank you for? Luring me into the jungle in the middle of the night? Leading me across that bridge to be attacked by killer ants? Setting those monkeys on me . . . ?"

"Oh, poor Hup," said Lola, ruffling his hair.

He pushed her away.

She pushed him back.

Next minute, they were rolling on the ground, fighting like jaguar cubs. It was evident that Lola had had rather more practice at this sort of thing and within a few minutes she had Max flat on his back and trussed up in a vine.

"So, Hup, admit that I am the better fighter."

"No."

"Admit it."

Max looked her straight in the eye. "I admit it, Monkey Girl," he said. "You are the better . . . *thief*!"

Lola tightened the vine around Max's body. "It's not stealing when you take back something which belongs to you," she said.

"Liar!" squeaked Max, his voice constricted by the vine. "If it belongs to anyone, the Red Jaguar belongs to the Ancient Maya."

"That's what I said."

"Right," said Max. "So you're over a thousand years old, are you? I suppose you live in that pyramid over there and chop up tourists for human sacrifices."

"Maybe I do," said Lola, raising her machete.

"You don't scare me," said Max. "Even I know that the Ancient Maya died out hundreds of years ago. It's a big mystery, The Mystery of the Maya. They vanished into thin air one day. Some experts think they were abducted by aliens in spaceships."

"What experts?" laughed Lola, relaxing the vine.

"I read it in a magazine at the supermarket. Apparently, the Maya are living in another galaxy now — like Elvis and Buddy Holly."

"What? How can such brilliant parents have such a stupid son? Do you believe every crazy thing you hear, Hup?"

"Well, I don't believe you're an Ancient Maya. They vanished. Everyone knows that."

"Is that so? Well, maybe *I'll* vanish and leave you tied up like a tamale."

She walked away and began pouring water on the fire.

Max tried to break free of the vine, but he wasn't strong enough.

"Hey, Monkey Girl . . . ?"

No answer.

"Lola . . . ? Lady White Flower . . . ?" he called sweetly. "Please untie me."

She came back and stood over him, hands on hips.

"OK," she said, "but only because I like your parents. But first, you have to understand that Maya like me and Maya like the guys who built this pyramid are one and the same."

"I don't get it," said Max dubiously.

"It's simple. There's no mystery. We didn't disappear. We just left."

"In spaceships?"

"On foot. It was a classic peasant revolt. It takes a lot of work to sustain a city in the middle of the jungle, you know. Our ruling classes weren't pulling their weight, so the workers decided enough was enough. So they left the cities and went back to farming their own *milpa*."

"*Milpa*?"

"The family cornfield."

"What happened to the ruling classes?"

"I guess they learned to grow their own food."

"Speaking of food," said Max, "do you have any?"

She ignored him. "There are still six million Maya in Central America today. So don't go saying stupid things like we all disappeared. Just because we wear jeans and eat pizza, we're still Maya, you know."

"You eat pizza?" said Max, salivating. "Do you have any?"

Lola slashed through the vine with her machete. Then, she reached into her backpack and pulled out a little parcel wrapped in a leaf.

"Here," she said. "No pizza on the menu today, Hup."

Max unwrapped the parcel and found a rough-looking tortilla filled with brown beans. He inspected it with distaste. "Haven't you got anything else?" he complained.

"You're welcome," said Lola sarcastically.

Max tried a bite — it didn't taste as bad as it looked. As he wolfed down the tortilla, he looked around. "What is this place, anyway?"

"It's just an old temple. It doesn't have a name. There are hundreds of them around here, waiting to be properly excavated."

"What a waste! If this place was in the States, they'd dig it out in no time. They'd have souvenir shops and snack bars and costumed interpreters. You could turn it into a Maya theme park. It'd make a fortune."

"And you think that's a good idea?"

Max shrugged defensively. "Why not?"

"Some people say the old temples are still alive," said Lola.

"Nah. I bet it's just a rumor to keep looters away." He looked sharply at Lola. "Are you a looter? Or a tomb raider?"

"No!" she said, shocked at the suggestion.

"But you stole the Red Jaguar. Are you working for the count?"

"No! I work with baboons, not snakes!"

Max became aware of several large black and brownish monkeys sitting in the nearest tree, watching them.

"Baboons?" he said. "Is that what they are?"

"The locals call them baboons, but they're actually howler monkeys."

One of the lighter colored monkeys dropped to the ground and sat down in front of Max, regarding him with an air of disappointment.

"What's the matter with him?" asked Max.

"*Her*," corrected Lola, stroking the monkey's head. "This is Seri. She and her brother Chulo woke you up. Your snoring was disturbing the whole forest."

"Oh, ha ha," said Max. "I'm amazed I got any sleep at all."

"What a lazy boy you are. I watched you on the beach. I've never seen anyone work so little and complain so much."

Max ignored the insult. "So it was you! " he exclaimed. "I knew someone was spying on me."

"I wasn't the only one. DeLanda's men are everywhere," said Lola, smoothing dirt over the remains of the campfire. She put her finger to her lips and cocked her head to one side. Max had no idea which of the many forest sounds she was listening to.

After a few seconds, she whispered: "The baboons say men are coming." She shouldered her backpack. "Can you swim?"

"Why?"

"There's a place near here, the Blue Pool, we can give them the slip . . . "

"In a pool?"

"It leads to an underground cave system. There are caves under the whole jungle. My ancestors thought they were the doors to the Maya underworld. You're not claustrophobic, are you?"

Max shook his head, without conviction. He didn't like the sound of this at all.

What should he do? Stay here? Go back? Run? Hide?

He had only one thought. More than his fear of the jungle, more than his fear of Uncle Ted or Count DeLanda, he didn't want to be alone. Meeting this girl felt like fate.

"Let's go then," he said, trying to sound casual.

She fished some waterproof zipper bags out of her backpack. "Here, put your flashlight and anything else in one of these."

While Max fiddled with the bags, Lola called to the monkeys. From the wistful tone of the growls, he guessed she was saying good-bye.

Then, with a nod at Max to follow her, she ran across the clearing and into the trees. After a while, the ground sloped down and they came to a large pool with a rocky cliff on the far side. The water was light blue in the shallows, darkening to a brilliant cobalt as the bottom fell away.

Lola waded purposefully in, with Max trailing cautiously behind. A few more steps and they had to swim. She seemed to be heading for the cliff face. As they got closer, Max saw a small opening in the shadow of an overhanging rock.

Lola swam straight into it.

Max swam to the mouth of the cave and held on to the side, afraid to go farther. All he could see was inky blackness. There was a strange sound like the hissing of gas.

"Come on, Hup," said an impatient voice from out of the darkness. "The water's shallow inside the cave. Just swim toward my voice."

A few strokes later, his feet touched bottom. He stood for a moment as his eyes adjusted to the dim light coming from the entrance. He could just see Lola several yards ahead, pulling herself up onto a ledge. Max splashed his way over to her and tried to scramble up beside her.

To his embarrassment, she had to give him a hand.

"Where are we?" he asked.

"Take a look," said Lola.

When they switched on their flashlights, Max saw that the ledge was in a huge cavern. In some places, the stream below them was narrow; in others, it spilled out into wide expanses of dark, still water. Minerals had seeped through the cave walls, staining them in rich metallic colors of blue, gold, silver, and red. Against this vibrant backdrop, white calcite formations rose up like abstract marble statues.

"It looks like a cathedral," gasped Max, in awe. It was then he realized that the hissing sound was coming from the hundreds — maybe thousands — of little brown furry bats that were clinging to the roof of the cave.

"Gross!" He turned to Lola, but she'd gone. He could hear her splashing on ahead. He quickly climbed down into the stream and followed her into the darkness.

"How much farther?" he asked, but she didn't answer.

They waded deeper and deeper into the cavern following the course of the stream. Bats swooped over Max's head, making him duck and hit his head on the cave wall. Most of the time, the water came up only to his ankles, but it was cold and the stones on the streambed were sharp, so the going was difficult. It was also slightly surreal, due to the ever-increasing amount of pottery they passed.

Pots had been placed in small pools, on ledges, stuffed between stalagmites, tucked into small niches: Anywhere there was a pot-sized hole, a pot was filling it. It reminded Max of his grandmother's house in Italy, where every available space was filled with china figurines. But the oddest thing about this display was that every single pot was cracked or broken.

"What's with the pots?" asked Max.

"Caves were sacred places," said Lola. "People came to this one to pray for rain. They would bring a piece of pottery with them and break it to release the spirits inside. It's a way of saying thank you to the gods."

Max had a mental flash of holding a Maya thanksgiving at Nonna's house and smashing all her china, when he heard a noise behind them. One glance at Lola told him she'd heard it too.

They upped their pace.

Presently, they entered an even bigger cavern where the stream formed a wide, shallow pool. In this chamber, the tops of the stalagmites had been cut off and the insides hollowed out. Max slipped and bumped into one of them. It rang like a bell with a low vibration that echoed through the cave. The other stalagmites in the chamber also began to resonate, creating a haunting melody.

"Idiot!" hissed Lola. "You'll lead them straight to us. Don't touch anything else. And stay on the edge of the pool."

"Wouldn't it be quicker to just wade straight across?" whispered Max.

In answer, Lola shone her flashlight onto the pool. Several skeletons were lying in the water, their centuries-old bones covered in a layer of calcite, which gave them a more fleshly appearance. Rising from the center was a small island on which a stone altar had been built. On the front of the altar was carved a fearsome figure with bulbous eyes, a long nose, and two curving tusks. In one hand, the figure held what looked like a bolt of lightning. In the other, it held a bowl containing a sinister-looking lump.

"What's in that bowl?" asked Max.

"A human heart."

"Oh."

Max's own heart was pounding as they circled the rest of the pool.

On the far side was a narrow cleft in the rock. As they drew closer, he heard a low rumbling. They turned sideways to squeeze through the gap, and as they inched along, the rumbling got louder and louder until it became a deafening roar.

"Not much farther now," called Lola.

The passageway gave another turn and opened into a tall, narrow cavern. They were on a stone platform overlooking a rushing, underground river. Facing outwards from each corner was the stone head of a snarling jaguar. In the center of the platform, steps led down into the raging torrent.

"It's a dead end," screamed Max. "We're trapped!"

"It's the Sacred River of the Jaguar Kings — our escape route!"

Max looked down at the whirling, surging, foaming maelstrom beneath them. It wasn't possible that anyone could survive in those perilous waters.

"No way!" he yelled.

"It's the only way!" she yelled back.

CHAPTER IX

IN THE DARK

"YOU'RE CRAZY!" SCREAMED Max, over the noise of the water. "We can't swim in that — we'll drown!"

"The water *is* higher than usual, after all the rain," conceded Lola. "But we won't be swimming. We've got a boat."

Max watched, puzzled, as she climbed up behind a cluster of stalagmites. She dragged a large bundle out from this hiding place and shook it out to reveal a six-foot rubber raft. Rolled up inside were two collapsible paddles and a foot pump.

"How did that get there?" asked Max.

"I bought it in Aguas Muertas, and hid it here before I took the Jaguar Stone. I had a feeling I'd need a fast getaway."

"You planned this?"

Lola nodded proudly.

"But look at the water. Nothing could survive that."

"Where's your sense of adventure, Hup? You pump, I'll pack. Now hurry!"

His brain paralyzed with fear and not knowing what else to do but follow her instructions, Max inflated the raft and assembled the paddles. Lola tied the backpacks onto the raft's handles and taped their flashlights to the front to act as headlights and leave their hands free for paddling.

She seemed to know what she was doing.

They dragged the raft down the steps and Lola held it steady while Max scrambled in on shaking legs.

Suddenly, they were caught in a powerful beam of light.

"Stop!" commanded a heavily accented voice from behind the flashlight. "There is no way out. Surrender now, or these will be the waters of your death. *Las aguas de tu muerte.*"

Max recognized the lisping tones of Count Antonio DeLanda.

He was ready to surrender there and then, but Lola jumped in beside him and started paddling furiously. They were swept away from the steps and into the darkness.

Bang!

A shot echoed in the cave and a red light high above them illuminated the raft as it careened and bucked in the churning water.

"What was that?" whimpered Max.

"A flare gun," said Lola, as she dug her paddle into the water. "They're lighting up the cave, so they can shoot at us."

Max started paddling like his life depended on it — which, of course, it did.

A long burst of machine-gun fire rang out and ricocheted off the cave wall. Max threw himself onto the floor of the raft.

"Sit up and paddle!" yelled Lola.

He took a deep breath and forced himself up. As he dipped his paddle shakily into the water, he braced himself for the bullet that would rip into his back at any moment.

But it never came. The swift current swept them out of De-Landa's view and the last they heard of him was a volley of Spanish curses echoing through the cavern.

There was no time to relax. The tunnel narrowed and the current strengthened, shooting them into a twisting passageway. They were bounced from one wall to another, until, soaked in spray, they were swept sideways into a large cavern. It was filled with so many stalactites and stalagmites that it looked like a forest of stone. Max wondered how deep underground they were.

"Where are we?" he shouted.

"Stop talking and concentrate!" snapped Lola. "These rocks could rip us wide open."

Bossy, bossy, bossy, thought Max.

At times, they glided through vast caverns where the water was calm and their flashlights caught blind catfish, eyes long since atrophied from centuries of darkness, lurking in the depths. At other times, the current was strong and they had no time to look at anything as they struggled to keep the raft off the rocks.

And all the time, Max was trying to keep his mind a blank, trying not to think about the blackness around them, the weird shapes of the rocks, what it would be like to fall into the water, the impossibility of ending this day alive.

They entered a place where the cave roof had collapsed, and they had to shade their eyes from the blinding sunlight that poured down on them. The water here was a sparkling green, and it flowed slowly as if reluctant to reenter the darkness.

All around the chamber, strange forms like giant hairy turnips twisted out of the water and up through the roof of the cave.

"What are those?" asked Max.

"Tree roots from above," said Lola. "They've burrowed down through the limestone to get to this river."

"I can't believe roots could bore through solid rock," marveled Max.

Lola turned around to look at him. "Life is hard in the rainforest," she said. "Everything is fighting for survival."

"Including you?"

She didn't answer, and they paddled on in silence.

All too soon, they left the sunlight and were once again slipping through the dark. The river was quiet now and the air was stale. It was getting harder to breathe. The cave ceiling came down lower and lower and they had to lean backward to pass underneath. Sometimes they had to lie completely flat on their backs, but they always made it through.

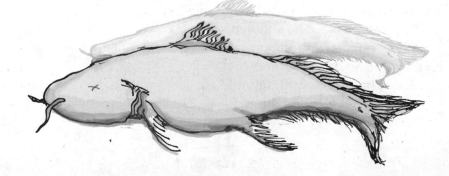

At last, the way ahead looked clear. They could see no more out-croppings hanging down, just blackness.

"Are we nearly there?" whined Max. "I've had enough. My arms are aching."

As they came closer, what had looked like a large tunnel filled with darkness revealed itself to be a solid wall of black stone.

And this time, there was no way through.

The raft lurched to a stop. The river disappeared under the rock.

"Now what? We're trapped! This is all your fault!" Max was panicking.

"It's *not* my fault," said Lola. "The water has risen with the storm."

"What are we going to do?"

"How do I know? Just don't freak out."

She pulled one of the flashlights off the front of the raft, leaned over the side, and shone the light along the surface of the water where it met the wall of rock.

"There's a gap farther along," she said at last.

"Are you sure?"

"Mmm," she replied unconvincingly.

They pushed and paddled their way along the rock face. As Lola had predicted, they came to a place where the raft could just about slip under. Lying flat on their backs in the pitch-black, they pushed themselves along, inch by inch, with their fingertips.

Sometimes, they heard the terrible sound of rock scraping on rubber as they got wedged under a particularly low overhang. Then they would have to try not to scream and calmly maneuver themselves to the left or the right, to find a place where the raft could squeeze through. (By unspoken agreement, Max did the trying not to scream, while Lola did the calm maneuvering.)

Claustrophobia didn't really cover it. There was no air, no space, no light. Max had thought that nothing could be more cramped than the chicken bus, but this raft was like a floating coffin. Except that he knew he wasn't dead yet, because he could hear the blood roaring in his ears. It was so hot, he thought he might dissolve like a lump of butter in a frying pan. He almost wished the raft would overturn, so that he could feel the cool water on his skin before he drowned . . .

No thanks to Max, they eventually floated out from under the dark stone and the cavern opened up again. He sat up and stretched his arms. It had never felt so good to be alive. But the roaring in his ears continued. If anything, it was getting louder.

"Hold on to the wall and keep us steady, while I fix the flashlights," said Lola.

As they bobbed on the water, Max realized that the roaring wasn't coming from inside his own head. It was coming from farther down the river.

"What's that noise?" he asked, shouting to be heard.

"Rapids," said Lola.

"Rapids? What do you mean, rapids?"

"Calm down, Hup, you're tipping the raft. Just go with the flow. Let go of the wall and let's get it over with."

Before he could protest, she'd pulled his hand away from the rock and they were off, slowly at first and then gathering speed until they became one with the roaring river. The twisting tunnel curved sharply down and they shot through it, whirling and pitching. The jumping beam of the flashlight made it hard to see what was ahead. Boulders loomed at them out of the darkness.

Max screamed all the way.

You'd pay a fortune for this at Disneyland, he told himself.

They struggled frantically to keep the raft off the rocks and centered in the main current. A sharp outcropping threatened them on the right. Max used all his strength to push off of it with his paddle. The raft hung there for a moment before veering back into the current. The paddle, still wedged in the rocks, was ripped from his hand.

Caught off balance, Max almost fell overboard.

He'd just scrabbled back inside when the raft was thrown into the air as they dropped over a small waterfall. He was pitched over the side of the raft and under the foaming water. The current swirled around him and raged in his ears. Everything was black. He couldn't breathe. He didn't know which way was up.

Then his knees hit a rock and he was somersaulted head over heels.

His lungs were gasping for air.

Suddenly, something pushed him from underneath and his head and shoulders shot up through the surface like a whale rider at Seaworld.

He was in some sort of underground lake now.

The water was still.

The rapids were behind him.

The raft was about ten feet away. He could see Lola outlined in a tiny circle of light, surrounded by the menacing dark on all sides.

He splashed over through the icy-cold black water, trying not to think about what might lurk beneath its surface.

"Give me a hand," he sobbed, pulling at the side of the raft.

"*A hand! A hand! A hand!*" His voice echoed back at him from all directions. This cavern must be huge.

"Hold on," called Lola. "The raft's full of water. We lost your flashlight, and I want to make sure we don't lose mine."

"Hurry, the catfish are biting my legs."

This wasn't strictly true, but in his imagination they were circling him like sharks. He was sure it was only a matter of time before they pounced.

"No they're not! Don't be such a baby!"

"*Baby! Baby!*" sang the echoes, as if the cave walls themselves were taunting him.

Lola helped him aboard.

"Where's your paddle?" she said.

"I lost it."

"You *lost* it?"

"I nearly drowned."

"But you didn't, did you? I think it's going to be OK, Hup, I think the Jaguar Kings are helping us. I can feel their presence."

Max remembered how he'd felt something push him to the surface. He was shivering uncontrollably, out of cold and fear. "Y-y-yeah, sure," he stuttered as cynically as he could through chattering teeth. "J-just get me out of here."

"I need you to get a grip," said Lola sternly. "We're coming to the tricky bit."

"The tricky bit? You mean those rapids weren't the tricky bit? You've got be kidding me!"

"Calm down, Hup, just chill. The Jaguar Kings will look after us."

"But, but —"

"Shhh," she said, holding up a finger and listening intently.

"What is it? I don't like this —"

"Be quiet."

Max fumed, but he did as she asked. After a minute or two, she began to paddle, slowly and quietly.

"Stay absolutely still," she whispered.

Max stayed as still as his chattering teeth would let him.

Lola paddled hesitantly onward. Then she stopped and listened again. She continued this way for a while, paddling and listening, paddling and listening, until she announced triumphantly: "This is the place! I've found it!"

"What place?" asked Max.

"The way out!"

"But we're in the middle of an underground lake."

"It's beneath us."

"Beneath us?"

"Can you hear that faint sucking noise? This lake drains from the bottom."

"No way!" said Max. "Forget it!" He was still shaken from his recent dip and being sucked through an underwater drain sounded even more terrifying than bodysurfing through the rapids of an underground river.

"Do you have a better idea?"

Max looked at her with terror.

"Then we have no choice," said Lola, unfixing the flashlight from the front of the raft and packing it away.

Darkness fell like dirt on a grave.

"Now slowly slide into the water," she said, "and don't let go of the raft."

"I can't do it."

"Yes, you can."

"No, I can't."

"Come on, Hup, if I can do it, you can do it. Are you going to let yourself be beaten by a girl?"

"I don't care," he said. "I'm not getting back in that water."

It all happened in seconds. He heard Lola splashing about, then he felt her wet arm around his waist. There was a quick scuffle and he was flipped into the water.

"I can't believe you did that," he spluttered as he surfaced and grabbed the raft.

"It was for your own good. Now hold on tight."

He didn't need telling twice. He was gripping the raft so tightly, his hands were starting to cramp up.

The water was just as cold as he remembered it.

There were strange sounds in the dark.

"Don't move," whispered Lola. "I'm slashing the raft with my machete."

"No!" he cried, but it was too late.

Weighed down by the backpacks, the deflated raft started sinking. It would have gone straight to the bottom if they hadn't been holding it.

"OK, Hup, deep breath," said Lola, "and let the current take you. The raft will pull us down. The Jaguar Kings will help us, I promise."

"I told you, I can't do it," said Max. The last thing he wanted to do was stick his head back under the water.

"We'll go on three," said Lola, ignoring his protests.

"I CAN'T DO IT!"

"One . . ."

"STOP!"

"Two . . ."

"NO!"

"Three!"

He heard Lola take a deep breath and then he felt the raft pulling him down as she disappeared under the water.

Max hesitated. He could let go or he could follow her.

He followed her under the water. He swam a couple of strokes. He could hear a roar coming up through the lake.

He started to panic.

He had to get out.

He let go of the raft and swam upward as quickly as he could.

His head broke through the water. He gulped huge mouthfuls of air. His arms flailed about. He breathed in deeply and tried to calm himself, treading water in the blackness. There was no difference between opening and closing his eyes. The darkness was so thick it was almost suffocating.

He'd lost all sense of direction.

He called Lola's name and it echoed back at him mockingly.

"Lola! Lola! Lola!"

He waited until the last echo died away. No answer.

He called again. The same echoes, the same blackness.

He was panicking badly now.

"Lola, Lola, Lola . . . "

Echoes surrounded him and closed in on him. He was completely alone. This was the single most terrifying moment of his life.

DeLanda's words filled his mind and mixed with Lord Six-Rabbit's curse. These would be the waters of his death. When he was too tired and too cold to tread water anymore, he would drown. Would they ever find his body? And if they did, would he have the mark of the Jaguar on his forehead?

He knew what he had to do.

He took a big breath, then chickened out.

He took another breath and forced his face into that black water. Max swam down.

One, two, three strokes. The roar was deafening.

Four, five, six strokes. His ears started to hurt and he felt dizzy.

Seven, eight, nine. He felt a searing pain as his hand smashed against a rock.

Ten, eleven, twelve. The current caught him and began to drag him down.

He started to panic again.

He had to get out. He had to breathe. He tried to swim upward, but it was too late. He felt as if a giant hand grabbed him, pulled him down, and squeezed.

He closed his eyes and gave in to the force.

Strangely, his last thought was of Zia's tamales.

CHAPTER X

STRANGE WEATHER

WHEN MAX OPENED his eyes, he was lying on his back in shallow water.

Somewhere in the distance was the sound of a rushing torrent, but the pool around him was as warm and still as a bath. A blue glow seemed to emanate from the water and it cast its unworldly light throughout the chamber, reflecting the ripples of the waves on the rock walls above him.

He was just wondering if this was a special watery heaven for people who'd died of drowning, when a familiar voice called him back to the land of the living.

"Are you going to lie around all day?"

He turned his head to one side and saw Lola sitting on a sand-bank, cutting the backpacks from the remnants of the raft.

"Did we make it?" he gasped.

"Yes," she said, "no thanks to you."

Max tried to sit up, but he sank back in pain. His hand was gashed and bleeding where it had smashed into a rock. He guessed the rest of him was covered in bruises.

"Some escape route," he grumbled. "I feel like I've been through a washing machine."

"You're alive, aren't you?" said Lola. "Stop complaining."

As he sat there nursing his wounds, Max realized what was odd about this cave.

"Why isn't it dark in here?" he asked. "What's that weird blue glow?"

"It's the light coming up through the water. The wall runs above the pool, but not below it, so the water flows under the wall and out into the sun."

It was beautiful, an enchanted grotto. The only thing that spoiled the tranquility of the scene was a crashing jet of water that shot straight into the pool from a large hole in the cave wall.

"How did we get here?" he asked.

Max followed Lola's eyes to the jet of water.

"We didn't . . . ?"

She laughed. "We did."

"But how?"

As she explained, Lola drew a diagram in the sand. "The lake is like a bowl, with a hole way down in the side. All we had to do was swim low enough for the current to suck us through."

"You could have killed us."

"But I didn't."

"How did you know about the hole?"

"My friend Hermanjilio told me. He said that Maya warriors used to prove their bravery by swimming through it, as some sort of initiation rite."

"Ha! So now I'm a fully fledged Maya warrior?"

"Never in a million years," said Lola. "Maya warriors were brave and fearless. And handsome."

Max made a face at her. "Well, at least the hard bit's over," he said. "If the water flows into the sun, we can just swim under the wall and we're out, right? "

Lola hesitated. "It's . . . er . . . not that simple. There's a *cenote* on the other side. Do you know what a cenote is, Hup?"

"Yeah. The police found one of Mom's earrings in the cenote at Ix Chel."

Lola heard the catch in his voice and came and sat next to him. "I'm sure your parents will turn up soon," she said sympathetically.

"I hope so," said Max. "We were supposed to be on vacation in Italy right now. This whole thing sucks."

"It can't be much fun for them either."

"Yeah, well, nobody made *them* come here. They weren't enslaved by their villainous, child-hating uncle until they made a

" 'Why isn't it dark in here?' he asked."

daring escape into the jungle, cheating death at every turn, only to be trapped like a hairball in the plughole of an underground sink."

"Wow," said Lola, moving away slightly. "You have a lot of anger."

"Can you blame me?" said Max.

"You're alive, aren't you?"

"Only just."

"I think you should stop complaining. Look, I'm sorry to say this, Hup, but it seems to me that you're a spoiled little rich boy who's spent his whole life watching TV and playing video games. It's time you grew up and realized that everything doesn't revolve around *you*."

"Wow," said Max. "You have a lot of anger, too."

"Yeah well, if you'd have grown up Maya instead of cosseted in your privileged little world in Boston, you'd know a bit more about hardship. You know, maybe life isn't meant to be easy."

Max considered this statement. He tried hard to answer it without shouting or losing his temper. "Yeah, well I'm not Maya, am I? And you're right, my life in Boston *was* easy. But last night I slept in a tree. Today, I did everything you asked of me. I'm hungry, I'm sore, I'm wet — what more do you want?"

Lola's tone softened. "How's your hand?"

"How do you think it is?" snapped Max.

Lola said nothing, but she looked hurt.

"I'm sorry," sighed Max. "It's hard to take in, that's all. In the space of one week, my parents have gone missing, I've discovered that my entire family is a bunch of crooks, and now I'm on the run from a gun-crazy, cape-twirling psycho who's trying to kill me."

"Don't take it personally," said Lola. "He's trying to kill me, too."

"That's true," Max admitted grudgingly. He gave her a weak smile and surveyed the forbidding stone walls on every side of them. "So how do we get out of here?"

"When I came with Hermanjilio, we rappelled down the cenote and pulled ourselves back up with the rope."

"Rope? We need a rope? Please tell me you have one . . . "

"Of course, I do! We'll be out of here in no time. It's a tough climb, though. You sit and get your strength back, while I go and check things out. I won't be long."

Lola pulled the rope out of her backpack and looped it around her. Then she strode into the water and dove under the dividing wall into the cenote.

Max sat back and studied his surroundings. He saw that the cave walls were painted with faded frescoes, and on the back wall, what he'd thought were natural formations were actually trees carved out of the rock. Their thick trunks stood to attention, branches intertwined, while their twisting roots formed a series of steps.

Before he could take a closer look, Lola reappeared.

"Bad news," she said, squeezing the water out of her hair. "The cenote's much deeper than I remembered. The sides are completely sheer. Even if you weren't wounded, there's no way you could make it. I'll have to go alone."

"But if you can climb it, surely I can?" protested Max.

"I hang out with monkeys, remember? I can climb anything, Hup."

Max's injured hand was throbbing. He knew she was probably right. But the thought of being alone in this cave freaked him out.

"You can't leave me here. What will I eat?"

"You'll be fine," said Lola as she filled her water canteen from the pool. "I'll leave you what's left of the tortillas. You can sleep the whole time if you like. I'll be gone two days at most."

"Two days? What if DeLanda finds me?"

"He won't find you."

"What if he finds *you*? If he finds you and shoots you? Then no one will know I'm here. I'll starve to death . . . "

"Do you ever think about anyone but yourself?" asked Lola.

"Oh come on, you can't say you're leaving me to rot in a hole in the ground and expect me to be happy," said Max. "I don't even know where I am."

"Well, if that's all that's bothering you, follow me," said Lola, jumping up.

She ran to the back wall and disappeared into the carved forest. Max followed her, weaving between the stone trees until he came into a room.

"What is this place?" he asked.

"It's an underground chamber. We're under the Temple of Chaak, the rain god."

"We're under a Maya temple? Then there must be a door to the outside?"

Lola shook her head. "Sorry, Hup. This temple was swallowed

up by the jungle hundreds of years ago and it's never been excavated. There must have been a door on the top platform once, but
the whole pyramid is completely buried under earth and trees. This
is the only way in — and out."

"So what did you want to show me?" he sighed.

As his eyes adjusted to the gloom, he saw that the room was circular with a low-domed ceiling. The walls had been polished
smooth and they glowed faintly green with a natural phosphores-
cence. In the middle of the room was a long stone table with raised
carvings on its surface.

"Look at this," said Lola, indicating the table. "It's a relief
map of the Monkey River Basin as it would have been a thousand
years ago."

It reminded Max of the table he'd played trains on when he was
little. But instead of stations and railway tracks, the surface of this
table had been carved into clusters of little pyramids, palaces, and
thatched huts. Five of the pyramids were inlaid with colored stones
and connected by a network of stone causeways.

"What's it for?" asked Max.

"I don't know," said Lola, "some ceremonial purpose, I guess.
Only kings and high priests ever came in here. If a peasant like you
found your way into this chamber, they'd skin you alive and rip out
your heart."

Max looked around uneasily. The room was cold and damp and
he was already feeling less than welcome. "Let's get out of here,"
he said.

"I'm just going to show you where we are before I go for help."

"Oh," said Max. "I thought we'd abandoned that plan."

"No," said Lola. "So pay attention."

"Isn't this map out of date?"

"Well, the old roads and the fields have gone, but the coastline
and the river and the sites of the temples haven't changed." She
pointed to one of the little pyramids, one colored white. "Look,
there's Ix Chel. Then follow the river down to the ocean and you
come to Aguas Muertas. There's the bay near your uncle's house.
There's that old temple where we first met in the jungle, and there's
the Blue Pool." She pointed to the red pyramid. "Here's Chaak,
where we are now."

"So where will you go for help?"

"Here," replied Lola, pointing to the green pyramid, "the old city of Itzamna. My friend Hermanjilio lives there."

"Is Hermanjilio your boyfriend?"

Lola laughed. "He's the archaeologist in charge of excavating Itzamna. I told you, he's a colleague of your parents. He was at Ix Chel with them."

"Isn't he missing too?"

"I don't know. But there's rescue equipment at Itzamna. If Hermanjilio's not there, I can winch you up myself."

"You don't seem very worried about him."

"Hermanjilio grew up in this jungle. He can look after himself — and your parents too, come to that."

"Do you think they might all have gone to Itzamna?" asked Max, tracing the distance from Ix Chel to Itzamna, from the white pyramid to the green, with his finger.

"I don't want to raise your hopes, but it's possible."

Now Max was tracing Lola's journey, from Chaak to Itzamna, from the red pyramid to the green. He noticed that Itzamna was in the middle, with the four other colored pyramids ranged around it. "What's the significance of the five colored pyramids?" he asked.

Lola looked flustered. "Who knows?" she said.

She was lying. She was definitely lying. But why?

And suddenly, he understood.

"Five pyramids, five Jaguar Stones!" he yelled. "My parents had the White Jaguar and the pyramid at Ix Chel is white. This place is red — and we have the red stone! Yes, I remember now — Uncle Ted called it the Red Jaguar of Chaak!"

"I think you're delirious, Hup. You should have a nice sleep while I'm gone," said Lola, making to leave.

"No!" shouted Max, pulling her back. "I'm right, aren't I? The red stone belongs in this temple somewhere. There must be a place for it."

He stepped back and looked at the table. With a bit of imagination, it looked like the back of a big cat standing on four clawed feet. At one of the narrow ends, where the head should be, there was a niche about the size of a Jaguar Stone.

"Look!"

"Forget it, Hup! You're wasting time! I have to go for help."

"And *I* have to see if the Red Jaguar fits in this table. I think the

 137

stones are connected with my parents' disappearance somehow. I have to try it!"

"No," said Lola, "don't get involved! Your parents may have meant well, but they should never have meddled in something they didn't understand."

"But they did understand," said Max. "They lived and breathed the Ancient Maya. It's *me* they didn't understand."

"Why is it always about you?" asked Lola.

Time to try a different tack.

"But aren't you curious?" asked Max. "Why did you steal the Jaguar Stone, if you're afraid to use it?"

"It's not for me," said Lola. "It's for Hermanjilio."

"Then you need answers as much as I do."

"He wouldn't want me to do this without him."

"He's an archaeologist, isn't he?"

"Yes," said Lola, suspiciously.

"Then I know he'd want you to take advantage of this unique opportunity."

She was listening.

" . . . And you don't want me messing around with the Jaguar Stone on my own, do you? Hermanjilio definitely wouldn't approve of that. If you try it with me right now, I promise I won't touch anything while you're away."

She was weakening.

"Look," he said, "probably nothing will happen. But at least you'll know."

She was nodding in defeat. "You win. Get the stone. But we have to be quick."

Before she could change her mind, Max ran and got the backpacks. Eagerly, he unwrapped the Red Jaguar.

"It's a bit chipped," he said, looking at it closely for the first time.

"You're bleeding on it," she said crossly. She pulled a bandana out of her back pocket. "Here, wrap your hand in this and give the stone to me . . . "

She was holding the Red Jaguar over the niche, looking for a way to slot it in, when it jumped out of her hand and clicked into the space.

"I told you!" said Max.

They waited for something to happen.

Nothing happened.

"Take it out. I have to go," said Lola.

"Wait — what's that?"

"Where?"

"There, the stone. Something's happening."

Lola gasped. "I think it's repairing itself."

Sure enough, where the stone had been chipped, it was slowly growing back to its original shape.

When it was whole again, the stone began to glow brighter and brighter. Then the map table itself began to glow and slowly come to life. The stone river started flowing in shining blue plasma. Many of the pyramids disappeared from view, to be replaced by luminous green jungle. Finally, a ball of yellow fire formed over the center of the table. It illuminated the whole room and warmed their heads with its heat.

"That fireball," whispered Max, "I think it's the sun."

"And the map's brought itself up to date," said Lola. "There's your uncle's place and the banana warehouse. And look at the Temple of Chaak — you can't even see it anymore under all the foliage. The jungle's taken over everything. Just like in real life."

Dark clouds formed over parts of the map and it began to rain. Max poked one of the clouds. It felt cold and moist and it moved.

"Look!" he laughed, "I'm the weatherman! I can move the clouds! I can make it rain anywhere I want! This is crazy!"

They amused themselves by directing the weather for a while, before the same thought occurred to them both at the same time. Their eyes met.

"You don't suppose —" began Lola.

"— that what we do here —" continued Max.

"— has any effect on what happens out there?" finished Lola.

"Let's test it!"

Lola studied the map and found the underground pool below them. She dammed the hole in the wall with her finger, so that the blue plasma jet stopped flowing. The noise of crashing water in the cave stopped immediately. Max stepped back through the carved trees to check. It was true. Not a trickle.

"Unblock it," he called. She lifted her finger and the water surged out again.

"That's incredible." Max was shaking his head in awe.

"And it still works after all these years," said Lola, her eyes shining. "Can you imagine the control my ancestors had over their world? They could make it rain. They could divert rivers. They could destroy their enemy's crops. I've never understood how they were able to sustain so many people in such a small area. This is the answer! They would never have had a bad harvest." She was almost dancing round the room. "And what a sense of power. It makes you feel like a god."

A shiver ran down Max's spine. "Just think what would happen if DeLanda got his hands on this."

Lola pulled herself together. "We have to stop him . . . I must go . . ."

Maybe it was the excitement of the moment or maybe it was just a lucky guess, but Max suddenly had a brilliant idea.

"Wait! Maybe we *can* get out upstairs," he said, scratching at the glowing green foliage that covered the miniature Temple of Chaak.

"You're a genius!" said Lola, as she helped him scrape off the centuries of growth until the little pyramid was bare again.

"Let's go!" said Max.

"OK," said Lola. "But brace yourself, Hup. It's creepy in there."

"Here comes the mumbo-jumbo . . ."

"Just don't say I didn't warn you."

Lola pulled out the Jaguar Stone, wrapped it up, and put it back in her backpack. Then she took out a flashlight and a candle. She lit the candle and handed it to Max.

"Hey! Not fair!" he protested. "I want the flashlight."

"Sorry, Hup, but it *is* fair. We lost your flashlight in the river."

"I want the flashlight! You take the candle!"

With a sigh of irritation, Lola gave him the flashlight and took the candle. She led him through a narrow doorway and into a long, passage that sloped steeply upward. The passage was flocked with a putrid green fungus and Max was glad when it finally opened up into a small, roughly hewn room. The ceiling was so low they had to crouch and the floor was cracked and uneven. The walls were stained dark brown, the color of dried blood. In the center of each wall, there was a low doorway, and above each doorway was carved a ghoulish face contorted in agony. Max had the sense that a lot of people had died in this room — and very unpleasantly.

"Which way?" he said.

Without waiting for an answer, he made for the nearest doorway.

"*Stop*!" screamed Lola, pulling him back. "Stay away from those doors — they're not of this world."

Now that Max looked more closely, he saw that the dark interior was scattered with skulls and bones. An evil presence seemed to lurk inside, something dead and yet alive, something that was trying to lure him in.

The hairs on Max's neck stood on end. "Get me out of here!"

Lola pointed to a dark square in the ceiling of the far corner. She pulled him across the room until they stood under a narrow shaft that shot up into blackness.

"How do we get up there?"

"Grab onto the side," said Lola, showing him some indentations in the wall.

"OK," said Max. Anything. He just wanted out of that room.

"Take your backpack off first," said Lola, "or you'll get stuck."

Max was shaking so much that he got tangled up in the straps of his backpack.

"I'll go first then," said Lola, in exasperation. "When I get to the top, I'll let down the rope and you tie on the backpacks. I'll pull them up, then you follow."

"Just hurry," said Max, still extricating himself.

As soon as he was free, he pressed himself into the corner and watched the glow of Lola's candle getting smaller and smaller as it receded up the shaft. He shivered. Was it fear making his blood run cold? Or was the temperature dropping?

He shone the flashlight under his own chin for heat and the icy darkness crowded in on him. What was that scratching noise? Fingernails? Rats? His heart beat faster and faster. He stamped his feet to keep warm and to frighten away anything that might be thinking of scurrying around his feet.

"Hurry!" he called. He could see his breath.

"Nearly there," he heard from far above.

By the time the end of the rope dropped down, a light frost had formed on Max's head and shoulders. His damp clothes were freezing against his skin. Fumbling with cold, he tied on the backpacks and gave the rope a tug. As soon as the packs vanished through the hole, he began to climb up after them. The darkness clutched at his feet like invisible fingers. It was hard going and his wounded hand throbbed, but his fear was greater than his pain. He thought about nothing but the need to maintain upward motion.

Eventually, he reached the room above. Lola helped pull him in, and he threw himself on the stone floor, breathing heavily. Relief coursed through him.

"Are you all right, Hup?" she asked. "I told you it was creepy down there."

"*Creepy*?" He looked at her like she was mad. "That wasn't *creepy*, Monkey Girl. That was every horror film, every nightmare, every evil thing that has ever existed in the world. It's like something is alive down there. I can't believe you brought us in here."

He looked back at the opening in the floor. A dark chill was rising out of it and spreading like dry ice. The room was starting to fill with a foul-smelling fog.

"Let's keep moving," coughed Lola.

"Me first," said Max quickly grabbing the rope and tying it around him.

Once again they had to climb a narrow shaft. Max complained all the way up, but eventually he arrived in a small square room with a high ceiling.

The top of the pyramid, at last!

A wave of heat engulfed him. It was like entering an oven.

His cold, wet clothes dried instantly in a haze of steam.

While he waited for Lola to tie the backpacks onto the rope, he fanned himself and looked around. All four walls were covered with life-size paintings of gods, kings, warriors, and bizarre animal people with crocodile heads and lobster claws. They were so grotesque, it took Max a moment to register the most disturbing thing of all about this room.

It had no door.

There was no way out.

CHAPTER XI

RAT-ON-A-STICK

"Phew," said Lola, pulling herself up. "It's hot in here."

"Like a furnace," agreed Max. "I need water." He pulled the canteen out of Lola's backpack and went to take a swig.

"No, Hup! We have to save it. We don't know how long it has to last."

Max shrugged and carried on drinking.

Lola grabbed the canteen out of his hand and screwed the cap back on. "You selfish pig!" she said. "There's hardly any left. That might be the end of our water."

"Who cares? We'll be out of here as soon as you open the hidden door."

"Slight problem, Hup."

"Come on, Monkey Girl, don't mess about. I'm going to melt in a minute."

Max studied her face. She wasn't smiling.

"No! Don't tell me you don't know where the door is . . . !"

Her expression told him that this was, indeed, the case.

"Your guess is as good as mine, Hup."

"What do you mean? You've been up here before, haven't you?"

"Yes, Hermanjilio, and I stuck our heads in once, but we knew the pyramid was buried under jungle, so there was no point in looking for a door. Besides, it was so hot, we didn't hang around."

Max stared at her in disbelief.

"Why did you drag me up here, when you knew there was no way out?"

"I thought I'd worry about that when we got here."

"Well, start worrying." He kicked the wall angrily.

"Oh grow up!" snapped Lola.

A lump of self-pity formed in his throat. He was going to die. He was too young to die. At least he would die with a girl by his side. And she definitely wasn't ugly. He pictured their bodies lying next to each other in this stone tomb, like Romeo and Juliet. He looked mistily at Lola.

"Don't stand there like a moron," she said. "Help me."

"Help you do what?"

"Find the door, stupid. It must be here somewhere."

Max cast a lethargic look around. His head was pounding from the oppressive heat. It felt like summer in the city, just before a thunderstorm.

"I have to have water," he begged. "I can't go on."

"Stop whining," said Lola, "and keep looking."

"It's not fair. Who made you guardian of the water?"

"Who made you such a baby?"

They searched the room from top to bottom, looking for a suspicious crack in the wall or a telltale current of air. But the walls were solid stone, and there was no air. The floor was starting to burn their feet.

"There *has* to be a hidden switch somewhere," said Lola.

After their third search, they'd still found nothing. It was getting hard to breathe. They stood on their backpacks to protect their feet and looked at each other in despair.

"I'm sorry, Hup, but we have to go back."

"No!" said Max, terrified of what might be waiting in the foul fog below.

"Yes!" said Lola.

Max shook his head stubbornly.

He forced himself to think.

Think.

Head hurts.

Too hot.

Think.

What if this was a video game? You wouldn't barge into a new

room and start poking around. You'd sit back and look for the clues. There were always clues.

He stared at the painted figures on the wall in front of him. "I bet *they* know the secret of this room," he said. He pointed at a particularly fearsome character with bulbous eyes, a long nose, and tusks. "Who's that ugly one on the end?"

"You've met him," said Lola, "that's the great Lord Chaak himself. We passed his statue in the Cave of Broken Pots, remember? He was holding a lightning-bolt axe and a bowl with a human heart in it."

Max did remember. And, as he stared at Lord Chaak, he began to feel a connection with him. It was the same feeling he'd had when he saw the metal case on the shelf in Uncle Ted's vault.

He went over to the painting and examined every inch of it.
Nothing.

He looked straight into one of Lord Chaak's goggly eyes.

"Show me," he said.

Nothing.

But the answer was here, he knew it. Call it a gamer's sixth sense.

"What do you know about this Chaak dude?" he asked.

Lola shrugged. "He's the rain god."

"Then maybe," said Max, "he wants to feel the rain on his skin. It's so hot in here. If you were him, wouldn't you want to feel cool, clear water?"

"You're crazy —" began Lola, but she didn't stop him as he took the canteen and poured the last of their precious water on the wall above Lord Chaak's head. Max watched expectantly as it streamed down the rain god's face and chest.

Nothing happened.

He shook out the last drop of water.

Nothing.

The water evaporated instantly. The wall was still as dry as old bones.

Max looked at Lola miserably. His throat was already so parched again that his tongue felt swollen.

"Sorry," he said. The word had never sounded so inadequate.

But Lola wasn't listening. She was totally focused on Lord Chaak.

"Blood!" she said. "He wants blood!"

She dragged Max back to the wall and ripped the bandana off his wounded hand. Ignoring his howls of pain, she pressed his cut hard against the painted bowl. Then she rubbed the bloodstained bandana into it as well.

"Greetings, Lord Chaak, from your people in Middleworld," she said. "In return for this blood, we ask for our freedom."

As the blood soaked into the limestone, there was a noise like a frog croaking. Then another and another, until the room echoed with a frogs' chorus. The atmosphere in the room seemed to lift slightly, and the air felt a little cooler.

Lola — who was still pressing the bandana against the bowl — yelped in surprise.

"What happened?" shouted Max, above the din of frogs.

"Electric shock —"

A string of red sparks made their way up from Lord Chaak's bowl to his lightning-bolt axe. There was a flash, a loud click, and the sound of stone rolling on stone.

Slowly one of the carved panels swung out.

Light flooded into the room, momentarily blinding them.

The sound of croaking grew to a deafening buzz as hundreds of frogs materialized out of the temple walls and leapt across the floor to the open door. For a few seconds, Max and Lola couldn't move for the sea of frogs around their feet. Then, like a wave rolling in to shore, the amphibian tide swept out of the temple and into the pouring rain, with a farewell croak that even Max could identify as pure pleasure.

Max and Lola stepped outside.

Rain had never felt so good.

"We did it!" yelled Max, whooping and punching the air. "We did it!"

A flock of parrots screeched disapprovingly as they flew overhead.

"We're a good team, Hup!" laughed Lola, high-fiving.

A team. He liked the sound of that.

He put his head back and tried to catch the rain in his parched mouth, dancing, whirling around, letting the downpour wash away the dust of the temple. He felt himself rehydrating like a packet of instant noodles.

His headache had gone.

His hand had stopped throbbing.

But his brain was still in shock.

Forget Lucky Jim's gun in his neck. Forget the underground river. Forget DeLanda's threats. Forget the sensation of being sucked into an underwater drain. There were a lot of contenders for 'Single Most Terrifying Experience of This Trip so Far,' but the Temple of Chaak had won the category hands down.

"Hey, Monkey Girl," he said, trying to sound cool, "I thought ruins were supposed to be a bunch of old stones. That place was definitely alive."

"I warned you," said Lola.

"But still . . . "

They were about a hundred feet up, on the top platform of a giant pyramid. The tips of other pyramids could be seen rising through the jungle canopy like distant islands in a sea of green. As the rain stopped, a rainbow formed in the distance.

"This was where they did the public bloodlettings and sacrifices," said Lola. "The royal family and the priests stood up here. The officials were on that platform halfway down and the common people watched from ground level."

Max shook his head in disgust. "Why were the Ancient Maya so bloodthirsty?"

"It wasn't like that," said Lola. "To them, blood was sacred. Blood was the breath of the soul, and the soul lived in the heart. They believed that our souls linked us to the world around us, and blood was the oil that kept everything running smoothly. Blood had to flow to keep the gods happy and the sun shining and the crops growing. Even the king had to shed his blood. The people expected it."

"They must have got through a lot of kings."

"No, the kings only gave a little blood, a token."

"Well, I think it's barbaric."

"Do you?" Lola looked at him thoughtfully. "You know, it wouldn't hurt you North Americans to make some sacrifices now and again."

"If you mean that we should go around cutting ourselves and ripping each others' hearts out, I think that would hurt a lot."

"Oh, ha ha. I was thinking about mahogany."

Max looked at her blankly.

"They come here, the illegal loggers, and start chopping down our trees. Before you know it, another chunk of rainforest has gone forever, just so someone in North America can have an expensive new table. What do you think the world needs more, Hup?" She pointed at the scene below them. "This rainforest and everything that lives in it — or some fancy mahogany furniture?"

Max didn't answer her.

"Hup?"

He wasn't listening.

He was standing on the edge of the pyramid, staring down into the jungle.

So this was how it felt to be the King of the Monkey River,

looking out over Middleworld. Above you, the heavens and the gods who spoke through you. Below you, the awestruck faces of your adoring people. In front of you, your helpless victim . . .

Lola touched his arm. "Let's go," she said.

As she skipped lightly down the stone steps, Max picked his way slowly behind her. It was so steep, he couldn't look down. In the end, he found the easiest way was to sit down and lower himself, step by step. Way below, he heard Lola calling to her monkeys, and a distant roar floating back over the rainforest in reply.

When he finally reached the ground, Lola was waiting for him, a length of thick vine draped over her shoulders like the snake lady at the circus.

"Look behind you," she said.

He looked.

The great stone doors of the pyramid had rolled silently shut and vines were already writhing their way across the platform. Earth was accumulating on the steps and trees were literally growing in front of his eyes.

"Wow!" he said. "It's all going back to normal. I guess the power of the map table fades when you take out the Jaguar Stone."

"Water?" asked Lola.

She slashed the end of the vine and passed it to Max. Following her instructions, he held it over his mouth like a hose. Sweet water came gushing out.

"You should learn to recognize this plant," she said. "Its Maya name is *Ha Ix Ak*." (Hah Eesh Ahk.) "*Ha* means 'water,' *Ix* means 'lady,' *Ak* means 'vine.' Lady Water Vine has saved many lives in the rainforest."

"I don't suppose she has a friend called Lady Pizza Plant?" asked Max.

"I'll look for some food," said Lola. "You get some wood and build a fire."

"I'm tired."

"Sorry, Hup, but it's the servants' day off. Just get on with it."

"Did anyone ever tell you that you're bossy?" said Max.

"Did anyone ever tell you that you're lazy?" said Lola.

"Yes," said Max proudly, "all the time."

"In the rainforest, lazy boys get eaten by jaguars. You must start the fire before dark to keep them away." She handed Max her machete. "Ever used one of these?"

"As a matter of a fact, I have," said Max.

"Really? Where?"

"Oh you know, son of archaeologists and all that . . . "

She didn't need to know that his previous experience with a machete was not actually in real life. He'd been swishing through a computer-animated jungle in Pyramid of Peril, that day his parents came home early.

Was that really just a week ago? It seemed like another lifetime.

Suddenly, Max remembered where he'd seen Lola before.

Level Two!

She looked like the girl who was taken hostage in the shoot-out. And now, here they were, having survived a real-life Pyramid of Peril! What a coincidence! For one brief moment Max entertained the possibility that his entire life was just a video game.

"Hey, Monkey Girl, listen to this . . . " he began, but she was gone.

He began to hack his way clumsily into the jungle in search of kindling. Swinging a machete wasn't as easy as it had looked on screen. But despite his lack of technique, he felt like a Hollywood action hero.

Max Murphy: Man of Mystery and Explorer Extraordinaire.

A movement caught his eye and he looked down to see a long, fat, brownish gray snake sliding out of the leaf litter toward him.

Max froze, not even breathing, and tried to remember everything he'd read about snakes in the in-flight magazine. He seemed to recall that the more garish they were, the more likely they were to be poisonous. This one was drab, apart from a yellow flash under its head. Reassured by this fact, he stayed absolutely motionless as the snake passed six inches to the side of his foot and slithered away into the bush. After that, he was more careful, probing the ground with his machete and checking overhanging branches for reptilian residents.

By the time he returned to the campsite with an armful of wood, the monkeys had arrived. Seri was sitting grooming herself while her brother Chulo, still wearing Max's baseball cap, was swinging languidly from a tree branch. Max's backpack lay open on the ground and both monkeys were chewing on the dreaded granola bars.

It occurred to Max that any self-respecting jungle action hero had a monkey for a sidekick. Time for a little male bonding.

"Good snack?" he asked in a friendly tone.

Chulo growled in a most unfriendly tone.

"No, I don't like those bars either," said Max. "Ever had pizza, Chulo?"

Chulo took off the baseball cap and covered his face with it.

"So you're a Red Sox fan too?" asked Max, reaching for the cap.

Chulo snapped at Max's hand and Max quickly withdrew it.

"Go Red Sox!" he murmured.

Stupid monkey.

As Max set about trying to make a fire, he could feel Chulo watching his every move. The monkey's critical gaze made him feel self-conscious and it took him a while to assemble his little teepee of twigs, as taught in Cub Scouts. As he paused to admire his creation before striking the match, Chulo jumped on his head and scattered the wood with his tail. Then he hopped about screeching with monkey laughter.

After this had happened several times, Max chased the monkey into the forest with the machete. Chulo jumped into the nearest tree and started lobbing fruit. The monkey's aim was deadly accurate, and a large papaya hit Max squarely in the back, sending him sprawling. Seri, meanwhile, paid no attention to any of it. Such mayhem was evidently beneath her.

Despite Chulo's attempts to disrupt him, Max finally succeeded in lighting the fire. He was feeling pleased with his newfound survival skills. Those spoiled little campers in Maine didn't have to contend with sadistic monkeys and haunted temples and trigger-happy Spanish aristocrats.

Lola's voice interrupted his thoughts.

"Who likes barbecue?"

She emerged out of the jungle, carrying a small animal that she'd skinned and gutted. The two monkeys raced to greet her, dancing about and leaping on her back.

"I caught dinner," smiled Lola, holding up the carcass.

Max made a face. "That's disgusting. It looks like a rat."

"It is a rodent," admitted Lola, "it's called a gibnut. It's a local delicacy. Even the Queen of England tried it when she came here. I'll skewer it over the fire and it will be the tenderest, juiciest meat you've ever tasted."

"I'm not eating rat-on-a-stick," said Max. "What's in your other hand?"

"Jackass!" said Lola.

"I only asked," said Max, offended.

"No," laughed Lola, "they're called Jackass Bitters — they're leaves for medicinal purposes. I'm going to boil them up to clean all your insect bites. They cure everything."

"I'd rather have some antiseptic and a box of Band-Aids."

"Stupid boy," replied Lola as she prepared the gibnut. "Most of the medicines you buy at the drugstore are made out of rainforest plants! It's just that here you don't pay for the packaging."

"I *like* the packaging," said Max.

"Spoken like a true city kid," laughed Lola.

"Speaking of packaging," said Max, "what kind of snake has a black head with a yellow flash underneath and a gray-brown body? It's harmless, right?"

"Where?" Lola looked around in alarm.

"I saw it in the forest earlier. It passed right by my foot."

She put a hand over her mouth in horror. "It sounds like a fer-de-lance. The locals call it the Three-Step because, if it bites you, that's how far you get before you drop down dead. It's one of the deadliest snakes in the world. You had a lucky escape!"

Max Murphy, Man of Mystery and Explorer Extraordinaire, went very quiet and pale and huddled closer to the fire. He wondered how he'd ever sleep tonight, among all those creeping, crawling, biting things.

"Sure you don't want some gibnut?" asked Lola.

It smelled delicious.

"Just a little then," he said.

Half an hour later, with belly full of succulent barbecued gibnut, Max fell asleep right where he was sitting.

Lola woke him at sunrise for a breakfast of wild papaya, gathered by the monkeys. Max could tell that Chulo begrudged him every bite.

"So what's the plan?" asked Max blearily, through juicy mouthfuls. "Why do we have to get up so early?"

"If we hike all day, we should get to Utsal by nightfall," said Lola.

Hike all day? Max groaned. He was still tired and aching from yesterday's exertions. "What's at Utsal?" he asked.

"It's on the way to Itzamna. It's where I grew up. I have a lot of friends there."

Max brightened up, imagining some sort of college town, populated entirely by pretty, giggling, dark-haired girls who would find a boy from Boston fascinating. "Sounds good to me," he nodded, glad to be heading back to the bright lights of civilization. He reached for the last papaya, but Chulo beat him to it.

"Hey, you've already had three," said Max, chasing the monkey away.

"Boys, stop fighting," laughed Lola. "Breakfast is over. We need to get going. It looks like the rains will come early today."

Max looked up. It didn't look like rain at all. There was one wispy little cloud in a clear blue sky. He started to argue, but Lola had already set off.

She walked so quickly that Max had to trot to keep up. He was breathless and panting when, twenty minutes later, the heavens opened and the rain came pouring down. But Lola still insisted that they press on.

She had a knack of springing from one dry spot to another while Max slogged behind her through solid mud.

"Can't you slow down a little?" he asked.

"No. You have to keep up, Hup, or we'll never make it in time." Bossy, bossy, bossy.

She was following a winding trail through the trees, and Max thought he spied a shortcut that would let him overtake her.

He stepped off the trail and instantly sank up to his knees.

"Help!" he screamed.

Lola surveyed his predicament from the safety of the trail. "It's quicksand," she said, calmly. "There must be an underground spring."

Max was flailing around and sinking in deeper and deeper.

"Help me! Get a branch and pull me out — "

"It's a myth," said Lola. "You can't actually *pull* someone out of quicksand, the suction of the mud is too strong. You have to get yourself out."

"I can't. I'm getting sucked under . . . "

"People only get sucked under in movies. Real people float in quicksand. Just relax, lean backward, and wiggle your feet."

Max tried to do as she said. To his surprise, his feet popped free, and he started floating.

"OK, Hup, now paddle with your hands . . . "

When he squelched back onto dry land, every inch of him was coated in mud.

"You look like the Creature from the Black Swamp," said Lola.

He flicked a clod of mud at her.

It missed and hit Chulo instead.

Max had a feeling he'd pay for that later. Guessing that the monkey wouldn't dare retaliate when Lola was near, Max stayed close to her as they hiked on.

He tried to make conversation, but it felt more like an inquisition.

"What do your parents do?" he asked.

"I have no parents."

"I'm sorry . . . "

"It's OK, I never knew them."

"What happened to them?"

"I don't know."

"How can you not know?"

She wheeled around. "Do you know what's happened to your parents?'

Touché.

He began a new line of questioning.

"How old are you?"

"I don't know."

"Do you go to school?"

"Hermanjilio is teaching me."

"Did he teach you to speak English?"

"Everyone here speaks English."

"What do you speak at home?"

"Yucatec."

"Is that the Mayan language?"

"It's one of them."

"Go on then, say something . . . "

"Kanaant awook!" (Khan-aunt ah-woke!)

"What does that mean?"

"Watch out!"

But it was too late. Max tripped over a large root and grabbed on to the nearest tree to steady himself. A searing pain shot through his hand. Several long needles were sticking into the fleshy part of his thumb.

"I bet that hurts," said Lola.

Max nodded. He couldn't speak for trying not to cry.

"That tree's called a Give and Take Palm," said Lola, slashing at the tree trunk. "The thorns *give* you pain, but . . . " — she peeled off some bark to reveal a layer of pink wispy fiber — "this stuff will *take* it away. It's the only thing that works."

Max winced as she pulled out the needles for him, one by one. "Where did you get that Ramones T-shirt?" he asked, to take his mind off the pain.

"A boy gave it to me."

"What boy?"

"A student from New York."

"Did you go to New York?"

"I will one day."

"So where did you meet him?"

"At Itzamna. Archaeology students come there from all over the world."

She pressed the pink fiber onto his injured thumb. The pain stopped almost immediately. "Better?" she asked.

Max had forgotten about his injury. "So is this New Yorker your boyfriend . . . ?"

Lola laughed and jumped up. "Come on," she said, "we need to move."

"How old is he?"

"We'd go a lot faster if you stopped talking and concentrated on walking."

She set a brisk pace and Max soon fell behind. This was the opportunity Chulo had been waiting for. When Lola was too far ahead to see what he was doing, the monkey started pelting Max with nuts, sticks, and bits of rotten fruit. Whenever a missile bounced painfully off Max's head, Chulo would screech with delight. Once he threw a small iguana, and instead of bouncing off, it dug its claws into Max's scalp.

Lizard Wars.

Lola saw none of this. But just as Max was wrenching the iguana off his head to hurl it back at Chulo, she happened to turn around. Her face was a picture of disbelief.

"I'm not even going to ask," she said.

"He started it," said Max, pointing at Chulo.

"You should be flattered," said Lola. "He has the crazy idea that you're a threat to his position as the dominant male."

"Why's it crazy?" said Max, puffing out his chest and trying to look dominant, but Lola had stomped off ahead, and Chulo soon resumed his bombardment.

It was a long and vexing day.

In the late afternoon, Max caught a comforting waft of smoky fires and cooking smells. At last, they were approaching Utsal.

Ice-cold soda was within reach.

He picked up his pace. All day, he'd been imagining a busy town with white-washed houses, nice clean bathrooms, and an air-conditioned pizza restaurant. As the hours went by, he'd added an Internet café, a gaming arcade, and an ice-cream parlor . . .

Now he was really salivating.

"Welcome to Utsal!" cried Lola happily.

All Max could see was a few shacks in a clearing on the riverbank.

"That's it?" he said.

"What were you expecting?"

Max was too disappointed to answer.

As they entered the village, a pack of scrawny dogs trotted out to bark at them. The dogs were soon joined by a gaggle of children. The children were closely followed by a rush of women in embroidered blouses and long skirts.

The women ran joyfully to Lola, arms open, black braids flying behind them. As they hugged her and poured out greetings in Mayan, the children clustered round Max. They were fascinated by his hair. The tallest one even pulled it to see if it was real.

Max's head was already hurting from the onslaught of monkey

missiles, and he was glad when the children suddenly ran off shriek-ing. At the same time, the women melted silently away and dogs slunk into the shadows.

Max squinted into the afternoon sun to see what had fright-ened them.

"It's Gandalf!" he smirked.

Lola wasn't laughing.

She was transfixed by the figure approaching them. He must have been at least a hundred and fifty years old. His hair flowed down in a thick white mane. His huge hooked nose protruded out of a face so deeply wrinkled, it reminded Max of a pyramid rising out of the tangled jungle. He wore a long embroidered tunic and a necklace of jaguar teeth. He leaned on an intricately carved wooden cane. Jaguar-skin anklets topped his ancient calloused feet. His bony finger pointed at Max accusingly.

Now Max wasn't laughing either.

His only thought was to get away, to run and keep on running until he had escaped the stranger's penetrating gaze. The closer the old man came, the more his eyes locked on to Max's brain. They read his mind, they burned into his soul, they reflected his past and present and future in their watery pink orbs.

These eyes gave new meaning to the term farsighted.

Yet, clouded as they were with cataracts, the old man's eyes were almost blind.

CHAPTER XII

THE FEAST

WITH ONE HAND pointing at Max and the other held up as if to stop the traffic, the old man cleared his throat. Even the birds in the trees stopped singing as the world waited to hear his words of wisdom.

"Pepperoni Supreme with extra cheese," he said.

Max gaped at him. That was exactly what he'd been thinking about before his mind went numb with terror. He started backing away uneasily.

The old man let out a booming laugh and turned to Lola.

"Your friend likes pizza, Ix Sak Lool," he said.

"You're right," she smiled, "as always!"

She grabbed Max's arm and pulled him forward. "Max Murphy, meet Candelario Ek, the village leader and wise man."

"All blessings, Max Murphy, and welcome to Utsal," said Candelario.

"Thanks," mumbled Max sulkily.

Candelario, still chuckling, turned to Lola. *"Biix a beel, chan aabil?"* (Beesh ah bale, chahn aahbeel?) he said. "How are you, little granddaughter?"

"Ma'aloob, tatich! Kux teech?" (Mah-ah-lobe, tah-teech! Koosh teych?) smiled Lola, "I'm fine, grandfather! And you?"

"These are unhappy times," he said, "but today is a day of blessings. Have you been keeping the days as I taught you?"

She shook her head. "I'm sorry, grandfather."

The old man clicked his tongue in disapproval. "No good will come of this, Ix Sak Lool."

"Will *you* tell me the day, grandfather?"

Candelario's face broke into a huge smile. It was obvious that he could not stay cross at Lola for any length of time. "Today is 13 Tooth, the day of the road that leads home. Welcome home, Ix Sak Lool. We have missed you."

"I've missed you too," said Lola. "It's good to be back."

Soon they were jabbering away to each other in Mayan.

Max, still dizzy from Candelario's scrutiny, sat down on the grass.

He looked at the village. It was just a few thatched huts on stilts, clustered around a large central square. All the huts had steps up to an open porch and most of the porches were strung with brightly striped hammocks.

He looked at the river, the famous Monkey River. It was wide, green, and fast flowing. There were a few dugout canoes upturned on the bank and a rickety bamboo landing stage for bigger boats.

A long-necked white heron settled on a tree stump to eat its catch.

Some women came down for water. Each one carried a large earthenware pot on her back, held by a woven strap over her forehead. As they walked back with their heavy loads, the women waved and called at the men who seemed to be building something in the square.

There was a sense of bustle in the air and a very good smell of food cooking.

Max's stomach rumbled loudly.

And still Lola talked on.

Just when he thought he'd have to jump up and drag her away, she came over and sat down next to him.

"Sorry about that," she said. "Candelario likes to talk."

"Is he your grandfather?"

"No."

"But you called him grandfather?"

"Yeah. He and his family kind of adopted me. So," she said, changing the subject, "do you want to hear the news?"

A wild hope surged in Max's heart. Had she heard something about his parents?

"Go on," he said expectantly.

"Hermanjilio came through here a few days ago," she said.

"With my parents?"

"Alone."

Max threw a stone at a passing iguana. He missed.

"You must be happy," he said. "Your precious Hermanjilio is safe."

"I wish Frank and Carla had been with him."

"Why should *you* care?" said Max sulkily.

"You know I care," said Lola. "Anyway, Hermanjilio's waiting for us at Itzamna. He'll be able to tell us what happened at Ix Chel."

"How far is it to Itzamna?" said Max in a flat voice.

"Just a few hours upriver. We'll hitch a lift."

"Whatever."

"Cheer up, Hup," said Lola. "Don't give up hope. I'm sure we'll find your parents soon. In the jungle anything is possible."

"I hate the jungle," said Max.

"It's been a tough day," said Lola. "But the worst is over, I promise you. We'll have an easy boat ride tomorrow. And tonight you'll be guest of honor at the feast."

Max looked up. "A feast?" he said.

Two little boys ran over. The bigger one shyly took Max's hand, trying to pull him to his feet. The smaller one watched from behind Lola's legs.

"This is Niko and his little brother Wilbert," she said.

Max stood up and nodded at the boys. Then he brushed himself down and combed his hair with his fingers. Niko did the same.

"You've got an admirer, Hup," whispered Lola. "Niko's copying everything you do. I think he's got a bad case of hero worship."

Max tried to hide his pleasure at this news. He'd often daydreamed about having an adoring younger brother who would hang on to his every word.

"Find Mister Max something to eat, show him where to wash, and get him some clean clothes," Lola was saying to Niko. "Then Candelario wants to speak with him."

"What if I don't want to speak with Candelario?" said Max.

"Don't be a baby, Hup. It's a huge honor to receive a private audience with a Maya wise man. Movie stars would pay a fortune for it!"

"He freaks me out. It's like he can read my mind."

"He *can*," she said. "See you at the feast."

Dusk was falling as Max washed in the river. Dusk, otherwise known as Mosquito Happy Hour, was not a good time to be naked in the open air. Niko and Wilbert kept guard for crocodiles, while Max swatted bugs and scrubbed away the accumulated grime of the last few days.

Since Niko had given him what looked like a handful of potato shavings to use for soap, he'd been skeptical about his chances of getting clean. But as soon as he dunked his hands in the water and rubbed them together, the shavings frothed up into a sudsy lather. Quite luxurious, actually.

"This stuff works pretty good," he called to Niko. "What is it?"

"Soap-root," answered the boy. "Also good for glue and fish bait."

"Right," said Max dubiously. But he had to admit that his hair felt squeaky clean and, in between the insect bites, his suntanned skin was peachy soft. He knew it was unlikely in a week, but he felt like he'd acquired some muscles too. In fact, by his usual couch-potato standards, he was feeling positively hunky.

Niko held out a clean T-shirt and jeans he'd borrowed from somewhere, and Max got dressed as slowly as he could, trying to put off the moment when Niko would take him to Candelario. When he could delay no longer, he found himself standing on the porch of a large hut at the edge of the village. Niko called out in Mayan and pushed open the door.

"*Ko'oten!*" (Koh-oh-ten!) called Candelario. "Come! I've been waiting for you, Max Murphy!"

Max went inside. The hut was dark and the air was thick with smoke and incense. At first, he couldn't see anything. Then, at the far end of the hut, he made out a large chair, like a throne, draped in animal skins.

It was empty.

"*Ko'oten!*" came Candelario's voice again.

Had he made himself invisible?

Max was halfway over to the empty chair when something caught his eye, low down on the other side of the room. It was Candelario's white hair shimmering in the candlelight.

" 'Sit!' "

"*Kulen!*" (Koo-len!) said Candelario, indicating a low stool like the one he himself was perched on. "Sit!"

Max sat.

For a while nothing was said.

Max looked around the room. Behind the old man was a long wooden table covered by a thick striped cloth. Its surface, like every other surface in the hut, was laden with flickering candles, statues, painted pots, and jars of unrecognizable, dried-up things. There were no windows and the walls were draped with animal skins. Masks, carvings, and animal skulls hung from the ceiling.

Through the dim light, Max saw it was a witch-doctor's lair.

The scent of incense was getting stronger. The fat wax candles flared and spat.

Max had the strangest sensation that this hut was no longer in Utsal, but spinning in space. If he ran out of the door at this moment, he would plunge into empty blackness.

He told himself he was imagining things, but he gripped the sides of his stool to steady himself.

What was he doing here? This room smelled worse than Lenny's bedroom. If only it *was* Lenny's bedroom. He'd give anything to be back in Boston right now, even if it meant playing dolls with Lenny's little sister.

"This is no time for playing with dolls, Max Murphy," said Candelario. "You must put childish things behind you."

"I wish you'd stop reading my mind. It's an invasion of my privacy."

"Your *privacy*?" Candelario roared with laughter, as he repeated the words to himself. "And do the yellow butterflies, as you say, invade your privacy?"

"Yes, as a matter of fact, they do."

"And what is it that draws them to you?"

"How do I know? Maybe it's the color of my hair."

"It is not your hair that attracts them, Max Murphy. They know that the gods have chosen you. They are asking you for help."

"Me? I don't know anything about butterflies."

"These butterflies are lost souls, trapped between worlds at the changing of *bak'tuns*." (He pronounced it bak-toons.)

"Are *bak'tuns* like coc-oons?" asked Max.

More laughter from Candelario. "A *bak'tun* is a period of time," he explained. "It is four times as momentous as your century, because it is four times as long."

"I see," said Max.

"You see nothing," said Candelario. "You are like a burrowing snake, enclosed in your own little world. It is time to take wing, Max Murphy, to soar far and wide like a hawk in the sky."

Was he talking about a return flight to Boston? Max hoped so.

The minutes ticked by and the old man said nothing more.

Max began to suspect he'd fallen asleep. His grandfather in Italy did that all the time, often in midsentence. He was just about to tiptoe out of the room when Candelario's eyelids shot open.

"Let us see what the gods have in store for you, Max Murphy."

Candelario unwrapped a deerskin bundle and shook the contents in his hand like dice. Nuggets of crystal and dried corn kernels fell onto the rug.

Max had a sudden flashback to Boston. Zia kneeling on the floor with her back to him, bits of something on the carpet in front of her and the Maya gods ranged around her. She'd said she was cleaning, but Max wasn't so sure. He was beginning to wonder about Zia. In fact, when he got back to Boston, he had quite a few questions for her. Like where did she get the Pyramid of Peril game? Who told her to buy his plane ticket to San Xavier? And how did she know his parents needed him?

A groan from Candelario brought Max back to the smoky hut in Utsal. The old man was peering at the crystals and corn kernels and shaking his head violently. He rearranged the pieces in different combinations, all the time frowning and muttering to himself, but — no matter what pattern he made — the results never pleased him. *"Bahlamtuuno'ob,"* he muttered crossly.

A bell rang in Max's head. *Bahlamtuuno'ob.* That was what Lucky Jim had hissed at him in the tunnel. And now that he thought about it, it was what the other diners had been whispering when Oscar Poot had told his tale. As Max tried to pluck up the courage to ask Candelario what it meant, the old man spat on the ground and began to wail an incantation.

His voice was high and unearthly and it swooped and soared in the room like a trapped bird. Max could almost see it thrashing around and beating the air with exhausted wings.

Then suddenly the voice was inside Max's head and he was the trapped bird. He was a hawk who longed for the wind and the sky and the wide open spaces. He was looking down on himself from the smoky ceiling. He saw a boy with reddish brown hair, small like a mouse, too scared to move.

Then the singing stopped and the hawk was gone and he was himself again.

Candelario poured out a cup of something, took a swig, and passed it to Max.

"Drink," he said.

"What is it?" asked Max.

"It is the sacred cup that we must share."

With shaking hands, Max lifted the cup. It smelled innocuous, like coconut.

"Drink," repeated Candelario.

Max took a sip. His head exploded. Suddenly, there were twice as many crystals and corn kernels on the rug. They danced a jig for him. "What does it mean?" he slurred.

"This time the gods have gone too far," said Candelario.

"What is it? Can you see the future? What do you see?"

"You face great danger, Max Murphy."

"Is DeLanda coming for me?"

"The legions of hell are coming for you."

"What are you talking about?"

"Your path will be perilous and difficult, but you will not walk it alone. It was not by chance that you met Ix Sak Lool. The gods have brought you together. Like the Hero Twins before you, you must work side by side to outwit the Lords of Death. It is not only your own lives that are at stake. The fate of this world hangs in the balance."

"What do you mean, the fate of this world?" asked Max. Half of him was terrified, half of him was convinced the old man was mad. "What about my parents?"

"The new *bak'tun* is almost upon us," said Candelario, ignoring his questions. "The time of change always brings trouble for humankind. But this time, the omens are dread indeed."

"But that's your world," protested Max. "It's nothing to do with me. I'm looking for my parents and that's it."

"The gods have chosen you."

"Well, they can choose someone else."

The old man leaned forward and wagged a gnarled finger at him.

"You are like the green macaw, Max Murphy. You flap your wings and complain loudly about nothing. The day is coming when you will be tested."

"Tested?" squawked Max.

"It is time for Lord Macaw to fly away," said Candelario. "From this day forward, you must be fearless, brave, and strong like Lord Balaam, the jaguar."

"I just want to go home," said Max in a small voice.

"The sapling's leaves just want to reach the sun, and yet, by doing so, they give the breath of life to all mankind."

"Please," begged Max, "stop talking in riddles. If you can see the future, just tell me — yes or no — will I see my parents again?"

"You will see them again," nodded Candelario.

Max sighed with relief. That was all he needed to know.

But Candelario was leaning over and beckoning him close. "You will surely see your parents again, Max Murphy — in this world or the next!"

The old man's laughter echoed round the hut.

Max's head was swimming.

The candles were blazing, the incense filled his nostrils, every carved mask, every statue, every animal skull seemed to be mocking him. He had to get out.

As he stumbled to the door, Candelario called out again.

"Max Murphy?"

"Yes?"

"Trust the baboons."

When Max got outside, he sat on the porch steps in the dark and tried to pull himself together. He told himself to see the funny side of it. Here he was, face-to-face with a Maya wise man in the heart of the rainforest, and the mantra he gets to guide him through life is *Trust the baboons*. He'd had better advice from a fortune cookie.

But no matter how hard he tried to make light of it, Max felt sick with fear. On the one hand, Candelario talked like someone in a bad kung fu movie. On the other hand, he seemed to know what he was talking about.

The legions of hell are coming for you . . .

Max shuddered and resolved to forget Candelario's words as soon as possible.

A mournful booming filled the air.

Had the legions of hell arrived already?

Max threw himself to the ground in panic, covering his head with his hands. Niko and Wilbert appeared out of nowhere and lay down next to him, copying his every gesture. They didn't seem at all perturbed by the noise.

"What's going on?" asked Max.

"They are blowing the conch shells, Mister Max," said Niko.

"Why?"

"To call the village to the feast."

Some pretty girls walked past and giggled to see Max sprawled in the dirt.

"Why are we on the ground, Mister Max?" asked Niko happily. "Is it a game?"

"No," snapped Max, as he got to his feet. He was too busy brushing off his jeans to notice the hurt look on Niko's face.

Niko and Wilbert led him back to the central square, which was now lit by flaming bamboo torches. Two long thatched canopies had been erected, one for the men and one for the women. The feast was to be served under these canopies on low wooden tables, with woven mats to sit on. Many village men were already seated and they shouted greetings to Max as Niko silently showed him to his place.

Max soon forgot the indignities of the conch shell incident when he saw his seat at the head of the table. He'd never been a guest of honor before and he was rather looking forward to it. He sat down cross-legged and beamed graciously at the other diners. Their brown faces smiled back at him, sunburned and wrinkled from working in the fields all day.

Max saw himself through the eyes of these peasants. How rich and cultured he must look to them. How jealous they must be of his good fortune to be born in the prosperous United States, two thousand miles north of this dump. How eager they must be to please him, to make friends with this mysterious stranger from the land of plenty.

They were all just sitting there, waiting politely, so Max thought he'd get the party started. He picked up a large gourd of pineapple juice and drank it down greedily, wiping his mouth with the back of his hand.

Niko looked horrified. "No, Mister Max," he whispered. "We do not eat or drink until we have given thanks."

Max rolled his eyes. Was everyone in the world obsessed with table manners? He surveyed the faces round the table. They weren't smiling at him now. In the shadows cast by the blazing torchlight, their strong Maya profiles echoed the carvings of the warriors on the wall at Chaak. If they were looking for a sacrifice victim tonight, he had a feeling he knew who'd they pick.

The thought made him shiver.

He looked around for Lola and saw her emerging out of the darkness with Candelario. Her hair was braided and she was wearing an embroidered blouse and a long skirt. She looked like all the other women in the village, except that she held her head proud and high instead of demurely cast down. She smiled as she passed by.

Max clicked his tongue approvingly, in what he hoped was a laid-back, playboy kind of style. "Chic!" he said, appraising her outfit.

There was a general gasp of horror.

As Lola escorted the old man to his place at the other end of the table, she said something rapidly in Mayan and everyone relaxed and laughed.

"What was all that about?" called Max.

"When you said 'chic,' they thought you said *xik*," explained Lola. The two words sounded exactly the same.

"So what does *xik* mean?"

"Armpit."

Max sighed. It was going to be a long evening.

"Oh come on, Hup, cheer up. I want you to have a good time tonight."

"Well, Candelario wasn't exactly a barrel of laughs," said Max.

Another blast of conch shell.

"Tell me later," said Lola, "I have to go."

"Where to?"

"The women's table, of course."

"But you can't leave me alone —"

"Niko will look after you," smiled Lola. "All you have to do is eat what you're given. That shouldn't be too difficult for someone who thinks about food as much as you do. And Utsal is famous for its cooking. Just remember, eat it all or you'll insult the village and we won't have anywhere to sleep tonight. Got it?"

"OK," said Max, meekly.

"And have fun!"

Candelario stood up and said a blessing in Mayan. It was very long and involved much bowing and passing of gourds and drinking of toasts. Everyone applauded, another toast was drunk and then someone banged loudly on the table. There was an excited silence as two smiling women carried in a big, black earthenware cooking pot. They set it down in front of Max.

A third woman brought a bowl and ladled some soup into it from the cooking pot. This, too, was set down in front of Max.

"*Hach ki' a wi'ih!*" (Hahch–key-ah-wee-ee!) chorused the women, giggling.

Max looked at Niko questioningly.

"They say they hope you enjoy it," the boy explained.

"Isn't anyone else eating?"

"You are guest of honor," said Niko. "You must eat first."

He looked in the bowl. It was some kind of bright red slop.

"What is it?"

"Specialty of Utsal — spicy soup with peppers," said Niko. He licked his lips and rubbed his stomach to show that it was good.

Max took a spoonful. It was spicy all right.

He took a swig of juice and looked around the table.

"Why's everyone staring at me?" he whispered.

Niko smiled. "They like to watch your enjoyment of this special delicacy."

Max took another spoonful. His gums started to tingle.

He put down his spoon.

He had two options. The first was to do what he wanted to do, and refuse to eat this pungent swill. The second was to do what Lola wanted him to do, and somehow force it down.

Around the table, every face was turned to him expectantly.

Feeling selfless and noble, he picked up his spoon.

The faces around the table broke into encouraging smiles.

Max took another spoonful.

It was the hottest thing he'd ever eaten. Sweat broke out on his forehead. When he swallowed, it burned all the way down to his stomach like a trail of molten lava.

He took another swig of juice but it was like throwing gasoline on a fire and the flames in his mouth flared up ten times worse. He discovered that the longer he paused between mouthfuls, the worse the burning sensation. The only way to survive this trial by fire was to empty his mind and eat as fast as he could.

Earnest faces willed him on. Even Candelario nodded his encouragement. What was it the old man had said? You must be fearless, brave, and strong . . .

Only a few more spoonfuls.

Max's lips had gone numb and his tongue felt twice its normal size. He thought his head might explode. He could no longer taste anything at all.

He put down his spoon in bleary triumph.

Well, one thing was for sure. He hadn't acted like a green macaw tonight.

He'd made a supreme effort to do the right thing. And it hadn't been easy — that soup was lethal. But now he could look forward to basking in the adoration of the villagers for the rest of the evening.

Max Murphy, Man of the People.

At the other end of the table, Candelario was smiling his approval.

Fearless, brave, and strong.

He had passed the test. Max smiled back — a flinty, heroic kind of smile, like a Maya warrior who'd just wrestled a jaguar and won.

But now Candelario's smile was turning to laughter, and his laughter was louder than the thunder of rain in the jungle. His shoulders were shaking and tears were running down his face. Everyone on both tables — men, women, children, toothless crones — was guffawing and slapping their legs. Niko and Wilbert were lying on the ground holding their sides.

Lola came over, wiping her eyes.

"What's so funny?" rasped Max through his swollen mouth.

"That soup," she laughed, "it's just a little joke they like to play on tourists. You should see your face! You did great, Hup!"

Her words were like salt on a slug. In an instant, Max's good mood shriveled up and died. His face, already pink, turned scarlet with rage. How dare these ignorant peasants make fun of him! They could have killed him with their vile concoction. As it was, his stomach would be on fire for days.

A giggling woman took away the dish of soup and set down a gourd of thin white liquid.

"Drink it," said Lola. "It will take away the heat."

He sipped it cautiously. It tasted like watery milk. It took away the heat.

"Better?" smiled Lola.

He looked at her accusingly. "I thought we were a team," he snarled. "I'll never forgive you for this." Another thought occurred to him. "And I suppose it was your idea of a joke to get Candelario to spook me out?"

"What? No, Hup —"

"You set me up!"

"But Hup —"

"My name is Max."

A platter of fried chicken was brought out and the woman served Max an extra large helping.

"I'm not hungry," he said, pushing the plate away.

"Oh come on," said Lola. "Where's your sense of humor?"

"It's back in Boston," said Max, "and I wish I was too."

Then he jumped up and stomped off into the night.

"I'll take you to your hammock, Mister Max," said a sad little voice by his side. With Wilbert in tow as usual, Niko led Max to one of the thatched shacks on stilts. "You sleep here," he mumbled, pointing to one of the hammocks on the porch.

"Is this your house?" asked Max.

Niko nodded. He showed Max how to sit on the edge of the hammock, pull the other side over his head, and stretch out backward until he was lying flat. The little boy was polite but subdued. Max assumed he was ashamed of his village for pulling the soup trick. It never crossed his mind that Niko was ashamed of *him*.

"Don't mind those idiots, Niko," he said. "When you come to Boston, I'll take you for some real food . . . "

But he was talking to himself. Niko and Wilbert had melted back into the night.

The hammock was surprisingly comfortable. The woven fabric shaped itself to his body and the gentle rocking motion made him feel weightless. He took off his sneakers and let them drop to the floor. Then he lay there, listening to the sounds of music, speeches, and laughter drifting over from the party. Soon, despite the spicy soup sloshing around in his stomach, he fell asleep.

He was awakened at dawn by the screeching of the birds. Niko's family were already up and going about their day. Still half asleep, Max slid out of his hammock. Someone had piled his clean clothes by his sneakers. He reached down to put them on, then suddenly yelled and pulled back his hand.

A huge, shiny, black scorpion was standing on the toe of a sneaker.

It must have been five inches long.

Its claws waved at him menacingly and its tail was up — poised to attack.

He guessed it would strike if he moved, so he stood there, frozen to the spot, emitting a low wailing noise to raise the alarm without alarming the scorpion.

Niko and Lola arrived at exactly the same time.

"Why are you making that noise?" asked Lola. "It's time to go."

"I can't move," said Max. "There's a scorpion on my shoe."

Lola and Niko crept over and looked at the offending footwear.

"It's a big one," said Lola, admiringly.

"Don't just stand there," hissed Max, "do something!"

"OK," said Lola. With one deft motion, she picked the scorpion up by the tail just below the stinger. "It's one of the biggest I've ever seen," she said admiringly. She carried the scorpion over to where Max was cowering in the corner and dropped it on his shoulder.

"Oops," she said.

CHAPTER XIII

MONKEY RIVER

THE SCORPION WAS climbing slowly up Max's neck.

"Get it off me! Get it off me!" he cried.

Niko set a wooden stool at Max's feet and carefully clambered onto it. Then he reached up to Max's neck, all the time making little kissing noises.

The scorpion crawled onto his outstretched hand.

"Look at that!" said Lola innocently. "It must be Selma. She's Niko's pet."

"He has a scorpion for a pet?"

"A lot of kids do. Big ones like Selma aren't dangerous. It's the little ones you have to worry about."

"You could have told me sooner," said Max.

"After your behavior last night, I thought I'd let you suffer."

"*My* behavior?" said Max in outrage. "What about that trick with the soup?"

"You need to learn to take a joke," said Lola.

"It wasn't funny," said Max. "And what about all that fate of the world stuff in Candelario's hut? *'Trust the baboons!'* I can't believe I fell for it all."

"I'm sorry about the soup, but I swear I didn't set you up with Candelario."

"Sure you didn't," he said, "just like you didn't recognize Selma. I'm never going to believe anything you tell me ever again."

"But Hup —"

"Don't call me Hup."

"Max —"

Lola's protestations were interrupted by Niko and Wilbert, who came out onto the porch proudly carrying a bowl of food between them.

"Breakfast," smiled Niko.

Max looked in the bowl. It contained a large helping of glutinous slop.

"Oh, I get it, another of your little jokes, eh?" He winked at Niko. "And what village specialty is this?"

"*Atole*," (Ah-toe-lay,) said Niko.

"Is that Mayan for stewed maggots, by any chance?" asked Max, with a big smile. "Well, I'm sorry, but you're not going to punk me again." He took the bowl and poured the contents over the side of the porch.

Six dogs appeared out of nowhere and began lapping it up.

Lola gasped. Niko's mouth opened wide in horror. Wilbert burst into tears.

"What's wrong?" said Max.

"That was their breakfast, you idiot," said Lola. "They were going to share their corn porridge with you. I can't believe you poured it away."

Looking at Niko's face, Max felt terrible. He would have given anything to turn back the clock and share a merry breakfast. "Can't they get some more?" he mumbled.

"More?" repeated Lola, contemptuously. "There *is* no more. Do you know how hard it is to grow corn in the jungle? We cook what we need and we don't waste any."

"You shouldn't have wasted that soup last night then, should you? Anyway, that porridge was disgusting. I did the boys a favor if you ask me."

Max winked at Niko again, but the boy's expression was like thunder. With a final black look, he grabbed his little brother's hand and dragged him off, still wailing.

Max pretended to shrug it off, but inside he was kicking himself. He liked Niko and he'd really enjoyed being the object of his hero worship. Stupid kid, he told himself.

But he felt bad. As he sat alone on the porch watching Lola say her good-byes and wishing she'd hurry up, he reflected on his week of social failure. It had been one disappointment after another. First, Uncle Ted had gone back on his word. Then Niko and Lola had let him down. What was wrong with everyone? Well, from now on, Max decided, he'd look after himself and not expect anything from anyone.

When Lola had finally finished kissing all the women and hugging all the children, Max followed her sulkily down to the river. Some girls were scrubbing clothes on the rocks, and they nudged each other and laughed when they saw him. He scowled at them, which made them laugh even more.

Candelario was waiting on the bank.

"Eusebio is taking his famous hot chili peppers to the market in Limón," said Candelario. "He will give you a ride upriver." The old man chuckled. "Please try not to eat all his chilies, Max Murphy, we saw how much you liked them last night."

"Ha ha," said Max, unpleasantly.

Lola glared at him. "Thank you for everything," she said to Candelario.

"You are most welcome, Ix Sak Lool," he replied, lifting her hand to his lips and kissing it. "Our hearts will travel with you until you return. Please pass on my greetings to Hermanjilio and give him this from me."

He reached behind him and produced a large bamboo cage.

Inside was a mangy little black rooster, huddled miserably in one corner.

"This is Thunderclaw," said Candelario. "Hermanjilio will soon have need of him."

"That's so gross!" snorted Max. "It's covered in scales!"

"Ah," said Candelario, "you refer to his battle scars." He smiled proudly. "The venerable Thunderclaw was once a great fighting cock. Most of his feathers were ripped out over the years, but he was never beaten."

"Poor thing," said Lola. "Well, if anyone can give him a worthy send-off, it's Hermanjilio. He can cook anything."

Candelario turned to Max and put a hand on each of his shoulders. Little electric shocks traveled up and down Max's body.

"Trust the baboons, Max Murphy."

Max curled his lip. Surely even Candelario realized that the baboon joke was wearing thin. He was trying to formulate a smart reply, when Candelario took a leather canteen from his belt, drank a little water, and spat it in Max's face.

Well, perhaps not spat exactly. To describe it more objectively, he walked round and round the horrified Max, spraying a gentle mist of water from his mouth until he'd made a ring of tiny rainbows around the boy's head.

"Get away from me!" shrieked Max, trying to shield his face. "What's wrong with you people?"

"You should be honored," said Lola. "Candelario has just blessed you with courage."

It didn't seem to be a joke. Max looked quickly from one to the other, but he couldn't catch them smirking. "I think you're sick," he said. "You're all sick in the head. I think this village is actually some kind of low-security mental hospital."

"I can't believe you just said that!" exploded Lola. "These people have shared everything they have with you. How can you be so ungrateful?"

"Let me think," said Max, sarcastically, wiping his face with his shirt. "They poisoned me, they made fun of me, and they spit on me. Yeah, you're right, I've had a lovely time. Remind me to send them a thank-you note."

Lola turned her back on him in disgust.

"I think Eusebio is ready to leave," said Candelario. "All blessings."

At the water's edge, a small, round man was loading big, round baskets onto a dugout canoe. When he turned to greet them with his big smile, twinkling eyes, and leathery face etched with laughter lines, Max recognized him as one of the chief merrymakers of the night before and took an instant loathing to him.

He wasn't overimpressed by Eusebio's vessel, either. He'd been hoping for a super-sleek white speedboat, but this was basically a hollowed-out tree trunk with an outboard motor at the back. Surely there wouldn't be room for all of them? The boat was already sitting low in the water from the weight of the chili baskets.

At Lola's call, Chulo and Seri materialized out of nowhere and settled themselves on the bow. Chulo bared his teeth at Max in passing.

There's some extra weight we could lose, thought Max.

Eusebio indicated that Max should sit in the stern with the chicken cage on his lap. Then Lola and Eusebio pushed the boat into the water and climbed in next to him. It was a tight squeeze, but soon they were all wedged in and on their way.

A little boy was sitting in a tree at the water's edge.

It was Niko.

Wilbert sat on another branch, lower down.

Max waved to them, but they didn't wave back.

Lola waved and they waved back enthusiastically.

Max pretended not to care. He dumped the chicken cage on Lola, put on his sunglasses, folded his arms, and stared fixedly upriver.

He was glad to be leaving this crazy village. What a nuthouse.

An early morning mist soon enveloped the boat and Eusebio had to concentrate on steering. They zoomed along in silence for an hour or so, until a weak sun broke through. "At last," said Eusebio, cutting the motor in midstream. Then he pulled out a small cooler from under one of the chili baskets.

Inside were some bottles of water and two tortillas stuffed with beans.

"Please," said Eusebio, "you are welcome to share my breakfast."

"No thanks," said Lola, "we're fine. We ate so much last night, and I'm sure Hermanjilio will have another feast waiting for us. You know how he loves to cook."

"Speak for yourself," said Max. "I'm starving."

With Lola looking daggers at him, he took a tortilla and gulped it down in three greedy bites.

"And for you, Ix Sak Lool?" said Eusebio to Lola.

"I couldn't eat a thing," said Lola, flashing warning glances at Max. "Please, Eusebio, enjoy your breakfast. You have a busy day ahead at the market."

"If you are sure —" said Eusebio.

"I'll have it," said Max.

"No!" yelled Lola, slamming down the cooler lid before he could reach the other tortilla. "I can't believe you, Max Murphy! A wild pig has better manners!"

"I'm sorry, Your Ladyship, what have I done now?" snapped Max.

"You were just about to eat all Eusebio's food for the day."

"How was I supposed to know?"

"Well, you could try thinking about someone besides yourself for a change! You spoiled the party last night, you hurt Niko's feelings, you're bad news wherever you go!"

"I got us out of the temple of Chaak, didn't I?" demanded Max. "And what about *your* manners? You told me to eat all the soup and you dropped a scorpion on me — where I come from, we'd never treat a guest that way."

"I'm surprised you have any guests — or any friends at all! The world doesn't revolve around you, you know. The villagers at Utsal work so hard every day of their lives. If they like to play their little jokes on spoiled, pampered tourists, I don't think it would hurt you to laugh along with them. You could have made a lot of friends last night. But you only know how to make enemies. You're the most selfish person I've ever met!"

"That's so unfair!" Max yelled back. "If I don't look after myself, who will? I certainly can't trust *you*! I'm taking care of number one — isn't that the law of the jungle?"

"Stop," said Eusebio. It was the first time Max had seen him without a smile on his face. "You are squabbling like baby parrots."

"Eusebio, I'm sorry . . . " began Lola.

But the boatman wasn't listening to her. He was staring at Max.

"What?" said Max defensively. "Why are you looking at me like that?"

"Candelario says that the gods have chosen you," said Eusebio. "It is a good joke, no?"

"No," said Max. "I don't think any of your jokes are funny. I just want to find my parents."

"Candelario says that first you must find yourself."

"The only place I want to find myself," said Max, "is at home in Boston, and as far away from here as possible."

"Candelario says that you have a difficult journey ahead."

"He probably meant this boat ride," said Max. "Can we just get it over with?"

Lola gasped at his rudeness.

Eusebio shrugged and started up the engine.

Max breathed out. Thank goodness that little spat was over and they were on their way again. But instead of continuing down the center of the river, Eusebio made for the bank. Then he cut the motor and tied the boat to the nearest tree.

"Please get out of my boat," he said.

"But Eusebio —" began Lola.

"It is the only way," said Eusebio. "Out. Please. Now."

When Max and Lola had reluctantly climbed ashore, Eusebio tied the boat to an overhanging branch and jumped onto land himself.

"Follow me," he said.

As they tramped through the forest, clambering over tree roots and ducking under branches, Max and Lola exchanged angry glances.

Eusebio paid them no attention. He seemed to be looking for something.

Suddenly, he stopped under a tall tree and pointed up at the flowers garlanding its branches. "Look, my friend," he said.

Max looked. Each flower had several long, greenish petals and one dark, heart-shaped petal. Not very pretty. Boring, in fact, compared to the tropical blooms in Uncle Ted's gardens.

"This is the rare black orchid, " said Eusebio. "In the United States, they fuss over it like a newborn baby. So how does this delicate little flower look after itself in the treacherous jungle?" The boatman reached up to pick one, but he wasn't tall enough.

"You're not supposed to pick them, Eusebio," said Lola. "They're a protected species."

"So much for looking after itself," muttered Max.

Eusebio waved his hand airily. "My point is," he said, "that the little orchid has trained itself to be the perfect guest. It lives in trees, like this hog plum, but it feeds itself from the air and the rain. It takes nothing from its host."

"I knew this was about the tortilla," said Max.

But Eusebio had already moved on. "Over here," he was saying, "is the trumpet tree — so called because my ancestors made trumpets from its hollow trunk." He handed Max his machete. "Hit it," he instructed.

Max whacked the tree as hard as he could.

"Aaaaaghhhh!"

He dropped the machete and jumped back as hundreds of angry ants came running out of the trunk and swarmed toward the machete marks.

"They live in the tree," said Eusebio. "The tree makes a special nectar for the ants, and in return, they attack anything that disturbs it."

"Uh-huh," said Max, backing away. He was getting seriously worried that he was stuck in the forest with a tree-hugging lunatic.

Eusebio had found another specimen. "The mighty poisonwood!" he cried. "Its sap will give you a rash that burns worse than pepper soup. But what do you think grows right next to it?'

Max looked at him blankly.

"The answer is gumbolimbo — otherwise known as the tourist tree, because its bark is always red and peeling!"

"I'm not really into rainforest humor," said Max. "Can we go now?"

"But a piece of gumbolimbo bark is the only cure for a poisonwood rash — and they always grow together!" explained Eusebio, as if he were sharing the secret of the universe. "Do you understand, my friend? We are connected to each other and to the Earth. Looking after number one may be the law of the concrete jungle, but it is not the law of the rainforest. Here, we must use our special skills to help each other. Our survival and our happiness depend on other people."

"Uncle Ted says hell is other people."

"That's the saddest thing I have ever heard," said Eusebio. "He is like a poisonwood without a gumbolimbo."

"I think he's happy being alone," said Max.

"Happiness and sorrow have much in common. I am guessing that your uncle has known great sorrow. You must help him to reconnect with the world."

"Me? I'm the last person he'd listen to. We didn't exactly part on good terms. He hates my father, and now he probably hates me too."

"You seem to make many enemies, Max Murphy." Eusebio looked him up and down with distaste. "I wonder why the gods have chosen *you* above all others?"

"I wish you'd stop saying that," said Max, wearily. "Nobody's chosen me. Your gods don't know I exist. This is your home, not mine."

"Ah," said Eusebio, "So you're a tourist here? A guest that takes without giving? Then I should introduce you to the strangler fig."

He pointed to a huge tree, with thick buttresslike roots. "It starts life as a vine, high in the top of another tree. Then it grows downward, stealing its host's food and light along the way, until its roots reach the forest floor. When it is firmly rooted in the ground, it tightens its death grip around its host's trunk and becomes a living coffin."

"I can't believe this," protested Max. "It was only a tortilla!"

"And you were welcome to it, my friend," smiled Eusebio, slapping him on the back. "But have you learned anything from our little nature walk?"

"Yeah," said Max, truthfully. "I learned that I should've brought sandwiches."

Eusebio roared with laughter. "Come," he said, "let us go back to the boat and share that last tortilla."

As they walked along, Max fell into step with Lola.

"I guess I have been acting like a tourist," he said, "I'm sorry."

She smiled at him. "Me too. I suppose I'd act like a tourist if I came to Boston."

Max's eyes lit up at the suggestion. "You'd like it there," he said. "No snakes, no quicksand, no rats-on-a-stick." He looked at her pointedly. "The people are normal too."

She ignored the insult. "Anyway, maybe you'll find it easier in San Xavier now that Eusebio has explained how things work around here."

Max snorted with derision. "That's the problem, though. Nothing *does* work around here. I don't know how they live in Utsal without cell phones and laptops and cable TV. It's the poorest place I've ever seen. They haven't got *anything*."

"They'd say they've got everything. They think they're rich."

"Why do they think that?" He grabbed her arm. "I was right, wasn't I? They *are* insane!"

"No! It's just that they've chosen the simple life. They don't want electricity in Utsal. They believe that the secret of happiness is to be surrounded by your family and friends and to have enough food to eat. They've seen what happens to Maya in the city. Ever since the Spanish came, we've been at the bottom of the social heap. Candelario thinks it's better to stay separate and be happy with what we've got."

"Candelario sounds like a defeatist to me."

"Maybe," said Lola, "or maybe he's a realist. There's a lot of discrimination against the Maya and you can't change that overnight. But you can refuse to be part of the system that feeds it. Once you get caught up in the consumer society, you're always trying to make more money to buy more things you don't need."

"I like buying things," said Max. "I *always* need more things."

"You tourists!" Lola laughed. "I've seen the rubbish you buy in souvenir shops. Authentic Maya pottery — made in China! More money than sense, the lot of you! Candelario thinks you're all doomed to unhappiness because you'll never be satisfied."

"Surely you don't want to live in a shack with no electricity?"

"No, I'm going to fight for my rights. I think you can have the best of both worlds. I'm proud to be Maya and I respect the old ways, but I also believe in progress and equality for women and a college education . . . that's why I'm studying with Hermanjilio at Itzamna. I'm hoping to get a scholarship."

"Shouldn't you be at Utsal making tortillas? Does Candelario approve of you going to college?"

"He's hoping I'll get it out of my system and come back and marry some boy he's picked out for me."

"You wouldn't, would you?" said Max, horrified.

"I think he'd like me to teach the village children." She shrugged. "Who knows what the future holds?"

"I know my future lies at the market," called Eusebio. "Hurry up, you two!"

When they got back to the boat, all was chaos and carnage.

A pitched battle was in progress between Chulo and a local howler troop. Missiles were raining down and screams of warfare filled the air. Chulo was crouched behind a cargo basket, lobbing chili peppers up at his enemies in the trees. They were retaliating with a barrage of bananas, cashews, and other unidentified fruits. Seri, meanwhile, sat demurely in the stern, using the lid of a basket to protect her head.

Lola leapt onto the boat and screeched something in monkey language. The monkeys in the trees dropped their ammo and slunk silently away. Chulo began to dance a victory jig, then remembered that Lola was watching him and grinned at her shamefacedly.

"I'm ashamed of you, Chulo," she said. "The whole point of being a howler monkey is that you're supposed to howl at each other instead of fighting. Now help me clear up this mess."

With Max in the bow and the monkeys sitting under Lola's watchful eye in the stern, they set off again. As they thrummed along between high walls of jungle, Eusebio pointed out the passing wildlife. It was like traveling through the pages of a children's picture book: there were freshwater crocodiles floating like logs, turtles sunning themselves on rocks, a bright orange iguana on a tree branch, a frigate bird with a chest like a plum tomato, kingfishers, storks, scarlet macaws, and always the clouds of yellow butterflies fluttering along the banks.

It was all so lush and unspoiled and peaceful, that Max could easily imagine he was the first explorer ever to navigate these waters.

His fantasy was soon disturbed by a whiny, nasal voice.

"Would ya look at that! See the cute monkeys on the canoe?"

Max looked back in the direction of the voice and saw a big cabin cruiser speeding up the river behind them. Its deck was thronged with overfed tourists in flowery shirts, and every tourist held a camera or a video camera. As the cruiser passed, it listed to one side with the combined weight of the shrieking mass who rushed to the railing to zoom in on Chulo and Seri. And then they were gone, leaving Eusebio's boat rocking in their wake.

"What the . . . ?" said Max, in shock.

"Tourists," explained Lola, "they come off the cruise ships. They're on the Mystery of the Maya tour. They dock at Aguas Muertas, take a quick trip upriver to take pictures of the market in Limón, stop at Utsal for lunch on their way back, and tick San Xavier off their list. Tomorrow, they'll be lying on a beach in Mexico."

"Don't they go to any pyramids while they're here?" asked Max.

"Nah, not in San Xavier. Our temples are hard to get to, and many of them haven't been excavated yet. But I expect they'll

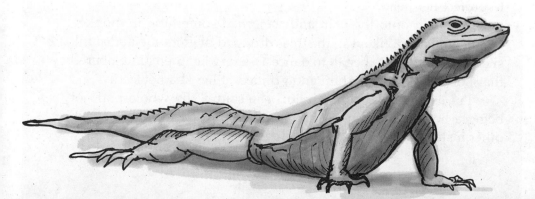

visit a pyramid or two in Mexico if it doesn't interfere with their sunbathing."

"Never mind the Mystery of the Maya," said Max. "It should be called the Mystery of the Tourist."

"You should know," said Lola.

Yeah, thought Max, I should know. Those are my people. But I don't want to be one of them anymore. Did they ever look at anything with their eyes, instead of through a camera lens? Did they ever understand what they were seeing? Did they even know what country they were in?

In that moment, Max understood why the villagers played the pepper-soup trick on tourists. He was glad the rowdy boatload who'd just passed by would soon be forcing down the fiery broth. That would shut them up for a while. He thought about himself, last night, sweat pouring down his face, trying to impress the natives.

Yeah, it was funny. It was really funny.

Lola and Eusebio saw him laughing to himself and waved at him across the chili baskets. He waved back enthusiastically. He suddenly realized how lucky he was to be on this boat and not the other one, even if he *was* getting a cramp in his legs and that cabin cruiser probably had a snack bar and a restroom with soft toilet paper.

It was time to take sides.

As long as he kept comparing San Xavier to Boston, he was no better than one of these tourists. Like it or not, the jungle was his only home right now and he was going to have to make the best of it. His parents were out there somewhere, and until he found them he wasn't going to think about his old life. Besides, playing video games alone in his room seemed kind of lame, when he could be zooming up the Monkey River with the wind in his hair.

He leaned back against the chili baskets to consider this momentous revelation. The sun was getting higher, the day was getting hotter. He closed his eyes. Soon, lulled by the throb of the engine, he fell into a waking dream.

It was a parade of disapproving faces, a lineup of everyone he'd upset, offended, or alienated recently — his mom, his dad, Oscar, Raul, Lucky Jim, the entire village of Utsal, and especially little Niko — all set against a hip-hop soundtrack of Uncle Ted saying, "He's a spoiled brat," over and over again.

Then a new sound joined the beat. A rhythmic *no, no, no.*

He opened his eyes.

"No, no, no!" yelled Eusebio, gesturing frantically from the back of the boat. "Your hand! Get your hand out!"

As Max had dozed, he'd dipped his hand lazily over the side of the boat. He pulled it in quickly. It wasn't the smartest thing he'd ever done, to trail such juicy bait in a river full of crocodiles. But then again, he reflected, perhaps he'd done a few things lately that weren't too smart.

It was late morning when Eusebio pulled the boat into the riverbank. Chulo and Seri leapt off the boat and headed into the trees.

"They know the way," laughed Lola. "They'll be there before us."

She hugged Eusebio, thanked him profusely, and showered her blessings on his family. Then she picked up the chicken cage and climbed out of the boat.

Now it was Max's turn to disembark.

He was dithering over whether to shake hands, when the boatman solved his dilemma by catching him in a suffocating bear hug.

"Good-bye, Max Murphy, all blessings," he said.

"Good-bye, Eusebio." Max took off his shades and handed them to the boatman. "Here, you need these more than I do. You're headed into the sun."

When Eusebio recovered from his surprise, he put on the shades, slapped Max on the back, hugged him again, kissed him on both cheeks, and roared off down the river.

"That was nice of you, Max," said Lola.

"You can call me Hup, if you like," he said.

Almost as soon as they began to walk, the rain started bucketing down. It was going to be another wet, miserable slog through the mud. Max remembered his new positive attitude. He gritted his teeth and followed in uncomplaining silence as Lola led him along a narrow path that snaked to and fro, up a steep hillside.

When they reached the top, the rain stopped as suddenly as it had started and the sun came out. The view was incredible. The forest spread out in every direction, from the banks of the Monkey River to the distant purple mountains. But all Max's tired body could focus on was the fact that they were not actually at the top.

There was one more hill to climb. On its summit, the upper terraces closer to the sky than the Earth, he could see the partially excavated ruins of a huge, stepped pyramid.

"That's the Temple of Itzamna," said Lola.

She started to run up the path. Then she stopped short and came back. "By the way, there's something you should know before we go up there . . . "

"What?"

"Hermanjilio is a little . . . " she searched for just the right word, "eccentric."

"What do you mean eccentric?"

But Lola and Thunderclaw had taken off up the path to the ruined city.

CHAPTER XIV

ITZAMNA

HUFFING AND PUFFING, Max followed behind, climbing slowly up the hill until he reached the Temple of Itzamna. As he got closer, he came face-to-face with a line of monstrous carved faces, taller than he was. One had a pig's snout, another had pop eyes and buck teeth. Some stuck out their tongues, others frowned and grimaced. It wasn't quite the welcoming committee he'd hoped for.

"Lola?" he called.

"Over here, Hup."

He followed her voice around the side of the pyramid and suddenly, spread out below him, was the glorious ancient city that had once ruled the Monkey River.

It wasn't what he'd expected at all. He'd thought Itzamna would be another boring archaeological site like the ones in his parents' photograph albums — a hodgepodge of taped-off trenches and rubble and piles of old stones, meaningless to anyone but the experts.

But this place was at once magnificent and welcoming, like coming home to the most beautiful city in the world.

The temple was built into the hillside. They were standing on a platform halfway up, about fifty feet above the central plaza. The top of the pyramid was another fifty feet above them. On this side, steep steps led down to the overgrown plaza. Through the middle of the plaza, a raised stone causeway, flanked with more ruins and grassy mounds, ran to another massive structure at the far end of the site. This too was only partially excavated and trees sprang from its upper terraces. But against the hazy backdrop of the forest, with the late afternoon sun bathing its white stones in pinks and purples, it looked like a precious jewel on a bed of dark green velvet.

"That's the royal palace," said Lola.

"It's awesome," he said.

"Yes," said Lola dreamily, "and to think it was all built without metal tools or wheels or draft animals."

"What?" said Max. "The Maya built their cities on top of hills, but they had no wheels to cart the bricks up?"

"It's a funny thing about the wheels," said Lola. "We did have them, but only on children's toys."

"You guys weren't as smart as I thought."

"Hey! There's not much point in having carts if you don't have any animals to pull them. And let's not forget everything we *did* come up with . . . like astronomy, the calendar, the concept of zero, stingless honeybees, barkless dogs, rubber balls, hot chocolate, chewing gum . . . "

Max's ears pricked up. "Chewing gum?"

"It comes from the sap of the chicle" (cheek-lay) "tree," said Lola. "If you're good, Hermanjilio might show you how to make it."

"Cool," said Max. "So where is he?"

Suddenly, from the far end of the plaza, an Ancient Maya king appeared.

He wore a richly embroidered tunic, belted at the waist with a woven sash. His straight black hair was pulled into a thick ponytail on top of his head with a gold ornament. Large jade spools bobbed from his ears as he ran toward them.

"Hermanjilio!" screamed Lola happily, handing Max the rooster cage and running down to meet this apparition.

"Biix a belex?" called Hermanjilio. "Are you OK? I've been worried about you, Lola."

"Ma'aloob, ma'aloob," called Lola, happily. "I'm fine! Have you seen Chulo and Seri?"

"Yes," laughed Hermanjilio. "They got here ages ago. They've eaten all the nuts in my store cupboard and now they're having a nap."

"It's so good to see you," said Lola, hugging him. "I've got so much to tell you!".

As Lola and Hermanjilio exchanged their greetings, Max tried to take in every detail of the archaeologist's extraordinary appearance.

He was in his forties, at least six and a half feet tall, and as muscular as an Olympic shot-putter. Piercing black eyes shone out of his leathery face. With his high forehead, prominent cheekbones, and splendidly hooked nose, he was another portrait out of time. Except, Max noted, no Ancient Maya king would have worn battered tennis shoes nor carried a wooden spoon.

So this was the last person to have officially seen his parents.

He coughed to get Lola's attention.

"Max!" she said. "Meet Professor Hermanjilio Bol, my teacher and my best friend. Hermanjilio, this is Max Murphy, Frank and Carla's son."

Before Max could say anything, a cloud of yellow butterflies descended on his head and shoulders.

"What an honor to meet you," said Hermanjilio, swatting at the butterflies with his wooden spoon. "These things have been everywhere since that massive rainstorm the other night. They certainly seem to like you, young man."

Max quickly flicked the butterflies away from his face and blurted out the question he'd been waiting to ask: "Do you know where my parents are, Professor?"

Hermanjilio shook his head sadly.

"Oh," said Max, visibly deflating. "Will you tell me what happened at Ix Chel?"

"As I said to the police, there isn't much to tell. The site was attacked —"

"Attacked? Who attacked you?"

"I don't know, Max. I didn't hang around to find out. There was a lot of shooting and I ran for my life. I didn't see what happened to Frank and Carla, but I assume they ran too."

"How do you know they weren't shot?" asked Max.

"I don't, for sure. But I have a good feeling about it. I think Frank and Carla are hiding somewhere."

He was the one who was hiding something. Max was sure of it.

"But you must have seen *something*?" Max insisted.

"I was too busy running away. I got separated from Frank and Carla, and there was nothing I could do. I'm sorry, Max. This whole business must be awful for you . . . "

Forgetting he was holding the wooden spoon, he went to put an arm round Max and accidentally poked him in the face with it. "Forgive me," he said, with a laugh so loud it scared the parrots in a nearby tree, "I've been cooking all day. Tonight, we're having a party to celebrate your safe arrival."

"A party?" said Max. "Who's coming?"

"Just the three of us," smiled Hermanjilio. "And Chulo and Seri, of course."

Despite his resolution to embrace life in the jungle, Max hadn't gone so far as to embrace the monkeys. He'd been rather hoping to meet some of those archaeology students Lola had mentioned — preferably female ones.

He looked Hermanjilio up and down. "Is it a costume party?"

"No," smiled Hermanjilio. "Pardon my appearance, but it's an academic experiment. My ancestors lived at Itzamna in the Classic and Postclassic periods. I've been trying to get closer to my roots by seeing life through their eyes . . . "

A hideous shrieking sound interrupted his explanation.

"Thunderclaw!" said Lola, "I completely forgot!" She lifted up the cage to show Hermanjilio. "It's a gift from Candelario."

"What is it?" asked Hermanjilio.

"His name is Thunderclaw. He's a black rooster."

"Does he have a disease? What are all those scales?"

"Old war wounds. He used to be a champion fighting cock."

"I wonder why Candelario would send me a chicken?" mused Hermanjilio.

"To cook?" suggested Max hopefully.

"But Candelario knows I'm trying to live like my ancestors, and they didn't have chickens until the Spanish came."

"Beats me," shrugged Lola. "He just said you'd soon have need of him."

"Well, we don't need him tonight, that's for sure," smiled Hermanjilio. "There's already enough food for ten people."

At this news, Max's stomach rumbled loudly.

"Come," said Hermanjilio, laughing. "Let's get you settled in and then we'll eat."

As he picked up Lola's backpack, his eyes registered the weight of the Red Jaguar. "You did it!" he said, in surprise.

"I told you I could," said Lola. "And it wasn't easy, either. The crazy count chased us all the way to Chaak. And you won't believe what happened there . . . "

"Come and tell me all about it while I finish cooking. But first, let's show Max to his room. Follow me . . . "

With that he strode off, holding the wooden spoon high in the air like a drum major leading a parade. Max and Lola followed behind until they came to a sudden halt in front of a huge tree.

"Look up," said Lola.

Max looked up.

Wow.

Above them, soaring up and up toward the jungle canopy, was an intricately constructed multistoried tree house, with thatched huts at every level linked by rope ladders and slatted walkways.

"This is fantastic!" exclaimed Max. "It's just like the Swiss Family Robinson!"

Lola looked at him with interest. "People live in tree houses in Switzerland?"

Before Max could explain, Hermanjilio cut in: "Lola, please show Max to my room. I'm not using it at the moment."

"But where will *you* sleep?" asked Max.

"Don't worry about me," said Hermanjilio. "I've been sleeping in the palace."

"The palace? Isn't that a little spooky?" asked Lola.

"Spooky? You mean haunted?" smiled Hermanjilio. "Well, there's definitely something in the air, particularly at night — latent vibrations or a sympathetic echo or something of that nature. And I've been having the most extraordinary dreams."

Lola shuddered. "Please be careful, Hermanjilio."

"I like it. It helps me imagine what daily life was like for my ancestors. I'm even grinding my own corn these days — which reminds me! I need to get back to my cooking! Please make yourselves at home."

Hermanjilio padded back down the forest path, silent as a hunting jaguar.

"He's eccentric all right," laughed Max. "What a weirdo!"

"Come," said Lola coldly, "I'll show you to your room."

They ascended the rope ladder in silence. When they reached the third level, Lola motioned that Max should go in. She pointedly avoided looking at him.

"What's the matter? What have I done now?" he asked.

Lola ignored him and started back down the ladder.

He thought quickly.

"Is it because I called Hermanjilio a weirdo? I'm sorry, Lola, I really am."

He saw that she'd stopped on the ladder and was listening to his apology, so he continued: "He took me by surprise, that's all. I was expecting the usual archaeologist type. You know, all beard and **khaki shorts.**"

Lola came back into the room. "Like your father, you mean?"

"I guess so."

"Could your father have done a better job of excavating this place?"

"Of course not, it's just Hermanjilio's 'going native' act that threw me."

"Hermanjilio *is* a native — and so am I."

"OK, OK! What are you so touchy about?"

"I just want you to understand that Hermanjilio is one of the most brilliant archaeologists in the world. He's Head of Maya Studies at San Xavier University and he's an amazing teacher. He's actually descended from the Lords of Itzamna, so he feels a spiritual connection with this place. One day he's hoping to open it as the first Maya-run site . . . Maya management, Maya tourist guides, Maya restaurant, Maya craft shop . . . " Lola's eyes were shining with pride. "He may not have a beard and khaki shorts, but Hermanjilio knows know more about Maya history than any foreign archaeologist."

"So that's what all this is about? You want me to say that your **friend in the dress is a better archaeologist than Mom and Dad?**

Well, maybe he is. But you know what? I couldn't care less! I hate archaeology! I just want to find my parents and go home. Can't you understand that?"

Lola looked him straight in the eyes. "Actually, I can."

He got it. "I'm sorry," said Max. "Will you tell me about your parents?"

There was a long silence.

Lola sat down and looked out over the jungle.

After a while she said, "I don't even know who my parents are. Hermanjilio found me in the jungle when I was little. Chulo and Seri led him to me. I was sitting in the white flowers of a mahogany tree. Hermanjilio took me to Candelario and he gave me the name of Lady White Flower. I lived in Utsal until a few years ago, when I persuaded Candelario to let me come and study with Hermanjilio. I've learned so much. Hermanjilio's a genius and I won't let anyone make fun of him."

Max nodded. "What an ass I am," he said.

"Yes, you are an ass." She wrinkled her nose. "And you smell like one too."

"So where's the river and the soap-root?" sighed Max.

"Aha!" said Lola. "That's the best thing about this tree house. If you admit that Hermanjilio is a genius, I'll show you how to work the solar-heated shower."

Max couldn't believe his ears. A hot shower was beyond his wildest dreams. "Hermanjilio is a genius," he declaimed passionately, ten times over, and he really meant it. Then he added for good measure, "You're a genius too!"

"Yum bo'otik teech!" (Yoom boh-oh-teek teych!) laughed Lola.

"Excuse me?"

"It means 'thank you.'"

Max bowed gallantly.

A crust of dry brown mud cracked off his clothes and fell to the floor in little pieces. Lola shook her head. "I don't know how you get so dirty," she said. "It's like you have a magnetic attraction to mud."

"They say it's good for the skin," said Max. "You should try it."

She raised an eyebrow.

"I mean . . . I didn't mean . . . not that you need it . . . " stuttered Max.

Lola laughed at his embarrassment and turned to go. "Look in Hermanjilio's closet," she said, "I think he has some jeans and T-shirts in among the jaguar skins."

The shower was wonderful, but clean clothes proved more of a problem.

Hermanjilio's jeans were too long even to roll up and too wide even to cinch in with a belt. Eventually Max found a pair of shorts that came down nearly to his ankles and tied the waist with a piece of rope. Then he put on the smallest T-shirt he could find, but it was still huge and looked like a tunic on him.

Dressed like this, he had no room to laugh at Hermanjilio's outfit. Oh well, at least he was clean and he smelled good. If only he'd brought his hair gel with him. He primped for a while in the mirror, but hunger overcame vanity — so he stopped worrying about his appearance, descended the ladder, and followed his nose to the food.

The scene that greeted him was magical. The plaza was lit with flaming torches and candles in lanterns strung through the trees. Fireflies the size of fairy lights darted across the path, and above it all, the jungle stars twinkled like diamonds.

Hermanjilio had set up a long table at the edge of the plaza. He'd spread large banana leaves for the tablecloth and decorated it with candles and pots of tropical flowers. It looked beautiful but Max had eyes only for the food.

There was plate after plate of succulent concoctions: a mountain of pastries, little fried dumplings, skewers of meat, avocado salad, tortillas, beans, sweet potato fritters, plantains, and a huge platter of tropical fruit.

Max stopped himself from reaching for a pastry. He would mind his manners and wait for the others. He was sure they'd be here any minute.

Come on, come on . . .

He started pacing up and down in front of the table.

Delectable smells made his mouth water.

He wondered what was in those pastries.

He gave in to temptation and tried one. Some kind of meat. It was delicious. Then a little dumpling. Double delicious. Another pastry and another . . .

"Aha! Caught you red-handed!" said Hermanjilio, gripping his shoulder.

Max coughed in surprise, spraying half-chewed pastry everywhere.

"I'm sorry, I was only joking, please don't choke!" laughed Hermanjilio. "Here, have some guava juice to wash it all down."

As his host poured out the juice, Max guiltily wiped the crumbs from his mouth. But there was no hiding the fact that the mountain of pastries was now a small hill. "I only meant to have a little taste. But it was so good, I couldn't stop."

Hermanjilio roared with laughter. "Help yourself, Max. You must be starving. From what Lola tells me, you've had quite an endurance test. Ah, here she is . . . "

Lola came into the clearing, followed by Chulo and Seri. She was wearing a pink and orange striped skirt, a lime-green flowery top, and a brightly colored woven shawl. A large pink flower was tucked behind her ear. Max thought she looked beautiful. Even prettier than all those cheerleaders at school who were totally out of his league. Who was he kidding? All the girls at school were out of his league. Suddenly he felt tongue-tied and awkward.

Come on, he told himself, say something witty and sophisticated. "You scrub up well."

He groaned inside. He couldn't believe he'd said something so clunky, but she didn't seem to notice.

"*Yum bo'otik teech,*" she laughed. Then she saw the laden table and clapped her hands like a little girl. "It all looks wonderful."

"Enough talking — let's give thanks and eat!" said Hermanjilio.

They feasted like kings. It had taken Hermanjilio hours to prepare the banquet, but it took only minutes for Max and Lola to wolf down their first helpings and come back for more. Table manners were forgotten tonight as they ate with their fingers and talked with their mouths full. After two days of living on their wits in the jungle, it felt wonderful to relax and make pigs of themselves.

Finally, when even Chulo could eat no more, Hermanjilio stood up and cleared the table. When he came back, he carried a flask of clear liquor that smelled to Max like a mixture of aniseed and gasoline.

"Maya elixir," said Hermanjilio with a wink. "Now tell me again what happened at Chaak."

"But I told you everything before dinner," said Lola, "three times."

"I know," said Hermanjilio, "but it's such an amazing story. I would have given anything to be there. Please tell me again."

As Lola told her story, he swigged the liquor from a gourd.

Before Hermanjilio could request another encore, Max jumped in: "Perhaps you'd tell *your* story now, professor, about the night my parents disappeared."

Hermanjilio winced and took another draft of liquor.

"We were attacked out of the blue," he said.

"Was it DeLanda's men?"

"I think so," said Hermanjilio. "All I can say for sure is that they were dressed in black, they were shouting at each other in Spanish, and they were armed with automatic weapons. They just came running out of nowhere, firing as they ran."

"And you think my parents got away?"

"I hope so."

Max tried not to lose his temper. Once again, he had the strong feeling that Hermanjilio was hiding something. If he couldn't get the truth out of him now, when his tongue had been loosened by elixir, he never would.

This was a case for Max Murphy, hotshot Boston lawyer.

"So Professor Bol," he said, "I put it to you that the last time you saw my parents, they were running for their lives?"

"Yes."

"And you don't think they got shot?"

"No."

"So you must think they escaped?"

Hermanjilio put his head into his hands. When he looked up, he had tears in his eyes. "I can't lie to you any longer, Max," he said. "Your parents didn't so much escape as disappear. There was a flash of light and they vanished into thin air."

CHAPTER XV

THE OATH OF BLOOD

"I DON'T UNDERSTAND," said Max. "How could my parents just vanish?"

"I saw it with my own eyes," said Hermanjilio.

"Where were you?"

"I was on top of the pyramid."

"Where were they?"

"On the ground, running toward the cenote."

"It doesn't make sense," said Max. "There's something you're not telling me."

Lola was staring hard at Hermanjilio. "There's a lot he's not telling you."

"Lola!" protested Hermanjilio. "You know I'm bound by sacred oaths to the Lords of Itzamna. When I started this excavation, Candelario blessed the site and made me promise to keep certain vows."

"But you said you didn't believe that stuff," said Lola. "You said you only went through with the ceremony to please Candelario."

"Since I've been trying to live the old way, my feelings on that subject have changed. There are things I can't talk about to outsiders."

"But Max *isn't* an outsider," said Lola, "he's in this up to his neck. He's seen the Jaguar Stones in action, remember?"

"I'm just trying to protect you both," said Hermanjilio. "There's something in the air. It all started that night at Ix Chel. I think the gods are up to something, something big, and I don't want you two getting mixed up in it."

"It's too late, Hermanjilio, we *are* mixed up in it. You have to tell Max everything. He'll keep your secrets. He just wants to find his parents. For my sake, please help him." She gave him her most irresistible smile. "Won't you do it for me?"

Hermanjilio sighed. He knew when he was beaten.

"I can only do it on one condition," he said. "The boy must take an oath of silence and seal it with a blood sacrifice."

Max did not like the sound of that.

"He'll do it," said Lola.

"I'll get the tools," said Hermanjilio, lurching off into the night.

"What tools? Why did you say I'd do it?" hissed Max to Lola.

"You want to know what happened to your parents, don't you?"

"Ye-es. But what did he mean, blood sacrifice?"

Before Lola could answer, Hermanjilio returned. He unfolded a cloth and took out a long, bony needle and a thin peel of tree bark. He passed the needle to Max.

"It's a stingray spine," he said, "sharper than cut glass. My ancestors passed them through their tongues and, um, other tender parts, to draw blood for their rituals."

Max swallowed nervously.

"Prick your finger," instructed Hermanjilio, "and let the blood drip onto the bark."

Max couldn't make himself do it.

After several failed attempts, Lola reached across, grabbed the stingray spine and jabbed his finger. She held it over the tree bark and squeezed out a few drops of blood.

"Now say these words," said Hermanjilio. *"If I should betray the secrets of the sacred stones, may the Lords of Death pluck out my living heart."*

As Max repeated the oath, a cold wind blew across the table, making the candles flicker and spit. Hermanjilio took the nearest candle and set fire to the bloodstained tree bark. They watched in silence as the smoke curled up into the night sky.

"The oath is sealed," said Hermanjilio. "I would advise you not to break it."

Max nodded earnestly. His face was ashen.

"I think he's got the message," said Lola, getting up to fetch more elixir.

"So be it," said Hermanjilio. "May Lord Itzamna forgive me." He beckoned to Max to sit closer and leaned in as if he was going to tell him a secret. *"Bahlamtuuno'ob!"* he exclaimed.

That word again.

Engulfed in a toxic cloud of elixir fumes from Hermanjilio's breath, Max turned his head away. His eyes were watering. "Baa-laam-toon-oh-ob," he pronounced. "I keep hearing that word. What does it mean?"

"Jaguar Stones, Max Murphy! It means Jaguar Stones!" Hermanjilio thumped on the table. "If you are to understand anything at all, you must first understand about the Jaguar Stones. Now, tell me, what do you know of them?"

Max wiped his eyes and thought for a moment. "I know there were five stones, I know my father had the White Jaguar, and I know what I saw at Chaak."

Hermanjilio nodded. "Five Jaguar Stones and five sacred pyramids. Each stone channeled the energy of one of the pyramids, and each pyramid represented one of the king's sacred duties. For example, he would take the White Jaguar to Ix Chel to get advice from his ancestors through the Vision Serpent —"

"Did Dad call up the Vision Serpent?" interrupted Max.

Hermanjilio looked annoyed. "Like all things in the universe," he said, "this story has a natural order. Now where was I?"

"Sorry," said Max. "You were explaining about the Jaguar Stones."

Lola returned with another flask of liquor and refilled Hermanjilio's gourd.

"So," he continued, "before recent events at Ix Chel, the stones had lain dormant for five hundred years. With all written record of them destroyed by Diego DeLanda, they had passed into legend. But I have always believed in their existence."

"Why?" asked Max.

"Just a feeling," said Hermanjilio. "It's like they're in my soul. I think a lot of Maya feel the same way. That's why I've sworn to track them down and put them on display, like the Crown Jewels of the rainforest. If I can restore the Jaguar Stones to my people, I believe the Maya will have a future as glorious as their past."

The night was getting cool. Lola huddled up to Max and draped her shawl over both of them like a blanket.

"Are you cold? Should I stop?" asked Hermanjilio, hopefully.

"No!" said Lola, rapt in the story.

"No!" said Max, rapt in the story and enjoying being under a blanket with Lola.

Hermanjilio fortified himself with elixir and continued. "Frank Murphy shared my obsession with finding the Jaguar Stones. So when he finally got his hands on the White Jaguar, he invited me to join him at Ix Chel for his experiments."

"What experiments?" asked Max.

"Frank wanted to try and activate the stone. Of course, I didn't think he'd succeed, because no one today knows how the Jaguar Stones worked. Little did I know he was bringing the instruction manual with him!"

"What?" said Lola.

"Dad found Friar Diego DeLanda's private journal," said Max.

"*What*?" repeated Lola, excitedly.

"It's true," said Hermanjilio. "It turns out that, before the wily old friar burnt our books, he copied down our secrets for his own use. Of course, the journal is very old and many pages are missing. But what remains makes it clear that DeLanda's plan was to steal the power of the Jaguar Stones for himself."

"And now crazy Count Antonio is reviving that family tradition," said Max.

"But this is incredible!" said Lola. "The knowledge in the journal must be priceless. Why did Frank keep it to himself?"

"Because, if it was genuine, it was one of the most dangerous documents in the history of mankind," said Hermanjilio. "Frank feared that some power-crazed madman would seek out the stones and put their power to evil use. He came to Ix Chel to end that possibility, once and for all. He wanted to find out if the journal was real or an elaborate fake. If it was real, he intended to burn it — just as DeLanda burned our books. If it was fake, he would hand it over to the authorities as a fascinating historical document. The White Jaguar, he would entrust to me."

"So Dad's a good guy?" said Max, in surprise. Since talking to Uncle Ted, he'd rather got used to the idea that his family were all crooks and criminals.

"Of course," nodded Hermanjilio, "one of the best. So, Lola and I went ahead to get things ready at Ix Chel. Along the way, I told her that Ted Murphy had found the Red Jaguar too. I was wondering how much he'd want for it when Lola got this crazy idea to simply repossess it in the name of the Maya people."

"But that's *stealing*," said Max, primly.

"Some people would say that all archaeology is theft," said Hermanjilio, with a shrug. "Do you want to hear the story or do you want a moral debate?"

"No! I'm sorry! Please, go on," begged Max.

"So when Frank and Carla arrived, Lola left for Aguas Muertas and the rest of us set to work. Once we'd cleared the vegetation from the top platform, we soon excavated the altar. It was in pieces — but, aided by the journal, we managed to reconstruct it. We saw the niche for the White Jaguar straight away. By this time it was nearly sunset. None of us could bear to wait another day, so we decided to attempt the activation there and then. The journal said they used blood from a human sacrifice to create conductivity. Even Frank drew the line at that, so we'd mixed up some wild turkey blood with chili and olive oil to get a good color and consistency. I remember passing the jar to Frank and him pouring it over the niche. He was nervous and his hands were shaking. He spilled blood all over that awful jacket of his."

"Hermanjilio!" interrupted Lola excitedly. "That must be why the Red Jaguar worked for us at Chaak! Max was bleeding on it! He'd cut his hand, he was dripping blood everywhere!"

"And that's what was on Dad's jacket!" said Max. "It was turkey blood!" Now he felt like he was getting somewhere. "So what happened next?" he asked.

Hermanjilio had a distant look in his eyes, reliving that terrible night. "It started slowly," he said. "The stone slid in perfectly. After a while, it began to glow and send out waves of white light. The waves cascaded down the sides of the pyramid, and soon the whole pyramid started to hum and vibrate under our feet. Then Frank pointed to the cenote. It had turned into a whirlpool of white light. Frank and Carla went down to have a closer look. That's when all hell broke loose."

"You were attacked?" asked Max.

"No, before that," said Hermanjilio. "First of all, the light in the cenote started twisting up into the sky until it formed itself into a huge white snake."

"The Vision Serpent!" gasped Lola.

"Yes! I was staring at it, transfixed, when I heard Frank and Carla screaming. Frank was covered in snakes. Then I looked down, and there were snakes around my feet, on the altar, the Jaguar Stone, the platform, the steps, everywhere . . . "

"Where were they coming from?" asked Lola.

"From the blood! Even the spills on your father's jacket were turning into writhing snakes! There was still some mixture in the jar and it was spewing out snakes like a volcano — all different kinds together, like you'd never see in the wild. Suddenly a fer-de-lance lunged at me and I literally thought I'd drop dead. I saw it sink its teeth into my leg and, although I felt no pain, I waited for death to take me. One step, two steps, three steps . . . four steps, five steps, six steps . . . I was still alive. I felt fine and I suddenly realized that the snakes were not of this world. They couldn't harm me. I was running down to help your parents when the sky turned black and a hurricane got up. I thought I'd be blown off the steps. Rain sluiced down, lightning shot in every direction, and thunder crashed overhead. Minutes before it had been a cloudless evening, and now it was the worst storm of my life. And that's when we were attacked." Hermanjilio took a deep drink of elixir. "They came out of nowhere, I didn't even hear the shooting at first because of the thunder, then I saw them . . . five or six gunmen . . . running across the plaza toward Frank and Carla, shooting as they went. It was hard to see through the rain, but it looked to me like Frank grabbed Carla's hand and they jumped into the cenote. There was a flash of light and they were gone. It was over in seconds."

"But there were no bodies in the cenote," Max said, "just my mother's earring." He thought for a moment. "They must have climbed out when it was over. "

"No," said Hermanjilio, "you don't understand. As soon as they hit the whirlpool of light, they were gone. Pouf! They dematerialized, disappeared!"

"And you just stood there watching?" said Max.

"It wasn't like that," protested Hermanjilio. "I was rooted to the spot in terror. When the gunmen started running toward the pyramid, I crawled down the back steps and escaped into the jungle. I was scared out of my wits. I didn't even go back up for the White Jaguar. With the snakes and the storm and the shooting, it was chaos. There was nothing I could do, Max. It all happened so quickly."

"But what *did* happen?' said Max. "It doesn't make any sense."

Hermanjilio's hands were shaking as he reached for his gourd. "I've been thinking about it ever since," he said. "I believe the cenote became a gateway to Xibalba that night." He pronounced it She-ball-bah, and the sound of it set Max's teeth on edge, like fingernails on a chalkboard. "I think that's where you'll find your parents."

"Xibalba?" repeated Max. "Is it far from here?"

Lola looked at him sadly. "Xibalba means Place of Fear," she said. "I'm sorry, Hup, but it's the Maya Underworld."

"The Underworld?" said Max. "Are you saying my parents are dead?"

As he put his head in his hands, a yellow butterfly landed on the table in front of him and started lapping up a spill of sickly sweet guava juice.

CHAPTER XVI

THE COSMIC CROCODILE

IT WAS IMPOSSIBLE to sleep. Several times, Max nearly fell out of his hammock as he tossed and turned, imagining the terrifying events at Ix Chel and trying to understand what it meant.

As far as he could work out, the good news was that his parents had not technically died. The bad news was that they were trapped in some Maya netherworld.

Two weeks ago, Max would have laughed at such a crazy idea. But after his experiences at the Temple of Chaak, he wasn't feeling quite so sure of himself.

But then again, even if Hermanjilio's version of events was true, how could two eminent archaeologists like his parents have got sucked into this mess?

It didn't make sense . . .

He finally drifted off to sleep as the rainforest dawn chorus struck up its overture. He was awakened minutes later by Chulo throwing mangoes at his head.

"If you were going to bring me breakfast in bed, Chulo, you could have chosen ripe ones," he complained.

There was no way he could get back to sleep, so he rolled groggily out of his hammock, pulled on some clothes and went down to the plaza. Hermanjilio was sitting at the table, deep in thought. There was a plate of tortillas and a bowl of fruit in front of him, but he didn't seem to have touched anything. Max sat down opposite him and sighed heavily.

"Bad night?" asked Hermanjilio.

"Yeah," said Max. "I can't get my head round this Xibalba thing."

Hermanjilio nodded sympathetically. "I'm sure it sounds crazy to you," he said. "But, around here, it's the only logical explanation."

Max sighed again. "I was thinking," he said, "that if a doorway to Xibalba opened at Ix Chel that night, couldn't we just go back there and open it again?"

Hermanjilio considered this suggestion. "It's a thought," he said. "But I don't think it will work. For a start, we don't have the White Jaguar. But even if we did, it's not that easy to bring people back. According to the Maya legend, the Death Lords must agree to release them — and they're not the most cooperative of folk."

"The Death Lords?"

"You swore an oath to them last night, remember?" said Hermanjilio.

"Yes, but I didn't know they were holding my parents prisoner."

"Well, I don't know that for sure, of course, " said Hermanjilio. "But the Death Lords are supposed to run most things in Xibalba."

"How many Death Lords are there?"

"Twelve," said Hermanjilio. He began counting off names on his fingers . . . "One Death . . . Seven Death . . . Blood Gatherer . . . Wing . . . Packstrap . . . Demon of Pus . . . Demon of Jaundice . . . Bone Scepter . . . Skull Scepter . . . Demon of Filth . . . Demon of Woe . . . and . . . one more . . . ah yes, Scab Stripper."

"Sounds like the lineup for a heavy metal festival," said Max. Then he had a horrible thought. "If my parents are in Xibalba, they won't meet these guys, will they?"

Hermanjilio shook his head. "I think not. There are nine levels of Xibalba, each more terrible than the last. You probably wouldn't run into the Death Lords until you reached deepest, darkest level nine. Your parents would be on the first level, which is said to be more like a waiting room."

Max thought about the waiting room at his dentist's in Boston. He imagined his parents sitting on those hard chairs, flicking through old magazines, blocking their ears to the sounds of pain from within, waiting nervously for their names to be called. Then, with a pang, he realized they were waiting for him, their son, to come and rescue them.

"How can I contact the Death Lords?" he asked.

"I don't know," said Hermanjilio, "it's usually the gods who contact mortals. They talk to us through dreams. The Maya Dreamworld runs parallel to the waking world, like two sides of a coin; so a dream is as real to us as getting a letter in the mail."

"But you're a university professor," said Max. "Surely you don't believe that?"

"Since I've been living at Itzamna, I don't know what I believe. In fact, I had a wild dream myself last night. I think it might have been a message from my ancestors."

Max took a banana and peeled it miserably. He was sick of all this Maya mystical garbage. He just wanted some solid facts. But if the only people who were willing to talk were Hermanjilio's dead relatives, he supposed he might as well listen.

"Did they mention my parents?" he asked, hopefully.

"I'm afraid not," said Hermanjilio. "It was about the Temple of Itzamna."

"That doesn't sound very wild," said Max.

"It is if you're an archaeologist," said Hermanjilio, laughing. "Anyway, I dreamt I was a priest at Itzamna, during the Golden Age. I watched myself entering a secret chamber in the pyramid and saw how to gain access in every detail. I've long suspected such a room existed, but I've never been able to find it. So, this morning, Lola and I are going to put my dream to the test."

It didn't sound very interesting to Max, but Hermanjilio could hardly contain his excitement. His face was shining like a child's on Christmas morning.

Just then, Lola clanked into the plaza, carrying armfuls of hurricane lamps.

"I brought as many I could find," she said, letting them drop onto the table, "but some of them have seen better days. Can't we just use flashlights, Hermanjilio?"

"No," he said firmly. "We're going to do this the old way — by the light of beeswax candles, just as my ancestors would have done."

Lola rolled her eyes. "Did he tell you about his dream?" she asked Max "Are you coming to look for the secret chamber with us?"

Max shook his head. After the Temple of Chaak, he hoped never to enter another Maya pyramid as long as he lived. "You go ahead," he said. "I haven't eaten yet."

"We'll leave you to enjoy your breakfast," said Hermanjilio. "Wish us luck!"

They set off across the plaza, then Hermanjilio wheeled round and came back. "By the way, Max, keep an eye on that boa up there. She's due to give birth any time, and it's really something you should see. Most snakes lay eggs, but boas have live young — as many as fifty or sixty babies, each up to two feet long! Can you imagine?"

Max looked up. A huge green snake was curled around the branch above his head. "Wait," he said, stuffing a tortilla into his mouth. "I'm coming with you."

By the time he'd found a decent lantern and grabbed a few more tortillas, Max had fallen behind. As he ran to catch up, he heard Hermanjilio's voice drifting back across the plaza, babbling with excitement: "I never imagined this temple could hold such secrets . . . a hidden chamber beside the ballcourt . . . I remember when we were excavating that area . . . the ground radar said it was solid rock . . . ha, and we believed it!"

"It may not work, Hermanjilio," said Lola. "Don't get your hopes up."

"I'm telling you, I have a good feeling," he smiled, "like everything's been leading up to this moment. Think about it, Lola. I've been looking for years and found nothing. Then — suddenly — *two* Jaguar Stones *and* DeLanda's journal! This dream is the cheese on the tortilla. You can't tell me it's all just coincidence."

"That's what worries me," said Lola. "Who — or what — is behind all this?"

"You're not getting cold feet are you?" said Hermanjilio.

"I'm just saying that you need to be careful, Hermanjilio. These temples can be dangerous places. It was pretty heavy at Chaak. And look what happened at Ix Chel."

"Yes, but this time we don't have a Jaguar Stone to stir things up."

"I'd just like to know what to expect in there."

"Me too," panted Max, catching up with them.

"Itzamna was the Lord of the Heavens," said Hermanjilio, "so his secret chamber is probably something to do with astronomy or astrology. He was definitely one of the good guys, so I wouldn't think there's anything to worry about."

They arrived at a flat, grassy space between two steeply sloping walls. One wall was set against the pyramid, the other had wide terraces built into it like bleachers.

"What's this?" asked Max.

"The ballcourt," said Lola.

"The Maya played baseball?"

"It was called Pokapok."

"Sounds like a kids' game."

"Except that the losing team and their supporters usually got sacrificed."

Now Max was interested. "How do you play?"

"It's like a cross between soccer, basketball, and volleyball," explained Lola. "See that stone ring sticking out of the wall? You have to hit the ball through it with your hip, knee, or elbow."

"Doesn't sound that difficult."

"Famous last words, Hup. The ball's as heavy as a solid rubber watermelon."

"Sometimes they did make it lighter," Hermanjilio pointed out, "by using a human skull wrapped in strips of rubber."

"Gross!" said Max, delighted.

"Apparently it improved the bounce," said Hermanjilio.

"Now that's what I call taking sport too seriously," laughed Max, looking more closely at the stone hoop.

"Ah," said Hermanjilio, "but this was literally a game of life and death. It was based on the Maya creation story." He pointed to some carved panels on the side of the pyramid. "Look," he said. "You can see it in action, right here."

"Who are the two dudes in loincloths?" asked Max.

"Those are the Hero Twins. They've been summoned to Xibalba by the Death Lords to play the ballgame for their lives. Their father has already played and lost."

"Do they win?"

"Yes," said Hermanjilio, "they trick the Death Lords and they rescue their father. He becomes Huun Ixim," (Hoon Eeshim) "the maize god. You know, maize was so important to Maya life that the upper classes used to squash their babies' heads between two boards to lengthen them like corn cobs."

"How did they trick them?" asked Max.

"The babies? I don't think they had much choice."

"No, the Hero Twins. How did the Hero Twins trick the Death Lords?"

But Hermanjilio wasn't listening anymore. He was peering at the carved panels. "Now, in my dream . . . if I press this glyph here . . . like so . . . the door should open . . . "

"Nothing's happening," said Max. "We should go back."

"Not so fast," said Hermanjilio. "The stone's getting warmer under my hand. I can feel a vibration . . . "

There was a grinding sound and the stone in front of them slid slowly into the ground, revealing a small dark tunnel.

"It worked! It worked!" Hermanjilio was almost crying with happiness. He stood back and surveyed the tunnel. "It looks a little tight," he said. "My ancestors were a lot smaller then me. Do you think I'll fit?"

"No way," said Max, shaking his head. "You'll get stuck for sure."

"You'll fit," said Lola, with absolute confidence. "If you fitted in your dream, I'm sure you'll fit now."

"I hope you're right," said Hermanjilio. He took a deep breath. "OK, let's light the lanterns and see what the chamber of Itzamna has in store for us. I'll lead the way."

Hermanjilio had to get on all fours to crawl into the tunnel. His body filled every inch. Lola went next and Max brought up the rear. As they made their way slowly down that suffocating passage, Max wondered what might be waiting for them at the end. Tombs? Skeletons? Evil spirits?

Hermanjilio eased himself out.

Then Lola.

Then it was Max's turn.

He could hardly bear to look . . .

But he needn't have worried. There was nothing. The tiny room at the end of the tunnel was completely empty.

"Well, that was a waste of time," he said, with relief.

"Time?" came a voice behind them. "What dost thou know of time?"

The three of them spun around to see a glowing red lightbulb hovering in the shadows. Wait, it wasn't a lightbulb, it was a nose. A bulbous, glowing red nose. A nose on an ancient, wizened face. As the rest of the hologram took shape, the nose and the face became part of a hideous old man. He had sunken cheeks and toothless jaws and stringy gray hair that fell to his thin shoulders. He wore nothing but a bejeweled cloth turban, a bead necklace, and a voluminous, intricately wrapped loincloth.

Hermanjilio recognized him immediately.

"My Lord Itzamna," he said, bowing down.

"Who art thou?" croaked the old man.

"My name is Hermanjilio Bol, my lord."

"What dost thou here?"

"I had a dream. I thought my ancestors had summoned me to this place. I am sorry to have disturbed you. We will leave you in peace."

Max and Lola — who had edged into the farthest corner and flattened themselves against the wall in fright — saw Hermanjilio try to take a step backward. But he could not move. He seemed to be rooted to the spot by an invisible force.

The old man laughed an eternity-of-smoking-cheap-cigars kind of laugh. "Thou wilt go when I say and not before. I must know who thou art."

"I spoke the truth, my lord. My name is Hermanjilio Bol."

"Place thy hand against mine," commanded the old man, holding up his palm.

Hermanjilio turned to look at Max and Lola. Sweat was pouring down his face. He looked terrified. They tried to give him encouraging smiles.

He put his hand palm-to-palm against the old man's hand.

And then he screamed.

Hermanjilio was changing. He was becoming different people. Always men, always Maya, always richly attired. As the different faces and bodies appeared in his place, all that was left of him was his scream.

When it was over, he slumped to the floor.

"What did you do to him?" yelled Lola to the old man.

"How darest thou address me thus? I am Itzamna, Lord of the Heavens! And thou . . . a mere female, if I am not mistaken!" He peered at her more closely. "Who art thou? Come here, wench. Hold up thy hand."

"You don't scare me," said Lola, her voice trembling. "You're just a hologram, some trick laid into the walls when this pyramid was built." The old man looked surprised to be spoken to in this way. His gummy old mouth started popping like a guppy fish. Lola swept past him to help Hermanjilio.

"Are you OK?" she asked. "What did he do to you?"

"I don't know," said Hermanjilio weakly. "It was the strangest feeling . . . "

"I did but show him his lineage," boomed the old man, recovering his dignity. "Arise Hermanjilio Bol, heir to the great city of Itzamna, son of nobles, chieftains, and priests, descendant of the illustrious warrior Lord Hurumak."

As Hermanjilio staggered to his feet, the old man foraged in the billowing folds of his loincloth. He seemed to be looking for something. Then, with a flourish, he produced a large bundle. It looked like a football, wrapped up in many layers of rags. He held it out, solemnly, to Hermanjilio.

"This day, Hermanjilio Bol, I entrust to thee the future of thy people. When the time is nigh, thou wilt know what to do. May good prevail, may evil be vanquished, may the sun rise again on the glories of Itzamna."

Hermanjilio took the bundle. He looked dazed.

"Open it," commanded the old man.

Cautiously, Hermanjilio peeled away the rags. And there, glowing in the lamplight with all the greens of the forest, was a Jaguar Stone of mottled jade.

He ran a trembling finger over the creature's head and it seemed to purr with pleasure. Hermanjilio, too, looked very happy. He got to his knees to thank the old man.

"I never dared to hope that one day I would hold the Green Jaguar of Itzamna. My grandfather told me it was lost in the days of the conquest."

"Not lost, merely biding its time. And now Hermanjilio Bol, go forth into the Chamber of Itzamna and accept thy destiny."

A doorway appeared in the inner wall. It was black and filled with stars.

Tears were streaming down Hermanjilio's face. "Thank you, thank you, thank you . . . this is the greatest moment of my life . . . I can't believe it . . . " He was babbling and laughing at the same time, as if he'd just won an Oscar.

"Go, Hermanjilio Bol!" commanded the old man. "Go, Ix Sak Lool and Massimo Francis Murphy! May you confound your demons!" He straightened up and pointed toward the doorway.

Max and Lola stared at each other in horror.

"How does he know our names?" mused Lola.

When they looked again, he was gone.

Hermanjilio seemed unphased by these events. He was cradling the Green Jaguar in his arms and stroking it lovingly, like a child with a new kitten. "Shall we go in?" he said.

"No!" said Max.

Lola looked unsure.

"Come on," wheedled Hermanjilio. "We've come this far. Let's just have a quick look . . . "

"No!" said Max.

"Well, please yourselves. But I'm going in . . . "

Lola hesitated for a moment, then she grabbed Max and pulled him through the door of stars behind Hermanjilio. There was a noise behind them. A stone descended from the lintel and sealed them in.

"Happy now?" hissed Max.

"Sorry," said Lola.

"I don't think Lord Itzamna means us harm," said Hermanjilio. "He's supposed to be friendly and peace-loving. Maybe there's another door on the other side."

They raised their lanterns to cast some light across the chamber. The room was so high that the ceiling remained pitch-black. But none of them noticed this fact. None of them noticed anything but the enormous cube — maybe thirty feet square — that commanded the center of the room.

Its base was a slab of shiny black stone. On each corner of this slab stood a huge statue of a warrior, his arms raised to support an identical slab. It looked like a massive ice-cream sandwich, with black stone wafers. But instead of a thick slice of French Vanilla, these wafers held a complex assembly — all in polished wood — of interlocking gears, wheels, and cogs.

"What is it?" said Lola.

"I've never seen anything like it," replied Hermanjilio. "Just look at this workmanship — every component is inscribed with glyphs."

"But what does it do?" asked Max. "Can you read the glyphs?"

"No, it would take me years to translate them all," said Hermanjilio walking round the machine. "But I think I recognize these four statues. They're the Bakabs, the sons of Itzamna and Ix Chel. It's their job to hold up the corners of the world. Lola, come here — have you seen this?"

He looked around for Lola, but she was nowhere to be seen.

"Lola!"

"Up here," she called.

She was standing on top of the machine.

"Come down immediately!" shouted Hermanjilio. "After everything I've taught you, I can't believe you'd climb on an artifact."

"I didn't climb on it," said Lola. "There are steps on the back wall."

Max and Hermanjilio followed her directions to a narrow staircase. It led them up to a small platform on the same level as the top of the machine.

"Jump!" called Lola, "I want to show you something."

They sprang across and found Lola kneeling over a low stone table in the center of the slab. Its surface was inlaid with a jade mosaic of a headless leaping jaguar and on the beast's shoulders was an empty niche. Above this were two rows of square windows. In each window was a carved stone glyph. Like the pictures on a slot machine, these carvings were attached to a roller that must have been linked with cogs to the machinery below.

"I know these glyphs!" exclaimed Lola. "The two on the bottom right are from the Calendar Round. They tell us that 7 Marksman was the eighteenth day in the month of *Sip*."

"Candelario would be proud of you," smiled Hermanjilio.

Lola groaned. "When I think of all the hours he spent drilling me on this stuff."

"He likes to keep the old traditions," said Hermanjilio.

"But it's as if the twenty-first century doesn't exist for him."

Hermanjilio nodded sympathetically, as he kneeled down to inspect the table. "He's just trying to protect you all. It's a hard world out there, Lola, and it's hardest of all for Maya kids. You know, I've had students who refused to be taught by a Maya — they think we're all crazy savages. Candelario's worried that if he allows them too much freedom, the kids of Utsal will abandon their culture. They're already torn between the world of their parents and the world of MTV."

"It's the same for kids in Boston," said Max. He remembered the last time he'd watched MTV with his parents. *"Is that a boy or a girl?"* . . . *"I don't know why they bother writing lyrics, you can't hear what they're singing anyway"* . . . *"That's not a skirt, it's a belt . . . "*

They used to drive him crazy. Now he'd give anything to hear their voices again, no matter what they were saying.

"It's not the same for kids in Boston at all!" protested Lola.

Her voice dragged him back from the cozy Murphy sitting room in Boston to this dark, smelly chamber in the middle of the jungle. He tried to concentrate on the matter at hand. "So what about the other glyphs? Do you know what they mean?" he asked.

"Ish," she said.

"*Ish*?" repeated Max. "Is that a Mayan word?"

"No," said Lola, "I know what they mean, sort of. I think the rest of the bottom row are from the old Long Count calendar, which measures the time elapsed since the creation of the world. You've got the *k'in* or days; the *winal* or months; the *tun* or years; the *ka'tun*, which are like our decades except they last twenty years; and, last, the *bak'tun*, which are four hundred years long and a very big deal."

"And the top row?" asked Max, sounding impressed.

"Names of gods," said Hermanjilio. "Each chunk of time has a different ruling god. There must be hundreds of them."

Max groaned. "I can't stand it. It's too complicated."

"All you need to know," said Lola, "is that the date showing on the machine was sometime in the ninth century."

"The last time it was used?" suggested Hermanjilio.

"Or when it stopped working?" said Max, hopefully.

"Shall we find out?" asked Hermanjilio, holding the Green Jaguar over the niche. "I vote yes."

"I vote no," said Max.

They both looked at Lola.

"I'm sorry, Hup," she said, "I guess I've been hanging out with archaeologists for too long. I'm scared, but I'm also curious to see what happens."

"Curiosity killed the cat," Max babbled nervously.

The Green Jaguar purred as Hermanjilio went to slot it in. Suddenly he drew back. "Blood!" he said. "We don't have any blood! I mixed up a batch when I got back from Ix Chel, but it's sitting on the shelf in my storeroom."

Lola clapped her hand to her mouth. "I thought it was salsa! I put it in my backpack with some tortillas!"

"Good girl!" beamed Hermanjilio. "I told you, this was meant to be."

Lola pulled a small jar out of her backpack and gave it to him.

"Come on, my little beauty," Hermanjilio coaxed the Green Jaguar, as he poured the thick red liquid over the niche. Just like the Red Jaguar at Chaak, the stone leapt into place of its own accord.

Hermanjilio blew out the lanterns and they were plunged into blackness.

A slight breeze brushed Max's face and the air in that dank chamber became as fresh as a morning at the seaside. There was a loud click. Then another and another. The machine was coming to life. The clicks continued, regular as clockwork. They were soon joined by whirrs and squeaks. As the noise of the machine increased, the whole huge cube began to rock gently from side to side. The stone table started to glow and the mechanism below them seemed to be glowing too. They grabbed on to the table as the cube began to buck like a mechanical bull. Was it trying to shake them off? Max was wondering how long they'd be able to hold on, when the machine seemed to find its groove and fell into a smooth vibration. They started to relax a little.

"Look," exclaimed Lola, "the glyphs are changing!"

Hermanjilio was giddy with delight. The carvings were turning so fast they were just a blur. Gradually they slowed down until each square had come to a dead stop.

"2 Jaguar!" yelled Lola, clapping her hands like a winner on the slots at Las Vegas. "It's brought itself up to date!"

"Is it just me," said Max, "or is this room getting bigger?"

Lola looked around. "Maybe it's a trick of the light," she said.

"It's no trick," said Hermanjilio. "The walls are moving back, and the floor."

"I don't like this," said Max.

"Me neither," said Lola.

"What wimps you are!" said Hermanjilio. "Think what a privilege it is to share this incredible experience. This might be the greatest moment of your lives."

Or the last moment, thought Max.

The walls and floor receded faster and faster until they could no longer be seen. Far below, tiny sparks of colored light began to rise in a circular motion. More and more sparks appeared, creating a spiraling column of lights around the machine. Suddenly the sparks clustered into luminous spheres and spun out across the blackness until they hung in twinkling constellations. Max, Lola, and Hermanjilio looked up in awe as faint translucent shapes began to form around the star clusters.

It was beautiful, hypnotic, poetic, amazing . . .

"It looks like a crocodile with two heads!" said Max.

"You're right!" cried Lola. "It's the two-headed cosmic monster!"

"This is incredible," said Hermanjilio. "We're standing in the Maya heavens!"

"What?"

"Think of it as an Ancient Maya planetarium," Lola explained. "Those lights are the stars and planets."

"I get that — but what's with the crocodile?"

"The Cosmic Crocodile represents the heavens; its blood is the rain."

"Why is it always blood with you guys —?"

Hermanjilio was trying to point something out, but his voice was muffled by what sounded like a big truck hurtling past on the freeway. It got nearer and nearer until a great ball of fire suddenly shot up behind them and made a huge arc over their heads.

Whoooooomph!

There was light and heat and a booming, terrifying noise.

Max shielded his eyes from the glare and peered through his fingers.

It was a jaguar.

A fire jaguar.

A massive flaming jaguar in midleap.

"What is that?" shouted Max.

"What's happening?" shouted Lola. She sounded as scared as Max felt.

Hermanjilio didn't look scared at all. He was shining with happiness. "It's the Sun Jaguar!" he laughed. "This is more than the night sky, it's the passage of time itself."

"Hermanjilio, did you touch something? What did you do?" shouted Lola, as the fiery beast disappeared behind the edge of the cube.

"I pressed the day glyph," said Hermanjilio. "and it moved one forward. The jaguar was the sun moving across the heavens. At night it crosses into the underworld."

It was dark again. Max leaned over the edge of the cube. There was something down there. Water. He could see the twinkling stars reflected in its glassy surface far below. "Is this some kind of time machine?" he said.

"I doubt it," said Hermanjilio. "I think it just shows the movements of the stars and the planets. It was probably designed to help the king predict eclipses, plan the best days for rituals, that sort of thing."

"So does the machine represent planet Earth?"

"There was no such thing," said Hermanjilio. "The Ancient Maya believed in twenty-three interconnected worlds. There were thirteen layers of Heaven, our world — which they called Middleworld, and nine layers of the Underworld."

"Like a club sandwich?" said Max. He wished he'd had more breakfast.

"Or a stack of tortillas," nodded Hermanjilio. "I'd guess this machine represents Middleworld. Somewhere below is Xibalba and somewhere above us are the heavens."

Whoooooomph!

Cue noise of truck and flaming jaguar.

"I just moved it forward again," said Lola. "It's 4 Sinner now . . ."

Whoooooomph!

"5 Thought!"

Max was staring down at the black waters.

"So Xibalba is down there somewhere?"

"No!" replied Hermanjilio quickly. "None of this is real, Max. You can't get to Xibalba from here. It's just a working model, an illusion."

Whoooooomph!

"6 Blade! This is fun!"

Ignoring Lola as she played with the glyphs and the flaming jaguar that rose and fell at her command, Max tried to get a straight answer out of Hermanjilio. "So is Xibalba real or not? How can I rescue my parents from a place that doesn't exist?"

"Who said it doesn't exist?"

Whoooooomph!

"7 Rain!"

Max felt exasperated. "But is it a spirit world, a parallel universe, another dimension?"

"It's all of those and none of them," mused Hermanjilio dreamily.

That was it. The final straw. Max had had enough of meaningless Maya double talk. He started to hatch his plan . . .

"Look!" said Lola. She was pointing at a bright star that was rising in the daytime sky.

Instead of twinkling, it seemed to bristle like a hedgehog. Suddenly, the star let loose with a barrage of flaming arrows. Max dropped to the floor and covered his head with his hands. Sizzling arrows fell on the slab all around him.

"What's going on?" he yelled.

"Venus!" said Hermanjilio. "The morning star!"

"I thought Venus was the planet of love?"

"Not to the Maya! Its appearance often heralds the outbreak of wars and military action. They used to schedule their battles by it."

"Why's it firing at *us*?" asked Lola.

"Move the day forward and maybe it will stop," suggested Hermanjilio.

Lola did so. The Jaguar Sun dove into the sea. Venus shone even more brightly. More flaming arrows hailed down. Max and Hermanjilio took cover with Lola behind the stone control panel.

As they huddled there, a disgusting odor filled the air.

Lola looked accusingly at Max.

"It wasn't me," he said. They both looked accusingly at Hermanjilio.

The smell — an eye-wateringly pungent cocktail of gas, bad breath, and cigar smoke — got worse and worse until it was too strong to be of human origin.

Whoooooomph!

Lola checked the glyphs. "They're going crazy!" she screamed.

In every window, the glyphs were spinning round. It reminded Max of the exciting moment when the odometer on his father's Volvo had changed from 99,999 to 100,000. (Extraordinary, he thought, that something like that used to be his definition of exciting.) Eventually, with much creaking and grinding, the glyphs came to rest.

"8 Marksman!" shrieked Lola, like a demented bingo caller. " . . . And the month is . . . Wayeb! — the five unlucky days between cycles!"

"This is big," said Hermanjilio, gravely. "The *kin*, the *tun*, and the *bak'tun* have all moved forward. We've just witnessed the Maya equivalent of a new millennium. But the worrying thing is . . . "

Max wasn't listening. He had it fixed in his head that this was his chance to get to Xibalba. Lola and Hermanjilio were engrossed in studying the glyphs. It was just a fascinating experiment to them. But he had parents to rescue. It was time for action.

Dodging arrows, Max crawled to the back corner of the machine and quickly slipped over the edge. His searching feet found the shoulders of a Bakab statue and his hands grabbed its head. He worked his way clumsily down the torso and legs, being careful to avoid the wheels and gears that were spinning at high speed just inches away.

When he landed on the black slab base, he looked into the water. It was as flat as a mirror. All he saw was his own reflection, with the erupting universe behind him.

What had he expected to see?

He'd had it all planned out.

If he could just get down this far, he was sure he'd see his parents looking up at him, holding out their arms, ready to be pulled back into the living world . . .

That's what should have happened.

What *actually* happened was that — just as Max was accepting his disappointment and thinking he should climb back up before the other two noticed he was missing — a flaming arrow shot straight toward his hands.

He let go.

He was falling.

He wished he was a cartoon character so he could scrabble back up through the air to safety. But he was Massimo Francis Murphy of Boston, Massachusetts, and he plummeted like a stone straight down to the dark sea of Xibalba, the Place of Fear.

This was bad.

He landed splat, flat on his back.

It was cold and damp. It didn't feel like water. It felt like tough black jello. He just lay there spread-eagled, flaming arrows sputtering and sizzling around him. He could see the machine in the blackness, hovering a few feet above him. There was something wrong with it. It was juddering wildly. Its wheels were roaring and screaming in pain. Gears were spinning out of it, end to end, into infinity.

Max cowered in terror, as the cosmic fireworks went into overdrive. Fireballs crashed and comets blazed, their fiery tails scorching everything in their paths. Stars collided in showers of burning sparks. A terrible meltdown was in progress and Max was fairly sure that it was all his fault. He'd disobeyed the rules. He'd tried to breach the fabric of the universe.

Stupid, stupid, stupid.

Every nerve in his body told him that whatever he was lying on was evil. A great rubbery mass of seething evil. It seemed to have some sort of power over him. He was dissolving into it. This black jello was sucking his soul. He was in a B-movie hell and he was going to die.

Then, through the smoke and explosions, he saw Hermanjilio's face above him. His mouth was moving, but Max couldn't hear his words. He was holding out his arm.

Focusing on nothing but Hermanjilio's outstretched hand, Max started to inch his way across the top of Xibalba.

He was close, so close, when five bony fingers closed around his ankle and started pulling him down. He was thrashing and kicking, but he couldn't break free. He felt heavy and drowsy, as if mercury had been injected in his veins. He felt he was dying.

"Fight it, Max, fight it!" Hermanjilio was shouting. He was hanging off the machine now, leaning out as far as he could, every muscle in his arm straining as he reached out to Max.

"Can't fight," mumbled Max. He was icy cold. His legs were numb.

He felt Hermanjilio's big warm hand close over his icy fingers.

"Let me go," he said.

He was the rope in a tug of war, and he knew that whatever was pulling him downward had won the battle. He tried to tell Hermanjilio, but the archaeologist wasn't looking at him. He was looking up, he was yelling something up at Lola. "Out! Out! Take it out!"

Hermanjilio's voice sounded distorted and far away. His words made no sense. Max wanted to tell him to relax, to let go, to stop fighting. It would be so much easier just to give in. He would sink peacefully down to Xibalba. Maybe he'd see his parents. Maybe he wouldn't. It didn't really matter anymore. Nothing mattered. He tried to disengage himself from Hermanjilio's grasp, but he wasn't strong enough.

Suddenly, with a bang that shook the universe, all the wheels and gears of the machine came to a screeching, cracking, shuddering halt. Everything went black.

The grip on Max's ankle released.

At that exact moment, his will to live came flooding back. He squeezed Hermanjilio's hand in the darkness. For a moment he hung there, between life and death. Then, grunting with the effort, Hermanjilio pulled him onto the bottom slab.

He could feel the life rushing back into his veins. His legs were tingling as they warmed up again. Hermanjilio was half holding him up, half hugging him.

"That was close," said Hermanjilio.

A faint light appeared above them. Lola was holding a lantern over the top edge. "Hermanjilio?" she called. She sounded like she was crying.

"I've got him," Hermanjilio called back. "Send down a rope!" He turned to Max. "Think you can make it?"

Max nodded and nothing more was said as Hermanjilio helped him to scramble shakily back up.

"I thought we'd lost you, Hup," said Lola when they got to the top.

"Me too," he replied.

They lit the rest of the lanterns and sat there, shell-shocked, just looking at each other. There were no stars, no planets, no Sun Jaguar. They were suspended in blackness.

Max was waiting for the other two to start shouting at him.

"I'm sorry," he began, "it was all my fault . . . "

"It was my fault," Hermanjilio cut in. "I brought you here."

His niceness made it worse. "You saved my life," said Max.

Hermanjilio shook his head modestly. "It was Lola who pulled out the Jaguar Stone. She saved us all. Did it bite you, Lola?"

"Yeah." She showed them the teeth marks in her hand.

"I'm so sorry," Max whispered, over and over.

"It's OK," Lola hushed him. "How were you to know?"

But he should have known.

And now they were adrift in eternity, because once again hot-headed Max Murphy hadn't thought before he'd acted. They sat in silence, each one trying not to panic, trying to think of some way to get back to the normal world.

They began to make suggestions, all of them bad.

Each time one of them drew breath to speak, the other two looked up hopefully, only to have their hopes dashed almost immediately. Most ideas were nixed by their creators before they were even formed.

"What if . . . ? No, that won't work . . . "

"Perhaps we could . . . nah, forget it."

"I'm sorry, I'm sorry, I'm sorry," Max said, over and over.

But sorry wasn't going to save them.

If only there was something he could do to put things right. He thought about what Eusebio had said in the rainforest. Something about using your skills to help your fellow creatures. Problem was, he didn't have any special skills. He was an idiot in an alien world and he didn't understand anything about anything.

"Think, Hup!" said Lola, in desperation. "What about video games? You got us out of Chaak by thinking like a gamer. If this was a game, what would you do?"

"Restart!" he yelled.

Hermanjilio and Lola looked at him blankly.

"All we've done is quit," he explained. "When a video game goes wrong, you quit and then restart."

"It's worth a try," said Hermanjilio, as he poured on the last of the blood mixture and slotted in the Green Jaguar again. Slowly, very slowly, the machine shuddered into life. The day glyphs spun back to 2 Jaguar and the Cosmic Crocodile stretched out across the sky.

So far, so good.

"Now, quit again," said Max.

Hermanjilio pulled out the Jaguar Stone. This time the walls, ceiling, and floor of the chamber came shooting back. The platform and steps reappeared. Then, most beautiful sight, the stone blocking the tunnel to the outside world rose smoothly up.

"Let's go," said Lola. She sounded exhausted.

As Max followed the other two out of the chamber, he paused and looked back. Apart from some bad decisions on his part, what had happened in there? Had he got any closer to his parents? What was it that had gripped his foot?

He shuddered and crawled into the tunnel back to reality.

He didn't know that the glassy surface of Xibalba had been a two-way mirror, nor that another face had been looking back at him as he'd lain there. He'd didn't know he'd been eye to eye with someone he would have recognized, someone who needed a mortal body to return to Middleworld, someone who'd grabbed his ankle and would soon have possessed the whole of him with his evil being.

But if Max had caught a glimpse of his opponent, he would have remembered the two great stone heads in the Villa Isabella. He would have recalled the story of Lord Six-Rabbit's embittered half brother who opened a doorway to the underworld and unleashed an army of undead warriors.

He would have recognized the face of Tzelek.

CHAPTER XVII

TRICK OR TREAT

AFTER HIS ORDEAL in the pyramid, Max just wanted to be alone. All afternoon, he lay in his hammock in the tree house and savored being alive. He tried not to think about the Temple of Itzamna, but he couldn't stop the images flooding into his brain. He cowered again from the hologram of the wizened old man, heard the booming of the Sun Jaguar, dodged the burning arrows and — the image he would most like to erase — fell headlong toward Xibalba.

He shuddered at the memory.

The Temple of Chaak had been physically challenging, like an ancient obstacle course, but the Temple of Itzamna had challenged his very being. His brain told him none of it was possible, but his eyes knew what they had seen. Somehow, the Green Jaguar had opened the door to another dimension where the laws of physics did not apply. It had taken the hunt for his parents to another level. Now there were no rules. Now he understood, for the first time, why people said that anything was possible in the jungle.

But was it real? Or just a theater of tricks and illusions?

His blood ran cold as he remembered the hand pulling him down as he fought to escape the clutches of Xibalba. He inspected his ankle. It was swollen and bruised. You could clearly see where five sharp fingernails had punctured his skin.

Suddenly, he didn't want to be alone anymore.

He climbed down the tree-house ladder and went to find Lola. She was sitting at the table, chopping a melon.

"Hey, Hup. Feeling better?"

"Not really," said Max. He held out his hands. "Look, I'm still shaking."

"What made you jump off anyway?"

"I didn't jump. I had this crazy idea I could get down to Xibalba and rescue my parents. Then I changed my mind and tried to climb back up, but I fell off anyway."

"I'm glad you're OK, Hup."

"I'm not OK. I'm completely freaked out. I can't believe you're taking it so calmly."

"I didn't feel calm when I was in there. But thinking about it afterward, I realized that I've seen it all before."

"What? Where? Where could you ever have seen anything like that?"

"In all the dreams and stories and legends I've heard since I was little. It was like watching the movie of a book you've read. Familiar, yet different."

"Have you ever actually seen a movie?"

"Of course, I have, you idiot," said Lola. "There's a multiplex in Limón. We may live in the jungle, but we're not that primitive."

"It's just that Eusebio made such a big deal about the simple life."

"That's Candelario's vision for the village. He's worried that if people get televisions and microwaves, the old ways will be forgotten."

"But you can't force people to live in the past."

Lola shrugged. "You can if they don't see a future. It's tough being Maya these days. We have to stick together."

"Like being in a gang," said Max.

"I guess," said Lola.

"It must be cool to know you belong."

"That's the thing. I *don't* belong because no one knows who my parents are. The Maya are obsessed with lineage. At least, the old folk are . . . "

"But you've left all that behind now. You live in the modern world."

"It didn't feel that way this morning," she said.

"I know what you mean," said Max. He looked around. "Where's Hermanjilio? I should thank him again for saving my life. He was like Superman in there."

"He's trying to get his laptop running. He wants to do some research on what happened in the pyramid. He's convinced it all means something."

"Hermanjilio has a laptop? He has electricity?"

"I told you he was a genius," laughed Lola. "He rigged up a small generator by the waterfall last year. It's a bit temperamental, but it does the job. He hasn't been using it lately, but he's gone down to the river to try and get it working again."

"Cool!" said Max. "Does he have e-mail?"

"No, we usually go to the Internet café in Limón."

"Maybe I should try to e-mail Uncle Ted," mused Max, "and let him know I'm all right."

Lola looked at him strangely. "If your uncle cared, don't you think he'd have come looking for you by now? Or sent that flunkey of his, Lucky Jim?"

"He's probably still angry with me," said Max, defensively. "But why do you suppose DeLanda hasn't showed up either?"

"Assuming he grabbed the White Jaguar at Ix Chel, he'll be too busy playing with his new toy. Your uncle's probably helping him."

"Why do you say that?" said Max, "Uncle Ted's not in league with DeLanda."

Lola said nothing but concentrated on slicing the melon.

Later, as Max sat eating his third slice, a disheveled Hermanjilio came running through the plaza. "Can't stop," he called, "got to fire up the laptop while the generator's running," and with that, he shinnied up the ladder to the tree house.

When they took him up some food, they found him hunched over the laptop, studying a Maya calendar program. Books and papers were strewn all around and he was ranting away to himself as he furiously scribbled down notes.

"Dinnertime!" said Lola.

When Hermanjilio looked up, he hardly seemed to recognize them. His eyes were big and wild and his long black hair was sticking out at odd angles. He looked like a mad scientist.

"I've been trying to make sense of what happened in the temple," he said.

"Maybe it's not meant to make sense," said Lola. "That machine was so old, I'd be amazed if it still worked properly."

"And I don't think I helped matters much," muttered Max.

"I hear what you're saying," said Hermanjilio, "but Lord Itzamna himself told me I'd find my destiny in there. It can't be just coincidence that the machine showed today's date when we activated it. And even before Max took his dive, the universe was behaving strangely. No, I have a feeling about this. Something big is happening."

"Venus was rising," Lola reminded him, "that's always bad news."

"Yes, and I'm guessing that accounts for the flaming arrows. But what about all those comets and fireballs? It was insane in there."

"Have you found anything on your computer?" asked Max, anxiously.

"It's not looking good," said Hermanjilio, "Do you remember how the calendar was moving forward and the days kept changing?"

Max and Lola nodded.

"And do you remember what day it was when the craziness started?"

Lola nodded again. "8 Marksman," she said. "I remember because Candelario calls it the most dreaded date in the whole 260-day Maya calendar."

"That's exactly what it says here!" said Hermanjilio, pointing at the computer screen. "And do you remember how the *kin*, the *tun*, the *bak'tun* and all their ruling gods changed on 8 Marksman as well? The omens could not be worse."

Lola was counting on her fingers. "Hermanjilio — it's 8 Marksman in six days' time!"

He looked like he might cry. "I don't know how this could have escaped my attention. I really must start keeping the days again. Grinding corn has been taking up way too much of my time . . . ."

"Will someone please tell me what it all means?" interrupted Max, plaintively.

Hermanjilio regarded him gravely. "What it means, young man, is that we have just six days until the *bak'tun* changes and the world enters a new age. The next four hundred years will be ruled by the god Ah Pukuh."

Ah-Poo-koo. It sounded like a cross between spitting and sneezing.

"Ah Pukuh!" said Lola in horror.

"Ah Pukuh?" echoed Max weakly.

"The god of war and violent death," explained Hermanjilio, "I've been reading up on him. Ah Pukuh is the king of the demons and he rules the ninth level of Xibalba. He's usually depicted as a skeleton or a bloated corpse, surrounded by dogs and owls. They say he stinks to high heaven. Apparently, he's also called Kisin — which means 'the flatulent one.'"

"That explains the foul smell in the temple," said Lola.

"I can't believe you thought it was me," said Max.

They started giggling, but Hermanjilio gestured for silence. "I don't think you understand how serious this is," he said. "Based on this conjunction, my ancestors would be predicting the end of the world."

"But it's the Ancient Maya world," said Max, "it can't affect us."

"It was the Ancient Maya world in the temple this morning, yet I distinctly saw a hand on your twenty-first century leg, pulling you down to Xibalba," said Hermanjilio.

Max went quiet and rubbed his ankle.

"But the pyramids are like worlds of their own," said Lola. "I can understand how the old gods might have power *inside* the temples, but not in the outside world. What we saw this morning was our ancestors' vision of the cosmos — not what's really happening up in the sky right now."

"Possibly," said Hermanjilio, "I just wish I knew more about it. Candelario's the expert on this sort of thing. Did he say anything to you about signs and portents . . . ?"

Lola shrugged. "He always talks that way . . . "

"Come to think of it," said Max sheepishly, "he did mention something about the new *bak'tun* and omens being . . . um, I think the word he used was *dread*."

"He did? Why didn't you tell me?" asked Lola.

"I thought it was one of your jokes," said Max. "I thought you'd asked him to scare me. He was chanting and groaning and throwing bits of corn around. He said the fate of the world was hanging in the balance . . . ."

"That settles it!" said Hermanjilio. "First thing in the morning, I'm going to Utsal. I have to tell Candelario about my dream and find out what all this means."

"Let's not talk about it anymore tonight," said Lola. "Who wants hot chocolate?"

It was real hot chocolate, made from roasted ground cocoa beans, mixed with water, cornmeal, and chili pepper. Max sipped it tentatively. The bitter, rich, spicy drink tasted nothing like the sweet chocolate milk they drank in Boston.

"What a day," sighed Hermanjilio, lying back and looking at the stars. "It was incredible. How about that Cosmic Crocodile?"

Another great name for a band, thought Max. He tried to trace the outline of the two-headed cosmic monster in the night sky. No matter how weird the Maya concept of the solar system, it was awesome to be gazing at the same stars they'd plotted on their charts a thousand years ago.

Hermanjilio guessed what he was thinking.

"Shall I tell you what the Maya see on a night like this?" he said. "Right above us are the constellations of Turtle, Rattlesnake, and Owl. Over there, where you see the Big Dipper, we see a bird called Seven Macaw. And your Milky Way is our World Tree, with its roots in the underworld, its trunk on the earth and its branches in the heavens. In legends, it's sometimes called the Road to Xibalba, but I guess you'd need a spaceship to drive down it."

"Some people believe the Ancient Maya flew off in spaceships," said Max.

"Not this stupid story again," said Lola, throwing a cocoa bean at him.

"Well, they *do*," insisted Max.

"Some people will believe anything," said Hermanjilio. "We've had a few New Age authors down here, trying to prove that our old stone causeways were landing strips for UFOs."

"You don't think my parents were abducted by aliens, do you?" said Max.

"No, Max, I don't," said Hermanjilio. "I think those authors spent a little too much time in the jungle, licking toads."

"Why would anyone lick a toad?" asked Max.

Hermanjilio chuckled. "The secretions of the cane toad, *Bufo marinus*, are supposed to have hallucinogenic properties. In fact, some Ancient Maya tribes made a drink out of sugar, fermented with live toads. You'd be surprised how many backpackers are out there, right now, harassing amphibians and trying to lick them."

"That's disgusting," said Max. Then curiosity got the better of him. "Have you ever licked one?" he asked.

Hermanjilio hesitated for a moment. "As a matter of a fact, I have," he said.

Lola looked up with interest. "You never told me that before," she said.

"It was a long time ago," said Hermanjilio, "I must have been about your age, Max. I was at loose ends one day and I'd heard about these hallucinogenic toads, so I thought I'd do a little private research. I sat around by the river and eventually I caught a nice big fat one. Plucking up courage, I ran my tongue over its scaly back. It tasted disgusting but I was determined to find out what all the fuss was about. I must have sat there for hours, licking the toad like a popsicle and watching the sun go down. Nothing unusual happened and I was thinking the experiment had been a failure, when the toad suddenly turned and looked at me. Then, as if in slow motion, it opened its mouth and spoke. Its words of wisdom have stayed with me every day of my life."

"What did it say?" whispered Max.

"It said . . . " answered Hermanjilio, in a furtive whisper, "it said . . . " — he adopted an amphibious croak — 'Stop *licking* me.'"

Max and Lola stared at him for a moment, then Lola burst out laughing. "I will never, *ever* believe anything you tell me, ever again," she spluttered.

"It wasn't true? You didn't lick a toad?" said Max, disappointed.

"Just a joke," smiled Hermanjilio. "One of the students told it to me, although his version took about twenty minutes."

After such a stressful day, it felt good to laugh, and they laughed until they cried, taking turns to imitate the angry toad. Max began

to feel safe again for the first time since they'd left the pyramid. But while he might have escaped the bony hand today, the fact remained that, one day soon, he had to go down to Xibalba of his own accord to find his parents. He knew for sure that he couldn't survive being pulled through that evil black jello. There had to be another way. But how?

"What are you thinking about, Hup?" asked Lola.

"Xibalba."

She threw another log on the fire. "What about it?"

"Well, how do people get there in Maya legends?"

"They get summoned by the Death Lords," said Hermanjilio. "And it's usually a one-way ticket."

"You said the Hero Twins survived," Max pointed out.

"They're allegorical, Max. They represent the sun and the moon."

"But until recently, you thought the Jaguar Stones might be allegorical."

"That's true," Hermanjilio conceded.

"And that's another thing," groaned Max, "how do the Jaguar Stones work? They seem to link everything together — truth and legend, past and present, this world and Xibalba. I'm sure they can help me rescue my parents . . . "

"If you want to understand the Jaguar Stones," said Hermanjilio, "you must understand the Maya. We believe that all things — plants, animals, stones — have a life force. Our pyramids are not just temples, but reservoirs for all this natural energy. The kings used the Jaguar Stones to channel this energy."

"Tell me again about the five sacred pyramids."

Hermanjilio used a twig to draw a map in the dirt. "There are five points to the Maya compass," he said. "In the north, at the Pyramid of Visions, the king summoned the Vision Serpent and called on the creative powers of the goddess Ix Chel. To the east was the Pyramid of Rain where he asked Lord Chaak for prosperity through good harvests. Here in the center, at the Pyramid of Time, he consulted the stars and sought wisdom from Lord Itzamna. In the south, at the Pyramid of Blood, he used the Yellow Jaguar to prove his true claim to the throne through Bolon Tz'akab, the god of royal lineage. And in the west, at Ah Pukuh, was the Pyramid of Death where the Black Jaguar oversaw military matters and inspired courage in battle."

"Wow," said Max, "they thought of everything."

"Yes, indeed. With the Jaguar Stones to help them, the kings of the Monkey River built one of the most advanced societies of the ancient world. But it all came crashing down after the reign of Lord Six-Rabbit. He was killed in a battle with his half brother Tzelek, and the Maya never seemed to recover from his loss. Many experts think that his successors grew so lazy that the people lost faith in them. Once the king could no longer predict the rain or placate the gods, he wasn't much use to them. So the priests hid the Jaguar Stones until better times — and worthier rulers — came along. But what actually came along was the Spanish Conquest. Friar Diego De-Landa found out about the stones and the rest is history . . . "

"Do you think you'll ever find them all?" asked Max.

"All five stones? Not a chance. It's always been said that one was destroyed in the final battle between Tzelek and Lord Six-Rabbit."

"The Yellow Jaguar?" guessed Max.

"No, we think the Yellow Jaguar is still hidden somewhere — in a cave or buried under a *milpa*. The stone that was destroyed was the most powerful one of all," said Hermanjilio. "It was the Black Jaguar."

"The Black Jaguar?" echoed Max.

"You're right to speak its name quietly," said Hermanjilio. "Tzelek was a master of the black arts. He stole the Black Jaguar and charged it with evil. He set up a rival court at Ah Pukuh and awakened the Undead Army that can never be killed. After Lord Six-Rabbit vanquished him, the great king's last act was to destroy the Black Jaguar so that Ah Pukuh's demon warriors could never again terrorize the mortal world."

"You're sure he destroyed it?" said Max.

Hermanjilio shrugged, "So legend has it."

Max tried not to panic. "So," he said, "the Yellow Jaguar is lost, *we* have the Red and the Green, and we're guessing that DeLanda has the White."

"That's two to one," piped up Lola. "We win!"

"The power of the Jaguar Stones is supposed to be cumulative," explained Hermanjilio. "If you had all five, you could probably rule the universe."

Max was getting increasingly agitated. "Did Dad burn De-Landa's journal?"

"No," said Hermanjilio, "he never got the chance. But he always kept it in that old jacket of his, so I assume it's gone to Xibalba with him."

"The police found Dad's jacket at Ix Chel."

Hermanjilio looked alarmed. "What? He must have ripped it off when the snakes appeared. Did the police find the journal too?"

"No, the pockets were empty."

"Then DeLanda has the journal," said Hermanjilio. He looked worried, but then he shrugged it off. "It's bad news, but the police will get him sooner or later. Meanwhile, he can't do much harm with only the White Jaguar."

This was the moment Max had been dreading.

"He has the Black Jaguar as well."

Hermanjilio and Lola gasped.

"Are you sure?" said Hermanjilio.

"I saw him showing it to Uncle Ted."

Hermanjilio and Lola looked at each other in shock.

"But if the Black Jaguar was not destroyed by Lord Six-Rabbit—" began Lola.

"— then the darkness is among us once again," finished Hermanjilio. He buried his head in his hands. "Now I understand the omens in the temple," he said. "If DeLanda has the Black Jaguar *and* the journal, he will know that the stone's greatest power is at the rising of Venus. He will know that in six days' time, Ah Pukuh will rule Middleworld. If he invokes the Curse of the Black Jaguar and releases the Undead Army, he will be invincible."

"We must stop him," said Lola. "We have two Jaguar Stones. What can we do?"

Hermanjilio repeated her question to himself. "What can we do? What can we do?" He thumped the table. "There is only one thing we *can* do. We must use the Green Jaguar to summon the immortal Lord Six-Rabbit. There's an old altar on top of the pyramid that was probably used for just such a ritual. We must bring him back to fight for us. Only he has the power to defeat the Black Jaguar."

"Lord Six-Rabbit?" echoed Max. "Bring him back? Bring him here? But he's a king of the Ancient Maya, the greatest there ever was! He's fearless and merciless! He's into cutting people's hearts out! He'll chop us down with his obsidian-bladed battle axe!"

"This is madness!" cried Lola. "It's too dangerous. You must talk to Candelario. There must be another way . . ."

But Hermanjilio had made up his mind. *"When the time is nigh, thou wilt know what to do.* Lord Itzamna himself said that to me. There is no more time for talking."

When he got up, he seemed like a different person. Gone was the eccentric, mild-mannered archaeologist. In his place, tall and proud, face ablaze with emotion, muscles gleaming in the firelight, stood a noble Maya warrior. He looked magnificent.

"This is my destiny," said Hermanjilio. "This is why my ancestors sent me the dream. This is why Lord Itzamna entrusted the Green Jaguar to me. I must go and start clearing the altar in readiness for the ritual."

And then he was gone.

Max and Lola looked at each other.

"I don't like the sound of this," said Max.

"Me neither," said Lola. "Maybe we can talk him out of it in the morning."

THE MORNING CAME rather sooner than either of them expected.

It was well before sunrise when Thunderclaw began to crow. (If you could call it crowing. Thunderclaw's idea of a wake-up call was less a cock-a-doodle-doo and more a series of hideous shrieks and cackles that belonged on the soundtrack of a Japanese horror film.)

After ignoring the cacophony for as long he could, Max stumbled out of bed. He met a bleary-eyed Lola making her way down the tree-house ladder.

"Thunderclaw seems to have settled in," she said.

"Yeah," said Max, "let's hope it's fried chicken for dinner tonight."

"Surely you couldn't eat Thunderclaw?" said Lola, who'd grown inexplicably fond of the mangy little fowl. "Not now we've got to know him?"

"Just watch me," said Max in an evil voice, before running into the plaza. "Here I come, chicky-chicken and I've got eleven herbs and spices . . . "

Lola ran after him, laughing wildly, and piled straight into him when he stopped dead a few steps later.

"What's happened here?" he said.

"Looks like we've been raided," she whispered.

In the early light, the camp had an eerie, deserted air. Upended boxes, crates, and files were strewn everywhere, their contents scattered on the ground. There was no sign of Hermanjilio.

"Why didn't we hear anything?" said Lola, surveying the mess.

"Blame that demented chicken of yours," said Max.

There was a rustling of branches above them. They looked up to see Chulo and Seri whimpering and clinging to each other. Lola held out her arms to them and made a series of low growls. The monkeys answered her, but stayed where they were.

"Something's frightened them," said Lola. "They won't come down."

"Where's Hermanjilio?" asked Max, looking nervously around for a corpse.

"Maybe they've kidnapped him," said Lola.

"But why?" said Max.

Their eyes met and they said in chorus: "The Jaguar Stones!"

"If DeLanda's got our two stones as well, we're in big trouble," said Lola anxiously. "In fact, the whole world's in big trouble."

"Do you know where Hermanjilio was hiding the stones?" asked Max.

"No," said Lola, close to tears. "I just hope he's all right."

"Who?" said a booming voice from behind them.

Their first instinct was to scream and run. Apart from his eyes, which were encircled in heavy black, the creature's entire body was painted bright red. He wore a red loincloth and his hair was styled into an extravagant topknot, decorated with strips of tree bark and parrot feathers.

"Hermanjilio!" exclaimed Lola. "You scared us!"

"First a banshee chicken, now a red devil!" said Max. "Is it Halloween today?"

"If, by that, you mean is it a day when the forces of evil are about to break free and run amok in this mortal realm, then yes, it is like Halloween," said Hermanjilio. "But I doubt you'll get any candy."

"Seriously, Hermanjilio, why do you look like that?" asked Lola.

"It's part of the ritual. I wrote a paper once on Ancient Maya Spirit Transmutation at university, but I never thought I'd have a chance to put my research into action. It's going to require some powerful magic to raise the spirits of the great Lord Six-Rabbit and his battle chief, Lord Kukab. It's important to do things as the ancestors would have done."

"Hermanjilio," said Lola, "this is going too far. Painting yourself red and putting feathers in your hair! How's that going to help anyone?"

"Look at it this way," said Hermanjilio, patiently. "If I'm wrong and this is all nonsense, then it's just a fascinating experiment in living history. But if I'm right, my paint and feathers might just save the world from four hundred years of living hell."

"I guess," she said. But she didn't sound convinced.

She gestured at all the boxes on the ground. "Did *you* make this mess? I thought we'd been raided."

"I'm sorry," he said. "I've been digging out my college notes and looking through my father's old boxes to see what I can find. It's all a bit of a rush. The ancestors would have taken weeks to prepare for something like this. Would you two mind tidying up a little? I must start fasting and meditating to achieve mental purity."

"Sounds like he's going to take a nap to me," whispered Max.

Hermanjilio winked at him. "It's true that I need to conserve my energy," — he adopted a Shakespearean tone — "for when the Sun Jaguar returns to the Underworld, I must arise and gather the creatures of the night: the silent killer who ensnares, the many-footed stalker, and the sacred flying light."

"What?" said Lola.

"At sunset, I'm going into the jungle to collect some bugs."

"Why?"

"You'll see. But while I'm away, you need to get yourselves ready too."

"Forget it," said Lola. "I'm not wearing body paint."

"That's for the High Priest," laughed Hermanjilio. "You'll be my acolytes."

"And what do they wear?" asked Lola suspiciously.

"Tunics."

"I'm not wearing a tunic," said Max.

Hermanjilio sighed heavily. "What you fail to understand," he said, "is that unless we stop DeLanda, you'll never see your parents again. Once the balance between good and evil is destroyed and evil gets the upper hand, they'll be left to rot in Xibalba with no hope of escape. So I suggest you stop whining and pay attention."

Max looked at his feet.

"Tunics it is," said Lola.

"Good. Now listen carefully . . . collect twelve red pods from the axiote bush and six long strips of bark from the balché tree. Then take out the axiote seeds, crush them, and soak them in water to make a red dye. While they're soaking, look in my office for a bolt of raw cotton. Then sew the tunics, one for each of you, and dye them red. You'll also need to dye two bark strips to make red head-bands. When you've done that, put the leftover bark to soak in elixir overnight. Ideally we'd brew our own balché liquor with bark and wild bees' honey in a sacramental canoe, but time is not on our side. Balché-steeped elixir will have to do."

"Got it," said Lola.

"Then get on with it," said Hermanjilio.

With that, he turned on his heel and they watched his tall red frame loping across the clearing toward the pyramid.

"How do you like that?" said Max. "No please, no thank you — and I'm not sure I want to take fashion tips from a dude who thinks red body paint is a good look."

"This is serious," said Lola. "You heard what he said about your parents. You want to rescue them, don't you?"

"You know I do."

"Well, unless you have a better plan to rid the world of the encroaching demon army, I think we should do as he says."

She cupped her hands to her mouth and started calling the monkeys.

"Am I the only one who isn't crazy?" muttered Max.

"I heard that!" said Lola. "Why don't you make yourself useful? You find the cotton. Chulo, Seri, and I will collect the pods and the bark."

He rolled his eyes, but he knew Lola was right. If — just if — Hermanjilio wasn't out of his mind and if — just if — a demon army was on the rampage, it was better to do something than nothing.

As soon as he reached the tree house, a torrential rain began to fall. As he watched the downpour from the window, he wondered if Hermanjilio's body paint was waterproof. If not, he'd be looking pretty silly right now. The image of Hermanjilio dripping a trail of red paint through the jungle made Max smile for the rest of the day.

NEXT MORNING, having once again been woken by Thunderclaw's maniacal crowing, Max and Lola inspected their handiwork. They had produced two reddish tunics, two red balché bark headbands, and a bottle of strong smelling balché liquor.

"Do you think this dye will ever come out?" asked Max, as he surveyed his crimson hands and forearms.

"It's strong stuff, isn't it?" said Lola inspecting her own impeccably clean limbs. "I'm glad I didn't get any dye on me."

"You're the cleanest person I've ever met," mused Max in wonderment.

Lola laughed. "I wonder what color Hermanjilio will be today?"

When Hermanjilio arrived, the first thing they noticed was that he was still red, albeit a little streaky. The second thing they noticed was that he'd either added beetle wings to his headdress, or he'd used a beetle nest as a pillow. And the third thing they noticed was that he held a plastic bag filled to bursting with a crawling mass of insects.

Of the species Max recognized, there were centipedes, ants, beetles, slugs, cockroaches, worms, maggots, and spiders of every size and color.

"I can see from your face, Max, that you're appalled," said Hermanjilio, "but I didn't have time to weave myself a bag, so I had to use a modern receptacle."

"Actually," said Max, "I was looking at what's *in* the bag."

"Ah," said Hermanjilio, proudly. "Come help me thread them onto skewers."

"I'll be right there," lied Max. "Let me just try and wash this dye off my hands. I wouldn't want to contaminate anything."

While Max pretended to scrub, Hermanjilio grilled the insects over the fire and ground their charred bodies into a black powder. He was in exceptionally high spirits for someone who was about to do battle with a demon army. Even when the daily downpour came, he took it as a sign that Lord Chaak the rain god was purifying the pyramid, ready for the rituals.

"But Hermanjilio," protested Max, "it rains every single day."

"There is rain and there is *rain*," said Hermanjilio.

When Max raised an eyebrow, he added, "As we Maya say," and went off with a shake of his ponytail to give thanks to Lord Chaak.

Despite his skepticism, Max felt excited, as if they were getting ready for a party. But what *were* they getting ready for? He couldn't imagine what the night held in store.

Just before midnight, Hermanjilio appeared in the clearing wearing the pelt of a huge jaguar over his loincloth. The pelt was a little moth-eaten and had obviously been handed down over the generations, but it was no less fearsome for that. The creature's snarling head sat on Hermanjilio's head and the rest of the pelt flowed over his shoulders like a cloak.

He had applied more thick red body paint and he wore a flamboyant creation of quetzal feathers and jade beads around his neck. Max didn't know whether to laugh or be terrified. As Hermanjilio checked over his basket of ritual paraphernalia, Max and Lola put on their new red tunics over their jeans and fixed each other's headbands.

"Here," said Hermanjilio, passing Lola a small drum to sling over her shoulder.

"I can drum," said Max.

Hermanjilio evidently had no interest in Max's percussive talents. "You take this," he said, handing Max the cage with Thunderclaw.

"Why . . . ?" began Max, but Hermanjilio gestured for silence.

"Let's go. We'll be conducting the ritual on the top platform of the temple."

The moon cast a pale light on the steep steps as they began the dizzying climb up to the top of the pyramid. Chulo and Seri tried to follow, but Lola kept shooing them back. Eventually, Hermanjilio grew tired of the constant commotion and signaled Lola to let the monkeys scamper behind.

That was all they needed, thought Max. Now they really looked like a traveling circus. Hermanjilio in his red paint and jaguar pelt, Lola with her drum and her monkeys, himself with a chicken in a cage.

*"The moon cast a pale light on the steep steps as they began
the dizzying climb up to the top of the pyramid."*

What a bunch of clowns.

Eventually the motley procession reached the top platform.

It was completely bare apart from a large stone bowl, which rested on a thick stone column. Around the column was carved a strange creature that was coiled like a snake but feathered like a bird. The creature's wide mouth gaped open, revealing two sharp fangs. Max couldn't help thinking that Chulo would fit beautifully between its huge stone jaws.

"Is that a snake or a bird?" he whispered to Lola.

"It's K'uk'ulkan, the feathered serpent."

"Is he a goodie or a baddie?'"

"It depends."

"On what?"

"On whether he gets enough red-haired boys to eat."

"Very funny. And my hair is brown."

"Be quiet, you two," called Hermanjilio, who was building a small fire in the bowl. "This is a sacred site." He instructed them to sit with the monkeys in a semicircle about ten feet from the altar. Then he stuck candles on the body of the snake to form a ring of light around the pillar.

Lola studied Max's tangled mop. "It's *red*," she whispered. Max opened his mouth to protest, but then he registered the admiration in her voice. "In the candlelight, it almost looks like it's on fire," she added.

"Silence!" commanded Hermanjilio. He raised his arms and faced his audience. "Here we go. Fingers crossed."

"Do you know what you're doing?" asked Max.

"Relax," said Hermanjilio. "I have a good feeling about this."

"Well, I have a bad feeling," said Lola. "Summoning the spirits could be very dangerous. I think we should stop right now."

"It'll be fine," Hermanjilio reassured her. "I studied this ritual in college, remember? Of course, we don't know the actual words the ancestors would have spoken, but we're fairly sure they used ground-up insects, sacred fire, and human sacrifice."

"Human sacrifice?" repeated Max weakly.

"Ah yes, did I forget to mention that part?"

Max and Lola looked at each other nervously.

"Hermanjilio," said Lola, sweetly, "you weren't planning on doing any sacrifices tonight, were you?"

"Of course," said Hermanjilio.

CHAPTER XVIII

THE CHICKEN OF DEATH

"RUN FOR IT!" screamed Max, jumping up and pulling Lola with him. Hermanjilio caught them both by the arm and held them in an iron grip.

"Are you mad?" he said.

"Are *we* mad?" said Max. "You're the one who's planning to sacrifice us."

Hermanjilio rolled his eyes in exasperation. "Of course I'm not planning to sacrifice you. That's why we brought the chicken."

"Not Thunderclaw — ?" began Lola.

"It is considered a great honor to be chosen for sacrifice," said Hermanjilio, impatiently. "Besides, Thunderclaw is a warrior. He wouldn't want to end up as a plate of chicken stew."

"Will the gods accept a chicken?" asked Max.

"Unless either of you would like to volunteer . . . "

They shook their heads firmly.

"Then the chicken will have to do. Remember, Thunderclaw is not just any chicken. Candelario said he was a great champion, a fearsome fighting cock."

The three of them regarded the wretched little creature in the cage, who was sound asleep. "He doesn't look very fearsome right now," said Max.

Hermanjilio sighed. "Give me a break, will you? I don't think

244

there's a precise science to these rituals. As I understand it, they're more about showing swagger and confidence than following any particular steps. The Maya gods are like children. They like costumes, special effects, and plenty of action. We just have to put on a good show."

"So you're going to bluff it?" said Max.

"In a manner of speaking. And now, if there are no further questions, please sit down again. I'd like to get started."

Hermanjilio opened several little packages of incense wrapped in banana leaves and put them into the fire on the altar. The flames flared up and cast an orange glow on his face. A thick pungent smoke billowed out. He began swaying back and forth, chanting in Mayan. Then he took a handful of the black insect powder and threw it into the flames. It sent crackling sparks flying in all directions.

In went more incense.

More smoke billowed out.

More black powder.

The smoke was now so thick that Max found it hard to breathe. Through the black clouds, he could just see Hermanjilio pouring his blood concoction inside the snake's mouth before he slotted in the Green Jaguar.

At Hermanjilio's signal, Lola began to beat on the drum in a slow rhythm that thumped like a heartbeat. The low-pitched *tum-tum, tum-tum, tum-tum* carried over the jungle and echoed back again. To Max, it seemed to reverberate through his body. His heart followed the rhythm — *tum-tum, tum-tum, tum-tum.*

Hermanjilio took the balché liquor and poured it over the fire and the snake. The fire sizzled and hissed. Blue and green flames flickered like snakes' tongues.

Then Hermanjilio moved back and sat between Max and Lola in the semicircle. He pulled a ceramic flute from inside his tunic and played a simple melody, the same four notes over and over. It was a hypnotic sound that seemed to work like a drug on the brain. The heartbeat of the drum and the song of the flute played faster and faster, over and over.

Soon Max felt a crackling energy in the air around him. It was as if the atmosphere had become electrically charged. The Green Jaguar started to glow. As it grew brighter and brighter, the head of the snake started to glow too. The glow spread down the back of the snake, feather by feather, down and around the coils to the tail until the whole creature was glowing with green light.

Max's eyes popped open. The snake had started to move. He was terrified.

"Stay completely still," muttered Hermanjilio, sitting immobile himself.

As Max watched, the stone snake uncoiled from the column and slithered slowly around the top of the platform. It came inches from where they were sitting. Then, apparently without seeing them, it formed its body into a large circle, nose to tail. Shafts of light rose up, one after another, within the circle formed by the snake until the whole area was one thick column of green light.

Within the column, wraithlike images of Maya people began to emerge, appearing faster and faster, until the whole column was writhing with ghostly figures.

Hermanjilio cleared his throat.

"It's now or never," he said, standing up in front of the column of ghosts. From where he sat, frozen with fear, Max could see the archaeologist's knees shaking.

"Spirits of my ancestors, we are in desperate need," boomed Hermanjilio, in his most commanding voice. "We beseech you to help us. Send us your greatest warlords. Send us the spirits of the mighty Lord Six-Rabbit and his fearless battle chief, the noble Lord Kukab!"

As Hermanjilio called out these names, the column of light grew brighter. Waves of green flames flowed out of the column, right across the platform and down the sides of the pyramid. When Max and Lola saw the wave of flames coming toward them, they looked at Hermanjilio in terror, but he just winked at them happily as if everything was normal. Chulo and Seri inched closer to Lola and put their hands over their eyes.

Max held his breath as the flames licked his legs. They were icy cold. When they touched him, he could remember things he had never experienced. Disconnected images of Ancient Maya life — a ballgame, a ceremony, a harvest, sights, sounds, smells — flooded into his brain. It was as if each flame contained the soul and the memories of a long dead Maya.

There was a deep, rolling rumble like distant thunder and the pyramid shook beneath them. Then two ghostly figures stepped out of the column of light. As soon as they did so, the column disappeared and the snake rewound itself around the altar.

One of the figures stepped forward, resplendent in an elaborate plumed headdress that was taller than he was. He was covered from head to foot in black body paint, and he held before him an obsidian sword, ready to strike. While the second figure hovered behind, the great warrior peered down at the trembling spectators.

"Who calls the mighty Lord Six-Rabbit and his fearless battle-chief, Lord Kukab, to walk again in Middleworld?" he boomed.

Mustering all his courage, Hermanjilio stood up and bowed.

"It is I, Hermanjilio Bol, direct descendant of the warrior Lord Hurumak, who summons you to the sacred stone of K'uk'ulkan."

"Hurumak! A fine fellow!" said Lord Six-Rabbit morosely. "We fought shoulder to shoulder many times, slashing and slicing our way across the battlefield. Those were the days! Descendant of Hurumak, I will hear thy petition."

The other figure, who'd been hanging back, now strode forward and pointed a gnarled finger at Hermanjilio. "Where are the human sacrifices? Do you dishonor us with no suitable offering?"

Hermanjilio's jaw dropped open. "Lord Kukab?" he said in disbelief.

It was true that the second warrior was not quite as formidable as the first. His gray hair hung in four long braids, he wore an ankle-length, fur-trimmed shift, and his face looked more like that of a cross-eyed old woman.

Lord Six-Rabbit spun round to face his fellow time traveler.

"Mother?" he bellowed. "What art thou doing here? Where is my battle chief, the glorious Lord Kukab?"

"He didn't hear the summons — he was too busy battling the Demon of Pus, so I thought I'd come along and keep an eye on you." She looked down at her astonished audience. Then she nudged her son sharply with her elbow.

"May I present my mother, Lady K'an Kakaw, First and Most Glorious Wife of the venerable Lord Punak Ha, King of the Monkey River?" said the warrior, as if he were announcing her at a ball.

Max, Lola, and Hermanjilio bowed their heads respectfully.

"Welcome back to Middleworld, your Divine Majesties," said Hermanjilio.

" 'So, Mortal, why didst thou summon us?' "

The old woman was still looking around with dissatisfaction. "But where are the bodies, the blood, the severed limbs?"

Hermanjilio took a deep breath.

"Your Divine Majesties," he began, "we would not insult you with a mere *human* sacrifice. To mark this most illustrious day in the history of Middleworld, we have brought a far greater tribute. If it pleases you, may I present the merciless and dreadful Thunderclaw, the Fowl of Fear, the notorious Chicken of Death?"

Max shot Lola a look of total incredulity. "Fowl of Fear?" he mouthed.

"Chicken of Death?" she mouthed back.

Hermanjilio grabbed the bamboo cage and opened it to reveal the scrawny, balding Thunderclaw who was still in a dead sleep.

"You are familiar with K'uk'ulkan, the serpent with feathers in place of scales?"

Lord Six-Rabbit and his mother nodded.

"Now meet his nemesis, the bird with scales in place of feathers. The Chicken of Death is a ferocious warrior who tortures mankind with his terrible shrieks. He struts through Xibalba with claws like razors, and the gods themselves tremble with fear."

He shut the cage door, as if to contain a mighty army.

Lord Six-Rabbit raised an eyebrow, "I believe I have read of this Chee Ken in the Codex of Tikal." He looked into the cage. "Is it true that with one slash of his talons he can rip off thine arm?"

"As you say, Your Majesty," said Hermanjilio solemnly.

"And with one peck of his beak, he can gouge out thine eyes?"

Hermanjilio nodded his assent.

"And with one shriek, he can banish thy soul to the ninth level of Xibalba?"

Hermanjilio nodded again.

Lord Six-Rabbit looked impressed. He whispered something to his mother, who peered at the bird in disdain.

"Is it not a bit small?" she said. "I would have expected something larger."

Hermanjilio was ready for this one. "With respect, Your Majesty, the chicken is like the scorpion: the smaller the body, the deadlier the bite."

"I see," she said. She seemed to have lost interest in the chicken. "So tell me, descendant of Hurumak, why did you summon us?"

"Us?" queried Lord Six-Rabbit. "They summoned Kukab — not thee, Mother."

"Listen, I could beat that milksop any day," said the old woman, sniffing in disdain. "His mother told me that he squealed like a stuck peccary when she had his teeth filed into points for his birthday. Talk about ungrateful."

"In truth, Mother, thou art the Demon of Gossip," sighed Lord Six-Rabbit.

Hermanjilio coughed to get their attention.

Lord Six-Rabbit fixed him with a haughty look. "So, Mortal, why didst thou summon us? What affliction besets my people in Middleworld?"

"In a few days, Your Majesty, the next *bak'tun* begins, and we face four hundred years under the rule of Ah Pukuh, the god of war and violent death."

The old woman shuddered. "He who has sockets without eyes and bones without flesh. And talk about body odor? It's no wonder he's never found a girl to marry him."

"Quite," said Hermanjilio. "But if I may continue, Your Majesty . . . "

She gestured her consent.

"It will be an age of misery, turmoil, and chaos. But that is not the worst of it. For dark forces have stolen the very same Black Jaguar that Lord Six-Rabbit, himself, once cast into Xibalba. As we speak, it is being readied, once again, to release the Undead Army of Ah Pukuh. And so, mighty Lord Six-Rabbit, Most Brave and Noble King of the Monkey River, we ask for your help in vanquishing this enemy and recapturing the stone."

The old woman turned to her son. "You should have destroyed that stone when you had the chance — and Tzelek with it. I knew that little runt would never keep his word. Now here we are in the same plight all over again."

"But, Mother, that is the nature of time," said Lord Six-Rabbit. "It runs in a circle. What has happened before, will happen again. History always repeats itself."

"All the same," she replied, "you could learn from your mistakes."

"I thank thee for thy counsel," said Lord Six-Rabbit frostily. "Let us hope thou wilt have less reason to reproach me this time around."

The old woman clapped her hands. "This time around? Then we're staying? Hurrah! I've been waiting twelve hundred years for something exciting to happen!"

Lord Six-Rabbit bowed to Hermanjilio. "This is a worthy challenge, Mortal. We will aid thee. Prepare the human vessels to give true form to our spirits."

"That is good news indeed, Your Majesty," said Hermanjilio uncertainly. "But what do you mean by human vessels?"

Now it was Lord Six-Rabbit's turn to look perplexed. He scanned the platform from left to right, until his eyes came to rest on Max and Lola. "Where are the royal personages in whom our spirits will reside? Surely thou dost not intend for the all-powerful Six-Rabbit and his venerable mother to dwell in these runtish bodies?"

Hermanjilio looked at Max and Lola who shook their heads vigorously.

"Divine Majesties," he wheedled, "forgive my ignorance, but is it absolutely necessary for you to possess a human body? Could you not continue in your present form, as spirits? Times are desperate in Middleworld, and we're a little short on royal personages right now."

Lord Six-Rabbit drew himself up to his full height. (He was tall for an Ancient Maya, at least five foot six, and his headdress added another three feet of iridescent quetzal feathers.) He threw back his magnificently sloped forehead and drew his sword.

"Fools! Dost thou not know that, once summoned, we cannot easily return from whence we came? When the Jaguar Stone is disengaged, we will vanish in the wind like smoke from a fire." He slashed his sword through the air. "That will *not* come to pass. Produce a host, or I will take thy body by force."

"Excuse me, your Divine Majesties," said Hermanjilio nervously. "Let me confer with my acolytes."

Hermanjilio, Lola, and Max stuck their heads together, whispering furiously. The only thing they all agreed on was that none of them wanted to be possessed.

All seemed lost until Max suddenly asked: "What about Chulo and Seri?"

Lola responded angrily. "I'm sure they don't want to be possessed either!"

"But it's perfect!" said Hermanjilio. "It's only for a few days, the battle will soon be over, and I'm sure Chulo and Seri will relish the experience. You've always said they were more like humans than monkeys. I promise they won't get hurt."

Lola looked doubtful.

"Frankly," muttered Hermanjilio, "we have no choice. This guy is going to skin me like a gibnut."

Lola relented. "But even if I agree, your new friends aren't going to buy it."

"Leave that to me." Hermanjilio bowed to the Ancient Maya spirits who were bickering loudly with each other. They paused in midquarrel to listen to him.

"Your Divine Majesties, please forgive us for setting this test. Knowing how much the Death Lords like to play tricks on us gullible humans, we had to make sure you were not demons in disguise. Now that you have proven beyond doubt your innate nobility, we can reveal the two honored bodies that we have brought for your possession."

"That sounds more like it," said the old woman. "Where are they?"

"May I ask Your Most Beauteous Highness," began Hermanjilio, receiving a flirtatious wink for the compliment, "to think once more of the noble scorpion. For while your new bodies may be small in stature, they are strong in muscle and brave in spirit."

The winking stopped abruptly, as the old woman looked round with mounting excitement. "Scorpions?" she asked. "Are we to have the bodies of scorpions? And maybe the head of a crocodile?" she added hopefully. "I've seen this fashion on some of the temple walls."

Hermanjilio seized his chance. "Although your Divine Majesty would look alluring in anything, the style these days is for something a little more . . . er . . . I believe the word in designer circles is . . . furry."

He cleared his throat and pointed to Chulo and Seri, who were engrossed in picking lice off each other and eating the proceeds.

Lord Six-Rabbit held up his hand and a shaft of light shot out illuminating the monkeys. "Jungle baboons? Art thou insane?" He pointed his sword at Hermanjilio's throat. "Idiot! I am the greatest warrior of the Jaguar Kings, a living god, and thou wouldst have me enter the body of a flea-infested baboon? Thou shalt die for this . . . "

Max could see that Hermanjilio was out of ideas. The archaeologist's eyes bulged in his red-painted face and his whole body was visibly trembling. Given that he was seconds away from having his throat cut, who could blame him?

Max looked at Lola. She was rooted to the spot, clutching Chulo and Seri to her, all three of them whimpering in terror.

In that split second, Max realized it was up to him to save the day.

In which case, they were sunk.

He didn't want to get involved. He especially didn't want to get hurt. He was an innocent bystander, this was a Maya thing, nothing to do with him.

But, as his brain tried to find excuses, his heart told him the truth. He wasn't a tourist anymore. He didn't have the option of watching from the sidelines. Hermanjilio needed his help. End of story.

But what could he do?

The Maya king suddenly grabbed Hermanjilio from behind and held the blade of his sword up against his throat. Hermanjilio made a loud gurgling noise. A trickle of blood ran down his neck.

Max had an idea.

It was worth a shot.

"Hey, Featherbrain!" he shouted, running over to the altar.

"Who *is* he?" gasped the old woman. "His hair burns like the torches of Xibalba."

"Hey, Featherbrain!" repeated Max. "Over here!"

Lord Six-Rabbit's plumed headdress quivered in anger.

"Who dares speak thus to Lord Six-Rabbit, supreme and sacred ruler of the Monkey River?" he bellowed.

"I do," said Max, putting both hands in the snake's mouth. "Because in exactly two seconds, I'm going to pull this Jaguar Stone out of here, and your little Maya butts are going to be ancient history."

Lord Six-Rabbit froze, his eyes on the Jaguar Stone.

"OK now, listen up," said Max, trying to sound braver than he was feeling. "I'm going to tell you the truth. This is not difficult to comprehend. We haven't got a human sacrifice. We haven't got two royal bodies for you. But we do have two healthy monkeys. And it's the monkeys or oblivion. You choose."

"Thou wouldst not dare," said Lord Six-Rabbit.

"Watch me."

"Son," said the old woman, "it is a persuasive argument."

Lord Six-Rabbit shifted uncomfortably. He had the strangest feeling that this moment was meant to happen. Deep inside him, some half-buried memory stirred like a long-forgotten dream. But a monkey? How could it be?

At that moment, Thunderclaw woke up.

It was nowhere near dawn, but that had never stopped him before. Lord Six-Rabbit and his mother watched in horror as the Chicken of Death arose and crowed its unearthly shriek.

Before Thunderclaw had finished his first chorus, the spirits of the great warrior king and his mother exchanged a glance of mutual agreement and flew into the mouths of the monkeys. Like a passing tornado, the force of it knocked the three humans and two monkeys off their feet. All five of them landed flat on their backs with a thud.

For a few moments, Max lay there, winded and terrified. He was aware of nothing but a green glow in the air and the perfume of incense. He closed his eyes. When he opened them a few seconds later, the night was black again. Only the light of the moon and stars remained.

He sat up and looked around.

Slowly the two bodies next to him sat up also.

Hermanjilio massaged his temples as if he had a headache. Then he rubbed his throat where the point of Six-Rabbit's sword had been. "Thanks for jumping in there, Max," he wheezed.

"It was nothing," said Max. But inside, he knew it was *huge*. He thought he'd probably stop shaking in a week or two.

"You were amazing, Hup," said Lola.

He grinned at her. He was feeling better already.

"So," came Hermanjilio's hoarse voice, "I thought that went well."

"What?" said Lola. "It was a disaster! You were nearly skewered by a spirit lord, Chulo and Seri have been possessed by who knows what, you brought back a little old lady instead of a battle chief — and you call that going well?"

"I saved Thunderclaw," said Hermanjilio, defensively.

"You mean Thunderclaw saved *you*," said Lola.

"It was all part of my plan," he sniffed. "I knew Candelario must have sent him for a reason. I'll send him back to Utsal tomorrow."

"I'll miss little Thunderclaw," said Lola.

"You'll be too busy looking after our guests," said Hermanjilio. "How are they?"

Lola shone her flashlight across the monkeys' immobile bodies. Then she knelt down and listened to Chulo's chest.

"Is he breathing?" asked Max, trying to sound like he cared.

"Yes," said Lola, "but they're both out cold. We'll have to carry them."

Between them, they hauled the heavy monkeys down the pyramid, across the plaza, and up the ladder to the tree house, where they laid them gently on mats.

"You guys get some sleep," said Lola, "I'll stay with them."

"Everything will seem better in the light of day," said Hermanjilio. But he didn't sound very sure.

CHAPTER XIX

MONKEY BUSINESS

LORD SIX-RABBIT was awakened by the sound of his own screaming. For a few moments he lay still on his sleeping mat, trying to shake off the memory of the dream. He told himself to calm down, but still his body trembled and sweat ran down his face.

A monkey . . . ?

Groaning, he sat up and ran his hands through his thick black hair. Then a thought occurred to him and he quickly examined his arms and legs. Upon finding them covered in monkey fur, he let out a muffled scream.

"It was no dream," he moaned.

On the other sleeping mat, Lady K'an Kakaw sat bolt upright and looked around in alarm. Then, seeing her own furry limbs, she instantly relaxed.

"It was no dream," she smiled.

She held out her monkey hands and tested her opposable thumbs. She clenched her fists and flexed her arms. Then she jumped up, stretched her wiry little body, and scratched herself from head to foot.

"Mother!" protested Lord Six-Rabbit. "Thou art a royal queen!"

"Yes, son, and I have a royal itch!"

"This vulgarity does not behoove thee. Thou mayest look like a flea-infested baboon, but thou dost not have to act like one."

"Well, that's a fine thing to say to your own mother."

Lady K'an Kakaw tried to look offended, but her attention was soon caught by a passing moth. She leapt into the air to swat it, only to fall flat on her face.

"Missed!" she chuckled. "A pox on my old crossed eyes!"

She'd been a cross-eyed queen and now she was a cross-eyed monkey. As a Maya queen, her crossed eyes had been a sign of beauty. As a monkey, they made focusing on small objects extremely difficult. She gamely scanned the room for another victim. Soon her skewed gaze came to rest on a large black fly and this time she did not miss.

Lord Six-Rabbit watched, appalled, as his mother caught the insect and popped it into her mouth. She saw his expression of disgust.

"What?" she said. "Why are you looking at me like that?"

"Mother, thou didst eat that fly."

"I'm sorry. Did you want it? Shall I catch another one?"

"Mother, we are royalty. We do not catch flies."

"No?"

"No."

"*I* do. And then I eat them."

"No, Mother! I forbid it. It is unconscionable."

Lady K'an Kakaw considered her son's words. "Hmmm," she said," as baboons, we're mostly vegetarian, I grant you. But who can resist a chewy little snack?"

"I am ashamed of thee, Mother. It is almost as if thou wert enjoying thyself."

She covered her monkey smile with her paw.

"Cheer up, son. Yesterday, we were just spirits floating in a time loop. Today we have living, breathing bodies again — what does it matter if they're covered in fur?"

She scampered over to Lord Six-Rabbit and stroked his bristly little head. "Anyway, I like this stuff, it's very fashionable. I used to have a monkey fur trim around the shoulders of my best robe."

She started making a strange gurgling noise and clutching at her throat.

"Mother, what ails thee?" said Lord Six-Rabbit. "Did the fly stick in thy gullet?"

Lola was lying low in her hammock watching them. She'd planned to give the guests a little time to settle in before introducing herself. But now she was seriously concerned about the welfare of Seri — or whoever was in Seri's body. She seemed to be deliberately choking herself.

In a flash, Lola understood the problem.

"Excuse me, Your Majesties . . . " she began.

The monkeys jumped in surprise, registering her presence for the first time.

"On thy knees, Mortal!" thundered Lord Six-Rabbit. "How darest thou speak to a divine king without permission? How darest thou even look at me? Thou shallst die for this! Mother, call the guards!"

While Lola bowed meekly down, Lady K'an Kakaw staggered to the doorway.

"I see no guards," she rasped, still holding her throat.

"This is an outrage," bellowed Lord Six-Rabbit. "What is this place? It does not look like a royal bedchamber. This sleeping mat was hard as flint. And where are the servants? I am overheated in this fur. Where is the bearer of the royal fan?"

He looked around the room expectantly until his disdainful gaze came to rest once again on Lola.

"Art thou alone?" asked Lord Six-Rabbit. "Where are the other servants and the guards? Explain thyself, girl! Speak!"

"Firstly, I'm *not* a servant. Secondly, if you want me to help your mother, you'd better ask me nicely," said Lola, coldly. Then, seeing the look of amazement on the monkey king's face, she added: "*Your Majesty.*"

The king was evidently lost for words. While he stood there open-mouthed, his mother fell to the floor, coughing painfully. She crawled over to her son and clutched at his legs, motioning that he should talk to Lola.

"So . . . do you want me to help her or not?" asked Lola.

"Art thou a shaman?"

"No. But I think I know what's happening. Seri is throttling your mother from the inside, to express her disapproval of the monkey fur robe."

"It was just a bit of trim," wheezed Lady K'an Kakaw.

"And who, pray, is Seri?" asked Lord Six-Rabbit.

"She's your mother's . . . er . . . hostess. Do you mind if I rub her back?"

Lord Six-Rabbit looked appalled. "Dost thou dare suggest that a commoner might touch the body of a royal personage?"

"Technically, it's Seri's body and a back rub might calm her down a bit," said Lola. "With due respect, Your Majesty, she needs help."

He looked at his mother's furry body, which was now convulsing on the floor.

"Proceed," he said.

Lola gently stroked the monkey's back, crooning in monkey language. For her guests' benefit, she said: "Calm down, Seri. Her Royal Highness is an honored guest in your body." A series of protesting squawks emerged from the monkey's throat. "I know, I know, it's not easy. You'll just have to learn to live with each other."

After a few final whimpers, Seri seemed to calm down and release her grip.

"Thank you, my dear," said Lady K'an Kakaw to Lola.

"I'm sorry about Seri's behavior," said Lola, "it's really quite out of character. All this has come as a bit of a shock to her and her brother Chulo."

"But my dear, I had no idea that baboons had feelings!"

"Of course they don't," sneered Lord Six-Rabbit. "They're the lowest form of life. Everyone knows that baboons are rejects from the Great Sky God's first attempt to make mankind. That's why they're all so ugly. Flat-nosed dwarves . . . "

Lord Six-Rabbit fell to the floor, clutching his throat.

Lola and Lady K'an Kakaw watched, fascinated, as the king and the monkey rolled around, slugging it out in the same body. Lola had never seen anyone try to strangle themselves and bite themselves at the same time.

"What's your name, my dear?" Lady K'an Kakaw was asking her.

"My Maya name is Ix Sak Lool."

"Lady White Flower?"

"Yes, but most people call me Lola."

"Lo-la." Lady K'an Kakaw rolled her tongue around it. "What does that mean?"

"It doesn't mean anything. It's just a nickname."

"Lo-la. I like it."

"Thank you," smiled Lola. "And your name means Yellow Cacao Bean, doesn't it?"

"No! How ugly that sounds! *K'an* can be 'yellow,' but it also suggests ripeness, something perfect and precious. *Kakaw* is cacao, but we used the beans for money, so it has a sense of treasure and riches. It's more like Lady Perfect Precious Treasure of Accumulated Wealth Through Judicious Trading of Cocoa Beans."

"That's pretty," said Lola, politely, "but it's a little long."

"Hmmm," said the monkey, thoughtfully, "what I need is a nickname, I've always wanted one . . . "

"Lady Precious? Lady Treasure . . . ?" suggested Lola. "I've got it! Lady Coco!"

"I love it!" said the monkey, jumping up and down with excitement.

"Over my dead body!" growled Lord Six-Rabbit. He'd managed to pacify Chulo, but his voice was still hoarse from the self-inflicted throttling. "I forbid thee to affect this ridiculous appellation."

"That settles it," said his mother. "Lady Coco it is."

Lord Six-Rabbit turned his back in disdain. He stalked over to the window, climbed on a chair, and looked out moodily, still furious at his mother. But as he stood there, his little body visibly relaxed. He put his head against the screen and inhaled.

"Aaaah," he said, "how I have missed the smell of sweet, wet earth."

Lady Coco sniffed the air. "Yes, these noses are so much better than our human ones. I can smell bananas and mangoes and . . . oh, that's disgusting! Is that you, Six-Rabbit?" She grimaced and sniffed again. "Oh no, it's me . . . this body stinks!"

Lord Six-Rabbit buried his nose in his own fur.

"By quetzal!" he said, coughing. "What a torment to have a sensitive nose when thine own body reeks like a dung heap."

Choking noises suggested that Chulo had taken offense again.

"Chulo, stop it!" cried Lola. "It's high time you had a wash. Here, let me show you the bathroom, Your Majesties. I think you'll enjoy the technology."

Lola showed the monkeys how to work the shower and, after some hesitation, put out the hand-milled French lavender soap that Hermanjilio had once brought back from a lecture trip in Europe. Just before she left the room, she turned to speak again. "Please join us in the plaza for breakfast when . . . "

Her voice tailed off as she took in the extraordinary sight in front of her eyes.

Lord Six-Rabbit, wearing a towel as a cloak, was standing on the sink surveying himself lugubriously in the mirror. Lady Coco was swinging and somersaulting on the shower rail like an Olympic gymnast. Somehow they'd managed to open every single bottle and jar in the cabinet, and the contents were daubed around the bathroom.

"I'll . . . er . . . leave you to it then," said Lola, backing out, but the monkeys didn't notice her.

She was still complaining as she helped Max set the breakfast table.

"You should have seen the mess," she fumed. "Well, if they think I'm cleaning up after them . . . "

"I wouldn't get on the wrong side of them if I were you," said Max. "They're not your cuddly monkeys anymore. They could have you sacrificed in the blink of an eye."

Hermanjilio emerged from the cooking hut with a plate of fried bread and a bowl of fruit. He was limping slightly and he looked dreadful, as though he hadn't slept a wink.

"I was just saying," said Lola, "that our guests have trashed the bathroom."

"Blame Chulo and Seri," said Hermanjilio. "It probably takes a while for this possession thing to take hold. I'm sure our guests will start acting like nobility soon enough. They just have to learn to control their inner monkeys."

"In that case," said Lola, "I think they're in the wrong bodies. Lord Six-Rabbit is serious like Seri. But Lady Coco's full of fun like Chulo."

"Lady Coco?" chorused Max and Hermanjilio.

"She wanted a nickname," said Lola. "I think it suits her."

"Well, if she's dropped all her airs and graces, maybe she'll clean up the bathroom herself," suggested Max.

"Just give them a chance to settle in," said Hermanjilio. "Last night was hard on all of us. I know I've got the worst headache of my life this morning and I didn't even drink much balché." He groaned and sat down at the table, laying his head on his arms. "Wake me up when our guests appear."

In fact, it was the reek of lavender that woke him. You didn't need a monkey nose to know that the two soft and fluffy specimens descending the ladder had used rather a lot of Lola's precious French soap.

She opened her mouth to protest, but Hermanjilio cut in.

"Lord Six-Rabbit! Lady Coco! It is such an honor to make your acquaintance. If there is anything we can do to make you more comfortable, you have only to ask."

But the king and his mother weren't listening. They were standing in the plaza, looking back and forth between the temple and the ruins of the royal palace.

"What is this place?" asked Lord Six-Rabbit.

"Itzamna," said Hermanjilio.

"Itzamna?" they repeated in bewilderment.

"Welcome home, Your Majesties," smiled Lola. She thought they'd be happy to hear this, but the monkeys looked distraught.

"It cannot be," said Lady Coco, looking round. "*Our* Itzamna was surrounded by fields and fertile terraces. Where are the markets, the houses, the workshops? Fifty thousand people lived in this city. Where are they?" Her gaze settled at the far end of the plaza. "My palace," she wailed.

Lord Six-Rabbit's liquid monkey eyes looked sadder than ever. He pointed mournfully toward the ruins at the other end of the plaza. "That overgrown mound," he whispered, "could it be the great Temple of Itzamna?"

Hermanjilio nodded.

"My father is entombed beneath those stones," cried Lord Six-Rabbit. "What enemy dared desecrate his memory?"

"That enemy was time, Your Majesty," said Hermanjilio. "The Golden Age of Itzamna was twelve hundred years ago."

"Twelve hundred years," repeated Lord Six-Rabbit wonderingly. "Like a whirlpool, time encircles me and confounds my memory in its bubbling waters." He looked Hermanjilio squarely in the eye. "It is my understanding that we were born many *bak'tuns* apart. And yet I feel I have known thee all my life. Who art thou, sir?"

Hermanjilio tried to avoid the monkey's intense gaze.

"My name is Hermanjilio Bol, Your Majesty. I am a descendant of Lord Hurumak. As the guardian of the Green Jaguar, it was I who summoned you here."

"Then I should thank thee, sir," said Lord Six-Rabbit, "for I am glad to walk in Middleworld again."

While the men were talking, Lady Coco had noticed the bowl of fruit and was looking at it longingly.

"Would you like something to eat?" said Lola.

"Yes please, my dear. Where is the women's table?"

"We'll all be sitting together."

"Disgraceful!" tutted Lord Six-Rabbit.

"Delightful!" smiled Lady Coco.

"Excuse me, Your Majesties, while I go and fry some eggs," said Hermanjilio.

Lord Six-Rabbit looked puzzled. "Lord Hermanjilio," he said, "thou hast the look of a noble warrior, yet thou dost act like a kitchen servant. Cooking is woman's work. Let us talk, man to man. Send the girl for the food."

Hermanjilio smiled meaningfully at Lola.

Reluctantly, she went to look for the frying pan. It wasn't that she minded cooking, so much as she was bad at it. She just hoped these fried eggs would turn out better than her last attempts, which had bounced off the plates like rubber balls.

Lord Six-Rabbit bounded over to the table and took the stool at its head, where Hermanjilio usually sat. Hermanjilio, who'd been making his way to the same place, was left standing.

For a moment, the monkey and the archaeologist locked glances in a battle of wills. Hermanjilio's gaze was bleary but un-wavering. Lord Six-Rabbit stared back as autocratically as a monkey could.

"Chill," whispered Lola to Hermanjilio, as she brought in the plates.

"Of course," said Hermanjilio, graciously ceding his place.

"What was all that about?" whispered Max to Lola.

"It's the dominant male thing again," she said. "They both think they're king of Itzamna."

"Wilt thou tell me about my people?" Lord Six-Rabbit asked Hermanjilio. "Tell me what has happened in Middleworld since that day, five hundred years ago, when thine own ancestors called upon me to curse the Spanish ship. Were we victorious?"

"Sadly not, Your Majesty," said Hermanjilio.

As Lord Six-Rabbit heard how the Jaguar Stones had been lost and all the great Maya cities were now in ruins, his monkey face grew sadder and sadder.

"Hast thou no good news for me?" he asked.

Hermanjilio thought for a moment. "The Maya held out for two hundred years longer than the Aztecs," he said cheerily. "In fact, if the Aztecs hadn't gone down so easily, the Spanish may never have conquered the Maya at all."

"The Aztecs! A flash in history's pan!" sneered Lord Six-Rabbit. "This tale of cowardice does not surprise me. They were always happier slaying children on their altars than fighting man to man on the battlefield. When the Spanish came, with their dastardly firearms, I'll wager they yielded like old women."

"Excuse me," said Lady Coco, "but an old *Maya* woman would fight to the death."

"'Tis true," nodded Lord Six-Rabbit. "So how did the Spanish breach our defenses, Lord Hermanjilio?'

"Most of the Maya killed by the Spanish did not die in battle."

Lord Six-Rabbit leapt angrily onto the table and grabbed a large banana that he brandished like a sword. "Dost thou imply that they died like cowards?"

"Not all. But brave as the Maya were, they could not fight the new diseases brought unwittingly from Spain."

Lord Six-Rabbit's shoulders slumped sadly and he let the banana fall.

Hermanjilio deemed it safe to continue. "You should also know, Your Majesty, that in some places they used your beliefs against you. They convinced your priests that your defeat was written in the stars. It became a self-fulfilling prophecy."

"You see?" said Lady Coco. "I've always thought it was ridiculous to put all your trust in fate. Astrology has its place, but so does common sense."

"I did not know thou wert such an anarchist, Mother."

"It makes my blood boil to think of my people being tricked like that. Just think what would have happened if we'd all stood firm."

"Like Nachankan," said Hermanjilio. "He stood firm. He was a great Maya chief from the north. When the Spanish demanded tributes from him, he said he'd give them *"turkeys in the shape of spears and corn in the shape of arrows."*

The two monkeys found this hilarious. They were still repeating it and slapping their thighs when Lola brought in the platter of eggs.

"Omelets! Delicious!" said Hermanjilio.

Lola glared at him. "They're fried eggs," she said. "They just got a bit broken."

Lord Six-Rabbit assumed command of the table. "Thirteen thanks for all our blessings and blessings yet to come," he began. He then thanked the wild turkeys that laid the eggs, the earth that grew the corn for the tortillas, the trees that bore the fruit, the rivers for water to drink, the air that gives man breath and so on, until he had given thanks for every minute aspect of his life in this reincarnation. By the time he'd finished, the eggs were looking distinctly cold and congealed.

"And we thank Lord Hermanjilio for his hospitality," added Lady Coco.

It was the last civilized moment of the meal.

Perhaps the hunger of twelve hundred years superseded the constraint of table manners. Or perhaps Chulo and Seri broke free and gave vent to their inner monkeys.

Whatever the cause, the breakfast was soon in chaos.

Lady Coco jumped straight onto the table and sat on top of the fruit bowl.

"Mother! Off the table! Hast thou lost thy mind?" shouted Lord Six-Rabbit.

Lady Coco considered this question for a moment, then lobbed a banana skin at her son, quickly followed by a ripe papaya that exploded on contact with his head and showered him with small black seeds. Lord Six-Rabbit jumped onto the table to retaliate and the two monkeys started wrestling, tails lashing, pots crashing, food flying until Hermanjilio and Max pried them apart,

"So these guys are going to save the world?" sighed Max. "They're not exactly the great warriors I was expecting."

Lord Six-Rabbit looked at Max and bared his teeth.

Lady Coco balanced giddily on the back of a chair and attempted a little decorum, an effect that was rather diminished by the raffia fruit bowl she now wore like a rakish straw hat.

"I do apologize," she said, trying to sound dignified. "I can assure you this is not our usual . . . "

Her concentration lapsed as she watched her son use his tail to grab a mango and bring it to his open mouth. "Let me try that," she screeched.

Soon both monkeys were fully absorbed in experimenting with their newly discovered prehensile tails.

It was the craziest breakfast Max had ever experienced.

At one point, Lady Coco bounced over to perch beside him. "And who are you, Young Lord? Are you of royal birth? Who is your father?"

"My father is an archaeologist," said Max. She looked blank, so he added: "He studies history."

"A wise man," said Lord Six-Rabbit, nodding sagely. "It is only by studying the past that we can predict the future. What has happened before will happen again." He upended the jug of juice. "Speaking of which, I feel a strange sense of familiarity. Art thou sure we have not met before, Lord Hermanjilio?"

Hermanjilio shook his head. "Perhaps I remind you of my ancestor, Lord Hurumak?"

Lady Coco turned confidentially to Lola. "His nickname was Hurumak the Heart Stealer," she murmured.

"Was that because he had a lot of girlfriends?" smiled Lola.

"No," replied Lady Coco. "It was because he used to rip out his captives' hearts with his fingernails. Kept them sharpened like claws for the purpose. You should have seen the surprise on his victims' faces!" She chuckled at the memory. "Mind you, his wife said those nails played havoc with her soft furnishings."

Lord Six-Rabbit was staring at Hermanjilio. "Not Hurumak, but someone . . . " He shook his head. "My memory fails me. I fear my brain was addled by the rituals. Tell me again, why didst thou summon me?"

"Your people need you," said Hermanjilio. "The cycle of destruction has begun again. A descendant of Friar Diego DeLanda has crawled out of the woodwork. "

"Then I shall curse him to hell as I cursed his loathsome ancestor."

"It's too late for that. He's got his hands on the Black Jaguar. When Ah Pukuh takes control of the new *bak'tun*, the way will be clear for evil to rule the world."

"There is no time to lose," said Lord Six-Rabbit. "Let us draw up our battle plans."

"Wait!" said Lady Coco, who'd been listening closely as she dangled from the tree by her tail. "In all that you have said, Lord Hermanjilio, there is one name you have not mentioned."

"And who would that be?"

"Tzelek!" She spat out the word like a curse.

"What does Tzelek have to do with it?"

"You said yourself that the *bak'tun* is about to change. Such an opportunity for chaos and destruction occurs only once every four hundred years. Do you really think Tzelek would miss that? Ah Pukuh is one of his closest cronies and they've made all sorts of plans together. It was common knowledge in Xibalba that Tzelek was hanging around the surface, trying to find a way through."

Max remembered the grip on his ankle in the Temple of Itzamna. Could it have been Tzelek . . . ? Just the thought of it made him tremble.

"Does your half brother have long, bony fingers?" he asked Lord Six-Rabbit.

"It may be so. But, at least his face, unlike thine, doth not resemble a wild pig's buttocks!"

"Excuse me?" said Max, shocked at this unexpected insult from the lips of royalty.

Lord Six-Rabbit appeared to be caught up in some internal power struggle. Finally, in a strangulated voice, he said: "I am sorry for my words, Young Lord. It seems my monkey host bears thee much ill will. He forces me to insult thee."

"That sounds like Chulo," said Max. "But what's his problem with me?

"Jealousy, Young Lord. He fears that Lady Lola favors thee above him."

"He thinks she likes me, does he?" smiled Max. Had Lola actually confided in Chulo, he wondered, or was this just monkey paranoia?

"Hup! Hup! With thy red hair and white skin, thou glowest in the dark like a matchstick!" his monkey rival taunted him through Lord Six-Rabbit's lips.

Max started to protest that his hair was brown, then changed his mind and blew the monkey a kiss. If Chulo's insults meant Lola liked him, they were music to his ears.

"Chulo!" admonished Lola. "We don't have time for this."

"At last, someone who understands the gravity of the situation," came a voice from the trees. Lola looked up and saw Lady Coco, sitting on a branch, chewing leaves.

"So when did Tzelek get through the gateway?" Lola called up to her.

"Who knows, my dear," answered Lady Coco, between

mouthfuls, "Maya time is different from yours. But I'll wager ten baskets of cocoa beans that he's here. I expect he glimpsed a hole in the gateway and squeezed through like the cockroach he is." She jumped down to the ground and licked her fingers. "You mark my words, if there's evil afoot in Middleworld, Tzelek is involved in it up to his villainous neck."

"Then the question we should be asking," said Hermanjilio, "is whose body is Tzelek living in? And I'm sorry to tell you that I think I know the answer."

"Is it me?" said Max in a small voice. "I think he grabbed my ankle in the temple and tried to suck out my soul."

"Surely you'd know if you'd been possessed by Tzelek," said Lola. "Do you get black moods? Do you think evil thoughts? Are you bad-tempered and irrationally angry?"

"Yes," nodded Max. "It's me, isn't it?"

"Of course it's not you!" sighed Hermanjilio in exasperation. "Let us not confuse the emotional turmoil of adolescence with the inner workings of one of history's most evil villains! Guess again."

Blank faces stared back at him.

"Isn't it obvious?" said Hermanjilio. "Who's been playing around with Jaguar Stones? Who has an interest in the black arts? Who would welcome an ally like Tzelek?"

"Count Antonio DeLanda!" burst out Max, in horror.

Hermanjilio nodded gravely.

"Well, that explains why he's been too busy to look for us," said Lola.

"This just gets worse and worse," groaned Max. "Now the evil descendant of one of the most evil men in history has been possessed by the evil spirit of an evil Maya priest. And my parents are caught in the middle of it."

CHAPTER XX

COUNTING THE DAYS

IT WAS TOO awful to contemplate: the fiendish Tzelek in league with the ruthless Count Antonio DeLanda. Between them, they represented twelve hundred years of absolute evil. Who knew what warped scheme they were hatching?

"But why did Tzelek come back? What does he want?" asked Lola.

"He wants what he has always wanted," said Lord Six-Rabbit, "to be the supreme and sacred ruler of Middleworld."

"It's such a cliché," said Max. "Why do baddies always want to rule the world?"

"Deep-seated emotional insecurity masquerading as a superiority complex?" suggested Lola.

They all looked at her in amazement.

"I'm thinking about majoring in psychology," she smiled.

"Whatever," said Max, "it's stupid. An Ancient Maya madman can't just suddenly appear and declare himself king of the world."

"When you have the Black Jaguar," said Hermanjilio, "you can do anything."

"But how?" pressed Max.

"Tzelek will call upon the Black Jaguar to release the Undead Army of Ah Pukuh," said Lord Six-Rabbit. "His timing is perfect. With his crony Ah Pukuh in charge of the new *bak'tun*, he will terrorize the world and install himself as king."

"But this time," said Hermanjilio, "we can assume that his power will not stop at the limits of the Maya realm. This time, all mankind will be enslaved under his dominion."

"If only his mother had given him more quality time," sighed Lady Coco. "Still, at least we know where and when he'll make his move."

"We do?" said Max and Lola.

"We do," confirmed Lord Six-Rabbit. "The place will be the Black Pyramid of Ah Pukuh, otherwise known as the Pyramid of Death. The time will be at the rising of Venus, the death star. And the day will be the dreaded 8 Marksman, on the eve of the new *bak'tun*."

"Why is 8 Marksman always so dreaded?" asked Max.

"Dost thou not keep the days, Young Lord?"

Max shook his head. "My school diary doesn't have the Maya calendar in it."

Lord Six-Rabbit looked shocked. "Then it is no wonder that Middleworld teeters on the brink of destruction. For if mortals have forgotten how to read the days, they are doomed to stumble through time like children wandering across a battlefield."

"If we could focus on the problem at hand," said Lady Coco, "the young lord was asking you about 8 Marksman."

"Ah yes. 8 Marksman is the day of the dead, the day that ends the cycle, the day when worlds collide, the day when the spirits may most easily cross back unto this earthly plane. It is a day of disaster and adversity — "

"Most importantly," interrupted Lady Coco, "it is in three days' time."

"And how long will it take to get to Ah Pukuh from Itzamna?" asked Max.

Lord Six-Rabbit and Hermanjilio spoke at the same time.

"One day," said the Ancient Maya king. "It is an easy march."

"Two days," said the archaeologist, "and it won't be easy."

They looked at each other in surprise.

"The straight stone roads your warriors marched on are long since overgrown," said Hermanjilio. "We'll have to hack our way through every step of the way. Trust me, it will take two days. We leave tomorrow."

They locked eyes as they had done before.

"Forgive me, Lord Six-Rabbit," said Hermanjilio, "but I think I should give the orders. I am, after all, more familiar with the present-day terrain."

"But thou hast never battled against Tzelek," said Lord Six-Rabbit.

"And you have never battled against modern weaponry. De-Landa's men don't fight with obsidian swords and wooden spears, you know."

"No firearms are a match for the fire of vengeance coursing through my veins."

"Let us hope that is the case," said Hermanjilio. "Nonetheless, Itzamna himself has chosen me to lead this mission. It is my destiny."

Lord Six-Rabbit looked away in anger. Then he looked down at his hairy limbs and the fight seemed to go out of him. "I bow to thy judgment. We leave tomorrow."

"And now, if you'll excuse me, I have much to do."

"Thou art dismissed," said Lord Six-Rabbit, imperiously.

As he watched Hermanjilio make his way back to the temple, he furrowed his monkey brow. "There are too many kings at this court," he said. "It may make things difficult at Ah Pukuh."

"Please forgive Hermanjilio," said Lola. "He's got a lot on his mind."

"Proud warriors once trembled when I spoke," mused Lord Six-Rabbit, surveying his monkey body with distaste. "They called me Godlike Jaguar Lord, Great Leader, He of the Twenty Captives."

"Only twenty?" blurted Max.

Lord Six-Rabbit, Lady Coco, and Lola turned in unison to glare at him.

"Do you have to show your ignorance at every opportunity?" asked Lola. "The point of Maya warfare was not to kill your enemy, but to capture the highest born. These weren't just rank and file soldiers, they were powerful kings and nobles. I'd like to see *you* try and capture one."

"Yes," added Lady Coco proudly, "twenty was the record. No one ever took more captives than my Six-Rabbit."

"Those days are long gone, Mother," sighed Lord Six-Rabbit. "How can I command respect in this bag of bones and fur?"

"You're the same person on the inside," said Lady Coco, landing on the table with a thump.

"Yes, Mother, I am the same. I am who I was on the day I was born and all the power of the Jaguar Stones cannot make me one day older."

"Why would you want to be one day older?" asked Max.

"Had I been born one day earlier on 5 Deer, I would have been selfish and dogmatic, taking what I wanted by force. Perhaps I would have had the will to destroy Tzelek. It would have saved the world much grief. But, unfortunately, I have always veered toward generosity. That is why I gave my half brother a second chance."

"You should thank your lucky stars," said Lady Coco, "that you weren't born one day later. 7 Water babies can be weak and sickly all their miserable lives." She turned to Lola. "What is your birth date, my dear?"

"I don't know," said Lola. She jumped up and starting clearing the table.

Lady Coco turned to Max. "And you, Young Lord, when were you born?"

"I don't know," said Max, "at least not in Maya days."

Lord Six-Rabbit and his mother looked at each other in alarm.

"What's the big deal?" asked Max.

Lola put down the dirty dishes. "Our royal guests believe that a person's character and destiny are decided by the day of their birth. You know, like a horoscope — except that a bad one could blight your whole life."

"And a good one could ensure wealth and success," pointed out Lady Coco.

"But it's insane," said Lola. "How could anyone look at a new-born baby and decide it's a liar or a thief?"

"That's just how it was," shrugged Lady Coco. "When your future's been decided by the gods, you don't question it. Besides, it's better to know what to expect."

"I can see your point," said Max. "Instead of agonizing about things, you'd be out there getting on with your lot in life."

Lola looked at him curiously. "I didn't know you agonized about things, Hup."

"I have hidden depths," said Max, trying to look enigmatic.

Lady Coco smiled. "We used to think of boys your age as little crabs who'd shed their first soft shell but had yet to grow the hard carapace of adulthood. It's a vulnerable time — for crabs *and* boys."

Lord Six-Rabbit nodded sagely. "What wilt thou be, Young Lord? Wilt thou study history like thy father?"

"No! Anything but that!" said Max.

"Then how wilt thou find thy true path?"

Max shrugged. "These days, we believe you make your own path. You can be anyone you want to be."

"How liberating!" cried Lady Coco.

"I have never heard such madness," said Lord Six-Rabbit.

"What day were you born on, Your Majesty?" smiled Max.

"6 Rabbit, of course," replied the king, lugubriously.

"Which means . . . ?"

"Children born on Rabbit days are lively and fun-loving," said Lady Coco. "6 signifies a good balance. 1 Rabbit could be a prankster. 13 could be a gambler and a drunkard. But 6 Rabbit is witty and playful."

"My people thought I lived up to my day name so well that it became my nickname," explained Lord Six-Rabbit mournfully.

Max burst out laughing. "I take it they were having a joke," he said.

"Explain thyself," commanded Lord Six-Rabbit.

Max stopped laughing. He realized to his horror that he, Max Murphy of the No Captives Whatsoever, had once again offended the greatest Maya king who had ever lived. "It's just that . . . well . . . " he stammered, "you're not exactly the life and soul of the party, are you?" Max had never seen a monkey look so angry. "And that's a good thing," he continued hastily, "no one wants a comedian for a king."

Lola scowled at him. "Have you lost your mind? Change the subject, quick!" she muttered.

Max plunged in again. "So what's your real name, Your Majesty?" he asked.

"Thou couldst not begin to pronounce it," growled Lord Six-Rabbit.

Max tried again. "Tell me more about nicknames," he said, trying to sound breezy. "Did everyone have one? What about your half brother, Tzelek?"

Lord Six-Rabbit regarded him in silence.

"Tzelek's nickname was Tze'lok," said Lady Coco, glancing anxiously at her son.

"Sounds the same to me," said Max.

Lola rolled her eyes. "*Tzelek*," she said, "means 'Basilisk Lord.' A basilisk is a kind of lizard. *Tze'lok* means a twisted leg or foot."

Lady Coco sniggered.

"I don't get it," said Max. "What's the story?"

"When Tzelek was a child, he tried to sacrifice his best friend on the altar at Itzamna," said Lady Coco. "The boy managed to break free, but in the struggle, Tzelek was knocked off the platform. He fell all the way down the pyramid steps. Sadly, he was unhurt, apart from a broken ankle that never healed properly. It left his foot as twisted as his brain. He used to drag it behind him in the dust. He left a trail like a rattlesnake."

"Really?" said Max. "How interesting."

He stole a glance at Lord Six-Rabbit to see if he was still angry. Lord Six-Rabbit's liquid brown eyes stared back at him. It was obvious that he hadn't been listening to a word of the Tzelek story.

Then the king slowly turned his gaze to Lady Coco.

"Were my people laughing at me, Mother?"

"No," said Lady Coco. "Never. Your nickname might have been a little joke, but it was meant as a sign of affection."

"It was a joke?" echoed Lord Six-Rabbit.

"Stop it, son. Your people worshipped you."

"They had to. I was a living god."

"No, son. They worshipped you for everything you did for them. You brought them peace and prosperity. You were a champion ballplayer, a noble statesman, a fearless warrior. There were those who said that no king could be greater than Punak Ha, but you proved them wrong. The people's only sadness was that you left no son and heir. Your people loved you, Six-Rabbit. They still love you. That's why they call on you."

"Thou hast never said such things before. Art thou laughing at me too?" Lord Six-Rabbit put his head in his hands. "This changes everything. I am a joke . . . "

"Oh, pull yourself together," said Lady Coco impatiently, "it changes nothing. You were a heroic leader who made the city of Itzamna into the glory of our age. And if people found you a little serious, so what? It's not your sense of humor that will win the day for us at Ah Pukuh."

"Let's give them some time alone," whispered Lola to Max. "Come and help me with the washing up."

As they cleared away the dishes, Max glanced anxiously at Lord Six-Rabbit. "Me and my big mouth," he said. "I think our royal champion is having an identity crisis."

"Better now than later," said Lola. "If Lord Six-Rabbit is questioning his true self, he needs to sort it out. When we get to Ah Pukuh, it will be a showdown between good and evil. Anyone not sure of their own heart may be lured to the dark side."

"Might I be lured to the dark side?" asked Max.

"You, Hup? I thought you'd decided to be a good guy."

"I'm trying," smiled Max. "But what if I'm meant to be bad?"

"Nah," said Lola.

"But do you believe all this Maya day stuff?"

"If I ever find out my birthday, I'll let you know," she said.

Back at the table, Lady Coco looked into her son's monkey eyes. "You must face the truth, Six-Rabbit. Tzelek is evil from his balding head to the toes of his stinking, twisted foot. Nothing you can say or do will change him. You must not give him another chance. Being wise and merciful is one thing, but this time you cannot waver. Tzelek must be stopped."

"I understand the situation, Mother."

"Then why didn't you finish him off last time?"

"He is my flesh and blood."

Lady Coco spat onto the ground. "I have never believed that," she said. "Your noble father, Punak Ha, could not have spawned that devil. Tzelek's mother was a witch. She was young and beautiful and she cast a spell over Punak Ha. I tried to warn him, but no one valued the opinion of a woman. I feel more respected as a baboon than I did as a Maya queen."

"Mother! What a thing to say!"

"You don't know what it was like for a woman at court. I was married to a great king, yet my days were spent making tortillas and weaving mats. My only official duty was to pull that awful thorn-lined rope through my tongue at the ritual bloodlettings. I didn't look forward to it, let me tell you. When Punak Ha died, I became invisible, like a living ghost. So I shut myself away and counted down the days until I, too, would die."

"Is that why thou hast come back with me, Mother — to make sure I cannot forget? I know you blame me for my father's death. Is thy existence still so empty that its only purpose is to twist the knife of guilt that lies so deep within my heart?"

Lady Coco saw the anguish in her son's face. "It is time you knew the truth, son," she said. "When your father died, I heard about Tzelek's plot to steal the throne. I wanted to help you, Six-Rabbit. I wrote you a letter to warn you . . . "

"What letter? I received no letter."

"Tzelek intercepted it. I had not realized that half the palace was in his pay. He came to see me in a blazing fury. *'Why does everyone love Six-Rabbit and not me?'* he said. *'My own father, Punak Ha, cared nothing for me. Now you, my father's widow, plot against me. I will not stand for it.'* He told me that if I ever again acted like a mother toward you or said one kind word to you, he would have you murdered."

"Mother, why couldst thou not tell me . . . ?"

"I didn't dare. I knew Tzelek would carry out his threat. So I slapped you and called you names and pretended I blamed you for Punak Ha's death. But I did it out of love for you. And all the while, I was trying to find out what Tzelek was up to and help you in unseen ways. I used to pray to the spirit of your father to show me what to do. He was so proud of you, Six-Rabbit. He *is* still proud of you."

"So you don't blame me for his death?"

"Of course not."

"But still, if only I had not gone hunting that day, Mother."

Lord Six-Rabbit's eyes were fixed on the ruined Temple of Itzamna, his father's final resting place. That pyramid had been Punak Ha's life's work. On the day of its dedication, his father had asked him to stand by his side on the top platform. It wasn't much to ask. But the young Six-Rabbit had slipped away to go hunting instead. How did he know that his father would come looking for him? Or that his father would be ambushed while calling out his name?

When Six-Rabbit had returned that night with his catch (an armadillo that was too small to bother cooking), the conch shell horns and the wooden trumpets were sounding their laments. The next day, Punak Ha's body was entombed in the pyramid and Six-Rabbit was crowned King of Monkey River.

The murderers were never caught.

Lord Six-Rabbit had sworn that day to avenge his father's death by becoming the most fearsome warrior the human world had ever seen. Gorgeous and terrible in his black body paint, jaguar pelts, and quetzal-plumed helmet, he had won every battle he had ever fought.

But he had never vanquished his own conscience.

"I am sorry, Mother. If I had only done as he asked and not gone hunting, perchance he would have lived."

"We don't know that, son. Perhaps it was his day to die."

"Dost thou believe our lives are written in the stars?"

"I believe in second chances, son. What has happened before will happen again. But this time, you can change the outcome."

"I cannot bring my father back."

"But you can honor his name by winning this great victory."

"Can I? Even the mighty Six-Rabbit may not be strong enough to defeat the combined forces of Tzelek and Ah Pukuh."

"But this time," smiled Lady Coco, "I will fight by your side. This is *my* second chance too, Six-Rabbit. When we arrive at the Temple of Ah Pukuh, I promise to be your most loyal and devoted warrior."

"May good prevail," he said.

"That's the spirit, son," smiled Lady Coco. "With you and me on the same team, those villains don't stand a chance!" She nudged him playfully. "Here's what I think of Tzelek and his cronies."

Lord Six-Rabbit watched in amazement as his mother, First and Most Glorious Wife of the Great King Punak Ha, pointed her bony monkey posterior in the air and noisily broke wind.

And then, for the first time in a thousand years, he laughed until his sides ached.

CHAPTER XXI

PREPARING FOR BATTLE

"As I SEE IT," said Max, "all that stands between mankind and the end of the world is two talking monkeys, a crazy archaeologist covered in red paint, and a couple of kids with blowguns? Am I right?"

"Wrong," said Hermanjilio. "I'll be wearing my black paint this time. Now keep practicing."

Max and Lola had been honing their blowgun skills for hours. It was late afternoon, and Max's cheeks were aching, but at least he was starting to hit the target. Lola had graduated to trick shots and several surprised parrots could vouch for the accuracy of her aim.

"But it's going to rain," said Max. "Couldn't we take a break?"

"What, and miss the chance to practice in wet conditions?" said Hermanjilio. While Max and Lola shot their blowguns in the pouring rain, Lord Six-Rabbit brewed up a potion to coat the tips of their darts. He and Hermanjilio had reached an uneasy truce in their power struggle and were attempting to get along.

"Could I not interest thee in something a little stronger, Lord Hermanjilio?" he asked as he stirred his mixture. "It pains me to waste this opportunity. If we added just one small poison dart frog, we could make enough toxin to slay DeLanda and all his men. It would make a fine offering to the gods . . . "

"A strong sleeping drug will be fine, Lord Six-Rabbit," said Hermanjilio. "These days, we tend to shy away from human sacrifice."

"Have it thine own way," muttered Lord Six-Rabbit. "But let us hope that Tzelek is equally well-versed in the etiquette of modern warfare."

When all was ready for their journey, they gathered around the campfire for one last meal.

"This meat is delicious," said Max, "what is it?"

"Iguana," said Lola. "Would you like another skewer, Hup?"

As Max chowed down on the juicy lizard, he marveled that his mother had ever called him a picky eater. He wasn't quite ready to sample the bowl of live termites that Lady Coco was passing around — ("Try them," she urged, "they taste like carrots and they're crunchy too!") — but he reckoned that, these days, he could eat Zia's tamales without complaint.

Once again, he thought back to that last day in Boston with his parents. How he'd turned up his nose at the tamales. How he'd felt unloved because there was only pizza and ice cream for dinner. He wondered if his parents would ever know how much he'd changed. He missed them so much. Somehow, he had to get them out of Xibalba. But first, he swallowed hard, he had to survive the coming battle at the Black Pyramid.

Everyone was quiet around the campfire, thinking about tomorrow's journey to Ah Pukuh. Hermanjilio tried to boost their confidence with tales of daring deeds from Maya legends, but his stories fell as flat as stale tortillas.

There was a sense of foreboding in the air, as if the evil that enveloped the Black Pyramid was already spreading its menace along the coast and through the jungle until it would eventually pollute the whole planet.

"Well, good night then," said Hermanjilio in resignation. "We leave for the Black Pyramid at dawn."

The rest of them murmured their good nights and began to gather up their things. But somehow, with Hermanjilio gone, the atmosphere lightened and they lingered under the stars.

"Look, son," whispered Lady Coco, "look up at the Moon Rabbit."

Max overheard. "The Moon Rabbit? You guys know about the Moon Rabbit? My mom used to make me wave to it when I was little."

Lady Coco smiled.

"Mothers have been pointing out the Moon Rabbit since the beginning of time, Young Lord," she said.

"It's funny," said Max. "I used to wave to it in Boston, but I could never really see it. Tonight it looks so clear. It really looks like a leaping rabbit."

"That's because you're looking at the moon differently now," said Lola.

"You mean, now that I understand more about Maya culture, I can see the moon through your eyes?"

"No," said Lola. "I mean that you're closer to the equator here. In Boston, you were physically viewing the moon from a different angle. I've heard that North Americans can see a man in the moon."

Lord Six-Rabbit looked up, surprised. "I saw a man in the moon once," he said. "And I was right here at Itzamna. Dost thou remember, Mother?"

Lady Coco nodded. "Perhaps it was a sign that one day you'd join forces with this young lord. Your destinies are surely intertwined. And with Ix Chel, the moon goddess, the great mother, watching over you, I know you will win the day."

"Ix Chel?" said Max, suspiciously. "Uncle Ted said she brings floods and storms."

"Like any woman, she has her moods," agreed Lady Coco. "When she's the old moon with a snake on her head and human bones on her skirt, she can be quick to anger. But as the new moon, with her pet rabbit on her lap, she's a beautiful young woman, creative and caring, a patron of motherhood, weaving, and medicine. It's the young goddess that has smiled on you both. She will surely protect you."

Max looked at Lola. She was staring up morosely at the Moon Rabbit. He guessed she was thinking of her own mother, whom she had never known.

He smiled at her sympathetically and reached out to touch her arm.

"I'm going to bed," she said, curtly.

Max got up to walk with her, but Lord Six-Rabbit pulled him back.

"Thou hast won favor with Chulo tonight, Young Lord," he said. "It seems that baby howler monkeys also look at the Moon Rabbit. He likes you better for that."

"Good night, Chulo," smiled Max. "Good night, Your Majesties."

"Good night," said Lord Six-Rabbit.

"Don't let the vampire bats bite!" added Lady Coco.

Max felt like he'd only just gone to sleep when Lola was calling him to wake up. He lay there thinking about the adventure ahead. He didn't want to leave the safety of the tree house and his fear felt like a lead weight pinning him down. As he dragged himself down the ladder, he reflected that their chances of success did not look good.

IT WAS A SOMBER PARTY that made their way through the jungle that day, following the overgrown course of the old Maya causeway. Even the monkeys, who usually kept up a constant chatter as they scouted ahead, swung silently through the trees. Everyone was tense and on edge. Every creature that rustled in the undergrowth made them jump and every new turning seemed fraught with danger.

They made camp before sunset by the banks of a wide cenote. The turquoise waters looked so inviting that Max decided to jump in and cool off. But as he sat down to take off his shoes, he saw a small lizard running across the surface of the water on its hind feet, like a miniature Godzilla.

At last, something to smile at.

"Look at that," he whispered to Lola. "How does it *do* that?"

"Amazing, isn't it?" she agreed. "Some people call it the Jesus lizard because it can walk on water. Something must be chasing it."

They sat stock still and watched as the little creature reached dry land and ran quickly up a tree.

"What are you two doing, just sitting around?" asked Lady Coco, crossly. "Come and help me get this fire going."

"Sorry, Your Majesty," said Lola, "but Max had never seen a basilisk before."

"What?" laughed Max, incredulously. "You mean *that* was a basilisk?"

"Where?" asked Lady Coco, scampering over. She scanned the cenote anxiously. "Has it gone? What are you laughing at, Young Lord?"

"When you said Tzelek was named after a basilisk," explained Max, "I was thinking of that dragonlike thing in Greek mythology. I didn't realize that the big scary priest is named after a tiny little lizard. You have to admit, that's kind of funny."

Lola and Lady Coco weren't laughing.

"Tzelek is well named," said Lady Coco. "You could learn a lot about him by studying his fellow lizards. They're all cunning escapologists and masters of disguise. They can change their colors and their patterns. Most of them will shed their own tails to avoid capture. The horned lizard even squirts blood out of its eyes to defend itself."

They became aware of being watched. A large green iguana, maybe seven feet long, had emerged from the jungle and stopped in his tracks to check them out.

"Shoo! Scram! Vamoose!" screeched Lady Coco, waving her arms at it wildly.

The iguana, seemingly unimpressed by its first encounter with a talking monkey, flicked its tongue at her a couple of times before lumbering right past her on its way down to the cenote.

Lady Coco shivered. "I sometimes think that all the reptiles in Middleworld are in league with that cold-blooded monster, Tzelek."

Max surveyed the huge scaly body of the iguana, as it drank from the cenote. As if sensing his scrutiny, it stopped drinking and slowly looked up, its hooded eyes appraising him without a trace of fear.

"Let's build a big fire tonight," said Max.

NEXT DAY, THROUGH rain and sun, they tramped steadfastly on. By late afternoon, the monkeys' noses had just detected the tang of sea air when a fierce storm blew up out of nowhere.

Struggling through the downpour, the bedraggled little militia worked its way along a ridge of hills toward the coast. When they rounded the last hill, they had a clear view to the ocean. Below them, the hill dropped away into jungle. Rising out of this jungle, set against a backdrop of black clouds and angry waves, was the city of Ah Pukuh.

It was every bit as forbidding as Max had imagined it.

As the thunder raged and the lightning flashed, he looked across at this ancient city that had taken the ways of darkness to its heart. Through the driving rain, he saw how it was built on a finger of rock pointing into the ocean. At the tip of the finger were the ruins of several overgrown buildings, dominated by a massive stepped pyramid.

The Pyramid of Death.

As Max watched, a bolt of lightning struck the pyramid and threw the stones into sharp relief. For a few seconds, the temple on the top platform was illuminated, and he saw to his horror that the façade had been carved into the shape of a snarling jaguar head. The dark void of the doorway was through the beast's gaping maw.

Would he ever have to go through that doorway?

Max's heart was beating wildly at the thought of what tomorrow might bring.

Then all was calm again.

The storm stopped as suddenly as it had started. The sky turned dusky blue and the birds began to sing. As the setting sun cast its glow over the pale green sea, it looked like a scene out of a travel brochure.

"It all looks so pretty now," said Lola, amazed at the transformation.

"Don't be fooled, my dear," said Lady Coco. "Malevolence hovers over this place like gas off a swamp. The very air is cursed. For it was here that the priests and sorcerers of Ah Pukuh developed their dark powers."

"And it was here, on the Black Pyramid," added Lord Six-Rabbit, "that Tzelek last raised the Undead Army and unleashed the fury that tore the Maya world apart."

"Look!" whispered Lola.

Squinting into the sunset, Max could see several armed workers moving about on the top platform of the pyramid. They had already cleared away most of the vegetation and it looked like their work was nearly done. From the roof comb at the very top of the temple, where vultures wheeled in search of carrion, a lookout guard was scanning the whole area.

"They look like DeLanda's men all right," said Max.

Lola was craning her neck, this way and that way, counting off the guards on her fingers. "I make it twenty," she said.

Max's head was pounding from the heat and the thunder and the fear. This is suicide, he thought, we should never have come here. We're hopelessly outnumbered. The guards will pick us off like ducks in a shooting gallery. Out loud, he said: "Twenty of them against five of us. That's four to one."

"The boy makes a good point," said Hermanjilio. "Tell me, Lord Six-Rabbit, as the most experienced warrior among us, what do you suggest we do next?"

"The first rule of war," answered Lord Six-Rabbit, "is to know thine enemy. I therefore propose that Mother and I infiltrate the camp to gather information. We will try to discover where the Black Jaguar is hidden."

"No!" cried Lola, "It's too dangerous."

"It's all right, Lady Lola," said Lady Coco. "I know you're concerned for Chulo and Seri, but DeLanda's men have no reason to shoot two friendly baboons."

"They don't need a reason," said Lola.

Lord Six-Rabbit stood straight and proud like the warrior he used to be. "Allow us to do the task we were summoned here to do," he said and started off toward the city.

"Don't worry," said Lady Coco, "we'll be careful." She gave Lola a quick hug before following her son into the valley.

Hours passed.

The rest of them made camp at the edge of the jungle.

Night fell.

Occasionally, a shout or a curse or a burst of raucous laughter would drift over from DeLanda's camp. But no monkeys returned.

"What's taking them so long? Why aren't they back yet?" fretted Lola.

"They can take care of themselves," Max reassured her.

Hermanjilio was less sympathetic. "Lola, you must get a grip on your emotions," he said. "This is a war. There may well be casualties."

Suddenly, a shot rang out.

Lola froze. "Chulo! Seri!" she cried.

There was a rustling in the undergrowth and before Hermanjilio could draw his knife, Lady Coco leapt into the middle of the campsite.

"We're doomed, we're all doomed," she wailed.

"What's happened? Where's Chulo?" said Lola.

"Here," said the voice of Lord Six-Rabbit. He stepped out of the bushes and sat down heavily by the campfire.

"Are you hurt?" asked Lola, "What was that shot?"

"I know not. 'Twas behind me . . . perchance a guard discharged his weapon at a tree squirrel. DeLanda's men are as jumpy as a barrel of bullfrogs."

"Now tell them the bad news," sighed Lady Coco. "Tell them what we heard!"

"What? What was it?" asked the others anxiously.

"The Chee Ken of Death," said Lord Six-Rabbit. "We did not see it, but we heard its infernal crowing. It seemed to come from behind the cooking hut. I doubt my sleeping draught will work on that scaly devil."

"A chicken? You were scared by a chicken?" said Max. He and Lola looked at Hermanjilio expectantly. Surely it was time to come clean about Thunderclaw?

Apparently not.

"Don't worry, Lord Six-Rabbit," said Hermanjilio. "I believe I am more than a match for this Chee Ken."

"Thou art truly a brave man, Lord Hermanjilio."

"To think you would attack a chicken single-handed," said Lola in mock admiration.

"Will you use a knife — or a fork?" asked Max, trying to keep a straight face.

Hermanjilio had the grace to look embarrassed. "Never mind the chicken," he said. "Were you able to find out where they're keeping the Black Jaguar?"

"I think so, Lord Hermanjilio. That lily-livered coward DeLanda is still hiding out at sea. It would be my guess that the Black Jaguar is with him."

"That sounds likely," mused Hermanjilio. "He probably won't show himself until the last minute. We must be ready to move quickly."

"So what's the plan?" asked Max.

Hermanjilio and Lord Six-Rabbit both opened their mouths to speak. The Maya king saw the resolve on the archaeologist's face and deferred to him.

"When the time draws near," said Hermanjilio, "we'll drug the guards' food and knock out any stragglers with blowguns. When DeLanda comes ashore, we'll ambush him, steal the Black Jaguar, and be long gone before his guards wake up."

"And then?" objected Lola. "Surely, he'll track us down and kill us? DeLanda-slash-Tzelek won't give in just like that. There's too much at stake."

"And let's not forget my parents in all this," said Max.

"First we find the Black Jaguar," said Hermanjilio. "Everything else will follow."

Max felt intensely irritated. These archaeologists were all the same. Worrying about their precious artifacts when they should be thinking about human beings. Still, at least they'd have a bargaining chip with DeLanda if they had the Black Jaguar. And if this stuff about Tzelek and Ah Pukuh were true, they might even avert the end of the world as we know it. Not a bad day's work.

"So how do we make a clean getaway?" he asked.

"I think I can answer that," said Lord Six-Rabbit. "I know this place like the back of my paw."

"Why would *you* know the Black Pyramid?" asked Max suspiciously. "I thought only bad guys hung out here? You're one of the good guys . . . aren't you?"

"I would like to think so," smiled Lord Six-Rabbit. "But while Ah Pukuh himself has always been the most cruel and feared of the Maya gods, the city that bore his name was not always rotten to the core. Before it was corrupted by Tzelek, in the days when good and evil were in balance, Ah Pukuh was one of the five sacred pyramids of the Monkey River. My father used to bring me here to celebrate victories in war. We would stand on the top platform and bow to the cheering crowds below. And then — pouf! — when the smoke cleared, we were gone!"

"How?" asked the rest of them, in unison.

"We would make our way down inside the temple to a secret passage, known only to the Jaguar Kings. It led to a labyrinth of caves and tunnels that crisscrossed the whole region. 'Twas possible to travel many leagues underground before emerging. There were exit points all over the jungle."

"Like a Maya subway system?" suggested Max.

"I know not about this subway, but I can tell thee it was a merry trick. The people loved it. 'Twas almost as popular as sawing the slave in half."

"Except that sawing the slave in half wasn't a trick," pointed out Lady Coco. "You really did saw him in half."

"But this passageway," said Hermanjilio, "why doesn't Tzelek know about it?"

"Try as they might, high priests did not know everything," said Lord Six-Rabbit. "In fact, given their talent for making mischief, we kings tried to tell them as little as possible. Passageways like this one were a closely guarded secret, passed down from king to king. 'Twas not just a matter of knowing the way. Ever-changing tests and traps are built into the walls — a trespasser would not survive."

"How do we know the passage is still there after all these centuries?" asked Lola.

"Good question," said Hermanjilio. "Lord Six-Rabbit, perhaps you could check it out for us? As a monkey, you'll be able to sneak around without suspicion."

"I would do so gladly, Lord Hermanjilio, but this stunted

baboon body cannot operate the secret door. One of thy number must accompany me. "

"I'll go," said Lola, without hesitation.

"Thou hast the heart of a true Maya warrior," said Lord Six-Rabbit, approvingly.

"Thank you," smiled Lola. "So where's the nearest entrance?"

"There are many places to exit the secret passageway, but there is only one point of entry."

Lola's smile was fading. "Don't tell me . . . "

Lord Six-Rabbit nodded. "We must enter through the Pyramid of Death."

"Rather you than me," said Max. Then he felt guilty because he could see that Lola was having second thoughts. "No, I'm sure it'll be fine," he said. "I mean it can't be worse than Chaak or Itzamna, can it?"

Lola turned to Lord Six-Rabbit. "Please tell me what to expect."

"Some things are easier to face if thou art not already dreading them."

"What is there to dread?" said Lola. Her voice was tight with fear.

"Tell her the truth, son," instructed Lady Coco. "Forewarned is forearmed."

"It is not possible to arm thyself against the terrors of the Black Pyramid," said Lord Six-Rabbit. "Particularly at this time."

Lola and Max were exchanging anxious glances.

"I don't like the sound of this," said Max. "It's too dangerous.

"If Lady Lola obeys my orders," said Lord Six-Rabbit, "we will complete our mission safely, I promise thee."

"So why can't you tell her what's inside?"

Lord Six-Rabbit sighed. "It is always perilous for a mortal to enter one of the sacred pyramids. But never more so than at the changing of *bak'tuns*. The pyramids hold gateways to the underworld, and at this time, they are all wide open. The demons roam at large and the spirit roads are as busy as a village on market day."

"OK . . ." said Lola, trying to sound casual, "so there are demons. Is that it?"

"No," said Lady Coco. "there's worse."

Lord Six-Rabbit tried to look as if he didn't know what she was talking about.

"Tell her, son," said Lady Coco.

"Mother, I do not think . . . "

"*Tell her!*"

Lord Six-Rabbit sighed. "The Black Pyramid is the last resting place of all thirteen generations of the Lords of Ah Pukuh. They were renowned for their military prowess, and by tradition, it was they who trained the armies of the Jaguar Kings. But when Tzelek took command of Ah Pukuh, he cast a spell on the ranks of the entombed. Their corpses became the earthly bodies for the Demon Warriors of Xibalba. The dead lords fought for Tzelek against my Jaguar Army in the battle that killed us both. Still they lie in the Black Pyramid, dressed in full battle gear, awaiting the call to arms. They feel no pain, they have no fear, they cannot die for they are dead already. I have no doubt that Tzelek will use the Black Jaguar to awaken them in the new *bak'tun*."

"But at the moment, they're still sleeping?" said Lola.

"That is my assumption," said Lord Six-Rabbit.

"So we have demons on the loose," tallied Lola. "And we have an undead army of zombie corpses. Anything else?"

"No," said Lord Six-Rabbit. "Unless . . . "

"Unless what?" said Lola, with a note of hysteria.

Lord Six-Rabbit took a deep breath. "As thou knowest, the god Ah Pukuh will rule Middleworld in the new *bak'tun*. We cannot discount the possibility that he has come to the Black Pyramid to prepare for his coronation. He may be in there at this moment, feasting with his cohorts and planning his reign of terror. So when thou dost ask what lies ahead, I can say only that I will protect thee. But as to what Ah Pukuh may have in store for us, thy guess is as good as mine."

It was Hermanjilio who broke the stunned silence.

"That's settled then," he said.

"You mean they shouldn't go?" said Max, relieved.

"No, I mean Lord Six-Rabbit will take good care of our precious Lola."

"I thank thee for thy trust, Lord Hermanjilio," said Lord Six-Rabbit.

"Meanwhile," said Hermanjilio. "I'll take a closer look at De-Landa's defenses. Lady Coco, please come with me and provide the necessary distractions."

"My pleasure," said Lady Coco.

"Just keep thy wits about thee, Mother," said Lord Six-Rabbit gently. "Remember, thou art my most loyal and devoted warrior. I need thee to support me."

"Don't worry about me, son," she smiled. "After a lifetime of waving off the menfolk, I'm ready for some action. And now, if you'll excuse me, I must go and practice my most entertaining baboon mannerisms."

They all got up to start preparing for their various missions.

"What about me?" asked Max "What should I do?"

Hermanjilio put a hand on his shoulder.

"To you, Max, falls the most important job."

"What's that?" said Max, warily.

"You will stay here and guard the camp."

Max could have cried with relief. He could have thrown himself at Hermanjilio's feet and kissed his battered old tennis shoes. Yes! Yes! Yes! He didn't have to go inside another pyramid. He didn't have to go anywhere near DeLanda's camp. All he had to do was keep the campfire going and toast the odd tortilla. Then he realized that Lola and Lord Six-Rabbit were listening.

"That's not fair," he said. "Why can't I go on a mission like everyone else? I've trained as hard as anyone. I'm ready to go into battle."

"Then take your orders, soldier," barked Hermanjilio. "You don't have the skills to move through the jungle without drawing attention to yourself. You'd endanger us all. We all have our own tasks to fulfill in this unit. You're staying here and that's final."

Max was so happy he could have danced a jig. He pretended to clench his fists in anger. "Yes, sir," he replied, in the surliest voice he could muster.

Lola and Lord Six-Rabbit shot him sympathetic glances.

He shrugged as if to say, "*You go ahead and enjoy yourselves, don't worry about me,*" and tried to smile bravely. Then he turned away quickly, so they wouldn't see his smile broaden into a huge grin. There would be no demons and zombies for him.

"Get some rest, everyone," said Hermanjilio. "We have a big night ahead."

CHAPTER XXII

THE BLACK PYRAMID

SOME TIME IN the early hours, Max was awakened by someone grabbing his shoulder and shaking him.

"Rise and shine," said Hermanjilio. "It's time to get ready."

"Ready for what?" slurred Max groggily.

"You can't guard the camp if you're sleeping."

Max rubbed his eyes and peered at Hermanjilio. At first he thought he was still dreaming. In the moonlight, all he could see of the archaeologist were the whites of his eyes and the pink of his mouth. The rest of him was covered in black body paint.

"Great camouflage, Professor," he said. "They won't see *you* coming."

Hermanjilio put his hands on his hips and turned his head sideways like a warrior on an Ancient Maya fresco. "They won't see me coming," he said, "because I am the invisible jaguar of the night."

Max laughed, then realized that Hermanjilio wasn't joking.

"Go get 'em, tiger," he said, under his breath, as Hermanjilio melted into the jungle with Lady Coco scampering at his heels.

Lola and Lord Six-Rabbit were getting ready to head off in the other direction.

"Art thou ready?" said Lord Six-Rabbit to Lola.

She nodded.

Max tried not to show his glee at being left behind. "Good luck in the Pyramid of Death," he said, trying to sound envious.

Lola looked at Lord Six-Rabbit.

Lord Six-Rabbit looked at Max.

"Art *thou* ready?" he asked.

Max's stomach sank into the ground. "But Hermanjilio said . . . ?"

"I do not see him here, Young Lord, dost thou?"

Lord Six-Rabbit tossed Max a blowgun. He dropped it. "But I can't come with you," he said, "who's going to guard the camp?"

"It can guard itself, Hup," said Lola. "Don't let Hermanjilio bully you."

"Thou wast trained as a warrior, not a night watchman. It is only fitting that thou shouldst join us on this skirmish. It will limber thee up for the main battle tomorrow."

"Yes, you looked so disappointed when Hermanjilio said you had to stay behind," said Lola. Her voice was filled with admiration and Max savored it for a moment, before pulling himself together.

"The thing is," he said, "much as I would like to come with you, it's out of the question. Hermanjilio is my commanding officer and I have to obey him. For all I know, this is a test he's set for me. I can't put my own selfish desires before military discipline. We all have our own tasks to fulfill in this unit."

Lola stared at him open-mouthed. "You're scared," she said.

"Am not," said Max.

"Prove it," she said.

Max hesitated. What should he do? Save his skin and let a girl think he was scared? Or bluff it out and face the horrors of the Black Pyramid?

"Ready when you are," he said, picking up the blowgun.

Lola slapped him on the back. "Way to go, Hup!" she said.

Almost as soon as they set off, he stumbled over a fallen branch and sent assorted jungle birds squawking out of the trees in fright.

"Maybe Hermanjilio was right about you," hissed Lola, crossly. "Watch where you put your feet!"

"Sorry," said Max. "Should I go back?"

"Keep marching, soldier."

Nearly an hour later, they approached the base of the Black Pyramid.

The closer they got, the more forbidding it looked.

DeLanda's men had cleared a way through the plaza and up the front steps, but dense jungle covered the rest of the site and gave them cover as they crept up behind the pyramid.

"Wait here," whispered Lord Six-Rabbit.

Max and Lola waited. The jungle around them was shrouded in the sinister monochrome of night. Black flowers, gray leaves, vines like industrial steel cables, thorns like barbed wire. There was no buzz of life, and the air was as thick and heavy as molten tar.

As they stood in tense silence, Max's heart was in his mouth. It nearly stopped beating altogether when Lord Six-Rabbit dropped silently out of a tree in front of them.

"There are two guards on the pyramid. One keeps watch from the topmost platform, one patrols the base," he whispered.

"Wait here, Hup," said Lola. "Let us deal with them."

Max nodded gratefully. He watched them go, then sat down on a log and waited. And waited. Each minute seemed like an hour.

At last, Lord Six-Rabbit returned.

"Follow me," he said.

With a heavy heart, Max followed him up the side of the pyramid. It was an easy climb for a monkey, but steep and difficult for a boy. By the time they reached the top platform, Max was sure someone would hear his breathless panting.

But they were safe. The guard was crumpled on the floor, a blowgun dart sticking out of his shoulder.

Lola appeared out of the shadows and Max helped her drag the sleeping guard through the jaguar's mouth, into the temple. Max shivered. Evil hung in the air like the smell of fried onions around a hotdog stand.

Once through the mouth, they entered a small, circular room.

"Light thy torches," commanded Lord Six-Rabbit.

They switched on their flashlights and gasped: The walls were made entirely of human skulls. While Max and Lola gazed around the chamber in horror, Lord Six-Rabbit pointed up to a particularly gruesome skull.

"One of thee must reach into its eye sockets," he said.

"How about we lift you up and you do it?" suggested Max.

"Art thou afraid of a carving?" said Lord Six-Rabbit. "These skulls are not real. They are cut out of the limestone."

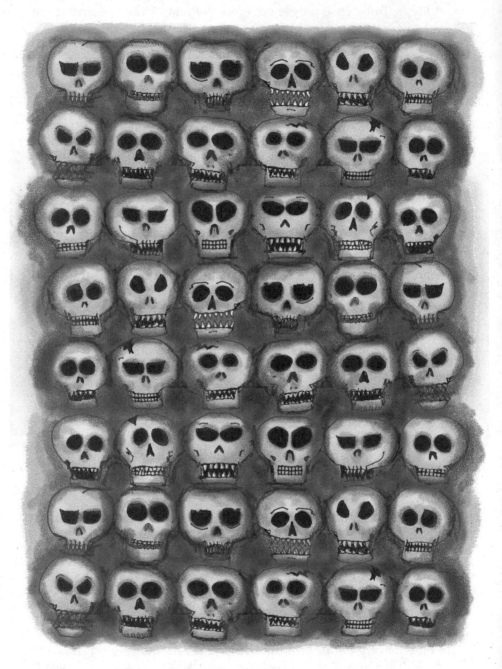

"The walls were made entirely of human skulls."

"They look real to me," said Max.

Lola pushed Max out of the way and wiggled her thumb and forefinger into the eye sockets of the skull. "I feel something," she said, "it's a lever."

"Good," said Lord Six-Rabbit. "Now push it down with all thy might."

There was a grinding sound and the wall began to rotate. As one panel of stone covered the doorway, another panel slid away to reveal a small opening in the back wall.

"Make haste and follow me."

Lord Six-Rabbit stepped through the gap, with Lola close behind him. The gap was getting smaller all the time, and Max slid through just before it closed up completely.

He looked back. All along the wall, holes were drilled into the rock to let observers peer through a row of eye sockets into the first room. Max wondered what horrors had been witnessed from this vantage point.

"From this moment, be on thy guard," said Lord Six-Rabbit. "The pyramids were always gateways between worlds. But remember that, as the new *bak'tun* draws near, they are more alive than ever. Watch thy step and do not deviate from the path. Trust nothing, not even thine own perceptions. Have no fear or they will use thy fears against thee."

"Have no fear?" repeated Max. "That's easy for you to say." He'd never been so frightened in his life. Even Lola was looking terrified.

Lord Six-Rabbit patted each of them with a gentle paw. "Stay close," he said.

The passageway spiraled steeply downward. The atmosphere was damp and musty. With each step, Max felt the air close in. He wished he had blinkers like a horse, so he couldn't see the walls on either side of him. They were covered from top to bottom in gory frescoes that looked horribly realistic in the dim light.

Muscular warriors in leopard-skin tunics plunged their lances into bulgy-eyed enemies. Cowering captives begged for mercy. A Maya priest held a human heart above the blood-spattered body of his victim.

Shuffling past these terrifying scenes, it was all too easy to imagine yourself as a captive being led to the sacrificial altar. They ran down the passageway for another twenty feet or so, until they came to a dead end.

"That's the end of that then," whispered Max, trying to sound disappointed.

"Wait," said Lola, "maybe this is one of those tricks Lord Six-Rabbit told us about."

In fact they were both wrong.

Lord Six-Rabbit stared intently at the floor and poked in the dust with his foot until he located some fingerholes in one of the flagstones.

"Help me, Young Lord," he said.

Together the boy and the monkey heaved up the ancient trap-door to reveal a staircase disappearing down into darkness.

"After you," said Max. Then, almost trembling with fear, he followed Lord Six-Rabbit and Lola into the unknown.

The staircase led them into an enormous chamber.

"There's another pyramid inside this one!" said Max.

"They used to build new temples on top of old ones, " explained Lola. "I guess it saved bricks. Or maybe it was a power thing for the new king."

"Silence!" commanded Lord Six-Rabbit. "Now the danger begins in earnest. We are entering the burial chamber of the Lords of Ah Pukuh. Woe betide the fool who dares disturb their slumber. Touch nothing. Tread only in my footsteps."

Max wanted to turn tail and run, but Lola pushed him forward.

"Don't look," she said. "Just follow Lord Six-Rabbit."

They began to work their way down the steep stairs cut into the terraced walls of the inner pyramid.

Max knew he shouldn't look.

He tried not to look.

He looked.

On both sides of the steps, reclining on every surface, lay the richly attired bodies of hundreds of dead Maya warriors. Some were nothing but crumbling bones. Others moldered in various stages of decay. But many of them looked fresh, as if they had only just died, their skin still glistening with body paint.

All of them wore battle gear, and clutched an arsenal of swords, axes, and spears.

It was too much. Max made a noise. A sort of muffled scream.

The eyes of the corpses who still had eyes opened in unison. With a creaking of bones, they sat bolt upright, even the skeletons. Their heads swiveled toward Max.

This time, Lola screamed as well.

"They will not hurt thee," said Lord Six-Rabbit. "I am sure of it." He didn't sound sure of it. "Only the Black Jaguar can bring them to their feet. But let us hurry."

Max and Lola did not need telling twice. They went flying down the rest of the steps until they reached the base of the inner pyramid. From there, more steps led down through a hole in the floor.

Max plunged through the hole after the other two and into another long narrow passage. Lola and Lord Six-Rabbit were already out of sight, ahead of him.

"Wait for me," he called. In his panic to catch up, he missed his step and fell flat on his face. The impact knocked his flashlight from his hand. He watched in horror as it skidded along the floor, bounced off a wall, flickered, and went out.

"Lola! Lord Six-Rabbit! Help me!"

Only the echoes of his own voice replied.

He got down on his hands and knees, gingerly feeling around on the dusty floor for the flashlight. Eventually, he found it.

Please work, he prayed.

It didn't.

"Lola! Lord Six-Rabbit! Where are you?"

This time he thought he heard a faint response.

"Lola! Lord Six-Rabbit! Come back!"

"Max? Is that you?" The voice was far away but getting closer.

"I'm over here! My flashlight's gone out."

Now he could definitely hear footsteps getting closer. He breathed a long and heartfelt sigh of relief. For a moment there, he'd thought he was a goner.

Far down the corridor, a light was flickering toward him.

"Max, where are you?"

"Straight ahead," he called.

Who was that? Was it Lola? It didn't sound like her. And yet he knew that voice.

"Stay there, Max! I'm coming!"

"Mom?"

The nightmare was over! Here he was, alone in the dark in the Pyramid of Death, convinced he was about to be captured by demons, and who should come along to rescue him but the person he loved most in the world! He was weak with amazement and happiness.

"*Bambino*! It *is* you! I thought I heard your voice!" Carla Murphy hugged her only son and kissed his head. "How can this be? I thought you were at camp with Lenny! I am so happy to see you, but what are you doing here?"

"What are *you* doing here?"

"We have so many questions for each other! But all that matters is that we're together again. Come, let's go and tell your father the good news." She took Max's hand and began to lead him down the passageway. "He's just down here with his friends . . . "

"What friends?"

"Oh they're such nice people. I can't wait for you to meet them."

What was going on? It crossed Max's mind that a group of nerdy archaeologists must have got together in the Black Pyramid to celebrate the new *bak'tun*. In which case it was up to him to warn them to get out as quickly as possible.

"Mom," he said, "I don't want to frighten you, but it's not safe in here."

"*Si, si, bambino*," she said, absentmindedly as she looked around to get her bearings. "Ah, here we are . . . "

Her candle illuminated a set of ornately carved double doors. She reached out to knock, but before her hand touched the wood, the doors were flung open. Max blinked with surprise as bright light spilled out into the corridor, bringing with it a pungent aroma and a wave of chattering voices.

A figure stepped out to greet them.

It was Lola.

"Hup!" she cried. "Isn't this fantastic? I was going to come back for you, but Carla insisted on getting you herself. She wanted to surprise you."

"And she succeeded," said Max.

Now that he could see his mother properly, he registered that she was wearing a long, embroidered dress with a huge jade necklace and a feathered headdress.

"That's quite an outfit, Mom!"

"Isn't it fun? Now come and join the party, *bambino*."

Max opened his mouth, but nothing came out. He didn't know where to begin. Taking an arm each, Carla and Lola escorted him into a large room lit by flaming torches. Someone had gone to a lot of trouble to clean it out and decorate it to look like a lavish Maya palace. Woven rugs hung on the walls and a roaring fire blazed in the hearth. All around the room, alcoves had been carved into the walls. If it had been a church in Italy, the figures of the saints would have looked down from these niches. But in this room, each space was filled by a large owl. At first Max thought they were stuffed, but as he moved, he noticed their unblinking yellow eyes were following him. At ground level, men dressed as Maya lords reclined on cushioned ledges or stood around in merry groups, filling the air with their cigar smoke and raucous laughter. The festivities were evidently in full swing.

On a raised platform in the center of the room was a stone table, laden with food and drink. Seated at this table, deep in conversation, were Lord Six-Rabbit and two other Maya lords. Lord Six-Rabbit appeared to be demonstrating to them the advantages of his monkey body. It was only when Max drew closer that he realized he knew one of the men.

"Dad?"

Like his wife, Frank Murphy was dressed in traditional Maya costume. He stood up when he heard Max's voice and beckoned his son over to join them.

"Max! What a wonderful coincidence! Six-Rabbit here has been telling me all about it! But you must come and meet our host! I know you're going to get on famously!"

Max had never seen his father so animated. He was usually a shrinking violet at parties, just looking for an opportunity to escape. But tonight he was smiling and talking ten to the dozen, like some cheesy TV presenter. He was certainly in his element, surrounded by all this Maya stuff, and Max guessed he'd been drinking elixir. But drunk or sober, it was good to see him. It meant this nightmare was over and they could all go home. Or better still, to Disneyworld and then home.

He hugged his father and shook Lord Six-Rabbit's paw, then waited politely to be introduced to the third Maya lord at the table.

He was obviously supposed to be someone very important because his chair was bigger than the others' and draped with jaguar skins. He was enormously, disgustingly fat and his chalky white skin was covered in hideous black bruises. He looked like a bloated body washed up on a beach, the corpse of a plague victim perhaps. To make the effect even more ghastly, he wore rouged cheeks and bright red lipstick.

As if this character's appearance was not striking enough, his tentlike tunic was covered in little bells that looked like they were carved out of real bone and jingled dully at their wearer's every move. As a finishing touch, his thick black hair was tied in an elaborate headdress, decorated with dried human tongues and shriveled eyeballs that bounced on their nerve cords as he spoke.

Max had never seen someone go to so much trouble for a masquerade costume. The fat suit alone must have cost a fortune and the makeup was incredible. No expense had been spared. He'd even brought along five massive, vicious-looking dogs that sat behind him in a semicircle, growling and slavering.

"Max, I'd like to introduce you to our host, Lord Ah Pukuh."

"Pleased to meet you," said Max, reluctantly going along with the joke.

Ah Pukuh held up a finger, as if asking Max to wait a moment. Then he leaned to one side, lifted up one of his huge buttocks, and noisily passed gas. The most noxious gas that Max had ever smelled. He thought he might faint from the fumes. Meanwhile everyone else in the room was laughing, cheering, and clapping. Max's mother was leading the applause. Was this the same woman who had a fit if Max drank from the milk carton? She'd evidently relaxed her standards since she'd been in San Xavier.

Carla indicated that Max should sit next to their corpulent host, while she and Lola took chairs opposite.

"Welcome!" boomed Ah Pukuh, as he sat down

Whoa! The blast of foul breath from the guy's black hole of a mouth nearly knocked Max right off the chair. He tried, surreptitiously, to cover his nose with his hand as the fat guy continued to speak. "Eat! Drink! Let us celebrate this joyous reunion! What will you have, Young Lord?"

"Nothing thanks," said Max, who was feeling queasy.

" 'Eat! Drink! Let us celebrate this joyous reunion!' "

"But I insist!" said Ah Pukuh. He clapped his hands. "Bring roast gibnut and hot chocolate for our guest!" he bellowed.

Immediately, a servant appeared with a loaded plate and a pottery goblet. The gibnut still had its head and tail attached. It lay on the plate like a burnt rat. Max surveyed it miserably as the servant filled his goblet with a viscous brown liquid the color of old blood.

"Dig in," urged Ah Pukuh.

Carla screamed with laughter. "*Dig* in! It's an archaeologist joke," she explained to Max. "Do eat something, *bambino*, you don't want to offend dear old Pookie."

Max gave the gibnut a desultory poke with his fork. He pushed back from the table in horror as the rodent opened an eye and turned its head toward him.

"Aaaaagggghhhh," he shrieked, jumping to his feet.

The rodent sat up, looked nervously from side to side, leapt onto Max's shoulder and sprang from there onto the floor. With a nod from Ah Pukuh, the waiting dogs ran after it and ripped it limb from limb.

Max was shaking all over. This guy was obviously a complete psycho.

"Mom," he whispered, "can we get out of here?"

"But why, *bambino*? The party has only just started. It will go on for days . . . "

"I just want to go home."

"Home? But, *caro mio*, this is our home now."

"What are you talking about? Do you mean we're going to live in San Xavier?"

"I mean, Max, that Pookie has invited us to live here, in the Black Pyramid."

"Can we just drop the joke, Mom? I'm tired. I've had enough. You have no idea what I've been through. I thought you might be dead."

"Dead?" Carla threw her head back and laughed. "We will never die now!"

"I'll drink to that!" cackled Lola, as they clinked their goblets in a toast.

"Mom, have you been drinking elixir?"

"Yes, and it's even more delicious than Chianti. Be a good boy and find me some more, would you?"

Max got up and went over to his father. "I think Mom's had too much to drink," he said. "I can't get any sense out of her. Will you tell me what's going on?'

"Of course, I will, Max. We have such good news for you."

"Good news?"

"Yes, jumping into that cenote was the best thing we ever did."

"It was?"

"If we hadn't done that, we'd never have met Ah Pukuh and the gang. We made friends with them in Xibalba. They're a great crew. And they'll be running the world soon, so we're in a very good position. It's all ours for the asking, Max."

"Thy father speaks the truth," said Lord Six-Rabbit. "It pains me now to think of all the time that I have wasted in pointless combat with my brother Tzelek. Far better that he and I should work together. The entire world will be ours to command."

"You've both gone mad," said Max. "Why are you obsessed with money and power and possessions all of a sudden?"

"Isn't that what everyone wants, Max? It's why we all go to work."

"No, it's not. You're an archaeologist, Dad. You love archaeology! You've always said you'd do it even if they didn't pay you."

"I've had it with old pots! Be honest, Max, haven't you ever wished that we led a more glamorous life? Or that we lived in a bigger house? What about a hot tub? An indoor pool? Or some of those plasma TVs you like so much?"

"Dad, you sound like the shopping channel. I thought you disapproved of the consumer society?"

"That's what I'm trying to tell you, Max. I've changed. Everything's changed. From now on, we're going to live like Hollywood stars. We'll take our vacations in the South of France or anywhere you want to go. We'll reserve a permanent suite at Disneyworld, if you like. We'll employ a chef to make you fresh pizza every day and all the homemade ice cream you can eat. How does that sound?"

"I don't want any of it, Dad. I just want our old life back."

"Oh come on, Max, there must be something you want. What was that game you kept asking me to buy back in Boston?"

"The new limited edition Hellhounds 3D?"

"That's the one. Limited edition, my foot! We'll commission the designers to create a special edition just for you — *starring* you, if you like — now that's what I call a limited edition! And you'll have all the time in the world to play it, because you need never go to school. You'll have enough money to buy everything your heart desires, so you can just laze around for all eternity."

Max was listening. Not going to school had certainly struck a chord.

"Professor Murphy!" scolded Lola. "Life isn't just about buying things."

"At last," said Max, "the voice of reason."

"Life is also about the things that money can't buy," she continued, "like revenge. Think about it, Max. Candelario really made a fool out of you with that pepper soup. Wouldn't you like to give him a taste of his own medicine?"

"And dost thou not hate the way Lord Hermanjilio orders thee around?" asked Lord Six-Rabbit. "Wouldst thou not like to turn the tables?"

"What about that teacher who failed you in Woodwork just because you sawed his desk in half?" put in his father.

"And that little blond girl across the street?" added his mother. "She thinks she's too good for you now, but when she sees you driving home in a red Ferrari . . . "

Max put his hands over his ears. "What are you all saying?" he cried. "I know I used to be greedy and materialistic —"

"— and selfish," interrupted Lola.

"— and selfish," added Max, "but I'm not like that anymore."

"Of course, you're like that," boomed Ah Pukuh from his throne. "All boys your age are like that. And I'm happy to say that most of them never grow out of it. Why, I can remember . . . " His reminiscences were drowned out in a barrage of flatulence.

"The question is, *bambino*," said Carla, "are you with us?"

"I'm your son, aren't I?"

"The continuation of that filial arrangement," said Frank Murphy, "rather depends on whether or not you decide to turn over a new leaf. You know, you've caused us a lot of trouble in the past, Max."

"I'm sorry about that, Dad. But what do you mean by *a new leaf*? Is there something in particular you want me to do?"

"Since you ask, there is. We would like you to sign your name in blood right now, committing your mortal soul to the protection of Lord Ah Pukuh. He'll be like a godfather to you and spoil you rotten. It's a good deal, Max."

"And, of course," wheedled his mother, "we'll be together for all eternity."

"Thy place is with thy parents," said Lord Six-Rabbit.

"I'm not sure," said Max. "It sounds creepy. I need to think."

The mood in the room changed instantly. The light hardened from a rosy glow of flames to a cold blue ashy glare. The laughter died down. The dogs began growling.

"He needs to think," said his mother, mimicking him.

"He's never thought before in his life," said his father. "Why start now?"

"What a loser," agreed Lola in disgust.

"Why are you all picking on me?" asked Max. "What happened to the happy reunion?"

"It might have been a happy reunion for *you*," said his father, pointedly.

"What do you mean?"

"To be honest, son, we were happier without you."

"The truth is, *bambino*, that we've never liked you, not from the moment you were born." Carla leaned over to Lola. "You know the type," she said in a stage whisper, "always crying and puking. The mess he made on my silk shirts! I used to pay strangers on the street to hold him so I wouldn't have to. Then there was the bedwetting and the nose picking and the whining. He made my life a living hell."

"Mom . . . ?"

His father put an arm around him. "The truth hurts, eh, son? But having you ruined our lives. We never risked having another child in case it turned out like you. I know you thought I worked long hours because I was so interested in the Ancient Maya. But, in reality, I just didn't want to come home to you. Half the time, I wasn't even in the office — I was at the movies or a ball game. Other fathers would be there with their sons, but not me. I couldn't bear to be near you. That's why I was so pleased to hear about Wilderness Camp. It was the worst place we could find. It's true they feed their campers on slugs," — at this Ah Pukuh clapped his hands in appreciation — "but what you didn't know is that, if their parents don't collect them, the guests are sold into slavery at the end of the summer. We thought we'd got rid of you for good."

Max's jaw dropped. He couldn't believe his ears. Occasionally, when his parents had refused to let him stay out late or said no to the most expensive sneakers, he'd suspected he was adopted. But he'd never dreamed they hated him this much.

"Why don't you sign?" said his mother. "Haven't you caused enough trouble?"

"Yes," said his father, smiling, "just sign the paper and we'll forgive you for everything and be a happy family. It's up to you, Max."

It was tempting to sign and have done with it.

He was afraid that, if he didn't, he'd never see his parents again.

Afraid that he'd be alone in the world . . .

Afraid that . . .

Afraid?

They will use thy fears against thee.

He closed his eyes and considered the evidence.

He remembered when he was little, sitting on his mother's knee and waving to the Moon Rabbit. He remembered when he was unjustly suspended from school, and his father had believed his version of events (for once) and taken him out to a movie. He remembered all those Saturday morning soccer games when they'd come and cheered him on in the rain. He remembered the night the laser printer broke down, and his parents had stayed up till dawn, trying to get his fifty-page project on state capitals printed out. He'd gone to bed in tears. But when he came down for breakfast, there was his project, all fifty pages, tied up in a big red ribbon.

Would they have done these things if they thought he was just a nuisance?

Then he remembered his mother's face on the evening they left for San Xavier and he knew beyond a shadow of a doubt that his parents loved him.

He opened his eyes.

He looked at the cruel faces around the table. Their eyes were filled with hate. How could he ever have believed those eyes belonged to his parents or Lola or Lord Six-Rabbit? He'd let himself be tricked by the demons of hell.

Mustering all his courage, he leaned over to Ah Pukuh. "Is that all you've got, Fatso?" he said.

Ah Pukuh laughed loud and long, like the sound of a saw cutting down trees. His multiple chins rippled and shook with merriment.

"I've only just begun," he said.

"Max, don't do this to us," cried his parents.

The flesh on their faces began to fall off in chunks, until he could see patches of white skull peeking through their rotting sinews. Lola touched his arm with a skeletal finger. "Save me," she said. "There's still time to sign."

"No," said Max.

And when he looked again, she was a decomposing corpse.

The stench was overpowering.

Max retched.

"I told you it wouldn't work," said the corpse of Lola. "We should have just ripped out his heart, like I said. Come on, Pus, you lost the bet. Pay up."

"Not so quick, Scab Stripper. How about double or nothing?" said the Demon of Pus, who had so recently been posing as Max's mother.

"Let's suck his brains out," suggested the remains of Lord Six-Rabbit, who was now just some bits of fur and gristle.

"Not for me, Blood Gatherer. I'm on a diet," said the skull of Frank Murphy. One of his eyeballs fell out, bounced on the table, and rolled onto the floor. An owl swooped down and carried it back to his perch.

"*You* may not be hungry, Jaundice, but the birds are ravenous," said Lord Six-Rabbit, alias Blood Gatherer. "Why don't we let them feast on his innards?"

"Stop!" shouted Ah Pukuh. "I grow weary of this sport. Let the dogs have him."

"Perfect!" said the Demon of Pus. "Apparently, the boy likes to play something called Hellhounds 3D. Now let's see how he likes the real thing."

The five massive dogs were snarling and foaming at the mouth, waiting for the signal to attack. Max was shaking. If only this *was* Hellhounds 3D and he could just quit out of it. But this was real life and he had no tricks left. And then he realized he didn't need tricks to deprive these demons of their power. All they understood was hate and greed and lies. He had something far more powerful. Or so he hoped.

Ah Pukuh clicked his fat greasy fingers.

The dogs leapt.

"I know my parents love me."

Max saw their yellow eyes and their sharp yellow teeth.

"I know my parents love me."

He smelled their foul breath and felt their burning saliva that dripped like acid from their foaming jaws.

"I know my parents love me."

Their bodies barreled against him and their claws knocked him down. He closed his eyes, bracing himself for the first bite.

"I know my —"

All was quiet.

He didn't move.

"Hup?" said a voice.

He opened his eyes slowly. He was back in the corridor, lying flat where he'd fallen in the dark. Lola was crouching over him, holding his flashlight.

"Hup!" she cried. "What happened to you?"

"You won't believe it," said Max, as she helped him to his feet. "I've just met Ah Pukuh. But I stood my ground. Lord Six-Rabbit would have been proud of me."

"You weren't scared, then?" she said.

"A bit. But Ah Pukuh is basically all talk."

Lola raised an eyebrow sardonically. "He's not the only one," she said.

"What do you mean?" said Max, baffled.

She pointed at his jeans.

He looked down. There was a large wet patch at the top of his legs. Had he really been so scared of the dogs that he'd peed himself? Probably.

He was mortified.

"There were these five huge dogs —"

"Oh, did the doggies scare ooo? Poor lickle baby!" she sneered. "We should've bwought some diapers for the lickle baby!"

"Stop it! I'm not a baby!" yelled Max. "You don't know what it was like."

"You're a bit old to go around wetting yourself, Hup. I'd see a doctor, if I were you. Just wait till the others hear about this —"

"No, please," begged Max, "don't tell them."

"Why not?"

"Because it's embarrassing."

"Are you worried about what they'll think of you?"

"Yes."

"Well, I can tell you what they think of you. They think the same as I do — that you're a jerk. A useless little jerk with stupid red hair and a face like a rat with acne."

"Lola! Stop it, please! I thought you were my friend!"

She snorted with derision. "Why would someone like me ever be friends with a jerk like you? I've been leading you on for a laugh, but now I'm going to tell you the truth. You're sad, you're ugly, you're boring, and you're disgusting. Even when you're not soaked in pee, you smell. You've got bad breath and those spots on your chin make me feel sick. Nobody likes you, Massimo *Francis* Murphy. Even your name is stupid. Everybody's laughing at you behind your back, and they'll laugh even harder when I tell them about this. If I were you, I'd just run away now while there's time."

Max sank back to the floor in misery. He felt as gutted as a fish on a slab.

It was so unfair. He could see that the old Max Murphy, the couch potato who'd landed at San Xavier airport, hadn't been much of a catch. But he thought he'd improved since then. His face was tan and his body was fitter. He'd tried to be a better person on the inside too, since that day on the Monkey River.

But, apparently, it all counted for nothing.

All Max's bravado melted away.

There was no point in going on.

Maybe his parents didn't love him after all. How could anyone love him? He was a failure. A creep. He'd always suspected that girls found him repulsive. Now his worst fear had come true.

Wait a minute . . .

His worst fear!!!

They will use thy fears against thee.

He looked up. Lola was grinning triumphantly.

"Give us a kiss," he said.

Her smile disappeared.

"Come on," he coaxed, "why not? You're not so hot yourself, you know. You've got a big nose and a bad haircut, and you're so bossy you give me a headache. I think you'd be lucky to kiss a hunk like me."

"What?" she said, incredulously.

"Face it, Monkey Girl," he said, "you can't get to me because you're not real. You're a product of my imagination. I don't have to listen to anything you say."

He just had time to grab her flashlight before she melted back into the walls.

Phew. That was a close one.

Max got to his feet and started to make his way quickly down the corridor. He shone his light in every direction, looking for the double doors that led to the chamber of Ah Pukuh, but he couldn't find them.

Running round a corner, he ran smack into Lola.

"Hup!" she cried. "What happened to you?"

She looked as white as a ghost. But was she a ghost or was she real?

"I met Ah Pukuh . . . " began Max.

He shone the flashlight on his crotch.

"What on earth are you doing?" she asked.

It was dry. She was real.

"Nothing," he laughed. "It's just that things got a bit weird for a while."

He told her all about the party, except for the bit at the end where her evil twin had appeared to him in the passageway. No need for her to know that his worst fear in the world concerned girls and what they thought of him.

"Poor Hup, it sounds awful. Let's get out of here."

"So, while we were separated, did Ah Pukuh get at you, too?" he asked.

She nodded.

"What with?"

She shuddered. "I'll tell you another time. Now, which way? This place has as many tunnels as a termite nest . . . "

"Wait!" said Max. "There's something I have to ask you."

"What is it, Hup? We have to hurry —"

"Do I have bad breath?"

"What? This isn't the moment to discuss personal hygiene," she snapped. "We have to find Lord Six-Rabbit."

"Thou hast found him," said the monkey, stepping out of the shadows.

Max peered into the monkey's eyes. "It is you, isn't it?"

Lord Six-Rabbit smiled. "Indeed it is," he said. "But am I to assume that the spirits have been testing thee with phantasms?"

Max nodded. "Did they test you, too, Your Majesty?'

"My test will be Tzelek," said Lord Six-Rabbit, gravely. "Remember, this is but a rehearsal. No matter what thou hast endured this night, worse is to come. So far thou hast been menaced with magic and illusion; on the morrow, thou wilt face the reality of pure evil. Until Tzelek is vanquished, each one of us is in immeasurable danger."

"Do you think we *can* vanquish him?" asked Max nervously, but Lord Six-Rabbit had bounded ahead down the passageway and didn't hear him. Max and Lola hurried after him, each lost in their own thoughts.

"So was that a yes or a no on the bad breath question?" he asked.

She stopped dead and made a noise like a cat when you tread on its tail.

"That bad?" he said, horrified, cupping his hand on his chin and trying to direct his breath upward so he could smell it himself.

But Lola wasn't paying attention. She was pointing straight ahead of them. "Look!" she said.

He looked.

Once again, the passageway ended in a solid wall. But this time there was no trapdoor. There was no way forward.

"We're trapped!" said Lola, reprising her tortured cat noise. "I just want to get out of here."

"Please don't say we have to go back," said Max. "Anything but that."

"Tsk, tsk," Lord Six-Rabbit chided them. "Hast thou no faith?"

Using faint indentations in the wall, he began to climb up the stones. When he reached the ceiling, Max and Lola were astonished to see his head and then his body and finally his tail disappear through the solid rock. A few moments later his head reappeared upside down.

"The passage is free to the caves," he grinned. "We have our escape route. Now follow me and do not hesitate."

Max prepared himself for pain as he forced his head up against the ceiling. To his surprise, it met with no resistance and he quickly climbed up into another passageway. The air was less oppressive here and he sensed that freedom was within their reach.

And so it proved. Lord Six-Rabbit led them easily through a long network of caves and tunnels, back into the sweet, wet, humming, buzzing, living forest.

The sun was rising by the time they returned to the camp. Max and Lola were dead tired and threw themselves down on the grass, prepared to sleep where they lay.

"Looks like Hermanjilio and Lady Coco are still out there," said Max.

"So he need never even know that you deserted your post, Hup!"

"Suits me," said Max. "What a night!"

"*Sí, qué noche!* A most interesting night," said a voice behind them.

They jumped to their feet and spun around.

A dark-haired man dressed all in black clicked his fingers loudly. Men with machine guns sidled out of the trees and surrounded them.

"*Senõr Murphy y La Bella Lola*," sneered the man. "I've been expecting you."

"Who are you?" asked Max, but he knew the answer.

"I am Count Antonio DeLanda," said the Spaniard, pointing his goateed chin in the air and making that melodramatic cape-flicking movement that Max had first seen at the hotel in Aguas Muertas.

"But the big question," the count sneered, striding over to Lola and grabbing her roughly by the jaw, "is who are you?"

As she fought to free herself from his grasp, he managed to turn her face this way and that, as if searching for a scar or a birthmark. "*Bueno*, it is as I thought," he laughed, obviously having found what he was looking for. "You will make a most prized offering to the Lords of Xibalba."

"Spanish scum!" she yelled and spat in his face.

He slapped her hard across the cheek. "Take them to the ship."

Lord Six-Rabbit had leapt into the trees when DeLanda had first appeared. Now Max could see him peering down between the branches. DeLanda followed his eyes. "And shoot the monkey," he added.

As Lola and Max were gagged and tied, a guard took aim into the branches. In a flash, Lord Six-Rabbit launched himself into the air and landed on the guard's head, sinking his sharp little teeth into his would-be killer's nose. The guard screamed in pain and dropped his weapon. Lord Six-Rabbit bit his hand for good luck, then sprang off his head back into the nearest tree.

"Imbeciles!" lisped DeLanda. "Shoot it, shoot it!"

Max and Lola hurled themselves into the nearest guards to make their shots go astray. The trees were peppered with bullets and Spanish curses filled the air.

CHAPTER XXIII

CAPTURED

WHUMP. WHUMP. WHUMP. The high-powered speedboat met each wave head on, as they raced across the ocean. Max and Lola were lying on the floor of the boat, drenched by rain and saltwater spray, their hands and feet bound with rope, their mouths tightly gagged.

Max looked across at Lola. Her hair was plastered to her face. She looked as seasick as he felt. He thought he might puke at any moment. How would that work with the gag? It was too disgusting to contemplate.

Just when he thought he could hold it in no longer, the boat stopped.

A white yacht towered over them.

Someone yanked him up roughly and hustled him into a cargo net. Before he knew what was happening, he and Lola were scooped off their feet and winched into the air. Next minute they were hanging a few feet above the surface of the ocean. Max thought he could see a shark fin cutting through the water toward them.

Would he rather be eaten first or watch Lola being eaten?

There was no time to decide, for the cargo net suddenly lurched, swung round and dumped them heavily on the deck, like two fat codfish.

When the goons in black had pulled them free of the netting, Lola was carried off in one direction and Max was dragged off in the other. Two guards manhandled him roughly along gangways and up stairways until they reached a red-carpeted corridor on an upper deck. Here the guards untied him and removed his gag.

"Where are you taking me?" asked Max.

One of the guards answered him in a torrent of Spanish. He was none the wiser.

"Is it to DeLanda?" guessed Max. "I have nothing to say to that pig."

The guards seemed to find this hilarious.

They nodded and leered and made disturbing finger gestures — were they warning him about some particularly twisted kind of torture? — as they pushed him toward a set of varnished wooden doors at the end of the corridor.

So this was it. The long-awaited confrontation with DeLanda.

Max wondered if the Spaniard had an onboard torture chamber. Well, at least if he was busy torturing Max, it meant he wasn't engaged in sacrificing Lola. Wow! Max got a lump in his throat as he realized that was probably the most selfless thought he'd ever had in his life. But what was the point of being a reformed character if a crazy count was just about to pull your fingernails out one by one?

Max's thoughts were spiraling into hysteria when the guards pushed him headlong through the doors.

He went sprawling onto a red carpet. When he staggered to his feet, he found himself in a plush, wood-paneled stateroom. There was a long table in the center of the room and red velvet banquettes around the edge. At the far end, a man was standing with his back to the room, looking out to sea. He was wearing a white linen suit.

"Uncle Ted!"

Uncle Ted turned round. His face looked even more furrowed. He had dark shadows under his eyes. He looked like he hadn't slept for at least a week.

"Uncle Ted, what are you doing here?"

"I could ask you the same question, young man."

"This is DeLanda's yacht! Are you in league with him? I might have known it!"

"I think we should start this discussion with an apology."

"It better be good," said Max.

He waited.

"It would be *you* doing the apologizing," clarified Uncle Ted.

"Me? For what?"

"Let me think," said Uncle Ted, sarcastically. "For betraying my trust, perhaps? For stealing the Red Jaguar? For doing your utmost to destroy my business?"

"Your business?" Max stared at him in disbelief. "Don't you understand that the world is about to end and you won't even *have* a business, if we don't stop your friend DeLanda before the new *bak'tun?*"

Uncle Ted looked alarmed. "What have they done to you? I heard you've been keeping bad company, Max. Have they brainwashed you?"

"Me, brainwashed? That's a good one. So how long have you been involved in this plot, Uncle Ted?"

"Plot?" Uncle Ted sounded genuinely puzzled.

"The plot for DeLanda-slash-Tzelek to take over the world."

"That's enough, Max!" said Uncle Ted. "Can you imagine how worried I've been? First your parents disappear. Then you run off into the jungle with a band of thieves. If this is what it's like to have children, then—" He stopped himself abruptly and continued in a colder, more businesslike tone. "All I'm trying to do is recover a valuable artifact for my client. If you'd just tell me what you've done with the Red Jaguar, perhaps we can sort it out without recourse to the law."

Max narrowed his eyes and looked hard at Uncle Ted. Either he was an Oscar-worthy actor or he really didn't know DeLanda's plans.

"Your client has been possessed by the spirit of an evil Maya priest. He's using the Black Jaguar to release the demon warriors of the underworld."

"Oh grow up, Max! I don't think you understand how serious this is. Larceny, assault, sabotage, property damage . . . you and your girlfriend are in a lot of trouble."

"She's not my girlfriend," muttered Max. "If you could just get us off this boat, I'll tell you everything . . . "

Uncle Ted ran his hands through his hair.

"I'm afraid that's not possible. The matter is out of my hands. Thanks to your delinquent behavior, Count Antonio DeLanda is calling the shots." Uncle Ted lowered his voice. "You know I'm no fan of the count, Max, but you've forced me to take his side. He's my client and I made a deal with him. Now he wants his merchandise and he's not going to stop until he gets it. He says that if I can't persuade you to give back the Red Jaguar, he will torture its whereabouts out of you. He's ruthless, Max. He'll stop at nothing. He'll kill both of us if he has to. So stop all this nonsense about the end of the world and tell me what's happened to the Red Jaguar. Or else it really will be the end of the world — for you and me."

There was a slight movement at the back of the room. Max turned around, once again expecting to see DeLanda. But it was Lucky Jim. He was sitting there, arms folded, gaze directed out to sea.

"Lucky, *you're* a Maya, you know I'm telling the truth. Or is it *you* who's in league with DeLanda? I don't know who to trust anymore."

Lucky Jim ignored him.

Uncle Ted stepped forward and looked closely into Max's eyes.

"Paranoia, stealing, delusions . . . have you been taking drugs, Max?"

"Of course not! I'm telling you the truth, Uncle Ted! You said yourself that anything can happen round here, that things are never what they seem. If you don't get us out of here, DeLanda is going to sacrifice Lola to Ah Pukuh."

Uncle Ted sat down heavily on a banquette. He looked like he was trying hard to keep his temper. "Let me spell it out once again. All the count wants — and all I want — is the stolen Jaguar Stone. If you return it quickly, you and your friend will be free to go."

"No, Uncle Ted, you're wrong! DeLanda doesn't just want the Jaguar Stone. What he wants is to rule the world! Don't you know what he's doing at the Black Pyramid? The place is crawling with his thugs. They're getting ready for the rituals."

"That's the most ridiculous thing I've ever heard. The count is preparing for a big party to celebrate the new *bak'tun*. He says he wants to ingratiate himself with the local populace and start making amends for the misdeeds of his forbears."

"You don't believe that, do you?"

"It's not my business, Max."

"It *is* your business! It's *all* our business! Someone has to stop him! I know you deal with some shady characters, Uncle Ted, but surely even you can recognize pure evil when you see it?"

"That's enough, Max!" Uncle Ted put his head in his hands.

Max turned back to Lucky Jim.

"Lucky, you know what I'm talking about!" he said. "You understand the power of the Jaguar Stones!"

Lucky Jim shrugged. He looked uncomfortable.

"You were right," Max continued, "the pyramids *are* alive! Last night, in the Black Pyramid, Ah Pukuh was celebrating his coronation. Tomorrow, he will rule the world . . . "

"You tourists should stay out of our temples," said Lucky Jim.

Max Murphy's very short fuse had been lit.

"No!" he yelled. "We've gone way past that. It's not about who's a tourist and who's a Maya. We're all in this together. You can't ignore history anymore, Lucky Jim, because it's playing out right in front of us. Your children will ask you why you didn't try to save them from the living hell that will be their lives when Ah Pukuh and Tzelek take the reins. Are you just going to blame it on the tourists? Or are you going to take responsibility and do something about it, while there's still time?"

Max's face, red with fury, was right in Lucky Jim's face. They stared into each other's eyes. Their noses almost touched. But Lucky Jim said nothing. He just sat there, impassively.

This made Max angrier than ever. "Is that it? You're just going to sit there and let it happen? That's the most selfish thing I've ever seen. At least, you could tell Uncle Ted that I'm not crazy."

Silence. But Max had seen something, a flicker in Lucky's eyes. Lucky Jim knew he wasn't crazy.

He took a softer tone. "We need you, Lucky! There's going to be a huge battle tonight between good and evil. The immortal Lord Six-Rabbit is out there right now. We used the Green Jaguar to bring him back. He's inside the body of a howler monkey and Tzelek is inside DeLanda . . . "

Max's voice trailed off as even he realized how ridiculous it all sounded.

Lucky Jim got up and left the room.

"Now you've really gone too far," said Uncle Ted, "making fun of Lucky like that. I'm disgusted with you, Max. I should have known better than to try and reason with you. Here I am, just trying to look after you . . . "

"Don't give me that," said Max. He was past caring what he said. "You hate me, like you hate my father."

Uncle Ted looked genuinely appalled. "That's not true," he said, quietly. "It took me a day or two, but I grew very fond of you, Max. You have a lot of spirit. You reminded me of myself at your age. Sure, you were a little spoiled, but I thought a few weeks in San Xavier would change that."

"I *have* changed, Uncle Ted."

"But, sadly, not for the better. Listen to yourself. Evil spirits, human sacrifices, demon warriors . . . I'm too frustrated to talk to you anymore. You should have stayed in your room that night, Max. You gave me your word and you broke it."

"But my word wasn't good enough for you, was it? I was *going* to stay in my room until I realized you'd locked the door. Why couldn't you have trusted me? You locked me away like a prisoner."

Uncle Ted sounded close to tears. "No, I locked you away like something precious. I just wanted to keep you safe, Max. Fool that I was, I allowed myself to care about you." The pain in Uncle Ted's eyes hardened into resolve. "But now I can see the error of my ways. I'm washing my hands of you, Max. I'll give you a little time to think about things, and then I'm handing you over to DeLanda."

With that Uncle Ted swept out of the stateroom.

The two guards, who had evidently been waiting outside the door, barged in and grabbed Max again. They looked disappointed to find him in one piece and did their best to injure him themselves as they pushed and pulled him through hatches and down ladders to the bottom of the ship.

At the end of a long metal gangway, a door was unlocked and Max was pushed in. He found himself in a small cabin with no porthole and no furniture, except for a sink and a metal bunk bolted to the wall.

Now what? Max checked every inch of the cabin for a way out. He pressed his head against the door, but he could hear nothing. He tried kicking it for a while, but no one came. He paced up and down. He lay on the bunk. As the hours went by, he grew more and more wretched. This waiting and not knowing was as bad as any torture the creepy count could have devised.

What was happening? Where was Lola? How would Hermanjilio and two talking monkeys be able to outwit DeLanda and all his men? The more he thought about it, the more his heart sank. Whichever way you looked at it, they were in big trouble. And there was nothing he could do to help.

As he lay on the bunk in that airless cabin, he gradually dozed off. He awoke with a start to the blaring of an alarm. There were men shouting and the sound of running feet all over the boat. Someone ran past his door and up the stairs. He heard motorboats starting up, revving their engines, and roaring off.

Then all was quiet again.

What was going on? Had something happened on shore?

Had Hermanjilio made his move?

Max banged on the door. He kicked the walls. He shouted. At last, exhausted, he threw himself back on the bed and lay there staring at the ceiling, his imagination running wild. After a while, he thought he heard a noise in the corridor. He held his breath and listened as closely as he could.

Yes, there it was again. There was something or someone out there.

He heard the lock slowly turning.

Suddenly the door flew open and a familiar figure half stepped and half fell into the cabin.

"Uncle Ted! What's happening?"

"Some kind of emergency . . . all gone ashore . . . good time to escape . . . "

Max took in his uncle's slurred speech, his unsteady gait, and the whisky fumes that wafted from his pores. "Are you all right, Uncle Ted?"

"Had a drink or two with the captain . . . to get him out of the way . . . he's sleeping it off . . . on the bridge . . . you must go . . . go now."

Before Max could ask any more questions, Uncle Ted lurched back down the gangway toward the stairs. When Max caught up with him on the deck, he was leaning perilously over the guardrail and pointing at something off to stern.

"That'll get you to shore . . . think you can handle it?"

Max peered over the side. A little boat with an outboard motor bobbed below, straining at its rope.

"I don't understand," said Max.

"'S easy . . . Zodiac inflatable . . . . jus' pull the cord and slam it into gear . . . "

"No, I mean, I thought you'd washed your hands of me. Why are you helping me to escape?"

Uncle Ted smiled drunkenly. "Turns out I *do* owe you an apology, Max. . . . the way they dragged that poor girl off . . . I think you were right about DeLanda . . . I should have listened . . . "

"Lola?" interrupted Max. "Where did they take her?"

"To shore . . . I think she was drugged."

"I have to go, I have to save her."

"Never mind her, Max . . . save your own skin . . . get as far away from here as possible."

"I'm going ashore to find Lola. Are you coming?" said Max, coldly.

His uncle shook his head. "'S too dangerous . . . they're armed to the teeth . . . what we should do," he staggered slightly. "What we should do, is call the police."

"There's no time! Don't you understand? DeLanda's going to sacrifice Lola to Ah Pukuh. We need to stop him now!"

Max was pulling his uncle toward the ladder down to the Zodiac, but Uncle Ted clumsily disengaged himself.

"Uncle Ted, come on. Lola needs us!"

"Sorry, Max . . . I'm not the hero type . . . no can do."

"Are you scared of DeLanda?" sneered Max.

"Yes," said Uncle Ted.

"So you'd let Lola die rather than face up to him?"

"We Murphys look after number one."

"Well, this Murphy has learned that you can't live your life that way."

"I tried to be a hero once . . . it went wrong . . . she died . . . my fault . . . if only I had just called the police . . . "

Max impatiently interrupted, gripping his uncle tightly by the arms to call him back from his drunken ramblings. "Where's Lucky Jim? He could help me."

"Lucky? I think you've really upset him, Max. He's locked himself in his cabin and he won't come out. I can hear him chanting and it smells like he's burning incense in there. If I didn't know him better, I'd think he was doing some sort of Maya ritual. I don't know what's come over him. I just hope *he* hasn't been at the whisky too." Uncle Ted hiccupped loudly. "S'cuse me."

"Please tell Lucky I'm sorry," said Max. "I wasn't making fun of him. I just wish he'd understood what I was trying to tell him. With Lucky on our side, we might have stood a chance against DeLanda."

"Do you want to try and talk to him?"

"There's no time," said Max, climbing over the side of the yacht. "Wish me luck."

"Max . . . wait!"

"Are you coming with me?"

"No, I just want to give you this."

Uncle Ted passed down a diver's knife on a belt.

"Good luck, Max."

When Max was safely aboard, Uncle Ted untied the rope and shouted down instructions. Max pulled the cord with all his might and the engine roared into life. After a few false starts when he butted the yacht like an angry ram, he got the hang of steering and the Zodiac sped away.

Soon Max could make out the shoreline and the sinister outline of the Black Pyramid. He headed straight for it, with the motor flat out. His heart surged, happy to be free again. His stomach, which apparently knew something his heart did not, shrank into a tight ball of fear.

What grisly sight would be waiting for him at the temple?

After a while, he heard the motor of a yacht behind him. The captain must have woken up and discovered him missing.

He told himself not to look back and willed his little boat on across the waves. But, as fast as his inflatable was, the yacht quickly gained on him. The bow got closer and closer until he could feel it looming over him and he had to look back. The captain was clearly trying to run him down.

When the bow was just a few yards behind him, Max turned sharply to the right. The yacht turned as sharply as it could. It was more maneuverable than Max had expected, but no match for the agility of a Zodiac. When the yacht had made the full turn, Max once again headed straight for shore.

He was confident that he could keep this up indefinitely. His only worry was that the captain might radio ahead and tell De-Landa's men to meet him in their high-speed motor launches.

In fact, Max should have been worrying about something else entirely.

Like the fact that, at that very moment, the captain was out on the flying bridge, aiming a high-powered rifle at him.

As the yacht closed the gap and loomed over him again, Max started to make his next turn when — crack! A bullet tore into the outboard motor sending bits of engine cover flying. The engine sputtered. Max turned sharply and started zigzagging to make himself a more difficult target. He was losing speed.

Crack! Crack! Crack!

Spouts of water shot up around his boat where the bullets had missed. Max silently thanked Uncle Ted for plying the captain with whisky. He was horribly aware that it would take only one good shot to deflate the Zodiac and scupper his escape.

But the damage was done. The outboard motor coughed and shuddered to a halt. He was dead in the water. As he pulled frantically on the cord, praying for the engine to start, he turned to see the captain leaning over the side taking aim. Max steeled himself. Even drunk, he couldn't miss now.

Suddenly, the captain pitched over the railing and into the ocean. In his place was Uncle Ted, with a big grin on his face. He threw a life ring to the flailing captain and took the wheel of the ship.

"Pull out the choke," Uncle Ted called down through cupped hands.

With the choke fully out and a few more tugs on the cord, the outboard motor roared shakily back to life.

"You look like the hero type to me!" shouted Max over the engine noise. He never knew whether Uncle Ted heard him or not. But, as the yacht veered sharply away, it gave a loud blast of its horn.

Max turned and waved, then once again headed for the shore.

CHAPTER XXIV

THE SHOWDOWN

IT WASN'T QUITE the James Bond moment that Max could have hoped for.

When he'd first sped away in the Zodiac, he'd planned to make straight for land and take cover in the jungle before anyone noticed him.

Unfortunately, it hadn't worked out that way.

Now he was puttering along in his bullet-ridden craft, stalling continually and leaving a trail of greasy black engine fluid. He suspected that he had a slow leak, as the boat seemed to be getting lower and lower in the water. Eventually the engine gave up altogether and he had to reach for the oars.

If one of DeLanda's guards spotted him now, he was a goner. But why hadn't they spotted him already? Or maybe they had? Maybe they were planning a reception at this very moment?

Max felt distinctly uneasy as he paddled the last few hundred yards to shore.

It was getting dark by the time he landed. He could make out the shapes of DeLanda's motorboats pulled up on the sand, about half a mile down the beach. But there was no sign of any crew. There was also, he realized, no sign of any way up to the Temple of Ah Pukuh. A line of cliffs, hidden from the water by a grove of palm trees, formed an impenetrable barrier between the beach and the jungle.

Don't panic, he told himself, work it out.

How had DeLanda's men got up to Ah Pukuh? There had to be a trail near their boat landing. He crept along through the palm trees, as fast as he dared. His only thought was to get to the pyramid and find Lola before it was too late. In a few hours, Venus would rise and DeLanda would initiate the rituals.

When he reached the motorboats, he was ready for trouble. He'd been expecting a guard or two, but he could see no one. Was it a trap?

He scanned the cliffs. He scanned the beach.

At last he saw a black shape lying face down in the sand. He moved closer and saw the telltale sign of a blowgun dart in the man's neck.

Good shot, Hermanjilio! he thought. One down, nineteen to go.

And then he saw the way up. A winding stairway had been carved into the cliff face. It was steep and narrow and completely exposed. Max hesitated. He knew that once he started climbing, he would be at the mercy of anyone above or below. But he had no choice. He had to risk it.

Trying not to look down, not to think about snipers, not to think about anything but getting to Lola, Max slowly made his way up. The steps were weatherworn and cracked. As he got higher and his head started to spin, he turned his back to the water and climbed up sideways, his fingers clinging painfully to the crumbling rock.

When he got to the top, he sat down for a moment to recover. The moon was rising over the sea. No sign of Uncle Ted and the yacht. A bright star hung low in the sky. Could that be Venus?

Max jumped up and headed inland. A path plunged into the rainforest and he guessed it would lead to DeLanda's camp. Mindful of Hermanjilio's disparaging remarks about his clumsiness, he moved as quickly and as silently as he could.

He didn't notice the body until he nearly fell over it.

The guard was sprawled across the path, with a blowgun dart sticking out of his neck. The Black Jaguar of the Night had struck again! A hundred yards farther on, Max found two more bodies, then another, and another. All felled by blowgun darts.

Maybe they could beat these thugs after all. Max was just starting to feel hopeful when he heard the crack of automatic gunfire ahead. The fight was still going on.

When Max got close to DeLanda's camp, he left the path and crept through the bushes. The last ten feet he covered on his belly, inching forward until he could spy on the camp from under a bush. Everywhere looked deserted. The rising moon cast a ghostly light over the scene.

Where was everyone?

Max lay still, his every nerve on high alert. He tried to filter out the cacophony of the rainforest and listen for voices or gunfire.

Suddenly, he had the unnerving sensation that someone was behind him.

He thought of the bodies on the path. Had those guards had the same sensation just before they'd been hit?

Slowly, very slowly, he turned his head and looked over his shoulder. Out of the corner of his eye he saw a movement. There was someone in the bushes.

Crouching now, Max pulled out his diver's knife. He scanned the undergrowth, but all he could see was the trembling of a fern frond that had recently been disturbed. His heart was beating fast. He listened hard, his ears straining for a clue.

Suddenly, out of the bushes, came a loud fart, followed by peals of laughter.

"Lady Coco!" whispered Max in delight.

She emerged from the bushes, her crossed eyes streaming with tears of laughter, just as Lord Six-Rabbit dropped to the ground out of a branch above her.

"I apologize, Young Lord, for the unseemly behavior of my mother," he said. "She has been making an exhibition of herself all day."

Lady Coco emitted another barrage.

"Ignore her, I beseech thee," said Lord Six-Rabbit.

"But what's happening? Where are DeLanda's men?" asked Max.

"They sleep like newborn babes."

"All of them? But how?"

"Last night, as we had planned, Lord Hermanjilio slipped into the camp. To our most glorious luck, the cook is a local man named Eligio — whom Lord Hermanjilio knows well. When he heard about DeLanda's evil plans, Eligio agreed to pour a bottle of my sleeping draught into the lunchtime stew. An hour later, all who had partaken of the stew were out cold."

"Result!" cheered Max. "Then what?"

"Eligio armed himself and hid in the jungle to wait for DeLanda. We pursued the stray guards who had not eaten the stew."

"Who's 'we'?"

"Lord Hermanjilio and myself."

There was a squawk of protest from Lady Coco.

"Mother helped too," sighed Lord Six-Rabbit. "Her duty was to create a loud and malodorous diversion of the kind you just witnessed. While the guards were transfixed in horror, Lord Hermanjilio and I would take aim with our blowpipes."

"Way to go, Lord Six-Rabbit!" said Max admiringly. "Those blowpipes are taller than you are!"

"Indeed," said Lord Six-Rabbit ruefully. "Lord Hermanjilio cut one in half for me. It is not as accurate as I would like, but it works."

"Excuse me," interrupted Lady Coco, poking a hairy finger into Max's chest. "Perhaps the young lord would like to compliment me on my diversionary skills. It's not easy maintaining such a high quality of flatulence, you know."

"I can imagine," said Max politely. "Way to go, Lady Coco!"

"Thank you," she said, with a regal air. Then she gave a few little toots of acknowledgment and jumped back into the trees to groom herself.

Max turned back to Lord Six-Rabbit.

"Did you get all the guards?" he asked.

"Unfortunately not. Due to the imprecision of my blowpipe, one of them was able to escape and make contact with the Spanish vessel."

"So that's why they all left the yacht in such a hurry," said Max.

"We were ready for them," smiled Lord Six-Rabbit. "When DeLanda landed with reinforcements, we ambushed them on the path."

"I fell over some of your victims! Did you get DeLanda?"

"It pains me to tell thee, but no. Instead of leading from the front like a noble Maya warlord, he hid at the rear like a coward. While we battled his men, he scuttled into the forest with Lady Lola and two of his bodyguards."

"Poor Lola! We have to help her! Where are they now?" asked Max.

"They're heading toward the Black Pyramid," said Lady Coco. "Eligio, the cook, has been taking pot shots at them to slow them down. We're hoping Lord Hermanjilio will get there first."

"I thought I heard gunfire. I hope the cook doesn't hit Lola by mistake."

"As I understand it, Eligio is not trying to hit anyone," said Lord Six-Rabbit. "He is merely taunting them, like a buzzing mosquito. Meanwhile, Mother and I are taking up position to attack DeLanda's flank if thou wouldst care to join us."

He made it sound like an invitation to tea and scones.

A shot rang out followed by a burst of automatic fire.

"Come," said Lord Six-Rabbit, "we must hurry."

They worked their way around the edge of the camp to the side of the pyramid. When they had taken cover behind a fallen tree trunk, Lord Six-Rabbit handed Max his cut-down blowgun and his last pouch of darts.

"Here, Young Lord," he said regretfully. "Thy lungs are bigger than mine."

"What will you do?" asked Max.

"Mother and I will collect some tactical ammunition."

Before Max could ask what he meant, the two monkeys had swung through the trees and vanished from sight.

Max was alone again. He surveyed the scene in the moonlight. Looking up at the Black Pyramid, he thought he could make out Hermanjilio lying low, blowgun at the ready. Max gave a little wave. Hermanjilio nodded, held his finger to his lips, and pointed across the clearing. Evidently, that was where DeLanda was expected to emerge.

Max waited nervously. He loaded one of the darts into the blowgun and carefully placed the other two in front of him.

Tucka-tucka-tucka!

Max ducked behind the tree trunk as the three men burst out of the forest in a blaze of machine-gun fire. DeLanda was pushing Lola along in front of him. His two bodyguards shot at anything and everything as they ran across the clearing toward the steps of the pyramid.

The noise was terrifying — guns shooting, men shouting, parrots shrieking — but Max tried to stay calm, waiting for the right moment.

He knew he would only get one chance.

And, armed with only a blowgun, he also knew the odds were against him.

In the end, it happened so quickly that he hardly had time to think.

Just as DeLanda reached the bottom step, the two monkeys let loose with a volley of stones from high above Max's head. The bodyguards paused to blitz the treetops with machine-gun fire. Max crouched behind the log, not daring to breathe, as leaves and twigs exploded and rained down onto the forest floor. An animal shrieked and fell through the branches, landing with a thud somewhere behind him.

It was now or never.

Adrenaline pumped through his veins as he fired his three darts in quick succession. At the same moment, Hermanjilio fired from the top of the pyramid.

Yes! Yes!

The two bodyguards staggered and then collapsed.

No!

DeLanda pulled Lola in front of him like a human shield. One arm was round her throat; the other pointed a gun into her back. She was swaying and moaning, as if her entire body was trying to fight whatever drug he had given her.

"Hold your fire!" DeLanda shouted. "One more shot and I will kill the girl."

Max kept completely still.

"And now, I will to count to three. *Uno, dos, tres.* If you do not step out with your hands up, your little friend is dead."

Max looked up at Hermanjilio but couldn't see him. What should he do?

"*Uno!*"

His mind raced. Each second seemed like eternity. If he didn't come out, DeLanda was probably ruthless enough to shoot Lola in cold blood.

"*Dos!*"

But if he did come out, DeLanda might shoot him in cold blood.

"*Tres!*"

"Stop!" yelled Max. "Don't shoot, I'm coming out."

"No . . . urgh," groaned Lola, as DeLanda choked her words by pulling his arm tighter round her windpipe.

Max slowly stood up and put his hands in the air. As he emerged from the underbrush, he took in the whole scene for the first time.

The full moon rising overhead. The brooding menace of the Black Pyramid. The two guards sprawled on the lower steps. DeLanda swiveling around to shoot him.

Max froze, waiting for the hail of bullets.

Then he saw a movement out of the corner of his eye, something soaring into the sky behind DeLanda. So unexpected was the sight that it took his brain a moment to register what it was.

A pineapple. It was a pineapple.

It sailed through the air in a graceful arc. When it reached its high point, it seemed to hang there for several seconds like a little UFO, hovering in the moonlight. And then the pineapple started its downward trajectory, plummeting to earth with increasing speed.

DeLanda became aware that Max was not looking at him, but at something above him. He turned to look up, only to catch the pineapple squarely in the face. It exploded, sending pineapple chunks and juice in every direction. DeLanda staggered and Lola groggily pushed him away.

Now Hermanjilio had a clear target and, as Max watched, a silent dart embedded itself in DeLanda's forehead. The Spaniard didn't even have time to flick his cape before he crumpled to the ground.

A loud whoop came from the jungle in the same direction as the pineapple. Max vaulted the log and ran toward Lola, who was slumped against the bottom step of the pyramid. Lady Coco swung out of the trees and got to her first.

"Lady Lola! Are you all right?"

Lola groaned. She put her hands to her head. "I feel like I've been drinking Hermanjilio's elixir," she said.

"DeLanda drugged you," explained Max, "but it seems to be wearing off. Luckily for us, his sleeping potion isn't as strong as ours." A loud snore erupted from the Spaniard. "Anyway, he's getting a taste of his own medicine now."

Lady Coco jumped up and down in excitement. "Did you see that?" she asked. "What a perfect shot! And I've had no military training, you know."

"It was incredible, Lady Coco," said Max. "You saved my life."

Lady Coco smiled modestly, but her crossed eyes were shining with pride. "Did you hear that, son?" she asked, looking around for Lord Six-Rabbit. "I promised I'd make a good warrior . . ."

"Enough talking!" came a booming voice from the pyramid.

They looked up to see Hermanjilio, making his way down. He seemed to be limping.

"Are you hurt?" Max shouted up to him.

"We will all be hurt," Hermanjilio called down, through cupped hands, "if we don't get the Black Jaguar and get out of here."

"The Black Jaguar? DeLanda must have it," said Max, running over to the count's prone body. When he moved the Spaniard's cape aside, he saw two large pouches hanging from a leather belt at his waist.

Quickly, Max cut them free with his diver's knife.

He looked inside the first pouch. A pure white light shone out as the moonlight danced off the translucent alabaster stone of the White Jaguar.

He opened the second pouch. A smell of rotting flesh filled his nostrils.

"I've found it," he called.

"Show me," bellowed Hermanjilio from halfway down the pyramid.

Max put his hand inside the pouch and there was a sudden vicious snarl. He screamed in pain as the needle-sharp teeth of a savage animal sank into his flesh. He pulled out his hand, expecting to find it bitten and bleeding, but there were no marks on it. He drew the drawstring tight to close the pouch.

"It's there all right and the White Jaguar, too," he called, holding up the pouches to show Hermanjilio. "We'll bring them up."

Max turned back to the group in triumph, but Lola and Lady Coco had no interest in the stones. They were looking around and calling into the jungle.

"What is it?" asked Max.

Lady Coco looked distraught. "My son, where is he?"

Max had a sinking feeling.

"Oh no," he said. "I heard an animal get shot and fall through the trees when DeLanda burst out of the jungle. It might have been Lord Six-Rabbit."

Hermanjilio was getting impatient. "What are you doing? This is no time for nature study! Bring me the stones and let's go . . . "

"Wait," called Max. "We have to find Lord Six-Rabbit. We think he might be . . . " He saw Lady Coco's anguished face, " . . . hurt."

"Hurry," commanded Hermanjilio.

Lola groaned. "I'm so dizzy," she said. "I'll sit on the steps and wait for you."

So they left the Jaguar Stones with her and went back into the forest to look for Lord Six-Rabbit. It was not an easy task. Very little moonlight filtered down to the rainforest floor and the thick foliage made it difficult to search. They found a Red Sox cap hanging on a branch, but no sign of Lord Six-Rabbit.

In the end, it was Lady Coco's finely tuned nose that located the spot where her son had landed when DeLanda shot him out of the trees.

They found his limp, blood-soaked body under a thorn bush.

Max put an ear to the brave monkey's chest and heard nothing but his own breathing. Tears welled in his eyes.

"Is he . . . dead?" whispered Lady Coco.

Max listened again. He held the monkey close and burrowed his ear into its fur. He could just make out a faint heartbeat.

"No," said Max with relief. "He's badly hurt, but he's alive."

Max tenderly put the Red Sox cap back on Lord Six-Rabbit's head. Then he took the monkey's limp body in his arms and carried him to the base of the pyramid.

"Lola!" he called, "Lola! We found him!"

No answer. She wasn't there. She must have felt better and gone up with Hermanjilio. She was probably showing him the escape route. Max cursed to himself. He'd been counting on her to rustle up one of her rainforest remedies.

Max laid Lord Six-Rabbit out in the moonlight where he could take a proper look at his wounds. He'd been shot through the arm and a second bullet had grazed his hip. It was bad, but not as bad as it had looked at first. Max took off his T-shirt and tore it into bandages while Lady Coco mopped her son's brow with a banyan leaf.

"Mama's here, Little Rabbit," she whispered in his ear.

When they'd done all they could to tend Lord Six-Rabbit's wounds, Max gathered up the injured monkey and began to stagger up the temple steps with him. It was surprising how much one howler monkey could weigh. Lady Coco tried to help, but it was slow going.

"Lady Coco," gasped Max, exhausted and only half way up, "I think you need to get Hermanjilio. Ask him to come down and help me."

She hesitated. She didn't want to leave Lord Six-Rabbit's side.

"He'll be OK," said Max.

Lady Coco licked her son's face tenderly, then bounded off up the temple steps. When she reached the top, she leaned over and waved, before disappearing from view through the cavernous mouth of the demon jaguar.

Max kept looking up hopefully, but no one appeared to help him.

Eventually he arrived at the top platform with no help from anyone.

He was breathing hard from the weight of the monkey and the steepness of the climb. He was tired and angry. He carried the monkey into the gaping maw of the doorway. As he lurched into the chamber of skulls, he was ready to give Hermanjilio a piece of his mind. How could he let Max struggle all the way up here on his own?

Then his resentment was replaced by a new feeling.

It was called fear.

Make that *terror*.

The hairs on the back of Max's neck rose up.

Something felt very wrong.

As his eyes adjusted to the darkness, he looked round the chamber.

What was that dark shape on the floor? He gasped as he made out the inert body of Lady Coco, a blowgun dart sticking out of her back.

Max had only one thought. He had to get out of there fast.

Still carrying Lord Six-Rabbit, he turned to go back.

As he did so, he caught sight of Hermanjilio's arm swinging down, the glowing Black Jaguar in his hand.

The stone hit Max hard on the side of his skull.

His head exploded into stars and he dropped to the ground unconscious.

CHAPTER XXV

HUMAN SACRIFICE

MAX STRUGGLED, BUT he couldn't move. He was pinned down to something. A hideous face leaned over and leered at him. She was the ugliest girl he'd ever seen. And as she smiled, he saw that she had fangs like a vampire bat.

There was a sickly smell of incense. He could hear the abrasive scraping of a knife being sharpened.

"Prepare to die, my little fool," crowed the Maya vampire girl. She licked his face.

Her breath was foul. Her tongue was rough and slimy. He pushed her away, but she kept coming back and licking him. He tried to scream, but she held her hairy black hand over his mouth.

He was still struggling when he woke up.

His head hurt. A monkey was licking his face.

Monkey spit! Gross!

He tried to protest, but a paw was clamped over his mouth.

"Make no noise," said the monkey.

A talking monkey!

Max tried to scream.

"Make no noise, Young Lord," repeated the monkey.

Max nodded. The paw was removed.

Max opened his mouth to scream as loudly as he could.

The paw was clamped back on.

"If he hears thee, he will kill thee," whispered the monkey.

Max had heard that voice before. He looked hard at the monkey. Its fur was matted with blood. It was wearing a baseball cap. It curled back its lips and attempted a reassuring smile, which made it look even more freakish.

"I am Lord Six-Rabbit," said the creature, "summoned from the Underworld to help thee . . . dost thou remember?"

It sounded familiar. Crazy, but familiar.

"I beg thy pardon if the ministrations of my tongue were offensive. It was the only way to rouse thee. Dost thou promise not to scream?"

Max nodded.

Lord Six-Rabbit removed his paw. Max considered screaming.

"No, Young Lord," said the monkey, wagging a hairy finger. "We have no time for games. We have to stop him."

"Stop who?" said Max, thickly. He was having trouble getting his thoughts together. His fingers explored the huge lump on his head. It felt wet and sticky. The slightest touch sent pain shooting through his brain.

Where was he?

He looked around. The walls seemed to be made entirely of human skulls.

That couldn't be good.

An eerie gray light flooded in through an open doorway. On the floor, he could make out the body of another monkey.

It was sleeping. Its name was Lady Coco.

How did he know that?

"Trust the baboons," said a voice in his head.

And then, in a flash, it all came back to him.

"Lord Six-Rabbit," he whispered, "are you all right? I was carrying you when . . . when . . . " his voice tailed off. He was about to say, *when Hermanjilio hit me* — but that couldn't be right. Could it?

"I am well enough, Young Lord," said Lord Six-Rabbit. "The force of the blow knocked me to the floor and brought me to my senses. I feigned death, but I saw everything. Come now, we must stop him . . . "

Lord Six-Rabbit helped Max to his feet.

"Stop who?" said Max.

"Tzelek!"

"Tzelek? You mean DeLanda-slash-Tzelek?"

"No, Young Lord, I mean Lord Hermanjilio-slash-Tzelek."

"What? I don't get it," said Max. "How did Tzelek get out of De-Landa and into Hermanjilio?"

"It doth appear that he wast never in DeLanda. It is my belief that when Lord Hermanjilio opened the gateway at Itzamna for mother and me, Tzelek sneaked through at the same time. He has been hiding inside Lord Hermanjilio since that night."

"But why didn't we notice?"

"It suited Tzelek's purpose to lay low. Like a strangler fig, he lived in harmony with his host until he had taken what he wanted. He has used Lord Hermanjilio to bring him to the Pyramid of Ah Pukuh this night and give him the Black Jaguar. Unwittingly, we have all done his bidding." Lord Six-Rabbit indicated the gray light beyond the doorway. "And now the rituals have begun."

The horror of the situation sank into Max's throbbing brain.

He crawled over to the doorway and peered out.

He was not prepared for the shock of what he saw and he had to clap his own hand over his mouth to keep from crying out.

Hermanjilio-slash-Tzelek was dancing rhythmically around the sacrificial altar.

The altar was a huge stone slab, supported at each corner by a column of human skulls. Set into the end facing Max was the body of a jaguar inlaid in black obsidian. On the headless shoulders of this beast, the Black Jaguar Stone now radiated its murky light. At its feet, the White, Red, and Green Jaguars added their own glow. The air stank of rotting flesh mingled with pungent incense.

In the center of this nightmare, lashed to the altar stone by her hands and feet, was Lola.

She was dressed in a blue tunic and her skin was daubed in blue paint. She seemed to be awake, but she was limp and lethargic. Her half-open eyes tried to follow Tzelek as he pranced round the altar, chanting. His dance was made all the more macabre by the strange, half-limping, half-lurching gait caused by the twisted foot he dragged behind him. In one hand, he carried a small stone bowl. In the other hand, he brandished a long knife.

Each time he circled the altar, Tzelek slashed his own ears and collected the dripping blood in the bowl. When it was full, he stopped in front of the Black Jaguar and let out a piercing howl. Then he lifted the bowl with both hands and dribbled his blood onto

the Black Jaguar. The pyramid started to vibrate, as if the whole structure was awakening. Tzelek cackled in delight.

Flames shot out of the stone and spread slowly over the altar. They engulfed Lola, but she did not seem to burn. The brightest flames were around the Black Jaguar. It was now white with heat and its eyes burned deep red.

As Max watched in horror, it opened its glittering mouth and roared. When the other Jaguar Stones roared in reply, Tzelek smiled like a proud mother.

Glowing eyes appeared in the black recesses of the skulls supporting the altar stone and their jaws began to chant a dirge. Rings of light pulsed in waves out of the altar, getting bigger and bigger like ripples in a pond. They rolled across the top of the pyramid and over the edges. They flowed down the stepped sides, vaporizing the vegetation and soil that still covered much of the pyramid. They reached the bottom steps where DeLanda's guards lay sleeping and consumed their bodies without trace.

When the pyramid was as clear as the day it was built, a gray light shone out of the cracks between the stones. Behind the altar, it looked as if the fabric of the world had ripped apart. A jagged black hole, a void of nothingness, shimmered like a supernatural heat haze. Bubbles of flame rose up from the altar stone and were sucked into the void.

Tzelek dipped the tip of his knife into the bowl of blood and traced an incision line on Lola's tunic above her heart. Still crouching at the doorway, Max was transfixed with horror. He nearly jumped out of his skin when Lord Six-Rabbit tapped him on the shoulder.

"The time has come, Young Lord," he whispered. "I will fell Tzelek with a dart. Thou shouldst be ready to pluck out the Black Jaguar from the altar."

"How? It looks white-hot."

"It will bite and scratch, but it cannot burn thee," said Lord Six-Rabbit, picking up Hermanjilio's blowpipe from the floor of the chamber. It was twice as tall as he was. He loaded it with a dart, dragged it to the doorway, lifted it, and took aim. His injured arm buckled instantly from the weight and length of the blowpipe.

"Blast this baboon body," he muttered. "Young Lord, I beg thee, hold the end of the blowpipe steady for me."

Max's hands were shaking too much. He couldn't do it. Lola would die.

"Kneel down. Let me rest it on thy shoulder."

Max suspected his shoulders were shaking too, but he obeyed.

Tzelek raised the knife high above his head. The obsidian blade glinted in the moonlight. Seconds before the knife was plunged into Lola's chest, Lord Six-Rabbit fired. The dart sped straight toward Tzelek's neck.

Max thought he would faint with relief. He crouched like a runner on the starting blocks, ready to sprint to the altar the second the dart hit its target.

Tzelek looked up and smirked.

The dart stopped in midair, inches from his face, and burst into flames. Then it dropped harmlessly to the floor.

Tzelek turned to Lord Six-Rabbit, hands on hips, and laughed.

"Oh, *puh-lease*! You've had twelve hundred years to prepare for this moment, Six-Rabbit, is that the best you can do? But then you have shrunk in stature since last we met. And you've given up shaving too, I see. I'm sure the ladies do not find you quite as handsome this time around. You pathetic buffoon! You can't stop me killing this girl anymore than you could stop me killing your father."

Lord Six-Rabbit froze, his monkey eyes fixed on Tzelek.

"Yes, it was I!" boasted Tzelek. "I killed Punak Ha! I would gladly have stood by his side at the dedication ceremony, but it was you he wanted. It was always you. So I killed him. And I vowed that one day I would have more power than either of you." Tzelek raised the knife again. "This is my day."

There was a bloodcurdling roar, like a soul in torment, and Lord Six-Rabbit sprang across the platform as if he'd been shot from a cannon. He propelled himself high into the air and landed on Tzelek's face. His tail wrapped around his half brother's neck while his paws gripped his head in a vice. A savage expression contorted his features as he sank his teeth deep into the evil priest's nose.

Tzelek screamed.

This was Max's chance. He raced across to the altar, thrust his hands into the flames, and grabbed the Black Jaguar Stone. It writhed and jerked and snapped at his fingers. Pain shot through him, but he did not let go.

Out of the corner of his eye, he saw something flying at him. The next moment, he was knocked to the ground by the body of Lord Six-Rabbit, which Tzelek had pulled off his face and flung at him.

Before Max knew it, Tzelek had him by the throat and the high priest's face was next to his. It was Hermanjilio's nose and mouth that breathed their fury on him, but the rest of the face he did not recognize. The eyelids were hooded like an iguana's, and Hermanjilio's gentle brown eyes were black coals glowing red with evil. Max could feel his life being squeezed out as Tzelek's icy cold hands tightened their grip and once again his sharp nails pierced Max's skin.

With one last, almighty effort, Max started beating the evil priest with his fists and kicking him wildly.

Tzelek's lip curled in scorn.

"You little worm," he sneered. "Do you think you can fight the mighty Tzelek? You disgust me. You are not even fit for sacrifice. Go and join your idiot parents in Xibalba!"

He raised Max above his head and prepared to pitch him into the black void. Max tensed, waiting to be propelled through the gateway.

So this was how his story ended.

Tukka-tukka-tukka.

A machine gun fired at close range. Tzelek staggered in surprise and dropped Max onto the stone platform. The High Priest spun around as Lucky Jim, gun in hand, took a flying leap at him.

"You're going back to Xibalba where you belong!" shouted

Lucky Jim as his huge body hit Tzelek high in the chest. The two men went flying together into the void.

There was no flash, no scream, no smell of burning.

All that remained was silence.

In a daze, Max lurched to his feet and tried to pull out the Black Jaguar. It scratched and clawed him, but he didn't care anymore. In one supreme effort, he wrenched it out and threw it down.

It was done.

Like a speeding car suddenly thrown into reverse, the whole pyramid shook from top to bottom.

There was a crashing sound like thunder. The stones of the pyramid jumped up and down; some even shot out of place. The edges of the black void were sucked back together. In an instant, the hole was gone.

For a moment, Max lay there, gasping for breath, replaying it all in his mind. Then he sat up and moved his head stiffly, like someone in a neck brace, to look around the platform for Lord Six-Rabbit.

The monkey king was slumped against the wall. He was covered in blood and chunks of his fur were missing.

Max crawled over to him and they sat there, exhausted, leaning against each other.

It was over. They had won.

"Tell me, Young Lord, who was that brave warrior who sent Tzelek back to Xibalba?" asked Lord Six-Rabbit.

"His name is Lucky Jim," said Max. "He works with my uncle. He was on DeLanda's yacht. I told him what was going on and I asked him to help, but he locked himself in his cabin. I thought he didn't want to get involved, but he must have been preparing himself for battle." Max clutched the monkey's arm. "We owe him everything. We can't leave him in Xibalba. We have to help him."

"All in good time, Young Lord. We have won this battle, but we have not won the war. First I must do what I should have done before and destroy the Black Jaguar. I will grind it into powder and scatter it to the winds, so that it can never again menace the mortal world."

Suddenly the altar stone began to rise, supported by a shimmering curtain of red light. All the relief Max was feeling evaporated in an instant.

"What's happening?" he cried hysterically. "Is Tzelek coming back?"

"Calm thyself," whispered Lord Six-Rabbit. "I know not what sorcery this is, but as long as the Black Jaguar is removed from the altar, Tzelek cannot return."

"So who's that?"

A curtain of light had detached itself from the altar frame and was forming, from the feet up, into the hologram of a person. A man. A man with muscular legs. He was wearing a white tunic and a white cape. He was carrying a scroll. His nose was huge . . . wait, it was not a nose, it was a curved yellow beak. His face was covered in feathers. He had the head of an owl!

Lord Six-Rabbit bowed his head respectfully and nudged Max to do the same.

The figure spoke slowly in a deep, echoing voice: "I am Lord Muan, messenger of the gods." (He pronounced his name moooo-an like a hooting owl.) "I bring a message for Massimo Francis Murphy from my masters, the twelve Death Lords of Xibalba: One Death, Seven Death, Scab Stripper, Blood Gatherer, Demon of Pus, Demon of Jaundice, Bone Scepter, Skull Scepter, Demon of Filth, Demon of Woe, Wing, and Packstrap."

The messenger paused for breath. He looked at Max for a response, but seeing that the boy was transfixed with terror and incapable of speech, he held up the scroll and began to read from it:

"Woe to thee, Massimo Francis Murphy, for thou hast disappointed the Lords of Death. They command me to ask of thee: Why hast thou changed?"

"Wh . . . wh . . . what do you mean?" stammered Max.

"When their lordships first observed thee, thou wast as greedy and selfish as one of their own. But now, like a snake shedding its skin, thou hast sloughed off the old ways that made thee special to them."

Max suddenly thought of Zia, her arms full of laundry, in the kitchen in Boston. *"They say you must go there,"* she was saying. *"They think you are special."* A horrible thought occurred to him. "The D-D-Death Lords didn't bring me here, did they?" he asked

The messenger looked down his beak at Max. "Of course not," he said. "What a looooooo-dicrous idea."

Max breathed a sigh of relief. For a moment there, he'd started to think that Zia was acting on otherworldly orders when she bought his plane ticket.

"It was not the Death Lords whooooo brought thee here," continued the messenger, disparagingly. "It was the gods. The gods have chosen thee."

"Why?" asked Max, fearfully. "Why me?"

The messenger surveyed him with distaste. "It is a curious choice, I grant thee."

"But what do they want from me?"

"I cannot speak for the gods. I come with a message from the Death Lords."

"Gods? Death Lords? What's the difference?" Max whispered to Lord Six-Rabbit.

"The Death Lords serve Ah Pukuh, but they are not gods themselves," he whispered back. "They squander their time playing games of chance and making foolish bets between themselves. They are compulsive gamblers, all of them."

A series of disgusting rasping noises was coming from the messenger. He looked at them with a pained expression. Then, slowly and deliberately, he stretched his neck forward and ejected an owl pellet. All three of them watched as the hard gray pellet rolled along the floor and came to a stop against the altar. Then the messenger cleared his throat and raised the scroll again:

"Massimo Francis Murphy, their Lordships had thought thee a kindred spirit. They wagered their entire stock of balché that, faced with the perils of the jungle, thou wouldst turn to the dark side for help. But thou hast confounded their expectations. Instead of mewling like a newborn kitten, thou hast fought bravely like a mighty jaguar."

"Thank you," said Max.

"Thank yooooooooo?" repeated the owl, incredulously. "Thank yooooooooo? How *darest* thou? My masters have lost their wager. *Why* didst thou change? Speak!"

Under the gaze of those piercing yellow eyes, Max felt like a small rodent that was about to eaten. "I . . . er . . . " he spluttered, "I don't know . . . I'm sorry . . . I'm just trying to find my parents."

"Ah, yes," said the messenger coldly, "Frank and Carla Murphy."

"You know them?" said Max in surprise.

"Of course. They are in the waiting rooms of Xibalba."

"What about Hermanjilio Bol and Lucky Jim?"

The messenger nodded.

"Are they OK?"

"They are a little too virtuous for our tastes."

"No, I mean, are they still living, breathing people? You haven't sucked out their souls or anything? They can still come back to Middleworld?"

"In theory, yes . . . "

Max brightened.

" . . . In practice, no."

"Why not?" asked Max.

"Whooooooo dares to ask why not?" hooted the messenger. "Thou hast defied the Lords of Death at every turn. Thanks to thee, my masters have lost all their balché. If they decide to flay thy parents alive and wear their skins as summer capes, it will be but a small punishment for thy calumny."

"Look, I really am very sorry," said Max desperately. "There must be something I can do to make amends?"

"No!" cried Lord Six-Rabbit, clamping a paw over Max's mouth. "Bargain not with the Lords of Death. Thou canst not win. Thou canst only lose thy mortal soul."

"I see *thou* hast not changed, Six-Rabbit — thou wast ever the wet blanket," said the messenger. "Let the young lord speak for himself. Tell me, Massimo Francis Murphy, what didst thou have in mind?"

"I'd do anything to free my parents."

"One moment," said the messenger. He seemed to be listening to voices in his head. Max assumed the Death Lords were giving him instructions, like ghoulish TV producers speaking from some cosmic control room. At one point he broke off to check a technicality with Max. "Thou didst say thou wouldst do *anything*?"

Max nodded.

Lord Six-Rabbit groaned.

The messenger stepped forward. He looked displeased. "This is most irregular, but it seems their Lordships have had a change of heart. They have decided to accept thine apology. They are prepared to release thy parents."

Max's face lit up. "Did you hear that, Lord Six-Rabbit? That's fantastic!"

Lord Six-Rabbit was unimpressed. "It is a trick," he said, "and it stinks like a rotting fish."

The owl narrowed his eyes. "Such cynicism is unwarranted, my old friend. For, in return for this extraordinarily generous gesture, my magnanimous masters ask only for one small favor, if they should ever need it."

"That sounds fair enough," said Max, eager to do the deal.

"No," said Lord Six-Rabbit, "the Lords of Death cannot be trusted. Who knows what this *small favor* might entail? Thou canst not make a pact with evil."

"I should mention," said the messenger, "that if thou shouldst refuse this offer, all four guests will be sacrificed immediately. What sayest thou?"

"I have no choice," whispered Max to Lord Six-Rabbit. "At least it will buy us some time to rescue Hermanjilio and Lucky Jim."

"I warn thee, Young Lord, do not underestimate the Lords of Death."

Max took a deep breath. "I will be honored to owe their Lordships a small favor in return for the release of my parents."

"Thou hast spoken wisely. My masters will contact thee at the appointed hour." Like a used-car salesman clinching the deal, the messenger took a moment to attempt a cheesy smile and then launched into the small print. "I am required by cosmic law to inform thee that the size of the favor can go up as well as down. If thou shouldst break this pact, thy parents will be dragged back to Xibalba and sacrificed forthwith."

Lord Six-Rabbit shook his head. "No good will come of this," he muttered, but the messenger was already melting back into the curtain of light.

"Do you think they will release my parents?" asked Max anxiously.

Lord Six-Rabbit said nothing.

"Say *something*," Max pressed him.

"I did not know thy middle name was Francis."

Max rolled his eyes. "I know you don't approve of this deal, but what else could I do? It was the only way. Why can't you be a little more supportive?"

Lord Six-Rabbit squeezed his hand. For a moment, the boy and the monkey slumped against each other in silence, recovering from their ordeal.

Then the hologram of the messenger came back into sharp focus.

"I forgot something," he twittered.

His owl head rotated 360 degrees as he scanned the platform. Max and Lord Six-Rabbit could only watch in horror as his yellow eyes settled on the Black Jaguar. With a flourish, he took off his cape, picked up the Black Jaguar and the other three stones, bundled them all into his cape, and vanished into the light.

"How can a hologram do that?" asked Max.

"I do not know," said Lord Six-Rabbit weakly.

"And what did he mean when he said the gods brought me here?" persisted Max. "Why would the gods choose *me*? What do they want?"

"Forgive me, Young Lord," sighed Lord Six-Rabbit, " but I cannot talk more. This baboon body has served me well, but now it needs to rest. Thou shouldst rest too. For the moment, it is over."

Lord Six-Rabbit stretched out his hairy little limbs and fell instantly into a deep sleep. Seconds later, Frank and Carla Murphy stepped cautiously through the curtain.

CHAPTER XXVI

MORNING

HIS MOTHER'S HAIR was greasy and matted. Her face was sallow. She looked tired and old. His father, who always looked a mess, was even more dishevelled than usual. But, for once, Max didn't care what they looked like. He was just happy to see them.

But was it really them?

Or had Ah Pukuh sent two more demons to fool him?

He watched them closely.

Please let it be them.

They were squinting in the early light. They must have come from somewhere dark. They were shielding their eyes with their hands and looking nervously around. His heart felt like it would burst with love.

Please let it be them.

His mother saw him first.

"Max?" she said.

He wanted to throw himself into her arms. If it had been a movie, there would have been violins playing and he would have run to her in slow motion. As it was, he just stood there awkwardly, staring at her matted hair.

Please let it be them.

"Mom . . . ? Dad . . . ?"

After his experience with the demonic doppelgangers in the Black Pyramid, he needed proof that these two hobos really were his parents. He needed to test them in some way. But he was so tired, he could hardly think. He rubbed his eyes and wiped his nose on the back of his hand.

"Massimo Murphy! Use a Kleenex!"

No one else in the universe would fuss about manners at a time like this.

"Mom! It's really you!"

She hugged him until he couldn't breathe, then she stepped back and looked at him. "But what's happened to you, *bambino*? Are you hurt? You have a big lump on your head. And what's that on your skin?"

Max looked down at himself. He was bare to the waist, having ripped up his T-shirt to make bandages for Lord Six-Rabbit. His arms were still red from dye, and his chest was smeared with black body paint from his tussle with Hermanjilio-slash-Tzelek.

"It's been a long night," he said. Now that it was finally over, his legs started shaking uncontrollably.

"Sit," said his mother gently, wrapping him in her arms.

"I'm very glad to see you, Max," said his father, "but what are you doing here?"

"Zia got me a ticket. She arranged for me to stay with Uncle Ted."

"Zia? Ted? But you were supposed to be in Maine . . . "

"Don't worry, Dad, it's been much more educational than Brat Camp. I know all about snakes and scorpions and quicksand — and I've learned a lot of Maya stuff, too." Max could hear himself babbling on like a preschooler, but he couldn't stop. It all seemed like a bad dream. "We used the Jaguar Stones to bring back Lord Six-Rabbit, but then we discovered that Tzelek had snuck back as well and last night the *bak'tun* changed and there was a major showdown and the Death Lords agreed to release you . . . "

He paused for breath.

"Oh *bambino*," cooed his mother, close to tears.

"Tell me everything, Max," said his father.

"Can't you see that the poor boy is exhausted, Frank?" said his mother.

Max opened his mouth to protest and then he realized that she was right. He'd never been so tired in his life. He smiled at her gratefully and they lapsed into a contented silence, each one savoring the moment.

Behind them, the altar stone sank slowly back into place.

"Excuse me," said a drowsy voice. "Could somebody please untie me?"

"Lola!" cried Max, jumping up and running to cut her free with his diver's knife.

To his relief, she looked fine — a little sluggish and hollow-eyed and covered in blue paint, but basically fine. He guessed that Hermanjilio-slash-Tzelek must have given her something pretty strong to knock her out for the sacrifice.

"Hey, Monkey Girl!" he said. "Are you going to lie around all day?"

She sat up slowly and looked around her. "What happened? Where am I?"

"Lola!" cried Frank and Carla warmly, as they rushed over to help her down. She peered at them, not recognizing them, and returned their smiles halfheartedly. Then, suddenly, it was as if the whole story came rushing back to her, and her eyes lit up with happiness. "Hup, it's your parents . . . that's wonderful!"

"Yeah," he said, "it is."

As they sat there, a new day was dawning in the rainforest. The air was fresh. The sea was blue. A flock of green parrots rose up from the trees and flew whirling circles above the pyramid.

All around them, the forest buzzed with the sounds of early morning.

But there was another sound that was getting louder and louder.

It was the sound of someone huffing and puffing up the steps of the pyramid.

A look of terror crossed Lola's face.

"It's not DeLanda, is it?" she said.

Frank Murphy leaned over the edge.

"No," he said. "It's my brother."

First Ted Murphy's hands, then his hat, and then his face appeared, as he hauled himself over the top step. He was red and sweaty, and his linen suit was filthy. "Good morning, all," he said, tipping his hat.

"Uncle Ted!" cried Max. "We did it! We won! But we lost Lucky Jim."

Uncle Ted nodded sadly. "He knew what he was doing, Max. He said it was time to accept his destiny." He patted Max on the shoulder. "I'm glad to see you in one piece, though. And who else do we have here? Frank! Carla! What a fine morning for a meeting of Murphys!" His eyes fell on Lola, still painted blue, and he stared at her oddly for a few seconds before regaining his composure. "And you must be the famous Lola? I'm so pleased to meet you. "

Frank Murphy nodded at his brother. Carla smiled, Lola shook hands drowsily.

"But what are you doing here , Uncle Ted?" asked Max.

"I came out with the police. They're rounding up what's left of DeLanda's men, and then they'll give us all a lift back to the villa. Is everyone fit to travel?"

Frank Murphy nodded. "It looks like no one was hurt," he said, "except for a couple of monkeys."

"Actually, Dad," said Max, "those two monkeys are Lord Six-Rabbit and his mother, Lady K'an Kakaw. We call her Lady Coco."

"What?" said Frank and Carla and Ted.

"I remember that bit," said Lola, still sounding dazed. "But who was that maniac pretending to be Hermanjilio?"

"Hermanjilio Bol?" said Carla. "Is he here? Is he all right?"

"It's a long story, Mom," said Max. "Can we get some food, first? I'm starving."

"Good idea," said Uncle Ted. "Raul makes the best brunch in Central America."

Which is how they came to be speeding along the coast in a po-lice launch, headed back to the Villa Isabella. The monkeys were laid out on banquettes. Frank and Ted were deep in conversation on the deck. Carla was trying to fix her disheveled appearance. Max and Lola sat at a table in the cabin.

"How are you feeling?" he asked her.

"OK, I guess, considering . . . " she said. "But it gives me the creeps, just thinking about it. Can you believe that Tzelek was in-side Hermanjilio, all that time?"

"Remember when he clashed with Lord Six-Rabbit and we put it down to the dominant male thing?" said Max.

"Yeah," said Lola, "I should have known Hermanjilio wouldn't be so childish. I kept wondering why he didn't take advantage of having a real, live Maya king at Itzamna, ask him more about the history of the site and so on. It all makes sense now. Poor Herman-jilio. I feel like I let him down."

"You couldn't have known. Even Hermanjilio didn't know."

"We have to rescue him, Hup."

"Yeah, and Lucky Jim. Any ideas?"

"Well, how did you get your parents released?"

Max lowered his voice to a whisper. "Don't tell Mom and Dad, but I promised to do a favor for the Lords of Death."

"What favor?"

"I don't know yet."

"It's been nice knowing you," said Lola.

"Thanks for the vote of confidence."

"It's just that the Lords of Death are ruthless, you can't trust them an inch."

"Yeah," said Max. "Well, I didn't have much choice at the time."

Lola nodded sympathetically. "Poor Hup," she said. Then she brightened up. "Maybe your parents can think of a way to outwit them. I mean, they've actually been to Xibalba."

"No!" said Max. "I told you, I don't want them to know about this. It will only worry them. Besides, the Death Lords will probably never claim their stupid favor. They'll probably forget all about it."

Lola didn't look convinced.

"Anyway," said Max airily, "I've got the gods to back me up. They've chosen me. Lord Muan and Candelario and Eusebio all said it. How can I lose with the gods on my side? The Maya gods are good guys, aren't they?"

"Not particularly," said Lola. "We're not so hung up on the heroes-villains thing. In fact, the same god can be good and bad, male and female, old and young, human and animal . . . "

Max sighed heavily. "That's great. Just great. Between the gods and the Death Lords, I think I'm dead meat."

He laid his head on his arms. Lola ruffled his hair. He didn't stop her.

"You'll help me, won't you, Monkey Girl?"

"I don't know about that."

"What? You can't just go back to your old life and forget all about me. We're a team."

"What about *your* old life, Hup? You'll want to forget that any of this happened when you get back to Boston."

"No chance," said Max. He was already imagining how cool it would be to tell the guys at school that he had a Maya girlfriend.

He took her hand and squeezed it.

She pulled it away.

"What are you doing?" she said.

"Oh, I just thought, you know, what with everything we've been through together, we could, you know . . . ?"

"What?"

" . . . Um, go out."

"Go out? Where?"

"You know, go out. On a date."

She looked at him like he was mad. "We're friends, Hup. Don't spoil it."

"Why would it spoil it?'

"I don't want to think about that stuff. Candelario's got a waiting list of boys who want to marry me and I don't want any of them. I just want to study and travel and be me."

"I didn't ask you to marry me," said Max grumpily.

"Let's vow to be friends forever," said Lola. "We can do an oath of blood if you like."

He looked at her and saw that she was joking.

But *friends*? A girl as a friend, but not his girlfriend? He'd have to think about that one. Meanwhile, he decided to tell the guys she was his girlfriend anyway. It's not like they were ever going to fly to San Xavier to check it out.

As THEY TRAMPED across the beach to the Villa Isabella, Raul was waiting at the door. His smile of welcome faded as he took in their appearance. For a second, Max thought he might shoo them all away like beggars. You could see his point. Max was black and Lola was blue. All three adults were filthy and the two men were carrying what looked like dead monkeys.

Raul quickly regained his composure. "Welcome back," he said. "Brunch will be served in twenty minutes."

Lady Coco stirred.

"I smell food," she said, springing out of Frank Murphy's arms, her nose twitching furiously to identify all the various cooking smells.

"It's a talking baboon!" exclaimed Raul.

"Raul," said Max, "may I introduce you to Lady K'an Kakaw, First and Most Glorious Wife of the great King Punak Ha and mother of the immortal Lord Six-Rabbit, Godlike Jaguar Lord, Great Leader, He of the Twenty Captives. That's him lying over Uncle Ted's shoulder."

Raul looked at Uncle Ted. He gave a little nod to confirm Max's story.

If there was one thing Raul had learned in a lifetime's butler-ing, it was to keep cool under all circumstances. He drew upon that training now, bowing low to the monkey as if it were the most normal thing in the world.

"I am honored to meet you, Your Majesty," he said.

"Likewise," she said, "but please call me Lady Coco. Now tell me, Raul, is that banana bread I smell? With just a little hint of nutmeg, if I'm not mistaken?"

"It is indeed," smiled Raul. "My secret recipe."

"Perhaps I can persuade you to share it," she giggled flirtatiously. "Would you be so kind as to give me a tour of the kitchens?"

"But, of course, Lady Coco," said the butler. "Follow me."

"Raul — such a manly name . . . " came Lady Coco's voice as they disappeared down the corridor together, deep in conversation.

"Apparently, monkeys have extraordinary powers of recovery," smiled Uncle Ted. "Looks like Lady Coco's fine. There's a vet on his way to look at Lord Six-Rabbit. Meanwhile, we should just let him sleep."

He laid the unconscious monkey down on a sofa in the Great Hall.

"Now, ladies and gentlemen," he said, "there's just time to freshen up before brunch. Let's meet on the terrace in twenty minutes."

Max and Uncle Ted got there in fifteen.

"I know it's rather out of character," said Uncle Ted, throwing open his arms, "but would you mind if I gave my favorite nephew a hug?" He looked about twenty years younger than he had on DeLanda's boat. "I'm so glad to see you, Max. I don't know what's come over me. Between you and me, I was even glad to see your father."

"Yeah, I saw you and Dad talking on the boat. Have you buried the hatchet?"

"Well, I don't think we'll ever be best friends again. But when you go through an experience like this, it does change your perspective somewhat."

"You know, you were a hero yesterday," said Max. "You saved my life."

"No, Max, you were the hero. You and Lucky Jim."

"What made Lucky come and help me? I thought he didn't want anything to do with the Ancient Maya."

"Lucky finally accepted his heritage," said Uncle Ted. "He's always thought the old ways were nothing but trouble. He wanted his people to join the modern world and leave all that superstition behind. But when he heard you say that Tzelek and Six-Rabbit had returned, he realized that the past and the future are all one. He said it was time to stand up and be counted."

"And now he's trapped in Xibalba —"

"Those Ancient Maya won't know what's hit them when they meet Lucky Jim!" chuckled Uncle Ted. "I have a feeling he'll be OK."

Lola came out onto the terrace and sat down next to Max. The skin on her arms was red from scrubbing, but it still had a distinct blue tinge. She was wearing one of Uncle Ted's linen shirts as a very fetching dress.

"This is a lovely house," she said to Uncle Ted.

Max struck what he hoped was a dashing pose. He thought he probably looked passably attractive at this moment — freshly showered, hair gelled, clean clothes — sitting on his prosperous uncle's terrace. He decided to have one more go at persuading her to be his girlfriend. Time to turn on the charm.

He gave her the dazzling, toothy, superhero smile he'd been practicing in the bathroom mirror.

"Are you feeling all right, Hup? You look a bit strange."

He stopped smiling.

Pay her a compliment.

"That blue paint really suits you," he said.

Lola looked appalled.

Try another tack. Something more intellectual. Engage her in conversation.

"So what was it like," he asked, "being a human sacrifice?"

"Max!" protested Uncle Ted. "What kind of a question is that? I'm sure Lola doesn't want to talk about it."

But Lola looked thoughtful.

"I wish I could tell you, Hup," she said, "but I honestly don't remember. "

"What? *Nothing*?"

"Well, I remember that you left me sitting there with the Jaguar Stones. And I remember Hermanjilio coming down to get them. I was still groggy from DeLanda's drugs, so he carried me back up the Black Pyramid. He was limping and dragging his foot like Tzelek." Her voice was little more than a whisper. "And then I remember him standing over me with those red eyes . . . "

She looked like she might cry.

Uncle Ted put an arm round her.

"It's OK," he said, gently, "you're safe now."

Safe. Such a cozy, comforting word. A word that would never apply to Max Murphy of Boston, Massachusetts, until he'd sorted out this deal with the Death Lords and found out what it was that the Maya gods wanted from him. And to think that, only a few short weeks ago, his worst fear had been eating fried slugs at Brat Camp.

His reverie was interrupted by the arrival of his parents.

"*Buongiorno*," trilled his mother, looking like her old, well-groomed, shiny-haired self. She'd wrapped one of Uncle Ted's white tablecloths around her as a long dress, with a hibiscus flower for a corsage. She was as elegant as any New York socialite arriving at a dinner party, and Max got up to pull out a chair for her.

"*Grazie, bambino*," she said in surprise.

He kissed her cheek and smiled to himself as he felt her astonished expression following him back to his place.

"A stay with you seems to have worked wonders on the boy, Ted," said Max's father, who looked only marginally cleaner than when he'd emerged from Xibalba.

"Thank you, Frank," said Uncle Ted, "but I'm afraid I can't take the credit. Your son is a remarkable young man."

"Pinch me someone," laughed Max's mother. "First Max kisses me in public, then Frank and Ted have a civil conversation. I think I must be dreaming."

Max's own dream at that moment concerned food and plenty of it.

His stomach gave a loud growl.

And then, like a dream come true, Raul appeared with a huge serving dish of crispy bacon and juicy sausages and a platter piled high with barbecued ribs and steaks. He went away and soon returned with scrambled eggs, fried eggs, fluffy hash browns, racks of thickly sliced buttered toast, baskets of banana bread, bagels, doughnuts and pastries, and a massive bowl of tropical fruit salad.

Max felt like a warrior returning to a victory feast. For the next few minutes, he forgot everything that had happened and concentrated on eating. It was only when he thought his stomach might explode that he applied his mind to the situation again.

"So what was it like in Xibalba?" he asked his parents.

"Wet and misty and cold," said his mother, "like Venice in winter. Everything was in black and white, except for the flaming torches on the street corners and the blood-red water in the canals."

"Hermanjilio thought you'd be in some sort of waiting room," said Lola.

"Exactly right," nodded Max's father. "It was quite bare, just a few stools, a few bloodthirsty murals. And there we sat, wondering what was going to happen, talking about you mostly, Max."

"What were you saying about me?" he asked.

"For one thing," said his mother, "we agreed that we would never again both go away and leave you alone. In fact, we're thinking about giving up digs altogether until you go to college. We want to enjoy every second with you while we still can."

Max laughed nervously. "You make it sound like I'm going to die or something."

"Don't even joke about it," said his father. "We've all had a lucky escape. When I think what could have happened . . . " He put down his knife and fork and looked at Max with misty eyes. "I've learned my lesson, I promise you. I've had a lot of time to think about things, Max, and I realized that, even before I was imprisoned in Xibalba, I was spending more time with the Ancient Maya than I was with my own son. From now on, we're going to do a lot more together, you and me."

"We are? Like what?" asked Max.

"Well . . . let me see . . . " his father cast around for a suitable activity. "You could teach me to play some of those exciting video games of yours."

"Actually, Dad, I think I've had all the excitement I can take for a while. But perhaps *you* could teach *me* more about the Ancient Maya. I hate to admit it, but they're not as boring as I thought they were."

His father beamed at him.

The future was looking good. The only cloud on his horizon was the little matter of his debt. "By the way, Dad," he said, trying to sound casual, "did you ever meet the Death Lords when you were in Xibalba?"

"I'm afraid so," said his father.

"They're supposed to stay in the ninth level," added his mother, "but they're always sneaking up. It amuses them to torture the wretches in the waiting room. They're like psychotic children. One day, they made us play dentists." She shuddered.

"Of course," said Max's father, "dental mutilation was all the rage in their day."

"You didn't have to cooperate," said Max's mother.

"It was all in the name of research." His father sipped his coffee and flinched.

"Is that tooth still sensitive to heat, Frank?"

He nodded sheepishly.

"What did they do to you, Dad?" asked Max.

At that moment, Raul came out and whispered something to Uncle Ted.

"Excuse me, everyone," he said, "important phone call."

Max's father waited until Uncle Ted had gone inside before pulling down his lower lip to reveal a small piece of jade studded into one of his bottom teeth.

"Cool!" said Max. "Can I get one of those?"

"No!" said his mother firmly. "It looks like a piece of creamed spinach."

"How about a nose ring? Or some body piercing? Or a tattoo?" wheedled Max. "It's very Maya . . . "

"No! No! No!" said his mother, throwing up her hands in despair. She was looking to Lola for support, when Uncle Ted came striding back onto the terrace.

"Bad news, I'm afraid, " he said. "That was the chief of police on the phone. Not only has Count Antonio DeLanda vanished without a trace, but his yacht has disappeared from police custody."

"So he's still out there, flicking his cape somewhere?" smiled Lola.

"I wouldn't make fun of him, if I were you, young lady," said Uncle Ted. "He's a dangerous man and he won't stop until he gets what he wants."

"But what *does* he want?" asked Max. "The Jaguar Stones?"

"Something even more precious," said Uncle Ted.

"Why are you staring at me?" asked Lola. "I don't know the answer."

"I'm afraid you *are* the answer."

Lola looked horrified. "Why are you saying this?"

"I don't want to frighten you, Lola," said Uncle Ted, "but after Max made his getaway, I searched DeLanda's yacht from top to bottom. I found these photographs."

He pulled an envelope out of his inside pocket.

"Photographs?" whispered Lola.

Uncle Ted emptied the contents of the envelope onto the table.

"These are just a few of them — there were hundreds. And they were all of you. Your face, your eyes, your nose, your ears . . . he seems to be obsessed with you."

"Yesterday, he was obsessed with killing me," she said. "When he was dragging me through the jungle to the Black Pyramid, he was muttering about offering me to the gods." She put her face in her hands. "And when DeLanda failed, Tzelek took over the job. Do you realize that two different people tried to sacrifice me yesterday? Why me?"

"Well, whatever DeLanda's up to," said Uncle Ted, "you can't go back to Itzamna on your own. It's just not safe."

Lola looked down at the table. "I'll be fine," she said. "I'm used to looking after myself."

"A loner, eh?" said Uncle Ted. "But what will you do?"

Lola shrugged. "I haven't thought about it. Maybe I'll go back to Utsal. I could carry on with my studies, sort through Hermanjilio's notes, get all his research ready for when he comes back." Her eyes were still fixed on the table.

"You can't go back to Utsal," protested Max. "Candelario will marry you off. Besides, you can't study without a laptop. They don't have electricity at Utsal."

"So I'll go to Limón," said Lola. "I told you, I'll be fine."

"You know, Lola," said Uncle Ted, "I used to think of myself as a loner too. Until young Max here changed my mind. This big house is going to very empty without him. So I was wondering if you'd like to stay here and I could be your guardian until Hermanjilio gets back. You could go to school in Aguas Muertas, and I'm sure we could persuade Max to come and visit us now and again."

"It's a great idea!" smiled Max.

"Lola?" asked Uncle Ted.

"It's very kind of you, Mr. Murphy," she began politely, "but I couldn't. I don't think . . . it's just that . . . well, Hermanjilio said . . . "

"What?" cut in Uncle Ted, gently. "What are you trying to say?"

"You're a smuggler!" Lola blurted out.

Silence fell around the table. Max thought he detected the hint of a smirk on his father's face, but no one said anything. They were all waiting to see Ted's reaction.

"Oh, that," he said. "The truth is that, after my brush with De-Landa, I've rather lost the taste for it." Max saw his parents exchange approving glances as his uncle continued: "I have no children of my own, Lola, and that's something I regret. If you would do me the honor of living under my roof, I promise you I will give up my little sideline. I might even take up painting again."

"Say yes! Say yes!" urged Max.

Lola looked around the table. Everyone, including Raul and Lady Coco, was nodding furiously.

"I'll think about it," she said. But she was smiling.

"Splendid!" said Uncle Ted. "That's settled then." He looked happier than Max had ever seen him.

"More coffee, sir?" asked Raul. "And perhaps you'd like to sample one of Her Majesty's muffins?"

"I beg your pardon?" said Uncle Ted.

His eyes fell on Lady Coco, who was standing behind Raul, wearing a child-size white apron and carrying a tray of little cakes.

"Cashew and mango," she said proudly. "I made them myself."

"I didn't know you could cook, Lady Coco," said Max.

"Ah yes, Young Lord," she smiled. "All Ancient Maya women, even queens, had to make the tortillas for their families. And my tortillas were famous throughout the Monkey River."

"Excuse me, Lady Coco," ventured Max's mother, "but I'd love to know what you think of the kitchen, here at the villa? It must be very different from what you were used to in the palace at Itzamna."

Lady Coco's little monkey face lit up like Times Square at Christmas. "It's amazing!" she gibbered, "Raul showed me everything! That mixing machine and the refrigerating unit and the cooking fire that turns on and off . . . even the greatest brains of the mighty Maya did not invent such things!"

Max chuckled to see the bemused expression on his father's face as he listened to the Ancient Maya queen singing the praises of modern household appliances.

Frank Murphy still hadn't got his head round the concept of a talking monkey. "They'll never believe this back in Boston," he said, shaking his head. "Speaking of which, are you looking forward to going back to Beantown, Max?"

Max considered the question. Not so long ago, back in Boston was the only place he wanted to be. But now he wasn't so sure.

"I guess so," he said. He looked at Lola. "But I'm going to miss this place."

"I hope normal life won't be too boring for you, after all these adventures," his mother said.

Normal? He thought about the word. What was normal?

His mother was wearing a tablecloth. His father had a jade inlaid tooth. They certainly weren't normal parents. But now he knew that was a good thing. He wasn't sure what he'd promised to get them back, but anything was worth it.

Wasn't it?

"Mom," he said, "I've been wanting to ask you about Zia . . . "

He wasn't sure whether or not his mother heard him, but next thing she was deep in conversation with Lola about Maya weaving techniques.

As Max waited for an opportunity to repeat his question, a yellow butterfly landed on his hand. He tried to flick it away, but it clung on.

"What do you want?" he muttered. "Leave me alone."

The butterfly waved its antennae at him.

"You're making a big mistake," he whispered, "I'm not the one to help you. I'd pick another champion if I were you."

The butterfly hovered in front of his face for a moment and then did a little dance, fluttering backward and forward between his chair and the glass doors that led inside. Even Max could not ignore its meaning. The butterfly wanted him to follow it.

Curious to find out what the insect was trying to tell him, he got up and wandered into the house. He was going to go up to his room, but a movement in the Great Hall caught his eye. He went in to check on Lord Six-Rabbit.

An extraordinary scene awaited him.

The monkey king was sitting on top of his own great stone head, staring across at the head of Tzelek. The vet had obviously been and gone, as the monkey was patched and bandaged.

"Thy devilish scheme has failed," he was saying to the image of his half brother. "But I know thou wilt not stay long in Xibalba. Like a rat who squeezes through the smallest of holes, thou wilt find a way back. And as long as Ah Pukuh rules the *bak'tun*, he will aid thee. So be it. Hurry back to Middleworld, my brother, for we have unfinished business. Once again, we shall take up arms against each other. What has happened before will happen again. There is still a great battle in the stars for us. But I warn thee, the world has changed and so have I. So go ahead and lay thine evil plans. I will be waiting for thee."

Lord Six-Rabbit saw Max standing there. "Come, Young Lord," he said. "I have much to teach thee and we have no time to lose. The new *bak'tun* is upon us."

"So Ah Pukuh is in charge now?" asked Max.

Lord Six-Rabbit nodded. "His reign has begun, but we have

stayed his progress. The Undead Army slumbers on and Tzelek is back in Xibalba. Thanks to thy courage at the Black Pyramid, Ah Pukuh has his hands full for the moment."

"And then?"

"Then is then, Young Lord."

"Lord Six-Rabbit, do you believe the gods have chosen me?"

"I do."

"But why?"

"I believe they have chosen thee to fight the evil that threatens Middleworld."

Max looked appalled. "Why me?"

Lord Six-Rabbit shrugged. "Even mighty kings do not question the reasoning of the gods. I am sure they will reveal their motives in due course."

"But it doesn't make sense. I'm just a kid."

Lord Six-Rabbit climbed painfully down from the stone head and stood facing Max on the ground. "Have courage, Young Lord. The Hero Twins were about thine age when they rescued their father from Xibalba."

"Yeah," said Max, in a small voice. "You'll have to tell me how they did it."

"I will tell thee everything I know," said Lord Six-Rabbit. "And then together, shoulder to shoulder, we will battle the legions of hell."

The legions of hell.

Max thought of Candelario. *"The legions of hell are coming for you,"* he'd said. *"Trust the baboons."*

"Help me, Lord Six-Rabbit," whispered Max. "I'm afraid."

"What talk is this, Young Lord?" said the monkey, kindly. "And thou a noble warrior? Did we not fight alongside each other on the Black Pyramid? And hast thou not learnt that *anything* is possible? Why, if the great Lord Six-Rabbit can cavort as a jungle baboon, who knows what else can happen? Perhaps a boy with hair as red as fire can outwit the powers of evil as easily as the blazing Sun Jaguar defeats the night?"

"My hair's brown, actually," said Max. "Do you really think I stand a chance?"

Lord Six-Rabbit bared his monkey teeth in what he hoped was a reassuring grin and hid his crossed fingers behind his hairy back.

"Of course," he nodded. "Now let us get to work."

TO BE CONTINUED . . .

Why have the Maya gods
chosen Max Murphy?

What favor will the
Death Lords ask of him?

Where is the crazy count,
Antonio DeLanda, and why
does he have pictures of Lola?

What will happen to Hermanjilio
and Lucky Jim?

Will Tzelek escape Xibalba
to wreak more terror
on the mortal world?

What is Zia's secret?

Where is the long-lost
Yellow Jaguar?

These questions and
many more will be
answered in
*The Jaguar Stones:
Book Two.*

APPENDIX

A GUIDE TO THE MAYA WORLD

GLOSSARY

AH PUKUH (ah poo-koo): A nickname, meaning "demon" or "devil," for the god YUM KIMIL, also known by archaeologists as God A. As the god of war and violent death, he rules over MITNAL, the ninth and most terrible level of the Maya underworld. He's usually pictured as a bloated, decomposing corpse or a cigar-smoking skeleton. His constant companions are dogs and owls, both considered omens of death. The Death God wears bells to warn people of his approach. (Possibly an unnecessary precaution, since another of his nicknames is Kisin or "the flatulent one," so you'd probably smell him coming, anyway.)

AH PUKUH

BAKABS (bah-kahbs): Four gods, all brothers, thought to be the sons of ITZAMNA and IX CHEL. Like Atlas in Greek mythology, the Bakabs are giants who support the four corners of heaven with upraised arms. Hobnil (hob-neel) is Bakab of the east and the color red (*chak*). Kan Tziknal (kahn tzeek-nahl) is Bakab of the north and the color white (*sak*). Sak Kimi (sahk kee-mee) is Bakab of the west and the color black (*ek'*). Hosanek' (ho-sahn-ek') is Bakab of the south and the color yellow (*k'an*).

BALCHÉ (bahl-chay): A ritual alcoholic drink brewed from fermented wild-bee honey, water, and the bark of the purple-flowered balché tree (*Lonchocarpus longistylus*).

BOLON TZ'AKAB (bo-lon tza-kahb): Meaning "nine generations," this is another name of the god K'AWIIL (ka-weel). He was a god of lightning as well as a patron of lineage, kingship, and aristocracy. Not the cutest fellow, he has a reptilian face, with a smoking mirror emerging from his forehead and a long snout with a leaf in it. He carries a lightning sword.

CENOTE (say-no-tay): A deep, water-filled sinkhole, like a natural reservoir. Cenotes are unique to the Yucatan peninsula where there are about 3,000 of them. The name is a Spanish corruption of the Yucatec Maya word *tz'onot* (tzo-note). Some cenotes are pools in underground caverns, while others are open shafts. Cenotes were an important source of drinking water for the

Ancient Maya. They were also thought to be gateways to the underworld and many ritual offerings, including human sacrifices, were thrown into their depths.

CHAAK

CHAAK (chaahk): Primarily a god of storm and rain, Chaak was one of the oldest and most revered of Ancient Maya gods. He has two tusks curving down from his mouth, googly eyes, and a long, turned-up nose. He usually carries a lightning axe in one hand and a human heart in the other. At the dawn of time, it was Chaak who used his lightning axe to split apart a sacred stone from which sprang the very first ear of corn. Forever after, it was Chaak who sent the life-giving rain to keep the corn, the staple food of the Maya, growing. The animal associated with Chaak is the frog, because it croaks to signal the coming of rain. Chaak is also known as Ah Hoya ("he who urinates"), Ah Tzenul ("he who gives food to others"), and Hopop Caan ("he who lights up the sky").

CHICLE (cheek-lay): A natural gum made from boiling up the milky juice of the Sapodilla tree. Chicle had been chewed by the Maya for centuries, but it didn't reach North America until 1869 when an exiled Mexican general called Antonio Lopez de Santa Anna introduced it to a New York inventor, Thomas Adams. Adams tried (unsuccessfully) to make it into toys, masks, rain boots, and bicycle tires before finally popping a piece into his mouth. He opened the world's first chewing gum factory shortly afterwards. The chewing gum market is now worth $2 billion a year. Having exhausted the natural resources of the rainforest, most gum is now made from synthetic rubber.

CODEX (plural CODICES): The name given to the beautifully illustrated books written by the Ancient Maya on subjects such as religion, astronomy, divination, kingly descent, agriculture, and history. The paper was made from the inner bark of fig trees and used in long strips, which were then folded accordion-style. The scribes made their pens from cactus thorns or the bones of small animals, and their paintbrushes from animal hair. It is hard to know how many of these priceless documents were burned by the Spanish; some say hundreds, some say thousands. (See DIEGO DeLANDA below.) Those that escaped destruction were buried in the ground or hidden in caves, only to rot away in the humidity of the rainforest. Today, as far as we know, only three complete books and the fragment of a fourth (found in a cave in Mexico in 1965) remain.

DIEGO DeLANDA: The overzealous Franciscan friar who arrived in the Yucatan in 1549 and set about destroying Maya culture. It was estimated that over 4,500 Maya were tortured during his inquisition to make them confess to idolatry. Of these 157 died, and many more were permanently crippled. Because he believed that their GYLPHS were the work of the devil (and also a subversive tool for any resistance movement), DeLanda banned the Maya's hieroglyphic writing system and forced them to learn to write

FRIAR DIEGO DeLANDA

their own language in the Spanish alphabet. But he wasn't done yet. On July 12, 1562 , at Mani, he staged his infamous auto-da-fé (literally, "act of faith"). On this dark day, DeLanda made one huge bonfire of their precious bark-paper books (known as CODICES) and thus reduced all written record of Maya history and learning to ashes. In his own words he explained it thus: "The people used certain characters or letters, with which they wrote in their books about the antiquities and their sciences; with these, and with figures, and certain signs in the figures, they understood their matters, made them known and taught them. We found a great number of books in these letters, and since they contained nothing but superstitions and falsehoods of the devil, we burned them all, which they took most grievously, and which gave them great pain." Even the conquistadors thought he'd gone too far and sent him back to Spain to stand trial. Ironically, the treatise that he wrote in his defense, *Relacion de las Cosas Yucatan*, is now our best reference book on the very culture that he tried to wipe out. Some say he regretted his actions in later years. DeLanda was absolved by the Council of the Indies and returned to the New World as Bishop of Yucatan in 1571.

GLYPHS: The name given to the roughly 800 different signs used by the Maya to write their books and stone inscriptions. The Maya writing system is considered to be the most sophisticated system ever developed in MESOAMERICA and, until recently, represented an insoluble enigma. Archaeologists have now cracked the code and know that each glyph represents an idea, a sound, or both. To date, about 85 percent of extant Maya writing has been deciphered.

GLYPHS

HERO TWINS: The twin brothers Xbalanque (sh-ball-on-kay, meaning "Jaguar Deer") and Hunahpu (who-gnaw-poo, meaning "Marksman") are the main characters in the Maya creation story. Like their father and uncle before them, the twins are challenged to a ballgame in XIBALBA by the LORDS OF DEATH. But where their father and uncle died in the attempt, Xbalanque and Hunahpu outwit the Death Lords and vanquish them. The Hero Twins become the Sun and the Moon, while their father is resurrected as HUUN IXIM, the Maize God.

HOWLER MONKEYS: Called baboons in present-day Belize and *baatz'* (botz) by the Ancient Maya, howler monkeys are the largest monkeys in the New World and the loudest land animals on the planet. Their roaring can be heard as far as three miles away. Only the blue whale (whose whistle carries for hundred of miles underwater) is louder. The best times to hear them are early morning and late afternoon. But if you're lucky enough to spot them in the wild, don't stand right under their tree. Like all monkeys, they have a habit of spraying urine to defend their territory.

HUUN IXIM (hoon ee-shim): The reborn father of the HERO TWINS and the Maya god of maize. Unlike the majority of Maya gods who can be young or old, good or bad, Huun Ixim (Maize Book) is always young and handsome, and his combed hair flows like corn silk. He has a flattened and elongated forehead, accentuated by a partly shaven head that resembles an ear of corn. Maya nobility often attempted to mold the skulls of their newborn babies into this shape by binding the infant's head between two wooden boards.

ITZAMNA (eets-ahm-nah): Son of the supreme god, HUNAB KU, and all-round good guy. Itzamna was Lord of the Heavens, Lord of Knowledge, Lord of Day and Night. He gave his people the gifts of culture, writing, art, books, chronology, and the use of calendars. As patron of healing and the sciences, Itzamna can bring the dead back to life. With IX CHEL, he is the father of the BAKABS. Itzamna is usually depicted as a toothless but sprightly old man.

ITZAMNA

IX CHEL (eesh chel): Like most Maya deities, Lady Rainbow had multiple personalities. As the Goddess of the Old Moon, she is depicted as an angry old woman with a coiled snake on her head, fingernails like claws, and a skirt decorated with human bones. In this guise, she vented her anger in

OLD MOON

destructive floods and rainstorms. But as the Goddess
of the New Moon, she is a
beautiful young woman who
reclines inside the crescent
moon with one foot dangling
over the edge, holding her
pet rabbit in her arms. Ix Chel
was the patroness of childbirth, medicine, and weaving.

NEW MOON

JAGUAR: The largest big cat in the Americas and the most ferocious. To the
Ancient Maya, it represented strength, power, stealth, and bravery. They
revered the jaguar (*bahlam*) for its remarkable ability to hunt on land, in the
trees, or in water, for its prowess in battle, and for its magnificent spotted coat
that reminded them of the stars in night sky. Today, due to the fur trade and
the destruction of its natural habitat, the jaguar is in danger of extinction.

JAGUAR STONES: The five fictional stone carvings that channeled the energy of the five fictional sacred pyramids. With the help of the Jaguar Stones
(*Bahlamtuuno 'ob*), Ancient Maya kings could supposedly control the
weather, predict the future, speak to their ancestors, prove royal lineage,
and gain military strength. Other writers have suggested that the Maya really did have supernatural powers that enabled them to transform into animals and to travel through time and space. As far as we know, their
accounts are also fictional.

JUNGLE/RAINFOREST: Although the words are often used interchange-
ably, there is a technical difference between jungle and rainforest. A tropical
rainforest receives at least four inches of rain every month, for nine to
twelve months of the year. It is home to more kinds of trees than any other
area of the world, most of them growing closely together. The tops of the
tallest trees form a canopy of leaves about 100 to 150 feet above the ground,
while the smaller trees form one or two lower canopies. Between them,
these canopies block most of the light from reaching the ground. As a result,
little can grow on the forest floor, which makes it relatively easy to walk

through most parts of a tropical rainforest. However, where the rainforest has been cleared, whether by nature or by man, a carpet of dense fast-growing greenery springs up in the direct sunlight. This is jungle, and its growth provides shade for the rainforest species to reseed and grow. Eventually, blocked from the light, the jungle dies out and the rainforest takes over again. This cycle can take one hundred years to complete.

K'AWIIL (ka-weel): See BOLON TZ'AKAB.

K'INICH AHAU (keen-each a-how): Each day, the Great Sun Lord traces the path of the sun across the sky. Each night, when he drops down into the Underworld in the west, he becomes the fearsome and nocturnal Jaguar God.

K'UK'ULKAN (coo-cool-kahn): The feathered serpent, a divine combination of serpent and bird, one of the great deities of MESOAMERICA. His Maya name (from *k'uk* meaning "QUETZAL bird" and *kan* meaning "snake") is probably a late Postclassic translation of the Aztec *Quetzalcoatl.*

LORDS OF DEATH: The Maya underworld, XIBALBA, is ruled by the twelve Lords of Death. According to the POPOL VUH (which was written in Quiche Mayan, a very different language from the Classic Mayan and modern Yucatec quoted elsewhere in this book), their names are One Death, Seven Death, Scab Stripper, Blood Gatherer, Wing, Demon of Pus, Demon of Jaundice, Bone Scepter, Skull Scepter, Demon of Filth, Demon of Woe, and Packstrap. They are usually depicted as skeletons or bloated corpses. The Lords of Death delight in human suffering. It's their job to inflict sickness, pain, starvation, fear, destitution, and death on the citizens of MIDDLE-WORLD. Luckily for us, they're usually far too busy gambling and playing childish pranks on each other to get much work done.

MAYA: The word most often associated with the Maya is *mysterious.* That's partly because no one really knows why they abandoned their great cities (almost overnight in historical terms); partly because most of their writings were destroyed by the fanatical Friar DIEGO DeLANDA; and partly because archaeologists have only recently begun to decipher their glyphs. But most agree that Maya civilization began on the Yucatan peninsula sometime before 1500 BC. It entered its Classic period around 250 AD, when the Maya adopted a hierarchical system of government and established a series of kingdoms across what is now Mexico, Guatemala, Belize, Honduras, and El Salvador. Each of these kingdoms was an independent city-state, with its own ceremonial center, urban areas, and rural farming community. In major cities like Tikal, which was inhabited from 600 BC to the tenth century AD, there were as many as 10,000 individual structures ranging from temple-pyramids to thatched huts. At its height between 600 to 900 AD, Tikal was home to an estimated 60,000 people, giving it a population density several times greater than the average city in Europe or America at the same time. Building on the accomplishments of earlier civilizations such as the Olmec, the Maya developed astronomy, calendrical systems, and hieroglyphic writing. Although most famous for their soaring pyramids, temples, and palaces (built without metal tools, wheels, or beasts of burden) they were also skilled farmers, weavers, and potters, and they established extensive trade networks. The Maya saw no boundaries between heaven and earth, life and death, sleep and wakefulness. They believed that human blood was the oil that kept the wheels of the cosmos turning. Many of their rituals and ceremonies involved bloodletting or human sacrifice, but never on the scale practiced by the Aztecs. For reasons we don't fully understand, Maya power began to decline around 800 AD, when the southern cities were abandoned. By the time the Spanish arrived in the early sixteenth century, only a few kingdoms were still thriving, and most Maya had gone back to MILPA farming in the jungle. Today, there are about six million Maya in Central America, making them the largest block of indigenous people north of Peru. However, with a legacy of repression, discrimination, and poverty from the colonial era, they continue to face formidable problems.

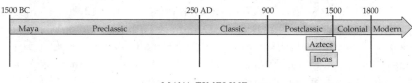

MAYA TIMELINE

MAYAN: The language family of thirty-one different, mutually unintelligible languages spoken by Maya groups throughout Central America.

MESOAMERICA: Literally meaning "central America," Mesoamerica is the name archaeologists and anthropologists use to describe a region that extends south and east from central Mexico to include parts of Guatemala, Belize, Honduras, and Nicaragua. It was home to various pre-Columbian civilizations, including the Maya, (from 1500 BC), the Olmec (1200–400 BC), and the Aztecs (1250–1521). The Incas of Peru in South America date from 1300–1533.

MIDDLEWORLD: The Maya believed they lived in a middle world (Yok'ol Kab'), sandwiched between the nine layers of the dark and watery underworld (XIBALBA or Xibnal, meaning "place of fright") and the thirteen layers of the bright and breezy upper world (ka'an, "sky"; or Ka'anal Naah, "Heavenly House").

MILPA (meal-pah): A tract of land cleared from the jungle, usually by burning, farmed for a few seasons, and then abandoned for a new tract.

MITNAL (meet-nahl): The ninth and lowest level of the Maya underworld; a place of eternal cold, darkness, and hunger. The ruler of Mitnal is AH PUKUH, otherwise known as God A and YUM KIMIL.

MOON RABBIT: Where North Americans see the face of a man in the shadows of the full moon, the Maya see a rabbit. This is partly due to the fact that people in the northern hemisphere view the moon at a different angle than those on the equator or in the southern hemisphere. What North Americans see as "the man in the moon" is actually sideways in much of Central America, which led the Maya, Aztecs, and others to see the image as a leaping rabbit. The man is entirely upside down in South America, which led the Incas to interpret the image as an inverted water jar. That same variation in vantage point also accounts for differences in how crescent moons are viewed. In the northern and southern hemispheres, the moon waxes and wanes horizontally, so North Americans depict crescents as parentheses; whereas on the equator, the moon appears to wax and wane vertically (and nearly so in the tropics), which may be why the Maya and Aztecs depicted the phases of the moon as bowls or cenotes. Returning to the Moon Rabbit: he was the pet of the young Moon Goddess, IX CHEL, who is often pictured holding him in her arms. The Maya credited the rabbit with the invention of writing, and rabbits are often pictured as scribes and artists.

MOON RABBIT

POK(T)APOK: A nickname for the ritual ballgame. (Its real name was probably Pitz.) The Maya ballgame was the first team sport in recorded history. It had elements of soccer, basketball, and volleyball, but it was more difficult than any of them. Players could not use their hands or feet, and the heavy rubber ball had to be kept in the air at all times. The aim was to knock the ball through a small stone hoop high on the side wall. Ball courts have been found in almost every Maya city. The game, which is central to the Maya creation story, had great religious significance. It has been called "the game

373

of life and death" because the losers (or sometimes the winners) and their supporters were frequently sacrificed.

POPOL VUH (poe-pole vooh): The Mayan Book of the Dawn of Life, the sacred book of the Quiche (kee-chay) MAYA who lived (and still live) in the highlands of Guatemala. The title literally means "Book of the Mat." Throughout MESOAMERICA, mats were symbols of authority and power, sat upon by nobles, governors, and high-ranking courtiers, but it is usually translated as the "Council Book." The Popol Vuh tells the Maya creation story and explains how the HERO TWINS rescued their father from XIBALBA. It was transcribed toward the end of the seventeenth century by a Quiche elder, writing in Quiche but using the Roman alphabet. It was then translated into Spanish by Friar Francisco Ximenez. His work lay unnoticed for 150 years until a group of European investigators stumbled across it in Guatemala City. One of them, Abbé Brasseur de Bourbourg, translated it into French and had it published in Paris in 1861, where it caused an immediate sensation.

QUETZAL (ket-sahl): This rare Central American bird (called *k'uk* by the Ancient Maya) was prized for its brilliant iridescent blue-green tail feathers that can grow up to three feet long and were a feature of royal headdresses. The birds would be captured and plucked, then set free to grow new feathers. The penalty for killing a quetzal was death. Today the quetzal faces extinction unless urgent action is undertaken to protect its habitat.

OBSIDIAN: This black volcanic glass was the closest thing the Ancient Maya had to metal. An obsidian blade can be one hundred times sharper than a stainless steel scalpel, but it is extremely brittle.

RAINFOREST: See JUNGLE.

VISION SERPENT: When Maya kings wished to communicate with their ancestors or with the gods, they would hold a bloodletting ceremony to summon the Vision Serpent. It is depicted as a great serpent, rearing out of the smoke, with the desired ancestor or god emerging from its mouth. It's a dramatic picture. But some experts suggest, less dramatically, that we should think of it more

VISION SERPENT

374

as a "vision centipede," since its skeletal qualities are probably meant to invoke the carapace of the many-legged insect.

XIBALBA (she-ball-bah): Xibalba, which roughly translates as "place of fear" or "place of phantoms," was the realm of the dead. Only kings and those who died a violent death (battle, sacrifice, or suicide) or women who died in childbirth could look forward to the leafy shade of heaven. All other souls, good or bad, were headed across rivers of scorpions, blood, and pus to Xibalba. Unlike the Christian hell with its fire and brimstone, the Maya underworld was cold and damp, and its inhabitants were condemned to an eternity of bone-chilling misery and hunger.

YUCATÁN: Located in southeastern Mexico between the Gulf of Mexico and the Caribbean Sea, Yucatán was the first homeland of the Maya. From here, they spread to Guatemala, Belize, Honduras, El Salvador, and other provinces of Mexico. Yucatán was called the "Land of Turkey and Deer" by the Maya, owing to its abundance of edible wildlife.

YUCATEC: A Mayan language still widely spoken by the indigenous people of Mexico's Yucatán Peninsula, Belize, and northern Guatemala. Yucatec is not, as many people claim, a direct descendant of Classic Mayan. It's actually a distant cousin but because it once assimilated large amounts of vocabulary from the ancient language, Yucatec and Classic Mayan seem more similar and more closely related than they actually are. In fact, if Classic Mayan were Latin, then Ch'orti' Mayan (spoken on the border of Guatemala and Honduras) would be Italian (a true direct descendant), while Yucatec would be more like English.

YUM KIMIL (yoom kee-meel): see AH PUKUH.

TEACH YOURSELF MAYA

A note on pronunciation:

VOWELS
a sounds like "ah" as in *father*
e sounds like "ey" as in *hey*
i sounds like "ee" as in *see*
o sounds like "oh" as in *toe*
u sounds like "oo" in *who*
Double vowels are held twice as long

CONSONANTS
ch sounds like the "ch" in *church*
tz sounds the "ts" in *gets*
x sounds like "sh" as in *shoe*

GLOTTAL STOPS
Try saying the word *butter* without the *tt*. The sound that replaces them is a glottal stop. In Maya, these are indicated by an apostrophe (i.e., *k'* or *tz'*) and they can change the meaning of a word completely. For example, *kan* is the number four, but *k'an* is yellow as in Lady K'an Kakaw.

MAYA PHRASEBOOK
The Ancient Maya spoke the language known as Classic Maya. The modern Maya in Middleworld speak Yucatec Maya, also known simply as Maya, which is one of the thirty or so Mayan languages still spoken in Central America today.

> *Biix a beel?* (beesh ah bale) — How are you?
> *Ma'aloob* (mah-ah-lobe) — Fine
> *Yum bo'otik* (yoom boh-oh-teek) — Thank you
> *Mixba'al* (meesh-bah-ahl) — You're welcome

MAYA MATH

Maya math was the most sophisticated counting system ever developed in the Americas. It allowed scholars, astronomers, and architects to make complex calculations, but it was simple enough to be used by market traders and illiterate farmers.

Where we use ten different symbols to represent numbers (1, 2, 3, 4 , 5, 6, 7, 8, 9, 0), the Maya used only three: a dot for a one, a bar for five, and a symbol (usually a shell) for zero. (The Maya were one of the first civilizations to understand the concept of zero.) Below are the Maya numbers from 0–19:

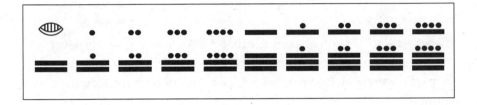

We use a decimal system, based on the number ten, but the Maya used a vigesimal system, based on the number twenty. So where we learn to count on our fingers, Maya children counted on their fingers and toes. In fact, the number twenty was very important to the Maya, so much so that the words for "human being" and "twenty" share the same root in most Mayan languages.

The Maya wrote their numbers from top to bottom rather than from left to right, but apart from that, their system was not so different from ours. For example, to write the number 34, we place a three in the tens column and a four in the ones column. The Maya put a one in the twenties column and a fourteen in the ones column.

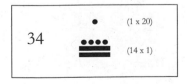

Adding and subtracting in the Maya system is simply a matter of juggling the dots and bars. To calculate 36 + 13, for example, you start by adding the units (i.e., 16 + 13). This gives you 29, so you leave 9 in the ones column and carry the 20 up, giving you a grand total of 2 twenties and 9 ones = 49!

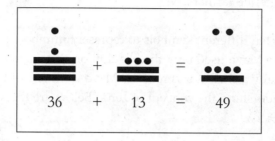

Clever, isn't it? When you consider that the Ancient Egyptians never cracked the concept of zero and that complex calculations with Roman numerals were way too complicated for ordinary Romans, you have to admit that the Maya win the Ancient Math prize!

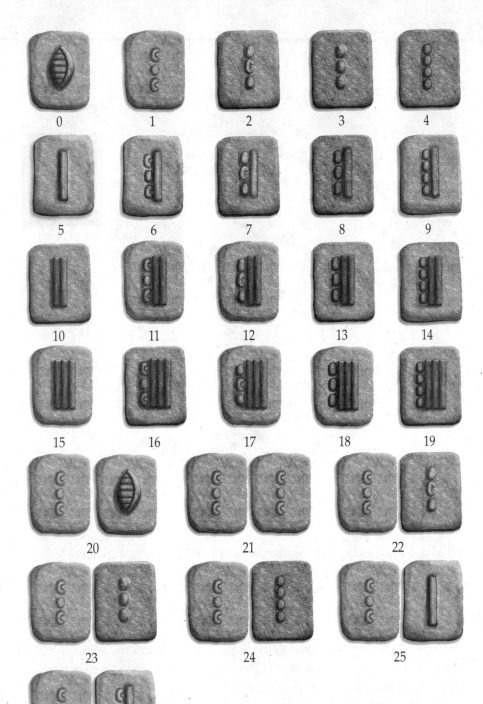

Chapter number glyphs from zero to twenty-six.

MAYA COSMOS

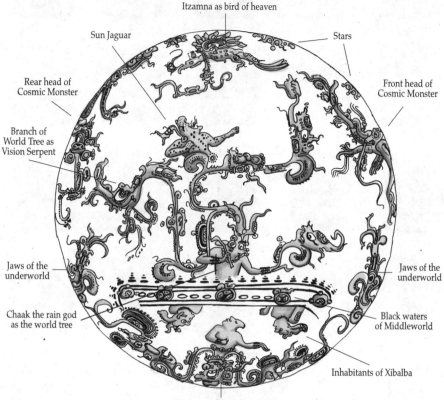

Itzamna as bird of heaven

Sun Jaguar

Stars

Rear head of
Cosmic Monster

Front head of
Cosmic Monster

Branch of
World Tree as
Vision Serpent

Jaws of the
underworld

Jaws of the
underworld

Chaak the rain god
as the world tree

Black waters
of Middleworld

Inhabitants of Xibalba

Waters of the Underworld

What did Max, Lola, and Hermanjilio see in the Temple of Itzamna?
This illustration (based on a painted plate from the Late Classic period)
depicts the three realms of the Maya cosmos: the heavens above,
Middleworld (the world of men), and the waters of Xibalba, the Underworld. In the heavens, the two-headed Cosmic Monster (or Cosmic
Crocodile as Max called it) contains the Sun, Venus, and the Milky Way.
In the middle of it all is the World Tree, which was brought into being
by the king during bloodletting rituals. With its upper branches in the
heavens and its roots in Xibalba, the World Tree was the doorway to the
otherworlds of gods and ancestors. Communication with these spirits
took place through the mysterious Vision Serpent. At the top of the
World Tree sits Itzamna, as the bird of heaven.

THE MAYA CALENDAR

The Maya were obsessed with the passage of time. They believed that events took place in repeating cycles — "What has happened before will happen again," as Lord Six-Rabbit puts it — and they developed a variety of astonishingly accurate calendars to track the movements of the sun and the stars. The Maya kings and priests used their elaborate calendar systems and their advanced knowledge of astronomy to help manage their kingdoms, to determine when to wage war, and to predict the future.

THE LONG COUNT

The Long Count is the Maya calendar system that is probably closest to our own. Just as our Gregorian calendar counts the days and years from zero AD, the Maya counted from the day when they believed this world

> Day = *K'in*
> Month of 20 days = *Winal*
> Year of 360 days = *Tun*
> 20 Tuns = *K'atun*
> 20 K'atuns = *Bak'tun*

began. (Which, in our terms, was August 11, 3114 BC.) However, to make things a little more complicated, their year was only 360 days long. It is made up of eighteen months (or *winal*), each consisting of twenty days (or *k'in*). The Maya called this 360-day year a *tun*. Since they used a twenty-based counting system, their equivalent of our decade was a *k'atun* and it was twenty years long. Twenty *k'atuns,* or 400 *tuns* was called a *bak'tun.* This was equivalent to our century — though, of course, four times as long. The Maya Long Count will last for 13 *bak'tuns* (5,126 years), giving us an end date of December 21, 2012, precisely on the winter solstice. What was supposed to happen after that date is not well understood. Some think that the Maya believed the world would actually end in 2012. However, there's a lot of evidence to the contrary — including predictions in the inscriptions of Palenque that K'inich Janaab Pakal's accession date would still be celebrated in our year 4025.

THE HAAB

Recognizing that the Long Count's 360-day year was 5 days short, the Maya devised another calendar called the *Haab.* To the eighteen 20-day months, they added a 5-day period called the *Wayeb.* These were considered to be days of uncertainty and bad luck when the portals between the mortal realm and the underworld dissolved and demons roamed the Earth.

IMIX (Waterlily)	IK' (Wind)	AK'BAL (House)	K'AN (lizard)	CHIKCHAN (Snake)
KIMI (Death)	MANIK' (Deer)	LAMAT (Rabbit)	MULUK (Water)	OK (Dog)
CHUWEN (Monkey)	EB' (Grass)	BEN (Reed)	IX (Jaguar)	MEN (Eagle)
KIB' (Condor)	KAB'AN (Earthquake)	ETZ'NAB' (Blade)	KAWAK (Lightning)	AHAW (Lord)

THE TZOLK'IN

The *Tzolk'in* was the sacred calendar, used to predict the characteristics of each day and determine the days for rituals, like a daily zodiac. It is still in use by many Maya today, and it has been kept, without interruption or losing a day, since the time of the Ancients. The calendar is made up of twenty day names and thirteen numbers. It takes 260 days (the average length of a human pregnancy) to go through the full cycle of name/number combinations. Each day name has a quality, some good, some bad. For example, *Imix* ("Water Lily") is full of complications and problems, and thus bad for journeys or business deals. The number (1–13) determines how strong the characteristic would be. So on 13 *Imix*, you might want to stay home.

THE CALENDAR ROUND

The Calendar Round brings together the *Haab* with the *Tzolk'in*. It takes 18,980 days to work thought the 260 *Tzolk'in* days and the 365 *Haab* days. This is about fifty-two years. The Calendar Round is usually depicted as a series of interlocking cogs and wheels — which, in Middleworld, was the inspiration for the time machine in the Temple of Itzamna.

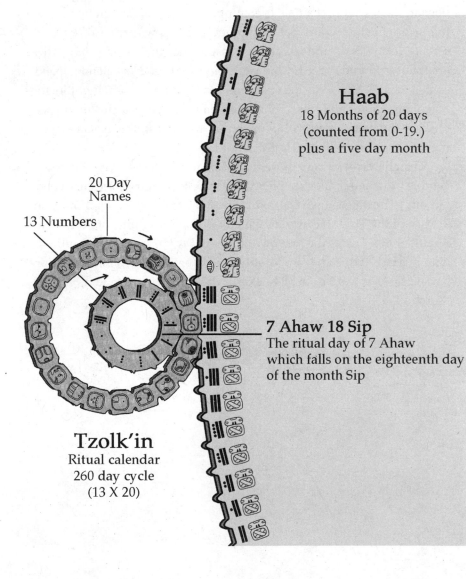

Haab
18 Months of 20 days
(counted from 0-19.)
plus a five day month

20 Day
Names

13 Numbers

7 Ahaw 18 Sip
The ritual day of 7 Ahaw
which falls on the eighteenth day
of the month Sip

Tzolk'in
Ritual calendar
260 day cycle
(13 X 20)

MONUMENT DATES

The Maya carved stone monuments to mark key points in the histories of their cities, whether for the inauguration of new buildings, the celebration of victories, the accession of kings, or the marking of significant passages of time. They carefully recorded the precise dates of these events in the carvings. Given the lack of other written sources, learning to decipher the date glyphs on monuments is an essential part of a Maya archaeologist's training.

In writing a date, the Maya began with an introductory glyph that flags to the reader that a date is coming. The glyphs that immediately follow are the long count dates and they show how many *bak'tuns, k'atuns, tuns, winals,* and *k'ins* have passed since the world began. These are followed by the specific day from the ritual *Tzolk'in* calendar. Next comes what is known as the supplementary series, which might include one of nine night gods who ruled each day, as well as a cluster of glyphs to show the precise day within the lunar cycle. Last, the mason carves the day and month of the *Haab* calendar.

The glyphs below are those that Max and Lola discovered in the Temple of Itzamna. (For simplicity, the supplementary series has been left out.) The date shown is 4,000 years since the beginning of time, on 7 *Ahaw* of the *Tzolk'in* calendar, which falls on the eighteenth day of the month of *Sip.* This is the first day of a new *bak'tun* — a very eventful date in Maya terms and supposedly the date when Lord Six-Rabbit first battled his evil half brother Tzelek. (In the Gregorian calendar, it is March 13, 830 AD.)

| Introductory glyph | 10 bak'tuns | 0 k'atuns | 0 tuns | 0 winals | 0 k'ins | 7 Ahaw | 18 Sip |

MAYA WRITING

The Ancient Maya writing system was extraordinary in that it could express anything that could be said in spoken language. Like ancient Egyptian hieroglyphs and modern Japanese characters, it had signs for both simple sounds and whole words. Maya writing combined logographs (symbols representing whole words) with symbols that represented phonetic syllables. The word jaguar (*bahlam*), for example, could be written as a symbol that looks like a jaguar's head, or as a cluster of three syllables: ba-la-ma. (The final *a* is silent.)

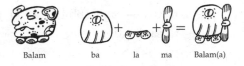

Balam   ba   la   ma   Balam(a)

There were over 600 logographs, but for reasons of style, the scribes often preferred to use syllabic writing. While the Ancient Maya language had around 100 phonetic syllables, there were as many as 200 symbols to represent these sounds. So, for most syllable sounds, there was a range of symbol choices. In an extraordinary mingling of language and art, the Maya scribes selected the glyphs that best fulfilled their aesthetic sense. The more frequently a word was used, the greater the variation seen in writing it, as the Maya didn't like to repeat a spelling or design within the same block of text. The symbols below are all possible versions of the sound *ma*.

In syllabic writing, the symbols representing consonant/vowel pairs or vowels were arranged in glyph blocks to sound out each word. In each glyph block the symbols were generally read from top to bottom and from left to right. Here are just a few of the many combinations possible.

SENTENCE STRUCTURE

In English, a basic sentence order is subject, verb, object — as in "Lord Six-Rabbit defeated his younger brother Tzelek." In Classic Mayan, the basic sentence structure is verb, object, subject — as in "Defeated his younger brother Tzelek, Lord Six-Rabbit." Of course, the Maya wouldn't mention a war without telling you precisely when it happened. (In Maya writing, dates are lengthy and verbs are short.) Moreover, their rulers liked to have long strings of titles to trumpet their importance. So the sentence below roughly reads: "On the change of the tenth *bak'tun*, on the day 7 *Ahaw* ruled by the ninth night lord, on the eighth day of a thirty-day lunar cycle and the eighteenth day in the month of *Sip*, he defeated Tzelek the younger brother — Six-Rabbit, Godlike Jaguar Lord, He of the Twenty Captives, Great Leader."

1. Introductory Glyph (Signals a date is coming)
2. Ten Baktuns (4,000 years)
3. Zero Ka'tun
4. Zero Tun
5. Zero Winal
6. Zero Kin
7. Ritual day Seven Ahaw
8. Ninth night god ruled this day
9. Glyph that goes in tandem with night god
10. Eight days into the lunar cycle
11. Thirty day lunar period
12. Eighteenth day in the month of Sip
13. He loses a war
14. Tzelek (Basilisk Lord)
15. The younger brother
16. The one who did it (defeated him)
17. Six Rabbit
18. God-like Jaguar Lord
19. He of the twenty captives
20. Great Leader

EASY CHICKEN TAMALES

Everyone in Central America has their own recipe for tamales.
Even Max Murphy would like this one.

INGREDIENTS

6 cups of Maseca corn masa mix for tamales

1 cup of corn oil

6 cups of chicken stock or broth

2 tsp salt

1 tsp baking powder

1 tsp cumin

1 green chilli, seeds removed, finely chopped

1 clove garlic, crushed and finely chopped

1 roast chicken, off the bone and shredded

1 jar of salsa verde or tomatillo sauce

1 bag of cornhusks

METHOD

1. Soften the cornhusks by soaking in warm water for at least three hours. You'll need to put something heavy on them to keep them under the water.

2. Marinate the shredded chicken in the salsa verde.

3. In a mixer combine the masa mix, oil, chicken stock, salt, baking powder, cumin, chili, and garlic. Mix until you have a soft dough. Add more chicken stock if needed.

4. With the wide end of the cornhusk toward you, spread a heaped tablespoon of masa into the center of a cornhusk (smooth side up) to make a three-inch square. Add two teaspoons of the marinated chicken and salsa verde onto the masa. Fold first the left side of the cornhusk over the filling, and then overlap with the right. Fold the pointed end toward you. Fold up the wide end over the tip of the pointed end. Tie with a strip of cornhusk or kitchen string to make a parcel. Continue until all the masa and chicken is used up.

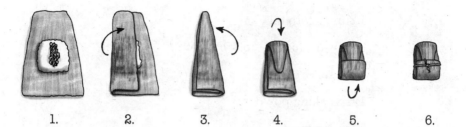

1.   2.   3.   4.   5.   6.

5. Place tamales in a large steamer and steam for about 40 minutes. You'll know the tamales are cooked when they easily separate from the cornhusk.

BIBLIOGRAPHY

The Ancient Maya: New Perspectives, Heather McKillop, W.W. Norton & Company, New York, 2006.

Ancient Maya: The Rise and Fall of a Rainforest Civilization, Arthur Demarest, Cambridge University Press, Cambridge, 2004.

The Broken Spears, The Aztec Account of the Conquest of Mexico, Miguel Leon-Portilla, translated by Angel Maria Garibay K. and Lysander Kemp, Beacon Press, Boston, 1992.

Breath on the Mirror: Mythic Voices and Visions of the Living Maya, Dennis Tedlock, University of New Mexico Press, Albuquerque, 1993.

The Caste War of Yucatan, Nelson A. Reed, Stanford University Press, Stanford, California, 2001.

Cartas de Relación, Hernán Cortes, edited by Mario Hernándes Sánchez-Barba, Dastin S. L., Madrid, 2000.

Chronicle of the Maya Kings and Queens, Simon Martin and Nikolai Grube, Thames & Hudson, London, 2000.

The Conquest of New Spain, Bernal Diaz, translated by J. M. Cohen, Penguin Books, London, 1963.

Courtly Art of the Ancient Maya, Mary Miller and Simon Martin, Fine Arts Museum of San Francisco, Thames & Hudson, New York, 2004.

The Fall of the Ancient Maya: Solving the Mystery of the Maya Collapse, David Webster, Thames & Hudson, London, 2002.

Final Report: An Archaeologist Excavates His Past, Michael D. Coe, Thames & Hudson, New York, 2006.

Handbook to Life in the Ancient Maya World, Lynn V. Foster, Oxford University Press, New York, 2005.

Howler Monkeys, Sandra Donovan, Raintree, Chicago, 2003.

Insight Guides Belize, APA Publications, HK, 1997.

Jungle of the Maya, Jim Wright, Douglas Goodell, and Jerry Barrack, University of Texas Press, Austin, 2006.

Lords of Creation: The Origins of Sacred Maya Kingship, Virginia M. Fields and Dorie Reents-Budet, Los Angeles County Museum of Art, Scala Publishers, London, 2005.

Lost Cities of the Maya, Claude Baudez and Sydney Picasso, Thames & Hudson, London, 1987.

Maya: Yucatec Dictionary and Phrasebook, John Montgomery, Hippocrene Books, New York, 2004.

Maya: Divine Kings of the Rain Forest, edited by Nikolai Grube, Könemann Verlagsgesellschaft, Cologne, 2000.

The Maya: History and Treasures of an Ancient Civilization, Davide Domenici, White Star Publishers, Vercelli, Italy.

Maya for Travelers and Students, Gary Bevington, University of Texas Press, Austin, 2000.

Mayan Cooking, Cherry Hamman, Hippocrene Books, New York, 1998

Montezuma: Lord of the Aztecs, C. A. Burland, Weidenfield & Nicolson, London, 1972.

The Myths of Time, Hugh Rayment-Pickard, Darton, Longman & Todd, London, 2004.

Popul Vuh: The Mayan Book of the Dawn of Life and the Glories of Gods and Kings, translated by Dennis Tedlock, Touchstone, New York, 1996

Rainforest Remedies: One Hundred Healing Herbs of Belize, Rosita Arvigo, Michael Balick, and Laura Evans, Lotus Press, Twin Lakes, Wisconsin, 1998.

Reading the Maya Glyphs, 2d ed., Michael D. Coe and Mark Van Stone, Thames & Hudson, London, 2005.

Secrets of the Maya, editors of *Archaeology Magazine*, Hatherleigh Press, New York, 2003.

Secrets of the Talking Jaguar, Martín Prechtel, Tarcher/Putnam, New York, 1999.

The Sport of Life and Death: the Mesoamerican Ballgame, edited by E. Michael Whittington, Thames & Hudson, New York, 2001.

Time Among the Maya, Ronald Wright, Grove Press, New York, 1989.

Time and the Highland Maya, Barbara Tedlock, University of New Mexico Press, Albuquerque, 1992.

The World of the Ancient Maya, John S. Henderson, Cornell University Press, Ithaca, New York, 1997.

Yucatan: Before and After the Conquest, Friar Diego de Landa, translated by William Gates, Dover Publications, New York, 1978.

ACKNOWLEDGMENTS

Th'l-oxaira to the illustrious and shimmering Professor Marc Zender, for sharing his immense knowledge so generously. Thank you to our editor, Sue Moore, and our designer, Julia Gignoux, and to Lisa Goldfinger for the cover painting. Thank you to Andrea Voelkel for her amazing illustrations, Niki Voelkel for the winning cover idea, and Christy Voelkel for all those long nights of reading aloud. Thank you to Jack and Mary-Anne and Peter and Hetty. Thank you to everyone who helped us in Belize, including Karina Martinez and Franklin Choco, our intrepid guides Geraldo Garcia and Hugh Daly, Clive Garbutt of Monkey River Village, and all our friends at the Turtle Inn and Blancaneaux. Thank you to Penny McConnel and Liza Bernard at the wonderful Norwich Bookstore for all their literary and business advice. Thank you to Jody Horan and Elise Foxall at the Richmond Middle School, Susan Voake at the Marion Cross School, and Lucinda Walker at the Norwich Library. Thank you to Jessica Carvalho, Lauri Berkenkamp, Deborah Schenck, Renée Barker, Philippa and Michael Earley, Greg Deyermenjian, Cee Greene, and Jason Parry. Thanks to Ali Al-Rawaf for his inspiring Iraqi nose. Thank you to everyone who voted in our cover contest, especially Graham Sharp. Thank you to our middle-grade advisory panel, particularly Andrew Pillsbury, Kyle van Leer, Rachel Allen, and Grace S. Gartel. Finally, a huge thank you to the incredibly intelligent and discriminating Peter Kraus — who liked the manuscript so much that he forced his parents to publish it.

YUM BO'OTIK TE'EX!

A NOTE ON THE TYPE

This book was set in Palatino, an old-style serif typeface named after Giambattista Palatino, a peer of Leonardo da Vinci and a master of calligraphy. Palatino is based on the humanist fonts of the Italian Renaissance, which mirror the letters formed by a broad-nib pen. It was designed by Hermann Zapf at the German branch of Linotype. Zapf optimized Palatino's design for legibility, producing a typeface that remained legible even on the inferior paper of the post-World War II period. Since its release by the Linotype foundry in 1948, Palatino has withstood the test of time as one of the most widely used and readable typefaces.

The display typeface is Old Claude, which simulates the effect of an old foundry type on handmade paper.

A NOTE ON THE PAPER

On behalf of the ancient rainforests and all their inhabitants, J&P Voelkel would like to thank the publishers for choosing to print the first edition of *Middleworld* on 100% postconsumer recycled paper. Not a single tree was chopped down to create paper for this book. In addition, to avoid releasing poisonous chemicals such as dioxins, lead, arsenic, and mercury into our waterways, this recycled paper was processed chlorine-free.

As a result of these choices, the first edition of *Middleworld* saved:

168 mature trees

117 million BTUs of energy

(equivalent to 15 months' worth of electricity for the average U.S. home)

14,724 pounds of greenhouse gases

(equivalent to the gases produced by the average car driving 12,870 miles)

7,848 pounds of solid waste

61,116 gallons of water

Environmental impact estimates were made using the Environmental Defense Paper Calculator. For more information, visit http://www.papercalculator.org